THE RUSSIAN DONATION

THE RUSSIAN DONATION

CHRISTOPH SPIELBERG

Translated by Gerald Chapple

amazoncrossing

Text copyright © 2001 Christoph Spielberg
English translation copyright © 2012 Gerald Chapple

The Russian Donation was first published in 2001 by Piper Verlag as *Die russische Spende*. Translated from German by Gerald Chapple. Published in English by AmazonCrossing in 2013.

Published by AmazonCrossing
P.O. Box 400818
Las Vegas, NV 89140

ISBN-13: 9781612184302
ISBN-10: 1612184308
Library of Congress Control Number: 2012913746

CHAPTER 1

Germany, Pentecost, Monday, June 12, six p.m. My patient Misha died on what could finally be called a warm summer evening.

A mouthwatering smell from a neighboring barbecue wafted into my living room through the open balcony door, though it wasn't as strong as it had been the previous weekend. German men had something infinitely more important on their minds tonight than grilling: watching our first soccer game in Belgium. I, for one, was well prepared. My beer was perfectly chilled, my crackers were within easy reach and only a week over their best-before date, and I had plenty of my favorite dip on hand. I could only hope that our boys on the field were equally ready. Sure, they were only playing Romania, but as the sports commentators never tired of pointing out, you still have to win.

I'm not even a particularly keen soccer fan and certainly no expert. But if millions of my countrymen find such an evening relaxing, who am I to disagree? Besides, it's less work than trying to have a civilized evening sipping wine, perusing the arts section of the newspaper, and carrying on an intelligent conversation. Who would I talk to anyway? Going and sharing a beer with my nouveau riche, SUV-driving neighbors was out of the question—and would only confirm my cynical opinion about the close correlation between economic success and stupidity.

I've been an Emergency Room attending physician for the past eight years, so it wasn't unusual for me to have spent most of the holiday weekend in the ER. Nonetheless, I still struggled with my place in the system. Patients are the reason hospitals exist, and it is thanks to them that the entire apparatus keeps functioning. If you think about it, it is the patients who ensure that doctors, nurses, kitchen and cleaning personnel, administrators, suppliers, and the pharmaceutical industry have a secure livelihood. In addition, patients facilitate doctors' further training and advancement by providing them with invaluable experience. In other words, I've never understood who is really serving whose needs in the hospital. OK, maybe I understand it, but I've never internalized it. I'm a Don Quixote in scrubs. I've learned that I may not be able to eradicate diseases, but I can stay out of nature's way if it's trying to heal a patient. Which it sometimes does, despite the combined efforts and textbook training of the various medical specialists on hand who benefit from disease.

In any case, I had done my bit for the survival of humanity on this Holy Pentecost weekend and was ready to settle into my authentically German evening of beer and television, television and beer. I'd been on night duty two days before, which meant that I'd fallen into bed dead tired when I'd gotten home the day before. I'd definitely earned my Teutonic evening, the kind of evening that only single people can properly enjoy: no arguments over what to watch, no bedtime stories for the kids, no danger of getting embroiled—particularly on an evening like this—in a discussion about "our relationship."

I even considered disconnecting the phone just to be safe, but the risk of being called in to sub on the night shift was practically zero; Abramchik was on call that night, and if he suddenly got sick, Adam was next, and it continued that way in alphabetical order. "Hoffmann" was quite a ways down the list, though I knew that the distance from *A* to *H* could shrink surprisingly quickly during holidays. I didn't turn the phone off because Celine occasionally dropped by on a soccer night. One of her most attractive qualities was that she always phoned ahead of time; she, too, was single and shared my respect for privacy. As an added bonus, she occasionally picked up a pizza or Chinese takeout on her way over.

Celine, unlike me, was a true soccer fan. She leapt up from the couch at every goal, miss, or foul and needed me to serve as the audience for her running commentary. She'd been known to get carried away and not pay the least bit of attention to what she looked like while she watched. Her short skirt sometimes rose up, offering a tantalizing glimpse of her ass, or her blouse might slip open, giving me a clear view of her perky little breasts. It was, of course, ridiculous for me to leer at her like that since we generally ended our TV-watching nights rolling around on the carpet or in bed, but I found it more fun to watch her than what was on the screen. "The ball is round," legendary soccer coach Sepp Herberger once said—my favorite profound analysis of the game; so was Celine's ass—and luscious too.

The national anthems had played, the teams' ends of the field were determined—and only five minutes into the game our boys had conceded the first goal. Good God! We'd even replaced the team captain!

When the phone rang three minutes later, I was already debating whether I was in the mood for pepperoni pizza or pork with bamboo shoots—but it wasn't Celine. It was the clinic; they needed me on the night shift. How'd they get to *H* so fast? Aha, Abramchik had called in sick, and it turned out the rest were on vacation or simply hadn't picked up. What idiot would answer the phone during Germany's first game in the final round?

I was tempted to use my standard lie, "My brother isn't home," which was the way I'd handled this type of situation in the early days of my residency, but the folks at the clinic have long since figured out that I'm an only child. Another fail-proof line that I'd been quite pleased with for a while—"Sure, I'll be right there, but I've had three beers…"—had opened me up to speculations of alcoholism. If I played that card now, I'd probably never have another emergency night shift slapped on me, but I'd also be definitively written off as a boozer. So much for pepperoni pizza and Celine's luscious ass and perky breasts on the rug in overtime.

I didn't bother to brush my teeth or shave, and I dawdled—in silent protest against my fate and my stupidity at having picked up the phone. When the phone rang a second time, I didn't even answer it. Whatever Celine had to say would only fuel my anger.

I got to the ER at about a quarter to seven. I'd only been on duty for five minutes when the paramedics arrived with the first case of the night. It was Misha, the Russian. Misha's skin looked yellow. And Misha was dead.

The ER of a teaching hospital, such as the one I'd had the honor to work in for the last eight years, was the eye of the needle patients had to squeeze through if they wanted urgent admission to our top-notch hospitals. It made no difference whether a patient came in on his own or was admitted by his family doctor. In the former case, his odds were sometimes better. Every clinician knew that doctors in private practice were, in their free time, specialists in real estate funds with high loss allocations, experts in tax-avoidance schemes in Liechtenstein, and well versed in the latest get-rich-quick schemes, but decidedly less knowledgeable about their patients. They either admitted them much too late, after mucking around with the wrong diagnosis until the patient was as good as dead, or else they sent in perfectly healthy people with an "abnormal ECG" or because "my lab has no idea what's going on." More likely a golf tournament had their name on it.

Some people do *not* want to be admitted to our top-rated hospitals. They've been tipped off that you don't have to wait for hours in the admitting room when you come in at night. They've learned that problem cases will be seen by five different specialists, that they'll get a real ECG and a pile of lab results, and even get X-rayed as a bonus—all within an hour or two of walking in the door. In private practice, such a rigorous battery of tests would take several stressful weeks, dozens of annoying phone calls, and countless hours reading dull magazines in generic waiting rooms.

I'd changed out of my clothes in the doctors' room and stashed them in my locker, along with my hopes for a relaxing evening. I was standing in my white coat, complete with my stethoscope and dosage notebook, ready to face whatever the night ahead might hold. Fortunately, I was taking over from Marlies. Other colleagues might lob an "Everything's under control" your way and disappear before you've even had a chance to put on your coat. Then, when you take a look around, you discover the beds are full of patients without their histories, test results, or any kind of plan, while people in the examination rooms are complaining that they've been waiting two hours for a doctor. With Marlies at least there were sure to be no surprises.

I knew it would be a quiet night until the end of the game. We all were following our team's comeback in Liège with one eye and studying the menu from the corner pizzeria with the other, hoping to have something delivered before the postgame turmoil got under way. One of the first things you learn in a hospital is to eat and sleep whenever you can, as it might be your last chance for a long time.

I was arguing with Nurse Sophie about whether I'd had lasagna al forno or the chef's spaghetti the last time when the automatic doors flew open and my colleague Schreiber stormed in. The ambulance paramedics were right on his heels with a stretcher on which I saw a patient with our All-Around Worry-Free Package:

he or she had been intubated and the chest was moving rhythmically up and down with the help of a portable breathing machine; several IVs were feeding meds of one kind or another into the body; and an ECG monitor was peeping sixty times a minute, nice and even.

Schreiber yelled, "ICU, ICU, the key!"

The paramedics asked for the score in Belgium.

Patients who arrive by ambulance in an emergency usually sail through directly to Intensive Care. A separate elevator leads up to the ICU, and those of us who work in the ER have the key. If a younger colleague is on call for emergencies, the doctor in the ER generally decides whether the ICU is really necessary before releasing the elevator key.

"What have you got for us, Schreiber?" I asked in a deliberately casual tone, every inch the experienced attending physician who doesn't ever lose his cool. After all, the guy on the stretcher wasn't my patient.

"Give us the key, Hoffmann! Whaddya want? The man's being ventilated, needs a jug full of catecholamine, and has a pacemaker. Do you guys really want to take care of him down here?"

Pretty sassy for a doctor who was just a month into his second year of residency, but I could tell that Schreiber was pretty stressed and releasing a jug of catecholamine into his own system right then. He was also clearly proud that he'd done the All-Around Worry-Free Package all on his own. He knew he could expect some praise for that.

"Well done, Schreiber. Now let me take a peek."

However, I could see only the patient's face and upper body; the rest of him was buried beneath a tangle of high-tech medical paraphernalia. The patient's pupils rested motionless in deep yellow eyeballs, and his upper body reminded me of a map, with large patches of dark bluish-red oceans forming around dirty yellow continents on the chest and shoulders. It was a case of advanced jaundice with massive hemorrhaging below the skin, probably the result of a total collapse of liver function—an extremely bad prognosis. A feast for the ICU and one that was almost certain to have a fatal outcome. Despite his color, the face looked familiar.

"You're right, Schreiber. Doesn't look good." I glanced at the screen. "Have you looked at the ECG monitor recently?"

The ECG monitor was blinking and peeping away rhythmically, which was a reassuring sound as long as you didn't look at the monitor. There it became clear that the cable from the pacemaker Schreiber had installed was giving the patient's heart a slight, well-meant jolt of electricity sixty times a minute, but that the heart could not be persuaded to work on its own. Patients often think that they won't die with a pacemaker, but they're wrong, as this case demonstrated. This patient was already good and dead.

Now Schreiber saw it too, and his paramedics recognized the problem as well.

"He was breathing fine a minute ago," they chorused.

Whatever gaps there might be in their training, paramedics have that statement hammered into them by the fire department really well. I looked at the patient's motionless pupils, then into Schreiber's innocent, Nordic blue eyes.

"Intubation, ventilator, and still he breathed his last. Amazing!"

"Well," Schreiber replied, qualifying his statement, "he had blood pressure back at the Kaisereiche."

It's about two miles from the Kaisereiche to the hospital.

"What was his blood pressure?"

"Oh, about forty, fifty systolic."

"Let's see the log, Schreiber."

Now I had him, and he knew it. Of course he didn't have a log; a doctor on an emergency call has more pressing matters to attend to during the call. The logs are written up the next morning over breakfast at the earliest, if you can even get around to it then.

"What do we do now?" Schreiber asked in a more subdued tone than before.

It was easy. The patient needed to go off to Pathology. That may sound simple, but it isn't. The real question was: Did they bring the patient in dead or had he taken his last breath one centimeter over the threshold of the ER? That would determine whether the ambulance or the ER would have to do the paperwork and see to it that the patient got transferred to Pathology. And that's precisely what the paramedics meant with their "He was breathing fine a minute ago."

"Go get yourself a cup of coffee, Schreiber. Come up with a few poetic lines for your log entry, and then we'll produce a beautiful death certificate together."

I felt a little sorry for Schreiber. The night shift in the emergency vehicle is bloody hard work. Because it isn't very popular, the younger residents are normally stuck with it—the argument being that they'll get all sorts of great experience. Schreiber had indeed learned something important tonight: even our All-Around Worry-Free Package couldn't protect a physician from having a patient die on him. Sometimes all the high-tech equipment in the world didn't do a speck of good.

The paramedics had washed themselves of the case; they were now having coffee with the admission nurses and watching the end of the second half of the game. They were off the hook as long as Schreiber was busy with his log.

We'd stuck the body in an examination room. While Schreiber was toiling away on his report, I took a closer look at the corpse. Again the face looked familiar, but I just couldn't place it.

"Where did you actually pick him up?"

"On Uhlandstrasse," Schreiber said, looking up from his paper, "in some sort of hostel for asylum seekers. All they told us was that he suffered a 'sudden loss of consciousness.' No wonder with all the vodka bottles lying around. But he's a bit too yellow to have simply been drunk. If you ask me, it was alcohol poisoning, which led to cirrhosis of the liver, or all the vodka was gone and he had taken solace in denatured alcohol. I couldn't find out anything more than that. There was a mob of people there, but they couldn't—or wouldn't—speak German."

"Did you find any papers?"

"Here. He had a passport in his pants."

It was a Ukrainian passport, in Cyrillic script, with a tourist visa from the German embassy in Kiev on one of the last pages that permitted Chenkov, Misha, born April 20, 1971, to visit the Federal Republic of Germany for three months. Those three months had run out a good year ago.

As I studied the passport, it finally clicked where I knew him from: Misha had done some cleaning in our hospital, whose entire cleaning staff was comprised of Russians and Ukrainians. He'd been a patient in my ward the previous October, but he'd disappeared one day and never returned, neither as a cleaner nor as a patient. He didn't have a family doctor, so I hadn't needed to write a medical report or come up with a diagnosis. Now he was lying before me, disconcertingly yellow and dead.

"What should I say the time of death was?"

Schreiber was apparently working on the most critical part of his report. We had to make a decision: DOA or did he die in the clinic?

"I need some coffee first. Let's get the death certificate done and then your log will write itself."

We went out to join the nurses and paramedics.

"Things are picking up, Dr. Hoffmann. You've got to take a look at a stomach in exam room one and a pill poisoning in two."

"What kind of pills?"

"It's an eighteen-year-old. Just a package of twenty Valium five. She's a bit tired, but she's responsive and her blood pressure's good."

Working with Nurse Sophie and her team was a godsend. I had total faith in her and knew that I wouldn't find a comatose, half-dead girl hiding behind her statement.

"Start program three. I've just got to finish up with this dead guy with Schreiber."

Program three is a strong gastric lavage that can be delegated to the nurses if the patient is awake. It's carried out for educational purposes as much as therapeutic reasons, our hope being that the patient won't be pestering us again anytime soon after being subjected to it.

I poured some coffee and we got down to business. Schreiber had no shortage of death certificates in his bag; they took up almost as much room as his medications.

"(a) Immediate cause of death…(b) As a result of…(c) As a result of (underlying disease)…" Woe to any death that didn't match the sequence prescribed by a German death certificate. The only way a frustrated physician filling out the certificate can get any revenge is by listing "cardiopulmonary arrest," "unnatural causes," or "cause of death undetermined." Writing in "cause of death undetermined" can set an inexorable series of events in motion. The corpse is appropriated, a criminal investigation has to be opened, and forensics might well have to perform an autopsy.

"What do you think?" Schreiber asked. "Should we check off 'cardiopulmonary arrest'?"

"How about 'death by medical treatment'?"

I instantly regretted my little joke. Schreiber looked like he was in bad shape. Posttraumatic stress. Well, he'd better get used to it.

"I was sure I had everything under control. He barely had any blood pressure, and he didn't have a regular heartbeat by the time we got to the hostel. But it all went really well. A quick subclavian for the IV, a neat internal jugular vein for the pacemaker, no bad puncture, no esophageal intubation. We had him pretty well stabilized when we drove off."

"He didn't have a chance, Schreiber. Nobody could have got him here alive. Not you, not me, not the pope. You did a good job, so don't blame yourself."

We took our coffee back to the exam room, where Misha was waiting to be shipped off to Pathology. Cadavers used to have a sort of suitcase tag tied to their toes, and it was that tag that somehow transformed a human being into an object. Now they wear special armbands, and Misha's had already been attached: "Chenkov, Misha, April 20, 1971." We had quite an efficient nursing team on the case. "You know, Schreiber, he was a patient of mine once."

Misha seemed to be watching us with his yellow eyes—somewhat apathetically perhaps, but as though he was eager to hear why he had to die.

"He was your patient? Why?"

"We didn't find anything serious back then. That's why I'm so interested in what he died of. I think we should say 'cause of death unexplained.' Then we'll get the details. Besides, it'll give other people something to do."

The typical sounds of coughing and retching penetrated the thin walls—that eighteen-year-old wouldn't forget her gastric lavage anytime soon.

"Have you drawn some blood for the study, Schreiber?"

He had. We were a teaching hospital after all, and one way we justified our existence was to carry out studies for science. Blood samples were regularly taken from ambulance patients, put into a centrifuge, and frozen. Doctoral students painstakingly gathered a variety of lab results from them later, then correlated the data with the patients' lives based on information taken from the ambulance protocols. A typical bean-counting study yielded a predictable result: we might find, for example, that sick patients with hardly any blood pressure and rapid breathing do not tend to leave this hospital alive, whereas healthy people with good blood pressure and normal breathing do. Since I worked in a teaching hospital, I was obligated to generate at least one publication each year. We couldn't do anything more for Misha; Misha, on the other hand, could, with a little blood sample, quite likely do something for me and my career.

Schreiber was staring at the death certificate; he was having difficulty with the section "moment of death—determination of death—day, month, year, time of day."

"Schreiber, give me that certificate." He gave me a puzzled look. "Look, 'Doctor,' the man died here. You brought him in here alive." Schreiber breathed a sigh of relief. "But you can return the favor. Be so good as to put his blood sample through the centrifuge right away, and put it in the deep freeze. Then it'll be time to head back out again. Berlin needs you; life goes on."

So I filled out the death certificate and signed it. I gave the time of death as 7:10 p.m., five minutes after he'd arrived at the clinic. I had no idea that at that moment I was almost signing my own death certificate, or at least landing myself in a heap of trouble. And as is the often the case with trouble, I had no one to blame but myself.

CHAPTER 2

That night the usual mix of people came through the door: the truly ill; the hypochondriacs; and a handful of people heading to Asia, the Caribbean, or wherever the next morning, who just wanted a quick check-up or vaccine—right away, please—for typhus, plague, or cholera. Sick people are the least of our problems; you either make a diagnosis and start treatment or you make a different diagnosis and transfer them to the relevant department. I'd stretched out a few times but only for long enough to be reminded how fantastic it is to lie in a real bed at night.

I met Heinz Valenta from the ICU and Hartmut from Surgery at breakfast in our cozy hospital cafeteria, which looked like some cross between a former East German restaurant and a gas station. Seeing them—gray and exhausted—chewing vacantly on their open-faced sandwiches and sipping their coffee, I got a pretty good idea of what I looked like right then; I haven't made the mistake of looking in the mirror after night duty for a long time, so it was something of a revelation. The television screen was filled with pictures of airplane parts strewn widely over a high plateau in Africa; an Airbus had gone down shortly after takeoff.

Our success stories from the night before suddenly felt petty by comparison.

We had to gobble down our delicious cafeteria rolls, which had become no fresher since our hospital kitchen had been privatized as "Hospital Catering Services." There wasn't any time allotted for breakfast after night duty, since the morning beds meeting took place right after the end of the shift. Blood had been drawn in the wards before the meeting and the lab results would be ready shortly. So we'd soon be able to send the more or less healed patients on their way to make room for a fresh batch. It's a huge tactical error to skip the morning meetings; that's when new patients are distributed among the wards, and the haggling is on par with what you'd find in an Oriental bazaar.

By the time Heinz Valenta and I entered the Internal Medicine meeting room, the bargaining was in high gear. As I sat down, I realized I still had the aftertaste of hard-boiled eggs in my mouth and discovered a new coffee stain on my white coat—I'd admitted two elderly patients who'd had strokes, and the ER day shift had to slough them off somehow.

The ward nurses are always admonishing the ward physicians before these meetings. "Just don't bring me any stroke patients!" It's easy to see why. They're a hell of a lot of work for the nurses, who are already overworked, and success, if any, is minimal and rare. They always end up in the wards that only sent their residents to the meeting—likely because the senior ward physician chose to have coffee with his nurses instead of attending.

The beds meeting was originally called the "morning conference," and its original purpose was to give the doctors a chance to discuss problem cases in the wards or ones that had come in on the night shift. For this reason, it was attended by the entire Admissions Committee (which we had nicknamed the "Central Committee"), comprised of the heads of our three Internal Medicine departments and Prof. Dohmke, who lorded over the fully automated—and recently privatized—lab as the medical director of the hospital.

The department heads and Prof. Dohmke hadn't done a night shift for years. Superbly well rested, they were always ready to dispense an abundance of advice in the morning. For that reason, doctors coming off the night shift had no desire to report on their various battles, large or small—whether it be their patients' intransigence or technological shortcomings—because if they had, they would then have been subjected to the committee's lengthy and scintillating commentary. As a result, the monotonous summaries of those who'd been on night duty made it sound as though our Best-of-All-Hospitals was a bastion of heavenly peace every single night.

"And who was on duty in the ER?"

I had nodded off by that time; the series of reports about the previous night traditionally ended with the doctor on duty in the ER.

"Nothing special in the ER," I announced a little late. "We had one death. A Russian from the CareClean Company crew who was a patient here last October. Looked like acute liver failure. Autopsy underway."

"Well, well, a Russian."

A typically profound comment from Prof. Kindel, the chief of Cardiology and my immediate superior.

"To be more precise, he wasn't actually Russian but Ukrainian. As I said, he's being autopsied."

"Interesting, Herr Hoffmann. Keep us informed."

My morning stupor was apparently in an advanced state after the night shift. Nobody in the room was interested in my yellow Misha and certainly not in whether he was from Russia or Ukraine. I could have told them anything—that he'd come from Mars with a liver virus imperiling all mankind—but as far as my colleagues were concerned, the meeting was over.

After the main battle over the distribution of new patients had been fought, the doctors just wanted to get over to their wards as soon as possible to rev up the daily hamster wheel. Of course I would never report on the autopsy, and nobody would ever ask about it. At least I hadn't mentioned that I'd checked off "cause of death undetermined." That would almost certainly have inspired a detailed lesson on the proper way to fill out a death certificate, and I, too, wanted to get the daily ward business under way soon.

"Good. If there's no further business…"

Even before Prof. Kindel officially brought the meeting to a close, the ward physicians were out of their seats and on their way to their patients.

The day turned out to be no more chaotic than usual on Ward IIIb; I got through it somehow, as I did whenever I had to work after coming straight off the night shift. After doing my patient rounds, I called Medical Records to have them dig up the old record for the late Misha Chenkov, but the line was busy as usual. So I filled out a request for the file and tossed it in the out basket.

By early afternoon, I had the ward largely under control and could begin to think about heading home—the patients who could be discharged had left, the patients who were to be moved had been moved, and the new patients had been admitted. I was lucky that the first-year resident was away on vacation, so he couldn't hold me up with his silly questions or know-it-all text-book wisdom. I asked Marlies, who was managing IIIc next door with Schreiber, to look after my patients in an emergency, and I asked my ward nurse Elke to keep family members off Marlies's back and all doctors except Marlies off the patients' backs. I'd had it up to here and wanted to go home. Home sweet home, where I could crawl into bed and get some sleep.

Even in my exhausted state, I remained curious. It was unlikely that Misha had already been autopsied, because, as the physician who signed the death certificate, I would have been notified. Nonetheless I made a quick call to Pathology and got Karl, the superintendent, or chief diener (orderlies in that department had been dubbed "dieners" because they worked with corpses).

"Karl, Hoffmann here. Have you guys already autopsied the yellow Russian?"

"He was from Ukraine, Doctor."

"Don't mess with me, Karl. Do you have him or not?"

"Your yellow Ukrainian is long gone. In one piece and without a scratch."

"No autopsy?"

"No autopsy."

"Did the state attorney's office take him over?"

"Why, Doctor? What would the state attorney do with him? The boys from the funeral home came and got him right away. I'm happy to get rid of the yellow ones fast. It might have been something infectious."

"How come there was no postmortem, Karl?"

"Why should there be, Doctor? Cardiopulmonary arrest, autopsy refused. It was short and sweet. He was our guest for just short of ten hours. We could hardly charge him the full rate for room and board."

"Karl, please wait for me. I'll be right over."

Though I'd worked in the hospital for eight years, I always found it hard to find the Pathology department. I made my way through the cafeteria on the first floor and found the elevator to the basement. After leaving the cafeteria, you can just follow your nose—the increasingly potent stench of formaldehyde points the way. Grieving family members arrive another way, following the shortest path from the Personal Records Department, where they are offered a few brief platitudes along with their documents for the Bureau of Vital Statistics and the funeral parlor. That route leads a few steps down into the basement and directly into the belly of the hospital, past Receiving, the laundry, and the garbage disposal center. I don't know that mourners even pick up on the proximity of Pathology to the garbage disposal center. In addition to the fact that these hallways aren't exactly reverential, there's another disadvantage: the inescapable stench of the recycling and garbage disposal centers prevents the bereaved from using the smell of formaldehyde to guide them. So if it's necesssary, our bedding launderers and garbage men show mourning stragglers, in silent sympathy, which way to go.

I knew Karl, the superintendent of Pathology, very well. The "intendent" part of his title was quite apt, since the dead are indeed often "tended" more carefully by him than they were in the wards during their lifetime. We've known each other for years, dating back to my state exams, when, for a small price—a bottle of supermarket brandy—he let me see the cadavers that were to be part of the next day's examination.

Karl might have a bit of an alcohol problem, but I knew he would never have misread a death certificate or gotten a cadaver and its certificate mixed up.

When I finally found Pathology, he was sorting through autopsy reports and histological findings.

"You look like you're in top form, Felix!" he said. "Were you on the night shift?"

We've been on a first-name basis since the business of the exam cadavers.

"I was, Karl. But when yellow Misha arrived, I was still relatively fresh and certainly able to fill out a postmortem document properly. So—why no autopsy? I checked off 'cause of death undetermined.'"

"From you? I don't have a postmortem examination request from you, Doctor."

"You haven't got a document for the yellow cadaver?"

"Of course I do. Do you think I can release the body any other way?"

"Can I see the request, Karl?"

Karl was a little unsure of himself now, but he was still precise. "You can see our copy. The undertakers have the original. How do you think they could put him in the ground without it?" Karl took the Postmortem Examination Documents binder off a shelf and gave me the top file. "Chenkov, Misha. Born April 20, 1971." Yep, it was the right document. The information was all correct—deceased the day before at 7:10 p.m.—but it wasn't in my handwriting. I read ahead. "Cause of death: cardiopulmonary arrest. Autopsy: refused." The signature read "Dr. Klaus Schreiber, Resident."

I returned the file to Karl.

"Something wrong?"

"Who refused the autopsy, Karl?"

"How do I know. Probably the family, who else. Ask Schreiber."

I stormed out to do just that.

I made my way directly to the doctors' room in IIIc, where I found Marlies and Schreiber. Marlies was dictating medical reports and making up for this hateful task with a piece of crumble cake; powdered sugar was sprinkled over her lips, the dictating machine, and the patients' files. Schreiber was packing up—a young father trying to get home on time.

"What happened, Schreiber?"

"What's supposed to have happened, Doctor? I had a crappy night shift in our fabulous emergency vehicle, I've discharged six patients and admitted seven, and I was flamed by Kindel while discussing X-rays. Apart from that, I have a wife and child, and I'm going home right now."

"I've just been over in Path. The yellow Russian from last night has already been picked up."

"So what?"

"He wasn't picked up by forensics. He wasn't even autopsied. A new postmortem document has suddenly appeared, filled out and signed by you. Cause of death: 'cardiopulmonary arrest. Autopsy: refused.'"

I thought I saw his hands tremble slightly as he was packing his things into his messenger bag, but that didn't mean anything: the man had been on his feet for thirty-two hours, after all.

"Felix, don't you think cardiopulmonary arrest describes the cause of death rather precisely?" Marlies intervened, a bite of cake raised to her lips.

"I want to know, Schreiber, why you filled out a new postmortem examination document."

"Because it's simpler that way."

"What do you mean by that?"

"'Cause of death undetermined' is something you talked me into. And that would have meant a long protocol, police inquiries, and who knows what else."

"Who told you that?"

"People who obviously want to do better by me more than you do."

"Bullshit! The only thing that happens if the cause of death isn't clear is that you get the autopsy results, and then you know the score. And besides, any possible inquiries would have wound up on my plate—I signed the document."

"See here, *Doctor* Hoffmann. Last night I had to fill out three other postmortem forms in the ambulance, and things went fine. One was a man around fifty whom we tried resuscitating for an hour, lying in his own shit. This morning I had to cut an old woman down off her clothesline. She'd been cold for hours and didn't smell real fresh either. And the last one, a half hour before the end of my shift, was an eight-month-old infant dead in his crib. His parents' screams are still echoing in my ears. But if you wish, dear sir, I will in the future deliver all my postmortem documents to you every morning. Or I can call you at night if you prefer."

His bag was packed. He put on his summer jacket and stormed out of the room in a rage.

"What was that all about?" Marlies asked, fishing the last of her cake out of the bag. The door was suddenly flung open and Schreiber stood in the entrance.

"By the way, in case you want to report me to the Central Committee, just go ahead!"

With that, he slammed the door shut.

"I don't know exactly what's going on," I said. "Schreiber dragged in a former patient of mine last night from the ambulance. An All-Around-Worry-Free Package but DOA. He was in my ward a few months ago, and I saw a few cuts and bruises on him, but nothing of any significance. Nothing that caught our attention in any case. Last night he arrived yellow as a quince and dead. I'd like to know what he died of. And now he won't be autopsied because Schreiber might have botched it up."

Marlies got up and put her hands on my shoulders.

"We'd be millionaires if we had a penny for every patient we can't properly diagnose or identify the cause of death. What's got into you? Why rip into Schreiber like that?"

She was right—why had I taken my exhaustion and frustration out on that poor kid? I probably just felt guilty about turning Misha's case over to a rookie resident. It had made sense at the time; after all, he had only been there for observation.

"You know, Misha was one of the hospital cleaners we hardly notice and never speak to. Maybe I didn't make enough of an effort back then or overlooked something important."

"Felix, of course I understand. A patient you thought was healthy is suddenly dead. It's our worst nightmare. But I don't know any doctor who goes to even half as much trouble with his patients as you do. Go home and include dear departed Misha in your bedtime prayers. You can't do any more than that. And leave little Schreiber alone. You don't want to screw up his grant for the States, do you?"

She was right; I didn't. I needed a nice little glass of brandy and my bed. Tomorrow would be a new day. I could worry about the death of my former patient then.

CHAPTER 3

I'd come to know Misha Chenkov the previous October when he'd been a patient of mine for thirteen days. He looked like he'd taken quite a beating when the police plucked him from the john in the Zoo railway station, though he claimed at the time that he'd just fallen down the stairs. He clearly belonged in the surgical ward for his wounds—cleaning of cuts, observation for possible hemorrhaging—but he wasn't a particularly interesting case for the surgeons. A roughed-up asylum seeker who spoke and understood hardly a word of German, he very likely had no health insurance, which meant filling out a whole stack of forms to sort out who would foot the bill.

So Misha became a "consultation form patient." The attending ER physician documents his treatment of this kind of patient on a green consultation form, never on the red ER form, which would indicate that he was a patient in that department. The idea is to delay admitting the patient as long as possible in hopes that further tests will force another department to admit him.

Hartmut was the surgeon on duty on that occasion. After sewing Misha up properly, he'd tried the ophthalmologists ("threat of blindness following trauma to the eye"), then the neurosurgeons ("suspected subdural hematoma"). No luck—all he got out of those were two more consultation forms. But he hit the bull's-eye with a routine chest X-ray. "Cluster of striped lines in the left upper lobe projection. Probably old scarring. But new, perhaps specific, changes cannot be excluded; comparison with previous X-rays required." Bingo! Covering your ass is the hospital doctor's Number One Rule; you therefore put in writing whatever cannot reasonably be excluded. Hartmut knew that he'd solved his problem with the magic words "specific changes." With an innocent smile, he'd then slid Misha's file over to me: "Specific changes in chest X-ray cannot be excluded, request exclusion of tuberculosis."

Of course Hartmut knew full well that I couldn't exclude fresh pulmonary TB at one in the morning, certainly not for a Russian who wasn't carrying his old X-rays around with him in the Zoo Station john. The TB ploy was especially troublesome because Misha would have to be isolated, and since there wasn't a free room in the isolation ward, I had to clear out an entire room in my ward and listen to the hue and cry of the patients involved. I got my revenge on Hartmut by calling him every hour to make sure there was no new hemorrhaging. Having dumped Misha on me, he should also be forced to suffer a bit.

Although TB bacteria had long ago been pushed off into the margins of society, they'd come back with a vengeance in Europe after the fall of the Berlin Wall and the Iron Curtain. Much like Albanian weapons dealers, Russian diamond smugglers, and Ukrainian drug lords, they, too, had benefited from the newly granted freedom to travel. And doctors everywhere once again found themselves reaching for their textbooks on infectious diseases, where we were reminded that our best chance of finding the little critters was in stomach juices or pulmonary secretions taken directly from the bronchial tubes.

In order for us to obtain the necessary sample, Misha had had to swallow a stomach tube first thing the following morning—for breakfast, so to speak; for dessert, we'd had to submit him to a bronchoscoping, which meant inserting a flexible tube into his bronchial tubes via his windpipe. Neither procedure was especially pleasant, but Misha offered no resistance to the stomach tube and only protested a bit during the bronchoscopy. I don't speak Russian so I couldn't explain to him what was going to take place in advance, and he didn't know enough German to refuse. Besides, it's rather difficult to register a protest with a tube in your stomach or a bronchoscope between your teeth.

Harald, my resident, who was fresh from medical school, was an interested bystander throughout these procedures. First-year residents, also called interns, are the answer to the financial misery of the health sector. Though they've completed all their medical study, they haven't a clue about real medicine. So the overworked hospital doctor has the honor—along with performing his regular duties of caring for patients, keeping the ward nurses happy, and hunting down missing test results—of training these rookies. The trick lies in the fact that an intern, with a few restrictions, is entered on the hospital books as a doctor but makes less than half of a normal doctor's salary. So hospitals can get two for the price of one. Which hospital CFO would ever pass up such a deal?

Of course Harald would have loved to have inserted the stomach tube and the bronchoscope himself. I couldn't even argue that he'd never performed either of these procedures before, and I realized that even I had to do them for the first time at some point—though perhaps with a somewhat clearer idea of the esophagus's anatomy than Harald seemed to have. I thought his rationale—that Misha's inability to speak German made him an ideal candidate for his medical training—was ludicrous, but that was typical of Harald. I assured him that his day—and his patient—would come soon, because among patients, as in the real world, there was no lack of assholes.

I received the report the next day from Bacteriology via the hospital's intranet: "No direct evidence of acid-fast rods. Culture initiated." Misha could only be considered definitively negative for TB if no TB bacteria grew in his cultures. Though we wouldn't know this for a good two months, we could at least take him out of isolation for the time being.

I took on the surgical care of his wounds myself, which didn't involve anything more than an occasional bit of iodine and a new dressing. I used my mother's old secret recipe to treat the large, somewhat infected flesh wound on his upper thigh: I didn't close the wound but instead poured a decent amount of sugar into it and let the wound granulate shut from within. This resulted in several serious arguments with Harald, who considered himself an expert in treating wounds, among other things, and insisted on both local and systemic coverage with antibiotics. I finally told him that if he were to use antibiotics on Misha, I would strictly adhere to this protocol of his when the time came to treat any of *his* wounds. At that, he stalked off in search of new victims for his medical experiments.

Actually, we could have released Misha after five days. His wounds had healed considerably by then, and no other illnesses had come to light in spite of the hundreds of cc's of blood we'd taken—or rather, that Harald had taken. Interns love to take blood and send it off in little tubes for a countless number of lab tests. The typical intern is astounded to read in the *Manual of Laboratory Diagnostics* how many different diseases—which he can scarcely identify—can be tested for with a patient's blood. And all you have to do is to find a nice vein, put a serious expression on your face, and make a few *x*'s on the lab label. Now, you may ask why senseless lab tests, which of course factor into a hospital's operating costs, are not prohibited. It's not a bad question, especially in a hospital with privatized laboratory services whose boss and part owner is the hospital's medical director, Prof. Dohmke.

As I've said, from a strictly medical point of view, Misha could have been discharged after a few days. But I was afraid I'd find him cleaning our floors again the next day and felt that he deserved a few days' vacation. Besides, I still didn't know why he'd been beaten up or by whom—he insisted on sticking to his story about falling down the stairs—but I thought it would probably be safer for him if he stayed out of circulation for a little longer. I knew that an insurance form would land on my desk sooner or later demanding an explanation for why Chenkov was still hospitalized. But I was sure that at least one of Harald's hundred tests would turn out to be at least marginally or even outright pathological. That basic law of statistics would help when it came time for me to fill out the questionnaire.

I was proven right. Misha had been our grateful, low-cost patient for a little under two weeks when I came out of the heart catheter lab one afternoon and found him receiving a blood transfusion, despite the fact that all previous test results had shown him to be perfectly healthy. Misha was silently and unquestioningly allowing the procedure to take place, just as he had when Harald had performed his battery of tests. Harald, meanwhile, was in the doctor's room studying the results of his daily lab triumphant strikes.

"We were right to keep the Russian here. We almost missed a severe anemia. I ordered a blood transfusion; the first bag's in already."

"So I saw."

Harald was beaming; he had finally saved a human life.

"It's good I did another blood count today. Otherwise we might have kicked him out onto the street with a hemoglobin count of five point five."

"Hemoglobin five point five?"

"Yes. Pretty low, eh?"

"Harald, when did you last do Misha's blood work?"

Misha's blood count had been spot-on normal two days earlier, just as it had been four, six, and eight days earlier, and whenever else Harald had marked "CBC" on the lab label. It was simple enough to do a computer match to find the right owner of the 5.5 hemoglobin reading, a stomach cancer patient who truly did need a blood transfusion. It seemed that Harald or the lab doing the testing that day had mixed up Misha's sample with the cancer patient's. Misha was lucky that the blood work had been done before the rest of the lab tests. I hate to think what kind of acute therapy Harald might have subjected our poor Ukrainian to if he'd seen those results. In any case, the time had come to discharge Misha before he came to any serious harm in our hospital.

But we never even had the chance to formally release him. By the next morning, Misha had vanished from my ward and never reappeared. Neither as a patient nor as a hardworking employee of CareClean Cleaning Services.

The next time I laid eyes on him was as a corpse in the ER, on the night of the Germany-Romania game. Now he'd never be able to tell me who beat him up in the railway station and why. Or why he'd left the hospitable care of our clinic without so much as a farewell. I didn't feel good about it. I wondered whether Schreiber had made some mistake during the emergency call that had done our Misha in. Maybe that was why he'd filled out a new death certificate preventing an autopsy; there was no doubt, however, that Misha had already been fatally ill at that point.

Had I been in a coma at the time? Had I missed something vital? Or had he been infected in the hospital? Had I entrusted Misha to Harald's questionable medical care because he was only a floor cleaner from Kiev? The uneasiness I felt might be difficult for a layperson to understand; it was a matter of guilt, yes, but also one of medical curiosity. And of my medical honor. To overlook an incipient illness, and a life-threatening one at that, is unacceptable. If I really had missed something back then, then it could happen again today, and more patients could die on my watch. I simply couldn't put the matter behind me.

Although the case could no longer be cleared up by an autopsy, an investigation of the patient's medical history could lead me to a correct diagnosis. The next step was for me to gather as much information as I could about the final months of Misha Chenkov's life.

CHAPTER 4

Almost eight months had passed since Misha's guest appearance as a TB suspect on my ward; now it was summertime, which coincided with the European Championship in Belgium and Holland. Celine had frozen the pizza that we hadn't been able to enjoy the other night and videotaped the Germany-Romania game. Since I'm not much of a soccer fan and already knew that the game ended one–all, we just ate our pizza and then made love: once during halftime (with Celine on top—*yes!*) and again during the second break before extra time (with me on top—*good!*).

Less fun was the fact that Harald had returned from his Greek vacation two days after Misha died, which once again slowed down the work on the ward. Meanwhile, Schreiber was avoiding me. I'd mentioned the death certificate to him once more but only got a snotty response. Admittedly, he was quite busy. He'd applied for a study grant at Mount Sinai Hospital in New York, which would be a big coup for his career, and would find out whether he could go in the coming weeks. These decisions are made by the Central Committee, so his best bet was to keep a low profile, work hard, use few expensive medications, and ensure that the patients in his ward didn't stay long.

We hadn't been public employees for a good year. Like so many others, our hospital had been turned into a corporation, and the pressure to cut costs had increased markedly since. We now received a computer printout once a month that compared the length of patient visits and the consumption of medications with the month the year before, and, even more importantly, with the same statistics for the other wards. Overruns of more than 5 percent led without fail to a summons before the Admissions Committee, and if they happened repeatedly, you might have to justify yourself to the hospital's COO, Dr. Bredow.

Although Misha was not a hospital expense this last time thanks to the fact that he'd passed on, I couldn't get him out of my mind. Ultimately, it was Gertrud Schön, a patient admitted with a diagnosis of "indeterminate jaundice," that prompted me to get back on the case—though her skin was only a pale yellow compared with Misha's deep yellow hue. Frau Schön seemed to be in no acute danger, and the diagnostic measures for jaundice can be found in any medical text. I decided that Harald should be able to handle Frau Schön, which would give me time to look into Misha. However, it turned out I had misread the situation. When I saw Frau Schön the next day, she had turned almost as yellow as Misha, and she was clearly not well.

Harald was, as usual, convinced that concern for a patient can be measured by the number of lab tests requested. As a result, he'd sent quarts of blood off to the lab for testing for hepatitis A, B, and C, hemolytic anemia, rat fever, typhus, toxoplasmosis, sleeping sickness, rickets, amoebas, yellow fever, Rocky Mountain spotted fever, and of course syphilis and AIDS as well. Unconvinced by Harald's belief that yellow fever and spotted fever were viable possibilities in this age of tourism, I glanced at Frau Schön's abdomen. The abdominal walls were tense but could still take a dent. I could produce a sharp pain in the right upper abdomen, directly over the gall bladder.

"It's distension of the liver, which is common with jaundice," Harald informed me.

"Have you asked your patient about gallstones, *my esteemed colleague?*"

"My esteemed colleague" is doctor speak for "you moron." Frau Schön had no way of knowing that and jumped in to help.

"I've always had gallstones, Doctor, but my family doctor said they didn't have to come out."

Despite his limitations, Harald caught on quickly.

"I've already ordered an abdominal ultrasound."

Had he really filled out and sent off the ultrasound request for Frau Schön's abdomen? If so, the form would now be languishing in a large pile of similar requests in our Gastroenterology Department and would have to wait its turn. But Frau Schön's abdomen couldn't wait that long. I had Harald cart the heavy ultrasound machine, a clumsy old crate the size of a small freezer chest, over from Marlies's ward.

A thick, fat gallstone was sitting directly in the choledochal duct; not a single drop of bile would get past it to the intestine, where it belonged. So the bile had found another way out and taken a direct path into the bloodstream, which was the cause of Frau Schön's "jaundice." Thanks to our surgeons, she was rid of her gallstone three hours later and only a touch yellow the next day when Harald and I paid her a visit in Surgery. She was effusive in her thanks to him, for caring for her so selflessly. Harald beamed.

As I've said, my guilt had resurfaced because of Frau Schön and her jaundice. Medical Records had still not sent me Misha's ward record from the October before, so I called to follow up.

"You must send me Form Number Four, Dr. Hoffmann, or I can't do anything. Surely you know that," an unenthusiastic voice explained.

"Sure, I know that. I did it three days ago."

"Then it would have to be here."

"Listen, I'll send you another copy. Can you please go and find me the record anyway?"

"How urgent is it, Dr. Hoffmann? It's vacation season and we're pretty short staffed at the moment."

"Nevertheless, I need that record."

"Is the patient back in the ward?"

"No, he's dead."

"Then you'll have to be patient for a few days. You're welcome to come down here and see the pile of requests. There are only two of us in the archives at the moment, and we've already got our hands full with acute readmissions. You must understand that, Dr. Hoffmann."

As part of his cost-cutting measures, COO Bredow had reduced the staff in the archives by more than half. I couldn't blame the pissant on the other end of the line and filled out a second request form like an obedient child.

Organizing Frau Schön's operation had wrought havoc with my schedule. By the time I was finally able to leave my patients to their fates with a clear conscience, the cleaning crew had already begun their night shift. Jurek was as usual cleaning my ward; I guessed that he was from Russia or Ukraine.

Jurek could speak a few scraps of German, and I always asked him how he was doing and wished him a good day when I crossed paths with him. But I had no idea what he'd done before moving to Germany. Had he earned a living as a janitor in his home country? Or was he an important but now redundant expert on ICBM flight paths, or a highly decorated physicist in his country's atom bomb program?

He wore a one-piece blue suit with a yellow logo on the back: "CareClean—Cleanliness Is Our Job." Bredow had contracted with an outside firm for the cleaning, just as he had done with the cafeteria. Another cost-cutting measure.

"How's it going, Jurek?"

The fact that we only knew these people by their first names—if at all—was not right.

"Good. Good. Thanks, Doctor. Must go."

His accent had improved noticeably since we'd last spoken. But that had been months ago.

"Did you know Misha from Kiev?"

"Misha, yes. Misha dead. You know, Doctor?"

"Yes, Misha's dead, I know. Did you know him?"

"We together worked here, Misha and me. And then he sick. He here, in hospital."

"And afterward, did you see him afterward?"

"Misha sick, work nothing. Much sick at end. Much yellow."

Our mutual language difficulties foiled my attempts to glean anything more about Misha's illness over the last few months.

"Did he have a physician?"

"A physician?"

"Did he have a doctor?"

"No, no. Misha doctor nothing. Resident permit not good no more. But you tell nothing, Doctor."

"Don't worry, Jurek, I'm not the Foreigners' Registration Office. Do you know where Misha lived?"

"Uhlandstrasse. In hostel. There many of us."

I didn't have anything planned for that evening, and Celine had her karate class that night. I considered treating myself to a glass of wine at a café in Fasanenstrasse, or taking a stroll down the Kurfürstendamm and admiring the legs of the young girls in short skirts and the unshakeable optimism of the young and not so young men who invariably tried to strike up conversations with them. Either way, I planned to stop by the hostel in Uhlandstrasse. Somebody there might be able to tell me something about the progression of Misha's illness since he disappeared off my ward the October before. I didn't have the exact address, but that wasn't a problem.

The room where the paramedics usually waited for their assignments was empty; the guys were probably off on a call or maybe just refueling at the nearest curry sausage stand. The ambulance call sheet file was organized by date. Call number 1726/00 on June 12 was from a Hostel Elvira at Uhlandstrasse 141. I changed my clothes and drove downtown.

It seemed as though all of Berlin felt like going out for a drink that night. Traffic crawled, starting at the Hohenzollerndamm, and I gave up on ever finding a parking place. The wannabe trendy types found it chic to double-park their secondhand BMWs wherever they felt like it, and Berlin's meter maids were nowhere in sight.

I finally had some luck at Ludwigskirchplatz. I found an illegal spot on the sidewalk, but I hardly cared if my fourteen-year-old VW Rabbit got keyed by some disgruntled passerby.

Uhlandstrasse 141 had survived the Second World War but not the modernizing craze of the 1950s. The stucco had been removed from the façade, along with the balconies, and the whole building was spattered with gray textured plaster. New layers of plaster had been added in recent years; the owner of Uhlandstrasse 141 clearly had other ideas about how to reinvest his rental income. The building made a depressing impression, as did the two young men in tracksuits hanging around the entrance.

Hostel Elvira sprawled over the third and fourth floors and was as run-down as the building itself. I noted the dirty patches on the wallpaper, the bare or missing light bulbs, and the fading paint peeling off the doors. The reception desk on the third floor was framed by handwritten notes in Cyrillic. I guessed that they informed the hostel's esteemed guests that they were only allowed one bath a week and should keep a close eye on their valuables. One of the notes was in German: "Room Rent To Be Paid In Advance Every Day." The owner of the Hostel Elvira had clearly realized that a clientele comprised of illegal workers is not very demanding and quite financially rewarding.

The man behind the desk, also wearing a tracksuit, was leafing through a Russian magazine. On my way over, I'd been mulling over whether I should say I was the public health officer, shove my medical ID under his nose, mutter something about the danger of an epidemic, and threaten to shut the place down. That suddenly seemed like a ridiculous plan, so I chose a somewhat more direct approach.

"Hello. I'm looking for Misha Chenkov. He's a friend of mine."

The man behind the reception desk looked at me without interest.

"*Ya vas ne ponimayu. Ya ne govoryu po-nyemyetski.*"

One of the few disadvantages of growing up on the western side of the Wall was that I didn't speak Russian. I automatically resorted to that silly phrase "I no understand," which makes it impossible for foreigners ever to learn correct German.

"I—seek—Misha Chenkov. He *tovarich* of me."

The Russian sort of shrugged and repeated his earlier comment.

"*Ya vas ne ponimayu. Ya ne govoryu po-nyemyetski.*"

"What room Misha? Can you show me Misha's room?"

No reaction. My I-no-understand-German was slowly beginning to annoy even me.

"Listen, my friend. I'm not the police and not from the Foreigners' Registration Office either. I'm a doctor. Misha Chenkov was my patient. In the hospital. Last October. And now he's dead. I'd like to find out why he's dead. What made him turn yellow? Did he run a fever? Did he occasionally go home to Ukraine? Did he have any visitors? Friends?"

No response; it was pointless. He probably didn't understand on purpose and certainly didn't care. He probably had some experiences with German authorities—and strict instructions on how to behave with strangers.

I considered shoving a few bills over the counter, but my briefcase was in the car. Or stolen by now.

"Have a good day, *tovarich*, and many thanks. You were a big help."

When I left the building, it was still almost as warm as at midday. As usual, I hadn't bothered to lock the doors of my Rabbit, but my briefcase lay untouched on the passenger seat. And my car hadn't even been keyed. So I set off to a little bistro in Fasanenstrasse and ordered a cappuccino. The coffee came from Italy, the waiter from Poland, and the clientele largely from Russia. Fasanenstrasse had always been an elegant street and was a fine example of how some things never change. It had been primarily inhabited by wealthy Russian exiles after the Communist Revolution and was once again colonized by Russians after the fall of the Wall. Hundreds of thousands of euros and rubles were converted every day in its exclusive clothing boutiques and even more exclusive jewelers, exchanged by Russians who, unlike their compatriots at the Hostel Elvira, had been winners in the transition to capitalism.

Russian mothers in garish makeup sat all around me, showing off the day's haul to one another while their children screamed and ran wildly around the bistro in miniature Armani outfits. I discreetly tripped a particularly loud brawler, who fell beautifully right on his nose but then only screamed louder than before. I paid the tab and drove home. My antisocial act—successfully tripping one of those innocent children without his parents' noticing—had made up for my lack of success at the Hostel Elvira.

CHAPTER 5

Though I'd by now sent three or four request forms to Medical Records, I was still waiting for Misha's file. I tried to call several times to light a fire under them, but it appeared that they'd decided to put an end to bothersome interruptions by taking the phone off the hook.

My colleagues were on edge: a big meeting with COO Bredow was scheduled for all the doctors and department heads that afternoon. No good could come of that. The grapevine's near consensus was that the agenda would focus on new cost-cutting measures; the only discrepancies in our speculations were about what form the ominous economizing would take. Most agreed that the pharmaceuticals and ward supplies budgets would likely be taking another hit.

It turned out to be worse than that.

The meeting was held in the cafeteria, the only room big enough to hold all of us. This did not, however, mean that Dr. Bredow sprang for cake for us.

Prof. Dohmke—as I mentioned earlier, the chief lab doctor and medical director of our salubrious institution—kept it short. It was after all the COO who was to break the unpleasant news, not that Dohmke seemed to have a problem with that.

"Ladies and gentlemen. You all know about our hospital's precarious financial position. Just how precarious you are about to find out, because Chief Operating Officer Dr. Bredow is going to describe the current situation and the consequent implications."

My colleagues from Surgery hadn't noticed his presence, so a murmur fluttered through their ranks. Bredow was an inconspicuous character. A short man who was always properly but unexceptionally dressed, he looked like a senior bookkeeper, which, in some ways, he was. Rumor had it that he'd come to us after earning his stripes as a successful cost-cutting commissar at a smaller hospital. He must have taken a course in rhetoric along the way, as his speeches always followed the same pattern: praise, blame, drop the bombshell, then come to a conciliatory but meaningless conclusion. He needn't have bothered with the praise, because it was clear to one and all that Bredow didn't like doctors, and that we didn't like Bredow.

Nevertheless, he began as expected with the praise: "I know, ladies and gentlemen, how hardworking and committed you all are. Allow me to thank you for your efforts to reduce costs. Drug costs have dropped substantially in almost every ward since last fall. In the ICU sixteen percent, Nephrology eleven percent, Gynecology eighteen percent. As you can see, there is great potential for savings if one makes the effort to find them. Unfortunately, a few departments have not yet embraced that goal."

My chief, Prof. Kindel, seemed just then to discover a detail in the painting hanging on the wall that had completely escaped him until now—in the last six months, we cardiologists had been 7 percent over budget on medications.

"But I am sure that these departments will now energetically follow suit."

Pause, new subject. More praise, but in this case self-praise.

"Our outsourcing policy has also been very successful."

Bredow was said to have taken a crash course in medical Latin before his first hospital job so that he could understand what doctors were talking about; he'd been hugely disappointed to discover that modern medicine was based on Americanisms. Now he'd probably taken a crash course in management English and it was payback time. But he translated what he meant for us right away.

"Outsourcing, the assignment of certain tasks to outside companies, has led to very considerable savings. For example, we spent twenty-three percent less for cleaning services last year and over thirty percent less in the catering sector."

I wondered what Bredow might outsource next. Maybe he'd fire us all and bring in doctors from a leasing company.

"Unfortunately, ladies and gentlemen, all these measures have not been enough to pull us out of the red. You know as well as I do that over a thousand beds in Berlin are to be axed. We are competing for our survival, and only the most frugal providers will make the cut. The question is, where else can we still find potential savings?"

Everyone in the room likely wanted to reply "Not in my department" to this rhetorical question.

"Consider this: our greatest expense is personnel."

The last bit of chatter in the audience died away. It wasn't the budget that was at stake, it was us.

"May I remind you that the number of physicians over the last fifteen years has increased by almost fifteen percent, despite the fact that the bed count has remained by and large constant. You have assured me time and again that new positions would lead to a reduction in overtime. Unfortunately, though, the opposite has been the case. You are billing more overtime than ever."

This was one of Bredow's typically snide remarks. The fact that we "bill overtime" doesn't mean that we really generate it, not by a long shot. I understood his threat to mean that he would check up on it. But I was kidding myself; he wasn't concerned with peanuts today.

"I'll be completely honest with you, ladies and gentlemen…" ("Hear, hear" from the back rows.) "I am afraid that if we cannot agree on several strict new measures, we will have to talk about layoffs in the physician sector."

Dead silence in the room. Bredow the magician had given us a quick peek into his top hat. And what we saw wasn't a rabbit but the antechamber to an unheated hell. But I'd gotten to know the method to Bredow's madness by now and knew that a big threat was just a tactic he employed to achieve a different objective.

"No one—and I least of all, let me assure you—has any interest in laying off physicians. Redundancies always lead to dire hardship. Nevertheless, avoiding layoffs will necessitate solidarity. Solidarity on your part. My department calculates that we can forego redundancies—at least for the time being—if we forego paid overtime."

The silence in the room took on a different quality as each of us set about making his own sober calculations regarding financing plans for a home, vacation plans, alimony payments, that new car…

Heinz Valenta, from the ICU, mustered all 235 pounds of himself out of his narrow seat and headed toward the door.

"Then I can go on vacation until Christmas, and that way I'll have been paid for all the overtime I haven't submitted yet."

"Please be seated, Dr. Valenta."

I was always astonished that Bredow knew every one of us by name; after all, there are almost fifty of us.

"You haven't understood the situation correctly. I am not talking about compensatory time off. Going forward, overtime cannot be compensated in any form, either financially or through time off. The hospital simply does not have the money."

"Maybe it's not that we are doing too much overtime but that your department is doing too little. Maybe it's simply a case of bad administration."

Heinz Valenta could allow himself remarks of that kind. For one thing, he'd married money, and for another, he, Marlies, and I were among the few doctors who had secure tenure positions dating back to before privatization. If layoffs ever took place, he wouldn't be among those on the chopping block.

Prof. Dohmke jumped to his friend Bredow's defense. His people were not under threat because there was virtually no overtime in his department. Almost every test was carried out by automated analysis, and diligent lab technicians took care of the rest. On the contrary, the lab doctors have the problem of killing time, without exhausting themselves, so that they can moonlight in private practice and earn enough to make up the difference between a two-door Opel Corsa and a Volvo convertible.

"I don't see how there can be all these overtime hours," Prof. Dohmke said. "As a young doctor I was in charge of a ward with more than forty patients all by myself. Our wards today have twenty beds and two physicians."

Now I was peeved too.

"It's simple, my dear Dohmke, because in your day a patient with an infarction, for example, would have to lie quietly in bed for four weeks, and then it took four more weeks to get him to stand up. Nothing else worked back then. These days, infarction patients average four days with us, and during that time they get between one and eight stents in their coronaries, twenty-four seven, and a pacemaker or defibrillator or resynchronization device implanted if they require it. It's the same thing across the board."

There was a hum of general affirmation. The other departments explained how they had been forced to raise the clock rate on the patient production line from year to year. Hartmut, from

Surgery, used the more businesslike term "patient turnover rate" so that Bredow could better understand him.

Prof. Kindel was the only one who kept his eye on the big picture.

"Colleagues! I do not think that the hard work and the need for overtime are being called into question. The point seems to be that the hospital simply hasn't got the money. So we have to forego paid overtime or reduce staff. And I think that, for reasons of solidarity, we can only choose the overtime solution."

Kindel was right, but it sort of smelled like a done deal among him, Bredow, and Dohmke. In any case, Bredow wasn't finished with us yet.

"That is exactly how I see it. Unfortunately, however, the loss of paid overtime alone isn't enough to keep all of our current medical staff. I am sorry to say that there will be no Christmas bonuses this year. And finally, going forward, we'll only be able to fill open positions after six months at the very earliest."

This news was not met with silence this time. Cries of "Third World hospital!" and "Put the administrators in the trenches!" were heard. Only Marlies from IIIc had the courage to give some official input.

"How are the cuts going in administration, Herr Bredow?"

People with PhDs generally don't use the title of Doctor, but Bredow laid great store by his.

"Rest assured, *Doctor*, that we in the nonmedical sector are employing all possible means of cutting costs."

"I can attest to that," I announced, "at least as far as Medical Records is concerned. It's practically impossible to get old patient files."

It was typical of Prof. Dohmke to butt in at this point. He simply hadn't said anything for too long.

"I can't imagine why, Herr Hoffmann. Are you talking about any situation in particular?"

"I'm talking about the fact I've been waiting for days for the file of a patient who was here in October. Just try calling Medical Records. Not a chance."

Marlies came to my aid.

"It's true that as a rule the patients have already been discharged by the time we get our hands on their old records."

It was typically artful of Bredow to spin these little attacks to his advantage.

"I'll look into it. But as you can see from these difficulties, we've already been forced to make tough personnel reductions in other sections. I thank you for your attention and your understanding."

The mood at the following morning's beds meeting was decidedly gloomy; most of us had announced the news to our loved ones at home the night before. I was in a lousy mood myself. I was not so worried about my finances; after all, I don't have to provide for a family and don't have any expensive hobbies. But I'd been on the night shift again and been up all night. As a forty-five-year-old, you don't bounce back from two night shifts in a week the way you did as a young intern. Night shifts were the clearest sign that I was past my peak. I routinely dozed off in these meetings and checked my hands for age spots. Prof. Kindel sat next to me, and I'd observed the appearance and increase in age spots on his hands with fascination in recent years. That morning he had more unpleasant news for us.

"The measures that Dr. Bredow announced yesterday have an immediate impact on our department because management has approved Schreiber's stay in the US. Of course that's good news for him, but it means that we'll have to absorb the increased workload caused by his absence."

I noticed that Schreiber wasn't present, though I'd seen him just the day before at the we-must-all-save-and-tighten-our-belts meeting. Marlies spoke up as one of those directly affected.

"This comes as rather sudden news. How do you propose to make this work, Herr Kindel?"

Kindel actually had some ideas, which was quite unlike him.

"Hoffmann has twenty-two beds on IIIb and you have twenty-nine. I thought you could take this Mr., uh, the intern, from Hoffmann. I'm sure that Hoffmann can manage his twenty-two beds on his own."

I was afraid Marlies would faint. She didn't, though. She's one tough lady.

The medical faculty appeared reluctant to get straight back to work after the meeting; in any case, I wasn't the only one who didn't hurry back to his ward as I usually did, but instead I went to the cafeteria for breakfast. Marlies came over and sat down with me.

"So what's that intern of yours like?"

"Congratulations, Marlies! He's an absolutely committed young colleague brimming with unconventional ideas."

"I thought so. Shit."

Of course I was delighted to be rid of Harald. But I was sorry that Marlies, of all people, was getting screwed.

"He's not that bad. He can draw blood, and you can send him off as often as you like to look for missing X-rays. He just needs your maternal guidance, I think."

"Oh, thanks a lot."

The way she said it, I feared that Harald wouldn't much enjoy his time with Marlies.

"Tell me, Marlies. How old do I look, really? Be completely honest."

Marlies made herself appear to be looking at me objectively.

"Midfifties maybe?"

"Could be true, I suppose, since that's the way I feel these days. Especially when we do all the heavy lifting while our young, ambitious colleagues are jetting off halfway around the world. I'm telling you, in a couple of years Schreiber will be chief somewhere and we'll be asking him for a job. When was his trip to the US actually approved?"

Marlies shrugged.

"In any case, he still didn't know anything definitive a couple of nights ago," she said. "That night when you got on his back about that silly death certificate, he had just complained to me that he was dangling in thin air."

We chewed our dry cafeteria rolls. Why there were never fresh rolls, no matter what the time of day, would remain the cafeteria's everlasting secret. I suggested that Bredow had probably bought day-old bread. Another cost-cutting initiative.

"I don't think so," Marlies said, washing down the rest of her roll with her coffee. "They do the baking themselves. But do you have any idea what they put into them? Take it easy today, you look god-awful."

I'd lost my appetite by then and trotted off to my ward.

The only enjoyable thing that day was being able to work once again without Harald's interference and medical advice. I had to draw blood and hunt down missing X-rays myself, but even so, I was done with my day's work by three p.m. Although the workday officially ends at four thirty, I'd worked all night. Besides, Bredow's new overtime policy didn't exactly inspire in me the desire to keep working just for the sake of it.

My car can more or less drive itself from the hospital to my apartment in Zehlendorf. After working the night shift and the entire next day, I often can't remember how I actually got home and which streets I took. It was only four in the afternoon when

I walked into my apartment, and I decided a nap wouldn't hurt. If I didn't wake up until the following morning, that would be fine. Otherwise I'd call Celine later to see if she was up for going out to enjoy the summer evening.

As I lay in bed, my neighbors gradually arrived home, slammed car doors shut, dropped off crates of beer, chitchatted. I tried earplugs, cotton and wax in my ears, a sleep mask—to no avail. I just lay there, increasingly awake and pissed off. Misha kept going through my mind: the blocked autopsy, the second death certificate, the file I still hadn't received. It was going on six when I realized that any further attempt at a nap was futile, and so I got up.

It wouldn't be fair to invite Celine out now. At the very least I'd be grumpy and might even end up picking a fight with her. It occurred to me that Schreiber still had a few medical books of mine—and that, with one foot out the door and outside the hospital, he just might give me the straight scoop on how there happened to be a second certificate. A bike ride out to Lichterfelde would surely do me good, and some oxygen might help me sleep better. Marlies hadn't known whether Schreiber planned to stop by the hospital before his flight. I figured I could just ask him myself.

Schreiber and his family lived in a building that had once been a villa. Dating back to the late nineteenth century, the residence had been divided into several separate apartments. Though it was nothing extravagant, it was nevertheless quite a step up from the one-room apartment in Neukölln he lived in when he was an intern.

I hadn't phoned ahead of time but it was only eight o'clock.

No one answered the first time I rang the doorbell, so I rang again, a little longer this time. Schreiber's wife, Astrid, opened the door a crack, as though I were a stranger.

"Klaus isn't home."

"And you're not allowed to let strange men into your home?"

I was hardly a stranger. I'd helped ensure that he got the attending physician's job at the hospital in the first place.

"Come in. Excuse the chaos. I'm sorting out what has to go to the States. The rest is going to my parents'. No, bunny, not in your mouth!"

Schreiber Junior was crawling on the floor amid heaps of clothes and file folders. Astrid was in her midtwenties, about her husband's age. They'd done their medical studies together, studied for their doctorates, and both taken the state exam. These days, however, she was a housewife taking care of their child, with another on the way. It looked to me like she was in her seventh or eighth month. Was it obvious to her that she would probably never work as a physician again? Although she was still wrinkle-free, she'd look quite different after years of children's birthdays, hot dinners for Schreiber, and parent-teacher conferences.

"Feel free to get yourself something to drink—if you can find anything, that is. I hope you have more luck than I've had—I can't find a thing at the moment."

The fridge was stuffed with baby food and a variety of vegetable juices. I finally found a Coke and sat down at the table.

"Are you looking forward to America?"

"Of course we are. It was just a bit sudden."

She didn't sound happy though. I glanced around and noticed that they'd redecorated. The brick-and-particleboard bookshelves had given way to polished wooden bookcases. The door laid across two sawhorses had been replaced with a proper wooden desk. The Le Corbusier–style chrome-and-leather armchairs were inexpensive imitations from Italy but a vast improvement over their furniture plucked from the streets in Neukölln.

"It was sudden for us at the hospital as well. We only got the news this morning at the beds meeting."

"Isn't that the way it always is? For months it was completely up in the air, and now we have to be on our way in a matter of days. Klaus has gone to visit his parents in Munich. Then he'll go straight on to New York from there next week."

"Klaus isn't even in Berlin?" I was shocked. "But he was at work yesterday."

"The Yanks sent a telegram. Klaus has to start right away, on July first."

"Can I have a look at that telegram?"

"Why?"

I couldn't come up with an answer. My question had just slipped out, and I was surprised by it myself. Astrid looked at me with irritation.

"They sent it to him at the hospital, probably directly to Dohmke. And he finally gave his blessing."

Schreiber Junior caused Astrid to forget her irritation toward me; the kid was busy rearranging the little piles on the floor that Astrid had carefully sorted out.

"Aren't you too pregnant to fly?"

"Klaus will be going ahead alone. He'll get his bearings, find us an apartment, and so on. Then I'll follow with our son and the baby."

"Klaus won't be here for the birth?"

"You can't have everything. Besides, who's to say you wouldn't have scheduled him for work right when I go into labor?"

Astrid was right. That sort of thing is a specialty of the house. In any case, it seemed she knew nothing or wouldn't tell me anything. Who knows? Maybe there really was a telegram from the States and the death certificate incident was just a coincidence. My lack of sleep was slowly catching up with me and I suddenly wanted to go home. I finished my Coke and stood up.

"It's too bad you can't talk to Klaus. You must know that you're his great role model at work. Is there anything I can do for you?"

Right. I hadn't told her what I really came for.

"I loaned your husband a few medical books for his most recent lecture. He definitely wouldn't have taken them to the States; they're way too heavy. Do you know where they are?"

Schreiber's study was quite orderly, and it didn't take long for me to find my books. Astrid walked me to the door. She didn't seem particularly sorry to see me leave. I gave it one last try.

"I don't think it's right for Klaus to have left you alone so suddenly with all this work to do. Surely he could have stayed for a few days."

Astrid didn't answer; we stood in the doorway for a moment in silence.

"Do you want to make things difficult for us, Felix?"

"What makes you say that?"

"Klaus told me that you and he had a fight recently. Are you jealous that he's going to America?"

"Not at all, Astrid. And I haven't come here to make things difficult for Klaus. I only wanted to say good-bye to him."

"That's nice. I'm going to phone him later, and I'll give him your regards."

"Yes, please do that. And thanks for the Coke."

I was almost down the stairs when Astrid called after me.

"Felix, you mustn't forget that there's a difference between being a single man with tenure and a young doctor with a family and a contractually limited appointment."

"No, I understand perfectly. Good night, Astrid."

She closed the door. I heard Schreiber Junior begin to wail in the background.

CHAPTER 6

Although I was none the wiser after my bike trip, it did help me get some sleep. Not enough though. I could hardly stifle my yawns as I followed the night shift reports at the beds conference the next morning.

It's astounding how quickly people adjust to new circumstances; otherwise, wars would last no more than three days, most marriages not much longer. My colleagues were already joking; the spontaneous slowdown they had experienced the day before was over and everyone rushed straight to their wards after the meeting.

It was noon by the time I went to check about Misha's records in Medical Records. As I should have known, an almost holy silence awaited me there, along with a sign indicating that everyone was away on lunch break. When I stopped by again later, I bothered the staff at their coffee and cake, but at least they were there.

"Oh, yes, the file for that Russian. You've certainly sent us enough requests. One would have been enough, you know."

I made a great effort not to say anything.

"Fine. Can I have the file now?"

"But here's the thing, we haven't been able to find it. Is it important?"

Despite all the cost cutting, there is still someone in charge of Records. "Frau Tönnig, Head of Medical Records" was printed on a small plaque on the door. I entered without knocking.

Frau Tönnig had paid dearly for her largely sedentary work in that she weighed well over two hundred pounds. And she was still going strong: unlike her staff, she had already completely demolished her slice of cream cake.

"Yes, what do you want?"

"I've been waiting for five days for a patient's file from your department. Today I'm told that it's disappeared."

"No files disappear in my department, *Herr Doctor.*"

"Well, your staff claims that the file can't be found."

"Then we don't have it. I have to put up with this all the time. You give us hell and we look day and night. And where does the file finally turn up? In your ward. Misplaced in one of your closets or at the bottom of your desk. Or one of your colleagues has taken it home to write a report or whatever."

This was clearly not the first untraceable file in our hospital and certainly not the first discussion of this kind for Frau Tönnig.

"Remember two years ago when that colleague of yours in Neurology resigned? How many incomplete files were found in his locker?"

Rumor had it that there had been over two hundred, but I pressed on regardless.

"I am certain that I closed the file properly and sent it down to you. Do you keep a record of files going in and out?"

Frau Tönnig lost patience.

"When do you think you'd get your files if we had to keep a record of every file's movements? I'm working with two interns, and I'm lucky to get people who even know the alphabet. Otherwise they learn it here, and when they halfway manage to get a handle on it, they move on and it all starts over again. You're welcome to complain to hospital management; why don't you go see Bredow at once? You'd actually be doing me a favor. Do you have to work with such an inexperienced bunch of transients on your ward?"

Our medical interns are at least as bad, I thought, but I refrained from saying anything.

"Please do go see Dr. Bredow. But let me give you a piece of advice: go through your desk and your cupboards first. That's where you'll find your file. Good day."

It had been a long time since my status as a physician had given me any semblance of authority. In any case, I did not get my file.

I was sure that I'd passed Misha's file on to Medical Records, but perhaps I'd done so before the interns had properly learned to do their jobs. My death certificate for Misha had also disappeared. I realized I'd better get to work securing whatever documentation was still available. I decided to start by copying Schreiber's report on Misha's emergency call. So I paid a visit to the paramedics' waiting room.

Too late. The file for emergency call number 1726/00 on June 12 to the Hostel Elvira wasn't in the folder anymore. Of course, these protocols can disappear too, but the loss rate of documents in Misha's case struck me as astoundingly high.

I phoned Celine to see whether she was up for joining me for a glass of wine downtown. She was, so we agreed to meet at Steinplatz at about eight. That gave me a good hour.

The apartment building at Uhlandstrasse 141 was the same sorry sight, and my reception in the hostel as cordial as before.

"Good evening. I'm here again regarding Misha Chenkov. It's very important."

The guy at the counter actually set his Russian magazine aside this time, though not to direct his attention toward me; he disappeared through a door behind the desk.

Perhaps I should mention that I can be rather stubborn. So I picked up his magazine and took a seat by the desk. Full-bosomed blondes advertised the indispensable necessities for survival: cars from Korea and Japan, TVs, VCRs, cell phones, and all sorts of other Asian goods. There didn't seem to be any Russian products for sale, or they were advertised without pictures so that I could hardly tell them from the obituaries.

I'd worked my way through about half of the magazine when Mr. Receptionist reappeared at his post behind the counter accompanied by two young men. They seemed to be the same ones who had been hanging around the entrance to the building a while ago.

I've always believed in the goodness of people. There was certainly a chance that he just went and got the two young men because he didn't speak any German himself.

"I'm here regarding Misha Chenkov. He lived here, didn't he? You'll remember him—he looked rather yellow recently."

The two young men hardly glanced at me. They were looking at my friend the receptionist, as though waiting for orders.

"I'm not here to make any trouble for you or anybody else. I just need to know when Chenkov got sick and why."

No reaction. I had to believe that at least one of the three understood German.

"It may very well have been an infection. Bacteria. He might have infected you. You might need to be inoculated. You may already be sick!"

Whatever the receptionist brought the two men in for, it wasn't to serve as interpreters. They ignored me completely and weren't the least bit impressed by my mention of a possible infection.

I leaned on the desk.

"Your guest register. Where's your register?"

There was a small notebook on the desk that the reception-ist now shut. He'd understood me perfectly well, but he wouldn't even consider letting me take a look at it. I noticed two tattered suitcases behind the reception desk. I pointed to them.

"Are those Misha's suitcases? I'd like to have them."

"*Nyet, èto ne tye chemodany, kotorye vy ishchetye.*"

"If you don't release those suitcases, you'll be guilty of theft." I topped that with, "We're in Germany after all!"

The two young men came out from behind the desk and let me know—wordlessly but unambiguously—that it was time for me to leave. Even though we were in Germany.

They were right; it was time for me to retreat. I hadn't been to my karate class in months. But I wanted to score at least a half point.

"OK. But I'll be back. And not alone."

The two men escorted me out the door of the building.

Apart from wobbly knees, my second visit to the Hostel Elvira had produced no results. But it hadn't been completely futile. I was dead certain that the concierge had been acting on orders with his I-only-Russian, I-no-understand routine. Whose orders? He'd made one mistake though. He should have admitted that Misha had lived there but told me that he had no friends, was always alone, and that I was welcome to take the suitcases. Then he could have given me any old suitcase with a few pairs of dirty underwear and holey socks. I'd have been none the wiser.

I walked to the corner of Kurfürstendamm and sat down on a bench to ponder how much things had changed. I'd begun my research into Misha's last days out of a guilty conscience and medical interest, but it was now clear to me that somebody was actively making all clues and documents concerning Misha Chenkov vanish.

I'd seen his corpse. There was no knife in the back, no bullet wound to the head. He'd probably died of liver failure, cardiopulmonary arrest—if you discounted the possibility that somebody had killed him with a nice slice of amanita mushroom. Simple liver failure. Who'd have any reason to hush up the causes? It occurred to me that there was still one way to find out.

I hopped in my Rabbit and drove back to the hospital. My date with Celine was forgotten.

Schreiber had replaced my death certificate for Misha with a new one, thus preventing an autopsy. It now looked to me as though he'd done that on orders from above rather than from any desire to avoid a possible malpractice suit. Had Misha's blood sample disappeared too, the one we'd frozen for our study? Misha's samples were numbered 958 to 962; they hadn't been crossed out in the book or taken from the freezer. Had they maybe been switched with others? I couldn't determine that on my own. I packed the samples in a cooler and called my friend Michael Thiel. He said I could come over right away.

Michael had worked in our lab as a senior doctor for many years. Some of our joint research projects had brought the hospital a pile of outside funding, and we got a few publications out of it, along with pleasant trips to conferences and a cute doctoral student now and then. Michael had never gotten along with his boss, Prof. Dohmke, and for that reason had drifted into the pharmaceutical industry a few years ago. Now he operated his own lab and wasn't doing badly for himself.

It didn't surprise me to get Michael on the phone in his lab at this time of night. He was a workaholic—in addition to the fact that he had to work hard to support two ex-wives and several children. I was there in twenty minutes.

"What's new, Felix?"

Michael's "What's new?" was as much a part of him as his expensive shirts and chic ties. He had to open the door himself because his lab techs had left for the night a while ago. Too bad,

I thought, since Michael always hired based on looks as well as qualifications.

"What's my friend Superasshole Dohmke up to these days?"

Our common dislike of Prof. Dohmke was perfectly common; I didn't know anyone in the hospital who could stand him. It may have been partly out of jealousy; rumor had it that Dohmke was financially involved in every test even before the hospital lab was privatized. In any case, whatever he did was enough for a swish villa in Dahlem and a fine holiday house on Lago Maggiore. I'd recently heard something about a private plane and a house in Florida. Although that may have been an exaggeration, it was clear that he hadn't suffered financially from the privatization of the hospital lab. Now Michael and Dohmke and their labs competed for jobs from the pharmaceutical industry, and Michael was keen to catch Dohmke or his lab making a big mistake. I had to disappoint him tonight: the lab hadn't made any blunders yet, and I'd been watching very closely.

"Well, OK. Then let's go and pour a little hydrogen sulfide into his swimming pool. It's a beautiful evening, perfect for a jaunt to the posh part of town."

"I'd be happy to, Michael, but another time. I've brought you some work."

I gave him the tubes containing Misha's serum.

"Where'd you get this stuff?"

"Believe me, you don't want to know."

It couldn't hurt to be a bit mysterious. After all, I needed Michael to work on this case for free. It worked; his eyes sparkled.

"And—can we pin something on Dohmke with this?"

"I don't know if we can nail anybody with this. But if we can, then Dohmke's a good candidate."

To each the motivation he needs. I was not ashamed of my little white lie.

"What are we looking for?"

"Good question. I think you should first run the yellow program. The hepatitis panel, alcohol, methanol, leptospirosis, all that stuff. You know, anything that makes it yellow."

"It's gonna cost you at least a dinner, Felix. Unless we nail Dohmke. Then I'm paying."

Michael put the tubes into a freezer and got out a couple of beers. We caught the second half of Germany against Portugal. It ended three to nothing in Portugal's favor. Germany was out of the European Championship. It was only after we'd properly mourned this national tragedy that I remembered my date with Celine. By then it was too late to call her.

CHAPTER 7

If an explanation for—or even any clues to—Misha's death were slumbering in the blood samples, Michael would be the man to find them. In the meantime, I was going to get to work tracking down any other traces of Misha's presence he might have left behind in Berlin. I went to try my luck with our hospital's personnel department.

Thankfully, Personnel hadn't been hit by the rigorous job cuts. It was still just as spacious and well staffed as when I had been hired eight years earlier, and the smell of fresh coffee wafted through the corridors.

Most of the patients' rooms overlook the operating rooms and lab wing, but Personnel has a magnificent view over the canal and the park. Personnel had successfully defended itself against a recent restructuring by arguing that "the patients are here for a few days or weeks, we're here forever." Officially, the rationale for leaving the patients' rooms where they were was the high cost of shifting the high-pressure oxygen and other pipes. However, all the supply lines in the patients' wing were torn out and relocated, and nobody could use the phones in our ward for close to a week.

I walked through the brightly lit corridors until I found a Fräulein Moser, the clerk responsible for employees *A–J*. Fräulein Moser was on the phone.

"Absolutely impossible woman, believe me. Did you read about it in the last issue of *Elle*?"

Unlike the occasionally successful nurses, physiotherapists, and technical assistants, the staff in Personnel quickly learned that this line of work wasn't going to land them a fine doctor husband, and, as a result, doctors rapidly became their explicit enemies. I patiently waited for "Fräulein Moser, Clerk in Charge" to finish her phone call. She eventually placed her hand over the receiver.

"What is it?"

"It's about one of our workers. Last name Chenkov. First name Misha. Nonmedical staff."

"I can't give you any information about other employees. In fact, about any employees in the hospital except yourself. The Doctors' Division handles you all."

"Chenkov is a patient in my ward. He can't say much at the moment. And even if he could, we probably couldn't understand him. We need his basic data, date of birth, insurance, and so on. Without it, we can't get anything out of his insurance company."

It could have been construed as a rather suspicious remark because since when—as Fräulein Moser might well have asked— do physicians worry their heads about their patients' insurance? But the insurance detail seemed to make sense to her. She worked on the same floor as our COO and surely was familiar with his mantra, "We're all in the same boat. The patients are our passengers, but the fuel that drives our boat forward is the health insurance company."

"I'll call you right back." She hung up. "What was the name?"

"Chenkov. First name Misha."

It was wondrously skillful the way her fingers flew over the keyboard in spite of her long fingernails.

"Chenkov...we don't have a Chenkov."

"But he worked for us. Or at least he was working here last October."

"Then he would definitely still be in the computer." Her ambition was aroused. "These foreigners often hardly know how to spell their own names. I'll go through all the Cs..."

She found nothing that sounded like Chenkov. Also nothing under S.

"What kind of job did this Chenkov of yours have here?"

"He did the cleaning."

"Sterilizing?"

"No, the floors and stairs and whatnot."

"You should have told me; it would have saved us both a lot of time. But you probably think that we've got nothing better to do all day in Personnel than do our nails and chat on the phone."

She'd pretty much spoken the truth.

"The cleaning service is run by CareClean; we've got nothing to do with them."

"You don't have *any* documentation on CareClean's employees who work here?"

"That's what I just said. Besides, everything related to outside companies goes directly through Dr. Bredow. He'd surely be happy to help you."

She was being unnecessarily rude, but I figured I might as well do as she suggested. By the time I closed the door to Fräulein Moser's office, she was already on the phone again.

Late that afternoon, I found a moment to drop in on COO Dr. Bredow, or at least on Frau Krüger, his secretary. He'd brought her with him from his last job; she's a kind, maternal type who doesn't harbor any fundamental antagonism toward physicians—quite the contrary in fact. She's a single mother, and her son's studying to be a doctor. She looks upon us as "her doctors" and has over time become something of an unofficial go-between for us and her boss. "Dr. Hoffmann, come in!"

Frau Krüger knows me from the time when I served as the spokesman representing the interns, and ever since then we've gotten along extremely well. Two other admin assistants were standing around with glasses of champagne, and the secretariat looked like a flower shop before Mothers' Day.

"What are you celebrating?"

"Have a glass, Dr. Hoffmann. It's the boss's birthday today. One of the big Os. The grand reception isn't until tonight, but as you can see, we've already gotten the festivities under way."

So Bredow was turning fifty. What was he planning to do in the next ten years? He'd been COO here for three years so far. Outsourcing had begun during his regime, and his ideas had helped transform us from a public institution into a corporation with private shareholders. Since we were no longer in public service, he didn't have to follow any collective bargaining agreements for new hires. It always came down to money. Though the hospital must of course offer a good product—in our case the restoration of health—its real objective is profit.

We were probably only one rung on his personal career ladder, a chance for him to prove that you could take a highly subsidized teaching hospital and make it a profitable operation. The next rung would be CEO of a large public health insurance company, or he'd switch sides and head up the private health insurance association, another not too poorly paid position. According to Heinz Valenta, Bredow's real goal was to become undersecretary in the health administration.

In any event, today he was turning fifty, and I knew well enough not to come at him with a dead Russian from the cleaning team. I politely refused the champagne, explaining that I still had a few things to do back in the ward.

"Too bad, Dr. Hoffmann, it's delicious stuff," Frau Krüger said. "You wouldn't believe how many things have arrived for the boss. It's fascinating to see who sent birthday greetings, aside from the pharmaceutical companies and biotech companies, of course. We could go swimming in all the bubbly. In any case, what can I do for you?"

"I wanted to have a brief chat with Dr. Bredow, but it's not so urgent that it has to be on his birthday."

"Not on your life, Dr. Hoffmann. It's like Grand Central here today. I could squeeze you in tomorrow in the afternoon. What is it about? Are you the spokesman for the residents again?"

"No, that's still Valenta. It's about a patient of mine."

"I hope you don't need the boss's medical advice."

That was a nod to Bredow, who had an MBA and was in the habit of enthusiastically butting in on medical issues during our meetings.

"No, the case isn't that desperate quite yet. It's more of a legal problem."

"Fine, I'll write you in for tomorrow at three. But call me before noon to confirm."

I thanked Frau Krüger and wished everybody a fun evening. It wasn't until I was leaving that it occurred to me that she might not even have been invited to his big shindig. I certainly wasn't.

Frau Schön returned to us from Surgery the next day, and my ward nurse Elke was rightly concerned. We had sent her to the surgeons all yellow and with a blocked gallstone, but certainly able to withstand an operation. Although Frau Schön was no longer yellow, she was in no condition to talk and as dehydrated as a prune. After the surgery, the surgeons had correctly infused her with two liters of fluid a day with the right number of calories in the form of sugar—it's what they always do—but they hadn't noticed that her blood sugar was steadily rising and that she was voiding at least three liters a day. She couldn't discharge anything more and was sliding slowly toward kidney failure.

A surgeon's natural reaction to pathological laboratory findings is to fill out a consultation form. This means that an internist is supposed to come and solve the problem. And someone had in fact taken pity on this form the day before and gone to see Frau Schön. Coming up with a sensible infusion plan was simple enough, but it would have involved the internist's trotting over to Surgery twice a day to check on her. Instead, he'd simply cut the Gordian knot, elegantly and expeditiously, with a brief note: "Transfer back to Internal IIIb tomorrow morning." And so Frau Schön was back.

With Nurse Elke's efficient help, we quickly came up with a reasonable treatment plan. We would pluck her from her prune-like state with a few liters of fluid and lower her blood sugar with a bit of insulin; sodium and kidney values would then regulate themselves. Harald would probably have put her on the kidney machine for a few hours first —he was crazy about little blinking lights and shiny chrome switches.

Frau Krüger called me up shortly before two to tell me that Dr. Bredow had time for me now.

Compared with the broom closets Bredow had assigned to the doctors as offices after the renovations, his headquarters was vast, reminiscent of photos I'd seen of Hitler's study. It was probably the largest room in the entire hospital after the cafeteria and the sterilization center.

But the COO of a large hospital is an important man these days. Even the once-powerful department heads now have to negotiate their contracts with the COO: their salary; how many beds they get for private patients; how much of the money they receive from those patients they have to fork over to the hospital; how many beds their department gets; how many doctors and nurses and how much lab capacity they have. The COO has become enormously important to the patients' well-being without their even knowing it. For instance, it is he who ultimately decides whether a new artificial kidney is purchased and whether it is profitable—thereby possibly determining whether a patient lives or dies. And Bredow made no bones about his importance and willingness to wield his power.

"Go right in. The boss is expecting you" were Frau Krüger's words of welcome.

Even the furniture reminded me of Hitler's: a heavy, three-piece upholstered suite wrapped around a smoking table, and a giant neo-Gothic desk anchored one end of the sprawling room. During meetings with Bredow I always found myself looking discreetly for swastikas in the carved wood furnishings.

"I'll be right with you, Dr. Hoffmann."

Bredow was probably the only person in the hospital who had his own bathroom adjoining his study. When he came out, he was still drying his hands.

"Nice to see you, Dr. Hoffmann."

Dr. Bredow seemed smaller in his immense study; he gestured toward one of his oversized wing chairs and sat down himself—his preferred seating arrangement for talks of an unofficial nature.

I wasn't sure whether I should belatedly congratulate him on his birthday; after all, there had not been a party at the hospital. Bredow spared me any further deliberation.

"Frau Krüger told me it's about a patient."

"Yes, that's correct. A couple of things have occurred that you should know about."

I told Bredow about Misha. I said that he'd worked in the hospital and had been my patient at one point.

"One day he suddenly vanished from the ward. As far as I know, he never reappeared for work; in any case, I didn't see him again until Pentecost Monday, when he showed up in the ER. Dead on arrival, probably fatal internal hemorrhaging."

I didn't tell him about my visit to the Hostel Elvira or about the two death certificates. As I said earlier, I suspected that Schreiber may have been acting on instructions. But whose? The COO was hardly a possibility, but I didn't see any reason to go into all the details.

"And you think, Dr. Hoffmann, that there's some connection between the fact that this..."

"Chenkov, Misha Chenkov..."

"That this Chenkov in October was treated in our ward and that he's now dead? Was he not treated properly here?"

"I can't exclude that possibility. It could be that we overlooked the start of an illness at the time and that we could be partly responsible for his death."

"Are you afraid there'll be trouble?"

"Lawsuits, justified or not, are never good for a hospital."

I really wasn't worried about a lawsuit, particularly from a Ukrainian with an expired residence permit. However, Bredow's job was not only to get money for the hospital but to keep it, and malpractice suits had become a popular specialty of lawyers in recent years. Dr. Bredow swallowed the bait.

"Is there family or anything else?"

"No idea. I never saw anyone when he was on my ward."

I didn't mention that, according to Schreiber's death certificate, an autopsy was allegedly refused. By whom if not by family members?

"Did many people come to visit him in the ward?"

"I don't know. But I can't remember anybody at the time asking me about the prognosis or when he'd be discharged."

Bredow appeared to be studying the carving in his desk himself.

"Did you find anything in his ward record back then that could make trouble for us?"

"That's one reason I wanted to talk to you. The ward record has disappeared."

"Disappeared?"

"It can't be found in Medical Records."

"Medical Records! Something must be done about that place. Frau Tönnig simply isn't up to the task. But you know as well as I do that old records are floating around all over the building. It's high time we had electronic records."

"I'm certain I sent Chenkov's file to Records at the time. In addition, the protocol from the ambulance about his call is missing from the ambulance call folder."

"Therefore, Dr. Hoffmann, it is not really an administrative problem. Those folders are *yours*! But they become *our* problem during the cost finding. You physicians must finally begin organizing your paperwork better. The ambulance protocols are what the cost center uses for billing the fire department and the Red Cross. They're useless. Last year, the fire department had two more hundred calls than were listed in your files. You might remember my circular about this."

Memos and circulars were Bredow's hobby; we received one or two each week. And whenever there was an argument between doctors and the administration, the administration could always point to some circular or other that nobody had read of course.

"And you say this Chenkov had been working for us?"

"Yes, he worked here in the building."

"Doing what?"

"He was on the cleaning staff."

Bredow relaxed.

"Those aren't our employees; they're employed by CareClean. We've got nothing to do with their people."

"I was already told that in Personnel."

"You've been there? Where do you find the time for all this?"

I noted the touch of indignation in his tone.

"Look, we were just talking about the dire state of our finances last week. You know as well as I do that the hospital is in trouble thanks to the new law on health structuring. It's not that I don't want to grant you your overtime pay. I want to give you every penny of it. But we simply don't have the money. If we hadn't moved some jobs to outside firms, we'd be much worse off. We're lucky that we haven't had to dismiss any physicians so far."

I noted his friendly grin as he worked the possibility of lay-offs into the conversation. And he seemed to be suggesting that I might be one of them if Misha's case caused trouble for the hospital.

"Who else have you talked to about this matter, apart from Personnel and Medical Records?"

I decided to avoid answering his question directly. His thinking was obvious: let sleeping dogs lie.

"I'm worried, Dr. Bredow, because I don't have any idea what the patient did after he disappeared off my ward. Did he keep cleaning here but in another department? Did he continue to work for CareClean somewhere else? Or was he sick the whole time? It's possible his jaundice was infectious and he's infected other people. Isn't there a list of people here who work for CareClean?"

Bredow shook his head. "I don't need one. CareClean handles everything."

"And what do we pay these people? Do they have sick pay?"

"Dr. Hoffmann, the interns' spokesman, just like in the old days. The whole point is that we don't pay these people a cent. We pay the outside company in question a flat rate and don't have to give it another thought. No payroll accounting, no expenses for Christmas bonuses or vacation pay. We don't need any criteria for staff sickness and vacations; it's not our problem anymore. How much money do you think that saves us? Money we need desperately for your salary."

"Are you sure that these people have decent health insurance?"

"You've said yourself that this Chenkov was cared for by us in the ward. We certainly didn't do that for free, at least I hope not. I'm sure that those firms follow the letter of the law. But it's really not our problem."

"I think we are somewhat responsible for people who work here, even if they're from outside firms."

"Dr. Hoffmann, I appreciate what you are saying but this is becoming a rather general discussion about the structure of the labor market in Germany, don't you think?"

Bredow checked his watch and stood up. I had no choice but to get up as well. He put his hand on my shoulder and pressed me gently toward the door.

"Don't worry, Dr. Hoffmann. If I've understood correctly, you didn't discharge this man, he discharged himself. For that reason alone, we're above reproach. You are a good doctor, I know, in fact one of our best. You definitely shouldn't blame yourself for anything."

We were almost at the door.

"If it makes you feel any better, I'll look into it myself to see if there's any threat to us. Just keep practicing your medicine and don't play the detective. You're more valuable to us as a physician. I'll keep you posted."

The meeting was over. Dr. Bredow said good-bye with a handshake. Margret, the senior lab tech in our blood bank, was in the waiting room. Was she bypassing Prof. Dohmke, her immediate superior? Or was she here on some other business? In any event, it was true: Dr. Bredow was a very busy man.

CHAPTER 8

That conversation with Bredow haunted me for the rest of that day and several days after it. I couldn't put my finger on it, but some things he had said left me with an odd feeling.

To begin with, it was remarkable that Bredow had even taken the time to see me even though I was no longer the spokesman for the interns or one of his department heads—they couldn't even always get an appointment with him. Could I thank my good relationship with Frau Krüger for that? Maybe, but ordinarily Bredow would have asked me to give my reason in writing to Frau Krüger and only get back to me after reviewing it. He also dismissed the issue of the missing files surprisingly quickly—he who loved written documents so much. I would have thought he'd have grabbed the phone right away and given Frau Tönnig hell.

I was most irritated about the fact that Bredow didn't probe into the medical history of the patient or ask any questions about the autopsy. We've all got liability insurance of course, but malpractice is simply bad for business. Besides, physicians' medical errors gave Bredow more power over us.

He'd paid attention throughout our conversation and asked sensible questions. But somehow he hadn't seemed to be fully present, as though he had other things on his mind—other than my dead Ukrainian, that is.

I waited until Friday afternoon for Dr. Bredow to call back, then I called Frau Krüger. She hadn't heard anything but said she would ask. After that, I went down to the cafeteria to grab lunch and ran into Marlies.

Friday is fish day—Hospital Catering Services hadn't changed that tradition either. The same boneless breaded square pieces were still served up, without offering the slightest indication of what living creature had served as the raw material for that perfect geometrical form.

Marlies had her first week with rookie doc Harald behind her. Her expectations were apparently fully confirmed.

"I think I'll kill him on Monday."

"Rope or nail file?"

"I don't know yet. It has to take a long time and really hurt."

Judging by the look on her face, however, Marlies had already decided on a very definite technique.

"Why don't you send him to the hospital library more often?"

"I already did that yesterday. Bull's-eye. He must have read some paper or other on high blood pressure because first thing that afternoon he changed all the patients' blood pressure medications. I'm going to go crazy!"

"Let me know when you want to kill him. I'll hold him down."

"I'll do that. And when you leave today don't forget to lock up your ward. He's on this weekend."

I hurried up with my piece of pressed fish. If Harald was on duty this weekend, I had a lot to do.

Patients generally don't pay attention if it's a weekday or a weekend, day or night. It's the attending physician's job on Friday afternoons to do whatever he or she can to preserve them in their current state through the weekend, and we gladly take up the battle with disease again on Mondays. In the interim, patients should avoid having the physician on weekend duty interfere with their care—because he's already pissed off at having to spend the weekend in the hospital and he wants to make use of the time to get through his long-overdue medical reports.

A weekend physician's reaction to being disturbed by patients who aren't his normal responsibility falls into roughly two categories: The more favorable option for the patient is that he does only what's strictly necessary and leaves anything else for the attending physician to resolve on Monday. It gets more dangerous if the doctor on duty is convinced that his colleague hasn't a clue about medicine and decides to use the patient as an example of the way medicine should work. Harald the greenhorn would make every effort to prove what a brilliant doctor he was. I didn't want to give him that opportunity.

Toward the end of the day, Frau Krüger called me. She said she'd talked to Dr. Bredow and he wanted to let me know not to worry further about the matter, that everything was in order.

"And what about the ward file?"

"Dr. Bredow said nothing about a file."

I thanked her for calling and wished her a nice weekend.

"Thank you, Dr. Hoffmann. And enjoy yourself at Prof. Kindel's."

Right. This was Kindel's last week as our department chief, and he'd invited us all to a farewell party at his house that night. I had to get home to shower, change my clothes, and get rid of the hospital smell. Just before leaving the hospital, I peeked in on Frau Schön. She looked much better, with some sparkle in her eye and a moist tongue. Her stools were moving, her glucose was only at about two hundred, and aside from potassium, her electrolyte levels were pretty much OK. Everything seemed under control for the weekend.

It was understandable that Celine didn't want to come to Kindel's party; she was perfectly happy to avoid an evening of clinical anecdotes. I was a bit late because it took forever to park, but I finally found a gap in an Absolutely No Parking spot on a turn-around loop and got to Kindel's house after a healthy evening hike through Lichterfelde.

The party was already in high gear. It exuded the dubious charm of the Just-Us-Guys Parties we used to have as puberty-stricken school kids as soon as someone's parents were away on a trip. In reality, it was only a carry-over of our daily morning meeting, only this time with canapés and drinks. The participants and topics of conversation were generally the same—the latest lab results for a given patient, swapping night shifts, or attempts to finish coordinating vacation dates.

As usual, Kindel had refused to have the party catered. Nobody held it against him that they wouldn't be served by deeply tanned, athletic, and stylish young people who generally looked better than the guests and inspired acute bulimia in the female guests. Kindel's argument against hiring party help was likely an economic one, and we could respect that. Around the hospital, frugality had lately become a more powerful measure for professional advancement than the mere bagatelles of medical knowledge. There were canapés of supermarket salmon and cheese cubes with grapes on top held together with toothpicks. We recognized the fake floral arrangement from our annual party at the Kindels' house; Frau Kindel had probably first deployed it for the baptisms of her two sons. She remained in the background and took care of supplying more canapés and drinks.

The guests had split up into three groups. Those around Heinz Valenta from the ICU generated a lot of laughter; he was probably regaling them with stories about the latest mis-diagnosis or documents mix-up, the last absurd directive from Personnel, or Bredow's most recent circular. Prof. Kindel stood at the center of the second group—it was his good-bye party after all. The largest group had gathered around Prof. Dohmke and was comprised of the opportunists and the truly desperate. It would ultimately be up to him if contracts got extended. Fully aware of the power he wielded as medical director, he held court right beside the buffet.

It had proved problematic to come up with a suitable farewell present. After working for many years and being handsomely compensated for his work, our boss had everything he could possibly want—and few interests outside of medicine. Three suggestions made the short list: a season soccer pass for all of Hertha Berlin's home games, a week in Mallorca all expenses paid, or golf clubs. The golf clubs won out because they would last longer.

Unfortunately, though, the clubs had to be carried in. Marlies had said she'd take care of buying them. The last to arrive, she looked as though dragging the clubs had done her in. I consoled her with the fact that Prof. Kindel would have to struggle with the damn things from now on. She replied that Kindel would probably have a golf partner—while he hit the balls, his wife would break her back lugging his bag around.

As usual Heinz Valenta had done little to help with the party or the gift, but he did make a delightfully witty speech and presented the golf clubs. Surprised at such kindness, Prof. Kindel claimed that words failed him and spared us a second speech.

Which was given by Prof. Dohmke. After his words, the future of the Cardiology Department looked grim. Prof. Kindel simply could not be replaced, not as a physician for his patients, nor for us as an instructor, nor for Dohmke as a colleague. We all knew this speech; he'd delivered it almost verbatim the year before when the head of Radiology retired. The following Monday, that radiologist had had to pick up his books, family photos, and correspondence files from Pathology, as Dohmke had his office cleaned out that very weekend.

After his fifteen years in our hospital, Prof. Kindel's official farewell would come in the form of a standard letter requesting that he turn in his hospital clothes and keys within three days, signed "Personnel Department."

When Dohmke finished talking, Kindel thanked him politely.

He was standing beside me and said, "You know, I'd imagined it would be much harder to leave that hospital. Not that I didn't enjoy medicine. It was interesting to watch the progression of cardiology and to follow the progress of the young residents."

It was true. He'd always taken time to train us. We'd learned from him to listen to our patients and, when in doubt, to believe the patient rather than lab tests or X-rays.

He went on, "But being chief is no longer what it once was. I certainly won't miss the never-ending battles for resources and positions. The administration may have lightened our workload a bit, but it hasn't made our jobs any easier. And everything's gotten even worse since the Hospital Financing Law went into effect. All of a sudden, we're expected to run a business, and we're not trained to do that. Those of us in Cardiology are still doing well because we bring in money for the hospital with the cardiac catheter."

Marlies had joined us and said, "But we're really *not* doing all that well in Cardiology. Suddenly Schreiber's off to the US for more training, and I've got a hyperambitious rookie intern around my neck. And what's going to happen when Schreiber comes back? He'll probably snag some great job somewhere else. Or he'll prance around here like some kind of all-star doctor while we're stuck with the routine drudgery."

Kindel had done some training in the States in his day and always liked to talk about it. I was afraid Marlies had stepped on a land mine.

"I don't see it that way," Kindel said. "My year in the US didn't hurt, and Schreiber's not the type to be too good to draw blood afterwards. Don't keep complaining, kids. It's such a great opportunity for Schreiber. It took me ages to get Dohmke to approve it."

While Kindel was sipping his wine, I replayed my conversation with Schreiber's wife, Astrid, in my mind.

"What's with the rush?" I said. "Schreiber hardly had time to pack his bags."

"You know Dohmke," Kindel said. "When he makes a decision, it always has to be implemented yesterday."

Although that was true, it didn't jibe with Astrid's version of what happened, with the telegram from the US announcing that Schreiber was to come immediately.

Valenta's and Dohmke's speeches were the party's highlights, and Frau Kindel's salmon-cheese-grape canapés had been all but exterminated. As is often the case, it was at precisely that moment that all hell started breaking loose at the hospital. Almost all of my colleagues suddenly received urgent calls that they were needed for an "emergency" around ten—and were lying in their comfortable beds snoring peacefully a short while later. The less strategic among us were forced to stick around for Prof. Dohmke's well-worn stories from the Stone Age of medicine, when he claimed to have missed being awarded the Nobel Prize by a whisker. When his audience had finally dwindled, he left too.

It was coming up on eleven, and I realized that I'd missed the right moment to make my exit. But I liked Kindel; he had always been a good role model for us, and it was his last night as our boss. I found myself sitting next to him. He'd indulged rather heavily at the bar all evening, and I suspected that saying good-bye to his work couldn't have been as easy as he claimed.

"A cognac perhaps, Hoffmann?"

"Maybe a grappa to help me sleep."

Trembling slightly, Kindel filled my glass up to the rim. He helped himself to a cognac.

"Sorry, Hoffmann. You've got to drink that carefully." His speech was slightly slurred. "Carefully…proceed carefully; don't rush things; that's the alpha and omega of medicine."

I was in for it. Kindel, with an estimated blood alcohol content of 1.5, was now going to fill me in on his entire life story in medicine. What an idiot I was not to have arranged for the hospital to call.

"Of course we're now quite overextended in terms of personnel. No question, you all are a hardworking lot. So you'll have to concentrate more than ever on what's important. You must learn to distinguish what is important from what is not."

"That distinction's not always an easy one to make, Prof. Kindel."

"You're right, there, Herr Hoffmann. But do I hear for instance that you're putting a lot of time into looking for a particular file?"

The bush telegraph in our hospital was astounding. How had Kindel heard I was looking for Misha's file? I suppose I had been making a big fuss over it, having personally visited Medical Records, Personnel, and Bredow. Kindel paused, but I remained silent. He didn't look at me and lowered his voice.

"You know, I'm not your boss anymore, I can't give you any instructions."

"What is it about that file?"

He nodded to himself in silence. In a few years, he'd probably be doing that constantly, but for the moment it seemed to be an exercise in concentration.

"I hear it's about a dead patient. That's just what I mean; distinguish between what's important and unimportant. 'Let the dead bury the dead.' Moreover…we're under close observation. We can't make any mistakes, particularly right now. Which hospitals in Berlin will be closed is a poker game that will take a while to play itself out…"

I glanced up at the sound of loud laughter, which was coming from the corner, where a congregation from the hard-drinking ICU was taking care of the liquid leftovers. Kindel was ruminating silently to himself. Had I underestimated his blood alcohol content, or was there something specific he wanted me to know? I waited but got no further clues. He only wanted to know who I thought ought to be the new manager of Germany's national team. It was time for me to take my leave.

Kindel walked me to the door unsteadily, holding me tightly by the arm as he walked alongside me.

"Dr. Hoffmann, about that file. I think you can use your working hours more wisely. But if you ever do find it, let me know. We can't be too careful at the moment."

However, Misha's file was not my most pressing problem just then. At that moment, I had to find my car.

CHAPTER 9

I'd drunk too much at Kindel's, naturally, and woke up on Saturday with a throbbing under my cranium that I wouldn't shake off until noon. I got up, showered, brushed my teeth, and did what I always did to restore myself: I trotted off to the bakery. I rang Celine's doorbell at nine o'clock on the dot for Saturday breakfast.

We have a fixed ritual on weekends: I get rolls and the newspaper for our breakfast on Saturday mornings. Unless we've got something going on, each of us recovers from the week any way we like until Sunday evening. For me that generally means lots of sleep and time in front of the TV. On Sunday evenings, we cook together, though in reality I do the cooking while Celine complains. That's still better than the other way around, because Celine—almost omnipotent otherwise—cares little (or not at all) about being a good cook. That weekend, however, we intended to head out to the Spreewald right after breakfast, a biosphere reserve southeast of Berlin comprised of alder forests on wetlands and pine forests on dry, sandy areas, and about a thousand miles of irrigation canals. Since Harald was on duty that weekend and I couldn't pop into the hospital from the Spreewald, I gave the ward a quick call before we took off.

I got through to Sybille, the student nurse who, according to the rumor mill, had something going with Harald. My worst fears were realized.

"Everything is in order, Doctor. Everyone is doing well except Frau Schön, the one who had the gall bladder operation, but the physician has already started antibiotics."

Celine wasn't thrilled about a detour to the hospital, but Frau Schön had by then experienced more than her share of trouble in our hospital. As I heaved our bikes onto the roof rack, Celine was still shaving her legs—a statement of silent protest.

Frau Schön looked bad. Her breathing rate was elevated, as was her temperature. Harald seemed to have it all figured out.

"Septicemia. I've already started broad-spectrum antibiotics."

"Did you take blood cultures first?"

"No. I didn't want to wait that long."

He'd never get it. If those antibiotics were to fail or there were complications, the blood cultures would at least have told us the pathogen we were dealing with. This chance had been blown.

I took a good look at Frau Schön. One of the best-kept secrets in diagnosing bedridden patients is to take a peek under the covers. A second, equally well-guarded secret is to have a look under all bandages. I did both. The incision from the operation looked innocent enough, but I noticed a small bump underneath it. The bump was bulging and warm. After administering a local anesthetic, I quickly cut the sutures; thick pus flowed out. I took a swab for sensitivities, rinsed the wound with hydrogen and covered it cleanly. I reduced the antibiotics to flucloxacillin.

"Shouldn't the scar be examined by ultrasound first?"

I didn't even bother replying to Harald's question; after all, I wanted to go to the Spreewald, not get put into the slammer for murder. Over his protests, I had him write down exactly what he was to watch for and when.

Celine and I finally set out into the beautiful day for Schlepzig in the Lower Spreewald. Schlepzig is popular with great numbers of storks, who make it their summer habitat.

Schlepzig also has a pretty little hotel called On the Green Banks of the Spree. It is owned by Torsten Römer, who used to work as a radiologist in our hospital. He saw early on that times were changing and now owns this hotel and lives happily with his family in the Spreewald.

Torsten gave us a hearty welcome and helped take the bikes off the car. We were given a pleasant room in the old barn with a view over the moor. Celine and I took a relaxing afternoon "nap," followed by a bike trip around the countryside.

It was a gorgeous afternoon. We watched as hundreds of dragonflies buzzing over the fishponds tried to impress their future partners with their crazy aerobatics, while countless frogs courted potential mates with their more or less melodious croaking.

Even the low-pressure system predicted for that evening petered out somewhere over the Oder River. Torsten had fired up the barbecue in the inner courtyard; the smell was mouthwatering, and it turned into a beautiful summer evening—in spite of the hordes of mosquitoes, which we accepted as tribute for a halfway intact environment.

Torsten joined us after dinner and wanted to hear the latest gossip from the hospital. But it quickly became evident that he was better informed than I was; his hotel was a popular weekend destination for other physicians at the hospital. I had heard that Prof. Dohmke came here regularly for weekend tournaments with his bridge club.

"Have you gotten a postcard from the States from the diligent Schreiber?" Torsten asked.

"I don't even know if he's in New York yet. I was surprised at the way he disappeared so suddenly. Of course we won't get a replacement and now have to do his work too."

Torsten pulled over another chair, put his feet up on it, and looked up at the night sky. "You must decide whether to have a career or to live life. I've decided to live life. How's Marlies supposed to manage her ward without Schreiber?"

Celine began intensely studying the night sky. She harbored a chronic suspicion that Marlies and I were having an affair, which was right only up to a point.

"Marlies is bearing the brunt of the misery resulting from Schreiber's trip. She's fighting a running battle with an overly keen intern that I've already had the pleasure of working with."

"Licensed to kill?"

I nodded. Torsten refilled our glasses; the wine was good and pleasantly refreshing. A collective groan occasionally came from the hotel because Italy versus Romania was on TV.

"Treasurer Bredow," Torsten said, "will soon cotton on that the hospital can save even more if he throws all of you out and only works with med students and interns."

"And after getting rid of us, he'll move on to the cost-intensive patients, the ones with tumors, or kids. They gobble up a pile of expensive medications and cost the hospital as much in nursing charges as a harmless appendix does."

Celine, always wanting to see the good in people, had a reasonable objection.

"Why has Schreiber been allowed to go off to America for further training if your bosses don't give a damn about the quality of medicine at the hospital?"

"Score one for her, Felix!"

"Maybe Schreiber has friends in high places at the hospital," I countered.

Torsten once again demonstrated the depth of his knowledge about the current state of the hospital.

"But those would have to be fairly new friendships."

Celine soon tired of our "What's so-and-so doing?" and went off to bed. We started to gossip in earnest. Bredow, Dohmke, Kindel…the surgeons, the gynecologists, the radiologists…and, of course, most importantly: Which doctor had gotten which nurse pregnant lately? Which lab tech had hooked whom? Torsten went off for another bottle of wine.

"How do you find it to be working for a private company now?" Torsten asked when he returned.

"A hospital is a hospital," I said.

"Typical doctor's point of view. Of course the patients are the same, their diseases are the same, your night shifts are the same. But don't forget, you're now working for a free commercial enterprise."

"If I listen to Bredow, I'm working for an enterprise on the brink of bankruptcy."

Torsten said he had a few ideas about how the hospital could make a pile of money.

"Wonderful: South Berlin Hospital, a center for the international organ trade! Karl hawks corneas to ophthalmologists and bones to trauma surgeons in the pathology cellar; upstairs the gynecologists flog embryos and placentas; we sell hearts and whatever other internal organs are in demand. It's on every other TV crime show these days, but it's not so easy to put into practice."

Inspired by the warm summer night and alcohol, we competed to come up with the best moneymaking scheme. I knew it was time for me to turn in when Torsten suggested using nuclear medicine to make mini atom bombs for the Third World.

Torsten's final interesting question was, who actually owned South Berlin Hospital Ltd.? Bredow was only the treasurer after all. I was surprised to realize that I'd never asked myself that question before.

"Do you know who, Torsten?"

"Not really. And I'm not sure I want to. I can only tell you that I don't like some of the bridge club characters who roll up here with Dohmke now and then."

Torsten was a nice guy, but even when he'd worked in the hospital he'd always been secretive, and we'd drunk enough by then. I didn't pry further and instead got up and stumbled carefully over the cobblestones to our barn. Celine was sound asleep.

I got up very quietly on Sunday morning so as not to bother Celine; it took her ages to leave the realm of sleep and find her way back to life. Celine collected seashells, and I had told her that you could find shells in the Spreewald. I'd bought a little bag of South Sea shells in Berlin, which I now spread around in the sand near where the boats were moored.

Torsten had arranged a surprise for Sunday breakfast. A Spreewald boat awaited us, complete with breakfast table, fresh rolls, and coffee in thermoses. The boatman punted us silently through the calm channels and woods; they had a fairy-tale-like aura, and I would hardly have been surprised if dancing elves had suddenly burst out from behind the trees. Celine wore a straw hat—normally part of the hotel's wall décor—and looked as though she had popped out of a Monet painting. With a bottle of chardonnay tied to a string behind us, we felt very much at ease.

Back in our room that afternoon, we took a deep siesta, then restored our energy with a strong espresso before our trip back to Berlin. Celine treated herself to an apple strudel with hot vanilla sauce; later that evening she'd blame it on me. We started back to Berlin in the late afternoon.

After a little while, traffic ground to a dead stop. Celine pulled her knees up and turned toward me, her back against the passenger door.

"Is something going on at the hospital?"

"What do you mean?"

"Because you practically never talk about work, especially not on weekends, and certainly not when I'm around. You're usually quite considerate in that respect."

"How do you think you know what I'm talking about when you're not there?"

"Don't be evasive. What's wrong at the hospital?"

I'd made a strategic error. I should have told Celine any old story from the hospital, maybe about Frau Schön and her gallstone, but my diversionary tactic had been precisely the wrong move. Celine knew me too well. Now I could only tell her the truth.

So I told her everything. I told her about Misha's death and Schreiber's second death certificate. About my suspicion that the sudden approval for his training in the US may have had something to do with it. About the missing patient file and the missing ambulance protocol. I told her about my chat with Astrid and her fear that I might cause trouble for her husband. I described my two visits to the Hostel Elvira and how I'd regretted not going to her karate class. I was able to recite my conversation with Bredow almost verbatim since I'd gone through it myself several times.

"He had his secretary tell me on Friday that everything was OK and that I shouldn't worry about it. Not a word about the missing patient's record. And then Kindel mentioned the file to me that night at his farewell party. Isn't that all very strange?"

The victims of the traffic jam had resigned themselves to their fate. A couple of men were playing cards on a camping table two cars in front of us; some kids behind us were playing hide and seek. Women were leaning on the guardrail watching their children and exchanging child-rearing tips. It was just another peaceful Sunday evening on a German autobahn.

Celine had been listening to me, her head tipped at a slight angle. And she hadn't interrupted me once—which wasn't like her.

"I think," she said after a pause, "something's pretty rotten in your hospital."

As I listed the various incidents for Celine, I became increasingly convinced that there might be something more to all this than just a series of unrelated coincidences.

"What are you going to do?" Celine asked.

"Do I have to do anything? I'm not responsible for the hospital but for my patients, and in that regard I can't complain about a thing. I get the medications I need for them, the appointments for the necessary exams, and the administration has yet to interfere. So why should I bother with a dead body from Ukraine?"

"You're right, Felix. It shouldn't bother you. But it does bother you. You may be telling me otherwise, but it's obvious that you're completely losing it over this Misha business. That's why you went to retrieve the files yourself. That's why you went to his hostel twice and almost got beaten up in the process. That's why you went and spoke with His Majesty himself, Prince Bredow."

"That may be. But perhaps now's the right time to get my damn nose out of this business before it gets burned."

"One burns one's finger. One gets hit on one's nose."

"I can burn what I damn well want. Even my nose. I saw plenty of burned noses when I did my time in surgery."

The men folded up their camping table, and the kids were shooed back into the cars. We weren't moving, but a giant crane was approaching from behind and the space between the cars wasn't wide enough for it. An elderly couple ahead of us flooded their engine in their excitement. We helped them push their car to the shoulder.

"The one thing that seems fairly clear," Celine said, "is that something's being covered up. What's normally covered up in a hospital?"

"Wrong treatment, wrong diagnosis, wrong leg sawed off, wrong arm sewed on. Wrong IV hung up, or the right IV inserted too fast because someone's in a rush to go off duty. Simple malpractice."

"And your Ukrainian? What malpractice needs to be covered up and who did it?"

"Haven't a clue. It doesn't make sense. If I'd screwed up back when Misha was my patient, I'd know. And besides, *I* would have made the files disappear instead of spending all those days stupidly running around after them."

"And Schreiber? After all, he delivered the dead Ukrainian to you. Maybe he didn't have to die at all. Maybe Schreiber screwed up or helped him die."

"Schreiber was my top pick too when the second death certificate turned up, even more so when the call protocol for the ambulance disappeared. But what reason could he possibly have for taking my October ward record out of circulation? And one thing's for sure: he couldn't have approved his trip to the States on his own."

Celine began to chew her nails. She was a mathematician and thus convinced that most problems could be solved if you just approached them the right way.

"We need some variables."

"I haven't the foggiest idea," I replied.

That was the God's truth. But I'd had a disturbing thought the night before.

"I've been wondering whether somebody's trying to pin Misha's death on me. The call protocol and the ward record can pop up anytime, in a slightly revised form, to show that Dr. Hoffmann has a patient on his conscience."

"And why would anyone want to pin a dead Ukrainian on you? Who's the last woman you've been screwing?"

"Celine! We've adopted a more American setup in the hospital lately; farewell to the good old lifetime job. Every one of my dear colleagues could be angling for my permanent position."

"Even your good friend Marlies?" Celine asked, looking innocent.

"Yes, even my friend Marlies. Or the administration, so they can replace me with a cheap med student. Anything's possible in the current corporate environment."

I said nothing for a minute and observed the goings-on on the autobahn.

"But I don't really believe that my colleagues are conspiring against me, especially since none of them could have approved Schreiber's leave."

Celine worked at her nails more intensely.

"So we must go up a level. If there's a connection there, then at least one level. Or two or three. I dunno."

Celine's hunting instinct was aroused. She assumed her I'm-thinking-about-this-very-hard position: hands folded around her drawn-up knees and her eyes focused straight ahead. Intense reflection almost always had the same effect on her.

"I think I have an urgent need to take a piss."

"You girls cannot take a piss. You'd like to, I know, but you can't. You can pee. Maybe even go pee pee, but not take a piss."

My love was already on her way to the shoulder.

"Chauvinist prick!"

Celine, who had indulged in more of the chardonnay than I had, headed into the bushes beside the autobahn.

We finally arrived back in Berlin late that evening. Celine stayed at my place, which was rare. As a rule we slept apart, in our own apartments. Our light supper consisted of cheese, salad, and vino. Just before nodding off, I remembered my buried seashells. Maybe somebody else would find my South Sea shells in the Spreewald and wonder how they could possibly have gotten there.

Celine woke me up in the middle of the night with a poke in the ribs; experienced night shift physician that I am, I was immediately wide awake. Celine was sitting up in bed and seemed to have arrived at a decision that she had to communicate to me at once.

"I don't think it's malpractice. It doesn't compute. Of course the hospital has to keep malpractice hush hush from the outside world or deny it, but they don't have to do so internally. And they wouldn't throw you out on account of malpractice. There must be something else behind it."

"So what's behind it?" I asked Celine. "A conspiracy?"

Celine loves conspiracies. To this day she's convinced that CIA biology labs are behind the AIDS virus and the agency's efforts to exterminate black people. In her eyes, German reunification was in reality a successful coup instigated by West German industry: in exchange for a pile of money, Gorbachev and the KGB handed it sixteen million car, video, and CD consumers. And it goes without saying that Lady Diana and her Arab friend Dodi's accident was staged by the British secret service so that the Queen didn't have to sit around the Christmas tree with an Arab son-in-law. It stood to reason that Celine would come up with a suitable conspiracy theory for my story as well.

"Yes, a conspiracy, if that's what you want to call it. That's what it is whenever several people band together to keep something secret. And I'm convinced that there's more than just a potential malpractice suit at stake."

"You could be right. Otherwise, we'd have a new conspiracy cropping up in the hospital every other day." I stood up. "Shall I get you some wine?"

I'd known Celine long enough to know that her theory couldn't wait till morning and got her a glass of wine. She took it without a word; she was busy with more important things.

"You remember the movie *All the President's Men*?"

"Sure. With the two buddies, Robert Redford and Paul Newman."

"No, they were in *The Sting*. *All the President's Men* was the movie about the Watergate conspiracy with Robert Redford and Dustin Hoffman."

For all her preoccupation with her new conspiracy theory, Celine was still a stickler for details.

"Anyway, you know what drove me crazy about that Watergate movie?"

"Surely not Robert Redford and Dustin Hoffman."

"How dumb those terrific *Washington Post* journalists were. They didn't really need that secret information from that FBI guy to hit on the idea to follow the money. If we both agree that it's not about malpractice, then that leaves love and money."

"What about revenge, jealousy, or other emotions?"

"You can classify them all under the two I just mentioned. Believe me, it's mostly about money."

Celine is more than ten years younger than I am. What had happened to her sense of romance? Or are women simply more realistic by nature?

"You mean," I said and quoted one of Dr. Valenta's favorite sayings, "it all boils down to money and cock size."

"Right on. And we can probably exclude love in your case. That leaves money." Celine inserted a dramatic pause. "And what, my dear fellow, is the good thing about money?"

One of her Socratic questions. I couldn't see where Celine, with her IQ of over 155, was going with this.

"That you can buy a lot of Smarties?"

"That it leaves tracks. Money has become largely virtual, a few bytes on your bank's computer. Billions whiz around the globe every day. Nobody knows where money is just now, or if it really exists at all, but every transaction leaves a trail. And usually a long-lasting one."

Despite my lower IQ, I could still follow her. But if it really was about money, then whose?

"I can hardly imagine that Misha was a Romanoff heir. He certainly wouldn't have been cleaning hospitals if he had been."

"Maybe he swiped drugs from the hospital?"

"I don't think so. Nothing's gone missing for a long time, and the drugs in the hospital are peanuts compared to the tons of stuff that's smuggled in from South America or Afghanistan."

"Let's go through it one more time." Celine tugged quite hard on her earlobe. "Someone is trying to get rid of any trace of your Misha. You mentioned another Russian on the cleaning crew."

"Jurek."

"Yes! He told you that Misha couldn't see a doctor because he was an illegal immigrant. And you also said that Misha only had a tourist visa for Germany, which had expired a while back. So he was employed by you people illegally. And that would surely have come out if he'd been autopsied and people were to look into where he might have picked up his jaundice."

An interesting point. If that were the case, I'd have to make inquiries with CareClean Cleaning Services. But Celine had already thought ahead.

"There must be more to it than illegal employment," she said. "Have a look at Potsdamer Platz. They'd still be excavating today it they hadn't had illegals from Poland, Albania, and God knows where else toiling away. Nobody would make such a fuss over illegal workers. And besides, his record, your death certificate, and the ambulance protocol have gone missing in the hospital, Felix, not in that cleaning company. I'm telling you, it's about money, and the key lies in your hospital."

"And where in the hospital am I supposed to look for this key and the money?"

I wasn't yet convinced, but Celine had warmed up to her idea.

"I told you. Money doesn't lie around in fat bundles these days, but it still leaves a trail. We've got to get access to your hospital's Accounts Department. With a little effort we'll find the money there, you bet your sweet ass."

Celine had a bellicose glint in her eye; I know it well. If anybody really was doing something crooked at the hospital, that person now had a very determined and stubborn opponent. Celine could pace herself, unlike me; the glint disappeared as quickly as it had come. She rolled over on her side and was asleep in minutes. An enviable trait. Why, though, did she want to bet my sweet ass and not hers? Maybe she wasn't quite so sure.

While I desperately awaited the sandman, my boozy conversation with Torsten Römer in the Spreewald flitted across my mind. He was right: my hospital was now a profit-oriented private enterprise, which was precisely why Celine's idea had a certain logic to it. It couldn't hurt to have a look at the company's books, but we'd need some help in order to do so; after all, I can barely cope with my tax returns.

That, however, was the second problem. We'd first have to somehow gain access to the documents from Accounts.

We came up with a plan over a quick breakfast. Our first course of action involved hacking the Accounts computer via the hospital's intranet. Our intranet was one of Prof. Dohmke's beloved projects, and sometimes it comes in quite handy.

Our plan was predicated on the assumption that a direct link existed between patients' billing and the record of both the bed occupancies and services performed for the patients; via patients' billing, there was a good chance we'd be able to link to *all* the hospital's accounts. Celine came to the hospital on Monday afternoon and sat down at the terminal in my office. Her math degree might finally have been about to prove its worth beyond her half-time teaching job.

"What's your password?"

"Celine."

"C'mon! You've got to give me your password so I can get into the system."

"I am. It's Celine."

Celine smiled. She couldn't know that I'd changed my password at noon that day. I thought it might make her happy. It did.

Using my access, Celine could easily not only retrieve lab data, X-ray results, and operation reports, but also the current bed occupancy on my ward and the patients scheduled for the next eight weeks. But when she tried to look up the occupancy dates in Surgery, the screen announced "Access Denied."

I began to have doubts about our brilliant plan.

"If we can't even retrieve data from the other wards, we'll hardly be able to get into Accounts."

"Access in a computer network signifies power, my dear boy. And if you mere attending physicians had the same access as your dear Prof. Dohmke, for instance, you would have the same power he does. But you don't, and he doesn't want you to have it. It's like the social organization of an orangutan herd. There's the alpha animal, who's the boss, and then the beta animals and the gamma animals. That's how these networks are organized too. You attending physicians have only gamma status in the system. What we need is Dohmke's access code."

"I think his wife's called Karin."

"Men aren't especially imaginative, but I don't think that's going to be enough."

True, "Karin" wasn't enough. Karin did happen to be the name of the wife or daughter or lover of another one of our attendings, but that just gave us gamma access as well.

"So what do we do now?"

"You could get us a coffee."

By the time I returned with the coffee, Celine was already off and running as an alpha user in the system. She spared me a detailed description of how cleverly she'd tricked the security system; she'd sent me for coffee at the key moment. Celine has pronounced alpha characteristics herself.

Now we could see the current and planned occupancies for Surgery, Gynecology, and all the other departments in the hospital. We knew the scheduling for the operating rooms and the medications available in our central pharmacy. We could print statistics as a bar chart or a table, in color or black and white, but we couldn't get beyond that.

"Are we not alpha users?" I said.

"Oh yes we are. But we can't get into Accounts on this terminal."

"And why not?"

"Two possibilities. They could have a firewall in the system, which works like a one-way street. It allows specific data to come into the central computer but not out. Or else they haven't linked Central Accounting to the hospital system at all. They could simply load the relevant data onto a CD and load it onto the Accounts computer. Then there's no physical connection to the hospital system. That's how I would set it up to protect my own accounts in case one of you doctors got a virus through an e-mail."

We were so focused on the flickering screen that we hadn't heard someone enter my office. It was Marlies.

Marlies and Celine hadn't met in person before. I hate introducing people to each other because I often can't recall their names at the crucial moment. In this case though, my problem was who to introduce first—my bourgeois upbringing at work.

They finally just introduced themselves to each other. My hesitation would almost certainly lead to an interrogation by Celine that evening. I tried to explain why she was here.

"Celine's giving me a tutorial on our computer system. I never wanted to admit to you all that I didn't understand a thing in that introductory course we all had to take."

Marlies examined the screen and was impressed.

"Hey, how'd you get into that? Occupancy numbers. Dohmke's big secret!"

Celine said with a smile that I would surely be happy to show Marlies the trick another time.

After mulling it over, we came to the conclusion that the inaccessible computer in Central Accounting probably wouldn't help us a bit. If something big was going on—shifting profits around, cooking the books, or whatever—it was unlikely that data was actually being manipulated in Accounts itself. It would make more sense for someone to give Accounts data that had already been manipulated.

Celine turned to me.

"Who's the most likely candidate to have fed Accounts doctored data?"

"Obviously our chief operating officer, Dr. Bredow."

Not only was he responsible for the hospital's financial management and a genuine MBA, but he'd also engineered the hospital's transition into a private company and was the one who'd implemented the new outsourcing policy. I recalled an instance a few months earlier when my overtime payment had been delayed because the data was temporarily with Dr. Bredow.

We had to get our hands on Bredow's computer. The question was how.

Celine thought I should try taking advantage of my good relationship with Bredow's secretary, Frau Krüger.

"What kind of relationship do you think I have with Frau Krüger anyway?"

"I don't know what sort of relationship you have with the women in your hospital."

"Frau Krüger could be my mother. Besides, if there's any fiddling around with Bredow's books, would he let Frau Krüger in on it?"

"So what do you suggest?" Celine asked, a bit insulted.

I had an idea. One advantage of my profession is that I get to interact with people with a wide range of professions and skills. Some patients did indeed leave the hospital in better shape than when they were admitted, and at least a couple of them were even grateful to their doctor for it.

My former patient Franz had a small lock-and-key service and was an old-school break-in artist on the side; he gained possession of valuable objects without using carjacks or crowbars, usually in collusion with the supposedly injured party, who split the insurance money with him. I'd cured Franz of a nasty salmonella infection a while back and had wangled him a suspended sentence with a medical report when his wife was pregnant. Franz was the sort of guy who meant it when he told you that he owed you one.

Sure enough, he handed me a key a few days later that was guaranteed to fit the lock to Bredow's office, along with half a homemade plum cake with greetings from his wife. He refused any payment.

I'd found out from Frau Krüger that Bredow would be off at a conference of the German Insurance Association in Dresden that weekend, so we planned our break-in for Friday night.

I would be lying if I didn't admit that we had butterflies in our stomachs. Celine and I wanted to fuel up with a burger before making our big strike, but all we could get down was a Coke.

It wasn't unusual for a physician to swing by the hospital at night. There might have been a patient emergency or a change in dosage on an infusion schedule. Maybe his favorite nurse was on night duty—there was always a room free somewhere. So we didn't have any problem getting into the hospital around eleven. Fatty Meyer sat at the gate, whiling away his night shift on the phone. He nodded at me and pressed the electric door opener. Although I was regularly at the hospital on night duty, there was something different about being there this time. I had visions of an alarm going off somewhere, of all the doors automatically closing (the hospital doesn't have any such thing), of Prof. Dohmke coming around the corner with a few hefty orderlies, and of the police waiting for us in Bredow's office. Of course, we didn't run into a soul aside from a couple of patients smoking surreptitiously.

The administration wing was completely dead. Franz's key slipped into Bredow's office lock without any resistance, and no alarm went off when we opened the door. We were inside.

I knew, as an attentive reader and watcher of mystery stories, what to do next. I left the door to the corridor open a crack until I'd carefully drawn the curtains. Only then did I close the door, locking it from the inside, and turn on the light. Celine was taking in Bredow's swank space.

"Impressive," she said. "What do you suppose the guy does with so much room?"

"No idea. Maybe he works on his golf handicap or races remote-controlled model cars."

I'd missed an unpleasant detail during my previous visits to Bredow's office: beside his neo-gothic desk was a table with not one computer but two. I had no idea why Bredow needed two computers or how we were to know which one to hack.

Celine carefully inspected the cables coming out of the back of each. I watched intently, even though I had no idea what I was supposed to be looking at. I figured my chances of picking the right one were fifty-fifty.

"I think this one here is our best bet," I said, trying to sound confident.

"Why do you say that?"

I couldn't use the color of the casing or the screen size as an argument, but I saw something at the last second.

"It's got one more cable."

"Exactly," Celine said.

I'd been accepted into the Club of Experts. But my triumph was premature.

"Exactly why I do *not* think that it's our candidate," she continued. "That extra cable is probably the connection to your intranet, same as the one you have in your office. So if there's cheating going on here and this guy Bredow wants to be on the safe side, then he should crunch his data in a computer that nobody can log in to over the net. Since this one has no connection, there's no way to hack it from the outside."

Why didn't I think of that?

"I considered that. But Bredow is sly. I bet he plugs the net cable into the other machine every night to fake out computer pirates like us."

Celine gave me a smile.

"You really think so?"

I swallowed my hurt pride by reminding myself that I'd at least obtained the duplicate key.

Celine sat down at the computer with no network cable and turned it on. The cooling fan began to purr softly.

"Well, let's just take a little look, my friend..."

The screen blinked on. A box demanding a password popped up. That didn't look promising, but I'd witnessed a sample of Celine's artistry only a few days earlier and knew better than to give up.

"Your friend is really one suspicious human being. He's protected his BIOS with a password."

I nodded self-confidently and made a mental note to look up what BIOS meant in the near future.

"And now?"

But Celine was already typing, entering a combination of letters that mystified me—"AWARD?SW"—but nothing happened. Then she tried the weird word "ikepeter"—without success. I waited expectantly for her third attempt, but instead Celine turned the computer off, conjured up a screwdriver from her backpack, and removed the plastic cover from the computer.

"What are you going to do? Are you going to dismantle the whole hard drive?"

I do understand a bit about computers, you know.

"That's not a bad idea," Celine answered, the screwdriver between her teeth, "but I think it'll be enough just to cripple this asshole's memory for a little while."

She took the screwdriver out of her mouth and used it to winkle a small battery out of the box. When she restarted the computer, the screen came on without a password request. I was impressed.

The first thing we did was to survey what programs were installed. We were looking for numerical data and knew we'd most likely find it in a database. We called up all Bredow's Excel files. And there we found what we were looking for. Celine read aloud.

"Accounts: first quarter; accounts second quarter...very tidy your Dr. Bredow; all neatly organized."

Celine clicked on "Open File." An on-screen prompt popped up asking for a password.

"Your pal really is a rascal. He's already protected his BIOS."

"It seems he'd counted on bad girls like you."

An impish grin appeared on Celine's face.

"On me? I don't believe it."

This time I was going to pay close attention to how Celine got access, but again I was disappointed, or more precisely, surprised. She pulled a little metal box out of her backpack and hooked it up to Bredow's computer. A message appeared on the screen: "External Hard Drive Recognized." Celine activated the program "Copy File." Her facial expression registered visible disdain.

"No copy protection, my friend? But that's very careless."

She copied Bredow's first and second quarter accounts files to her portable hard drive.

I felt somewhat superfluous and poked around on Bredow's desk but didn't find anything of particular interest. I then tried opening the desk drawers and was rewarded for my efforts. Why would a person secure his computer but not lock his desk?

Celine's hard drive signaled that the copying was successfully complete.

"We're done here," I said.

"Not quite," Celine responded. "We still have to cover our tracks."

"Right." I saw a second opportunity to demonstrate my digital savvy. "We mustn't forget to reset the date and time after we've reinstalled the buffer battery."

"Wouldn't help much," Celine replied. "Bredow would notice that he isn't being asked for his password when he boots up."

Instead of replacing the battery, Celine put in another one, a dead one. She explained to me later that Bredow would trace any unusual computer behavior to a dead battery.

"So if we don't leave the hard drive behind or knock over any flowerpots, we're pretty safe," she said.

We packed up and checked that we hadn't left anything behind. Celine is not keen on jewelry, so no lost earring in the seat cushions on Bredow's desk chair would betray us. I turned out the light, opened the curtains, and we made it to the door in the dark without bumping into his yucca plant.

I had unconsciously slipped into a cautious, sneaking gait, and Celine drew my attention to the fact that an attending in his own hospital doesn't normally tiptoe through the corridors. Nevertheless, it struck me that an alibi might be a good thing, and besides, I was holding something that I didn't want to bring home with me. So I checked on the two patients in the ICU I'd admitted that morning. Contrary to rumors claiming the opposite, it is not unusual for an attending to occasionally look in on his patients in the ICU.

Both of them were doing very well, but there's always room for improvement, so I changed a few details in their infusion schedule.

That documented my handwriting on that date at that time in the unlikely event that somebody decided to check up on the reason for my hospital visit.

In the meantime Celine was in the bathroom, which is her normal reaction to stress. I was astonished that her bladder hadn't caught up with her in Bredow's office. By the time she returned, I had stuffed my souvenir from Bredow's desk in a cupboard in the ICU.

Fatty Meyer was having a cup of coffee in the reception area with Nurse Gudrun from surgical First Aid and pressed the door opener for us again with little fanfare. The two of them would likely come to the same conclusion about what Dr. Hoffmann from Cardiology had been up to in the hospital late at night with an unknown young woman.

I drove Celine and her hard drive home and fell happily into bed afterward. Celine was without question the hero of the day, or would be if she could crack the access code to Bredow's accounting file. But I too had made myself useful in Bredow's office.

I'd just been killing time when I was inspecting his desk, but imagine my surprise when I found, in the second drawer on the left side, the file "Chenkov, Misha, born April 20, 1971, Ward

CHAPTER 10

It was Saturday, the morning after the first break-in of my life. And my first robbery as well, if I didn't count that bottle of Chablis the summer before and the screw I grabbed at the hardware store the previous fall. (About that Chablis: I'd waited for the salesperson for over ten minutes; as for the screw, I didn't consider the lifting of a single M5x60 screw from a package of fifty to be theft. Robbery is selling M5x60 screws in packages of fifty when any normal person needs no more than two.) A SWAT team hadn't stormed my apartment during the night.

I biked over to the bakery and bought the usual rolls for Saturday breakfast, which would be at Celine's place this time. The supermarket opens at eight on Saturdays, so I picked up a week's supply of Vino Trentino—eminently quaffable at under three euros a bottle. I grabbed a second case of six as well, since I knew that Celine and I probably had a labor-intensive weekend ahead of us. Herbert, a former physicist and now the only alkie in the immediate neighborhood, gave me a friendly nod.

As I unlocked Celine's door, laden with rolls and wine cartons, I was once again reminded of how different we were. I would have been glued to my computer all night long trying to dig up the password for Bredow's data files; Celine, on the other hand, was in the shower, her backpack containing the hard drive lying untouched in the hall. Thankfully, she'd already turned on the coffee machine. I poured myself a cup and started to do some thinking while Celine ran around half-naked looking for her things.

How significant was it that Misha's file had been in Bredow's office drawer? I was the only one who knew that it was no longer in his desk drawer. I knew it hadn't been there by accident, and there was no question of Bredow's not being aware of it. Had Bredow taken them to task in Medical Records? Had Frau Tönnig found the file after all? Or had it been in Bredow's care the whole time, ever since Misha's arrival on June 12, or even before that? Had it been sitting in his drawer when I'd met with Bredow in his office?

Under normal circumstances, I would have expected Bredow to call me in a few days to inform me of the file's reappearance. But he wouldn't find it now, so he wouldn't call. I had to get that file back into his drawer ASAP. For the time being, it was safely buried beneath the heap of files for deceased ICU patients. I couldn't picture any of my colleagues having a sudden urge to process that stack.

We got down to work after breakfast. I was well armed for figuring out the password. I'd found out Bredow's date of birth quite recently thanks to his birthday celebration. Without attracting any suspicion I hoped, I'd gotten Frau Krüger to supply me with the first names and birthdays of his wife and two sons as well.

"Try 'Margret,'" I told Celine, "That's his lover. Birthday August fourteenth."

Celine threw me a quick glance and tried all the names and dates I'd given her. But neither his family nor his girlfriend did the trick.

"Let me try."

Celine stepped aside. I tried the names and birthdays backward. No luck. Then I tried "Big Boss," "Mastermind," "Imperator," and various other titles that I imagined matched Bredow's self-image.

"Put yourself inside the perp's head. Think the way he does." Another lesson from my home study course in TV crime shows. But Bredow probably had a different self-image from the one I thought he had.

"Now let Auntie Celine have another go at it."

"I've always wanted to see a genuine cryptologist at work."

"Well, it isn't cryptology, properly speaking. That's when the entire text is encrypted. Then we'd really be in trouble. So what we need first is a password with eight numbers or letters, or a combination of numbers and letters, which is somewhat more common."

"How do you know it has to be eight?"

"Here." Celine tapped around on the keyboard. "You can see it on the memory slot for the password. That's a disadvantage of this system. Every number or letter takes up a certain number of bytes."

"And how do we find these eight numbers or letters?"

"If we were really good at it, we'd get the computer to tell us. Because the computer knows the eight strokes that are entered as the password."

"And how do we get the computer to tell us the password?"

"I don't know exactly. I could try but I'll probably have to ask Manfred to help."

"Who's Manfred?"

"I know him from math class. A computer genius. A hacker. And a friend." Celine flashed me an innocent smile. "I'll have to be a bit nice to him of course, so that he'll help us."

We'd been together long enough to know each other's weak points.

"Probably a stay-at-home, hollow-chested type, pale and pimply."

"Correct. Looks a little like you, actually."

"Thanks a million. What can we do for the time being without our genius?"

Celine took a CD from her box of disks and put it in her CD drive.

"As we just did with your hospital computer, we'll have this little program do some of the work for us."

"Decrypt III—The Ultimate Hacker" appeared on the screen and asked if it could get to work. After Celine had defined the parameters, it got down to business.

"And what does this program do?"

"I hope it'll dig up the password. It's not really a deciphering program, but Manfred says it finds about eighty percent of all passwords. It simply takes patience and computer speed. But it can take some time—several hours possibly."

There was nothing more we could do for the time being. It was shaping up to be a beautiful day, so Celine packed up her swim things and we stopped by my place to pick up my swimsuit and then headed out to the beach on the Wannsee. Marlies had promised to do my patient rounds on Saturday and I'd agreed to sub for her the following weekend.

The beach was the usual sunny-weekend hell. Serious-looking dads with artistic pretensions were building sand castles that their little kids were only permitted to enter with the greatest of care. Lithe young girls were pointedly ignoring the lecherous looks of puberty-stricken youths and older men, dreaming all the while of being discovered as future models. The largely outnumbered full-figured girls wore the briefest of bikinis and ignored the lack of lecherous looks with equal concentration. The boys showed off their muscular torsos while playing beach volleyball and attempted to establish contact with the future models by aiming misplayed shots in their direction, while men my age patiently waited behind a newspaper for an opportunity that would probably never arrive.

In brief, it was a typical summer's day on the beach. Though it was no different from any other sunny beach day anywhere in the world, warm days in Berlin are rare, particularly on weekends. This gave the day a special intensity and compelled us all not to miss a single ray of sunshine or the possibility of a summer romance.

It took some stamina for us to find a free spot out of range of whining children or arguing parents. But our efforts were rewarded. Three young beauties right beside us were discussing their chances of passing their upcoming biology exam. I allowed myself to enjoy our spot's optical delights out of the corner of my eye while Celine thumbed casually through a magazine.

"Could it be that you ought to be on a list of child molesters, my good man?"

I didn't even try to play dumb.

"What do you mean 'child molester'? How old do you think those three are?"

"Sixteen, seventeen, eighteen at most."

"And when you were seventeen, let's say even sixteen, were you still playing with dolls and thinking that children were brought by the stork?"

"No. In my century there was sex education."

Every now and then Celine likes to emphasize our age difference.

"And—that was it? I mean, just theory?"

"That's none of your business. Maybe I was a nymphomaniac at fourteen. You'll never know."

"Does that mean you still are?"

Celine laughed, gave me a slap on my still well-shaped butt—my opinion, of course—and ran to the water. She jumped into the Wannsee, apparently immune to the cold, and swam off with powerful strokes. I hesitated, stepping cautiously into the water to avoid sudden cardiac arrest from the shock of too-sudden contact with cold water. But soon we were floating around together in the Wannsee, swimming and splashing and slinging seaweed and mud at each other.

Celine stayed in the water while I returned to our spot to relax in the sun—though I wasn't completely relaxing because the three young ladies were slathering each other with sunscreen. My dreamy observations came to a jarring halt when a bathing cap of cold Wannsee water was unceremoniously dumped on me.

"Pederast!"

"One more comment like that and you'll have to put on your sunscreen yourself."

She lay down on her stomach and held out her sunscreen to me.

"I'd rather have skin cancer than a voyeur like you putting on my sunscreen. I'd be sure to get a skin fungus. Or a rash. Or cellulitis. And don't be too rough, please, I'm a delicately built woman."

"You've already got cellulitis."

"I do not!"

"Yes you do."

Of course she didn't have cellulitis, but then I also wasn't a dirty old man, or only minimally, and she surely had a little cellulitis somewhere.

Celine removed the upper half of her bikini and now, if not before, drew the eyes of my voyeuristic colleagues like magnets. I bent over her, filled with a male's pride of possession, and distributed the sunscreen over her attractive back and slim thighs.

"I hope you don't have an erection?"

"An erection? Why should I? Are you saying I'm a cellulite fetishist?"

The timeless atmosphere of a hot summer's day at the beach was at its peak, and the classic sounds floated through the air, lulling me into a peaceful stupor. While I was contemplating whether I was already on my way from being an attractive physician in the prime of life to a dirty old man, I fell asleep.

When I eventually woke up, I felt like a hermit crab that had forgotten to molt. I hadn't used any sunscreen and knew that I was in for an uncomfortable night. I tickled Celine's nose with a blade of grass. I had to unburden myself of my latest theory on the case we now shared. When Celine woke up, however, she was not interested in new theories but in tracking down some coffee. We dragged ourselves over to the beach café and ordered two cappuccinos. Our expectations of Wannsee gastronomy were low, so we were pleasantly surprised when our cappuccinos were served promptly, hot, and with real foamed milk instead of whipped cream.

My theory was to try to link Bredow and Misha. Bredow had turned over the cleaning of the hospital to CareClean, and CareClean employed foreigners almost exclusively. If, say, a large number of these foreigners were employed illegally at starvation wages without any benefits, CareClean's owners might turn quite a handsome profit. And if, say, Bredow was part owner of CareClean, he wouldn't want to see this lovely source of income threatened by an investigation into the death of an illegal employee. I had one more theory: Bredow could use the possible link between the hospital and CareClean to transfer profits and losses back and forth for the purpose of lowering taxes.

Celine was drinking her cappuccino; some of the milk foam stuck to her upper lip.

"It's possible. Let's see if we can track down any evidence of that in Bredow's books."

Celine was right of course: Why speculate when the facts were hopefully waiting for us on the hard drive? Nevertheless, I decided to pay a visit to this CareClean company very soon.

We went back to our spot, where the young Turks had succeeded in establishing contact with the three girls, packed up our things, got on our bikes, and headed back to Celine's place to see how far her hacker program had gotten us.

When we arrived, the screen was beaming Bredow's password at us: "minister." Interesting—had Bredow confided his career goal to his computer? Or was "minister" a sign of startling self-irony?

Within seconds, we had Bredow's accounts up on the screen. Everything was quite well organized: revenues from primary insurance and supplementary insurance; revenues broken down by departments and wards; revenues from private patients, outpatients, and ward services.

We decided to investigate "Revenues: Private Patients." Our private patients had contributed over €2.5 million to our hospital's welfare (and therefore to my livelihood as well), assuming they paid their bills—which Bredow had assured by bringing in a collection agency.

After that we trawled through the revenues from insurance company patients. This is where the hospital took in money for certain per diems and so-called major medical charges for one-time treatments such as operations. That added up to about €3 million in quarterly revenues. Another nice chunk of change.

Celine entered "CareClean" as a search item with no success. We hit the jackpot under "Expenses: Building cleaning," which came to €75,833.20 in May alone. But that didn't tell us much. Surely the entire sum didn't wind up in Misha's colleagues' hands, but how could we see whether a portion of the profit might have flowed back to the hospital or to Bredow directly?

"Maybe you know somebody who knows what he's doing with this stuff?" I said.

"You mean an accountant or someone like that?" Celine put on a cute little smile. "It's possible."

"And how nice would you have to be to this guy?"

She stroked the top of my head.

"I don't know. Besides, who told you it's a man?"

I let the subject drop for the time being and opened the Personnel Expenses file. While it was not directly relevant I admit, who wouldn't want to know what the department chiefs earn or how highly Bredow remunerates his own efforts? But we were disappointed here as well: the file only distinguished between physicians, nurses, technical staff, and administration. Even so, it was some comfort to see that administrative personnel expenses, rightly so or not, were lower than those of physicians.

It became clear toward dinner time that our campaign was a flop. We hadn't found Celine's money trail; her friend, male or female, with some competence in accounting might pick up on a couple of things we'd overlooked, but I doubted that we'd score any real breakthrough.

"I'm hungry as a wolf," Celine said.

I took that as a sign that she thought, too, that we'd reached an impasse. We ordered a pizza and polished it off with some of the wine I'd purchased that morning. Suddenly we were both exhausted, and I decided to stay the night.

Celine, naked but for her nail polish because of the warm night, fell asleep immediately, but sleep proved elusive for me thanks to my uncomfortably taut sunburned skin. I went out to the balcony to let the cool night breeze waft over my skin and considered our next moves. I came to the conclusion that we would probably have to break into Bredow's office one more time. And that the time had come to pay a visit to CareClean Cleaning Services.

Come Sunday morning, I'd hardly slept a wink, but Celine was full of energy and insisted on going though all the hospital's payments once again, even more thoroughly this time—remittances to privatized sectors, to providers of medicines and office supplies, to construction and repair companies, and whoever else profits from our patients and their illnesses. By noon we knew that Bredow had spent almost 30,000 euros to have a bathroom installed in his office and more than 170,000 to upgrade the administration's office—not the patients' rooms—with air-conditioning. But we didn't find any transfers to numbered accounts in Liechtenstein or the Cayman Islands, payments for new X-ray equipment that had never been installed, or a new addition to the hospital that didn't exist.

Celine soon hit upon the same realization that I'd had the night before: in order to track down any irregularities, we had to be able to compare the data we had with data from previous years, before the hospital was privatized. Though Celine wanted to head off to Bredow's office immediately, I wasn't wild about the idea of a second break-in. She confessed that illegally trespassing in someone else's office aroused in her an almost carnal lust.

"I think many burglars do it just because they like it, because they enjoy the forbidden. It's like a drug."

"But," I replied, "they say that many criminals would commit their crimes over and over again because they harbor an unconscious desire to be caught."

"Typical psychologist twaddle. That might be true for those types who kill women or sex offenders but not for serious thieves like us. And who's going to catch us? Besides, we're not filching anything, at least not really."

I resisted the urge to point out that Celine's carnal lust came pretty close to the definition of a sex offender's.

Celine wouldn't relent.

"It's Sunday so nobody's working in administration today—there couldn't be a better time. You're just a coward."

It's true I was still jumpy from the last break-in—I broke out in a cold sweat every time the phone rang—but a sensible argument occurred to me.

"But nobody in administration also means that our friend Bredow could be there, knowing he'd be undisturbed. His weekend conference would be over by noon at the latest."

Celine might still have thought me a coward, but she realized I had a point. We agreed that I should have a chat with Frau Krüger to come up with a more suitable time.

"Yeah, OK, not today then. But I'd still like to get outside today." She suggested another outing to the Wannsee. "The water will do your sunburned back good."

At that moment, I had no intention of lying in the sun ever again, but Celine was already packing her swim things.

"By the way, I've figured out why you're doing this," she said.

"What?"

"Why you're so gung ho. Why you're even willing to break in to Bredow's again."

She'd asked me earlier on the autobahn about my motives, but I hadn't had much of an answer for her at the time.

"You're surely not just worried about the death of an old patient anymore," Celine said.

"But somebody's trying to pin it on me!"

"I don't believe that's it, at least not the main thing. Maybe you're not clear in your own mind how much you've identified with your hospital. That's my point: it's *your* hospital, as far as you're concerned. And you take it very personally if something's amiss there."

Celine's analysis was pretty much right on.

While Celine pushed off toward the Wannsee, I drove to the hospital and checked my patients in the ICU for a second time—a

paragon of commitment to medicine. Valenta was hardly surprised to see me. He's been an ICU physician for a long time, and
half his patients are in the ICU as a direct consequence of his
colleagues' more or less glaring mistakes. He's learned to practice
imperturbability.

I fumbled around in the ICU's filing cabinet, wished Heinz
Valenta a relaxing day, and drove home with Misha's file well hidden in a grocery bag. I took several cold showers to soothe my
back, took a backless kitchen stool out onto my shaded balcony,
and took out Misha's file.

I usually got a good overview of my patients' medical history
and the current state of my efforts to effect their recovery. Once
they'd been discharged, though, I generally put most patients
completely out of my mind; my ward was limited to twenty-two
patients, and I focused my attention on those currently requir-
ing my services. Because I never knew when I'd have a chance to
write up the requisite report to the GP and because some details
could be forgotten over the course of a long hospital stay, I kept
fastidious records, making at least one brief note per day on the
illness's progression and my treatment plans.

Nothing seemed to be missing in Misha's file. I glanced over
the green consultation forms from that first night with a smile,
remembering when Hartmut from Surgery had tried his luck
with the ophthalmologists and neurologists and finally, after the
X-ray verdict—"New and specific changes cannot be excluded"—
fobbed the patient off on me. I'd left the inquiry into Misha's medical history to Harald, who'd compensated for his incompetence
with a barely decipherable "physician's handwriting" that I'm sure
he imagined was integral to being a proper doctor.

I couldn't recall how Harald had overcome the language bar-
rier while investigating Misha's medical history; perhaps he'd
gotten help from Jurek from CareClean. In a manner typical of
students, he'd cobbled together a case history of crucial details

about Misha's childhood illnesses, his parents' and grandparents' illnesses, an appendix operation at twelve, and so on. Information that had absolutely no bearing on an alleged fall downstairs in Zoo Station or "linear abnormalities in the left lobe" of his chest X-ray.

The physical examination results were there, in my handwriting, and there was little more than an occasional note— "changed bandage" or "no complications"—in the daily record. Thanks to Harald, the portion of the file containing the lab tests was quite thick; he'd marked the famous blood work reading of hemoglobin 5.5 with a red exclamation mark and right after it—ever organized—the tally sheets for the transfusion and from the blood bank. More blood work had been done after that as a control, and it revealed a normal hemoglobin reading of 14.3 that afternoon. At the end was my note: "Patient stopped treatment in the ward according to his own wishes."

Nothing in the file indicated why Misha had gotten sick later, nor why anybody would want to take the file out of circulation. If it really did hold a secret, then I hadn't discovered anything more than Celine had in Bredow's accounts. I planned to photocopy the whole file the following day and return the original to Bredow's desk during our next visit.

The pain from the tight, tender skin on my back worsened toward evening, and I was shivering besides, despite the fact that it was seventy-five degrees outside. I made myself a mulled wine and sat down on the edge of the bed. At some point I fell asleep.

CHAPTER 11

CareClean Cleaning Services was located in a two-story office building at Allee der Kosmonauten 116, in an old industrial area deep in the eastern part of Berlin. It was a *Plattenbau* structure, one of those lovely prefab buildings built in East Berlin during the socialist period; once monuments to a plan to compete with the best in the world, these structures were now nothing more than a sad legacy of socialism.

Several companies had put up cheap aluminum name plates at Allee der Kosmonauten 116. CareClean was located on the third floor and was accessed by a common stairway with concrete steps and living room wallpaper. The building still smelled of the German Democratic Republic; though the separate components of the odor were indefinable, it was an unmistakable smell that one couldn't get out of one's clothes for days after visiting the Workers' and Peasants' Paradise, as it was called at the time.

CareClean had replaced the usual lightweight door of laminated beaverboard with a reinforced metal version and several locks. The company's letterhead bearing the motto "Cleanliness Is Our Job" was stuck on the door in the place of a nameplate. No business hours posted, no doorbell.

No one responded when I knocked. I pressed down the latch, and the door opened onto a wide hallway that had been converted into a kind of waiting room, with a few backless benches and tin cans that had been converted into ashtrays. The walls were covered with the same chintzy wallpaper as the building's corridor; the rose wreath pattern was only disturbed by some notices in Cyrillic script, the previous year's calendar from a cleaning products company, and a request from the "Free" German Federation of Trade Unions—the FDGB—reminding people that membership dues were to be paid by July 1, 1989. The clientele sitting on the comfortable waiting room benches consisted of three men in their mid to late twenties who scrutinized me only briefly with tired eyes before going right back to earnestly perusing out-of-date TV magazines.

A single door led out of the waiting room to what I imagined were the corporate offices. There was another notice in Cyrillic stuck up on it. I knocked, and again no one responded. I opened the door and entered a small office. Nobody had taken the trouble to replace the FDGB office furniture—the blue Formica desk, a green plastic visitors' chair, and a gray telephone. The only evidence of German reunification was a modern computer screen and a comfortable-looking five-legged swivel chair. Judging from the weight of the woman seated in it on the far side of the desk, the chair had obviously been chosen with current safety regulations in mind. She didn't look up when I came into the office, and she simply muttered something incomprehensible to me in what I assumed to be Russian.

"Sorry, I don't understand."

Only when I spoke did the fat lady look in my direction. She scrutinized me through her thick glasses. Some years ago, she had probably had to stand up for a moment when a newer model of her desk chair arrived, but apart from that, it looked to me as though she'd been born in this room and never left it.

"We are not hiring at this time. And we don't have office hours at the moment. It says so on the door."

"I'm sorry. I don't know Russian."

"I don't care if you speak Russian or Chinese. No office hours now."

With that, she considered the matter closed and went back to her work, or maybe it was a recipe.

"My name is Dr. Hoffmann. I am a physician. I'm here regarding one of your staff, Misha Chenkov. He worked for you at South Berlin Hospital. And he was a patient in my ward."

"Chenkov…says nothing to me. Besides, I am not permitted to give you any information about our employees."

I had heard the same answer from Frau Moser in Personnel. There may have been differences between West and East Germany, but the international solidarity of administrative employees was certainly not one of them.

"And…who might be able to help me?"

"Our boss, if anyone. But I doubt he'd tell you anything."

"And what is your boss's name please?"

"That's none of your business!"

"Is it a company secret? Can I ask him myself?"

I motioned with my head toward the upholstered door leading into the next room. I didn't think that CareClean needed more than two rooms and that cozy waiting room for administrative purposes.

"You cannot go in. Besides, the boss is not in."

I wasn't so sure about that. However, I did find myself wondering what the head of a cleaning company had to do in his office all day, especially with such a competent secretary. Unless, that is, this mysterious boss were listening, in the most exemplary socialist manner, to our conversation through a monitoring device from the good old days.

"Fine. Then I'll wait here for your boss. When will he be back?"

"You can't wait here; I must work. Besides, I don't believe that Herr…that the boss will be in today."

"Now listen very carefully, my good woman. We're talking about a case of pulmonary tuberculosis here."

I wasn't really lying; after all, the possibility of overt pulmonary tuberculosis was the reason Misha had landed in my ward after his supposed fall downstairs.

"So we're concerned about tuberculosis," I continued, "and therefore with the Federal Infectious Disease Act, which has been in force here since the Wall came down. And pulmonary tuberculosis is an infectious disease. So I need more than just information about your employee Misha Chenkov; I need it for all the people he worked with or might have lived with."

The secretary looked at me. Because of her glasses, I couldn't tell whether I'd rattled her the least little bit.

"Tell me Doctor…"

"Dr. Hoffmann."

"Tell me, Dr. Hoffmann, tuberculosis like this, or possible tuberculosis, is that not a matter for the public health officer?"

I'd underestimated the fat lady. I should have known better than to underestimate the intelligence of a former Socialist Unity Party member. After all, these people managed to keep their sixteen million citizens on a short leash for over forty years. If my suspicion that the boss might be listening behind the padded door was correct, then he was probably rapturous over how reliably his collective was still functioning. All I could do now was attempt an elegant exit.

"I thought the CareClean company might be interested in an unofficial arrangement. But if you prefer, we can of course proceed via the public health officer. As you wish."

"Yes, *Herr Dr. Hoffmann,* I am certain that our boss will appreciate your concern for our employees. But he would prefer to speak with the public health officer if that should prove necessary. Good day."

Nothing had changed in the waiting room. I couldn't tell whether the three men waiting there had made any headway in their magazines. My appearance at CareClean reminded me of my visits to the Hostel Elvira, with regard to both the proceedings and the results.

But unlike at the hostel, I was not escorted out of the building. I'd parked my Rabbit in the building's parking lot, but decided to wait a bit before driving off. In any reasonable detective novel, the fat lady would now appear in some haste and jump into her car. I would follow—unobserved, naturally—and apprehend her and her boss and solve the case. Of course, nothing of the sort happened. In the film version, she would have grabbed the phone as soon as I left the room. I couldn't say whether that's what happened.

I waited about another fifteen minutes, but all was quiet. I noticed a familiar-looking dark blue BMW parked in the next row, but I couldn't place it. I didn't feel like lingering in the lot with only the farm news on my single-station car radio for distraction, so I decided to leave. Besides, I had an appointment to keep that evening. With Celine. And in Bredow's office.

We met at Luigi's, our regular Italian joint. Celine was still enthusiastic about the prospect of breaking into Bredow's office a second time, and she developed an impressive appetite whenever she got excited about something.

"Could be," she said cheerfully, "that we'll get caught this time. And then we won't get a thing to eat for days, or at least nothing decent. Do you have the faintest idea what they dish up in jail?"

I didn't. And I didn't want to know. Celine ordered several antipasti, garlic sole, and zabaglione for dessert. I settled for a pepperoni pizza.

"You'll be sorry, you know, in the slammer," she said.

"We're not going to the slammer. And if we do end up there, I won't be sorry anyway because there's definitely no pizza there."

"That's fine. If you're sure that we're not going to wind up behind bars, you've got nothing to worry about. Enjoy your meal."

It was Luigi who ultimately ensured that we even got around to the break-in. At this point, given our different degrees of enthusiasm for the endeavor, we might easily have started arguing and our evening plans might have gotten completely derailed. Despite his twenty years in Germany and his ten years as a married man, Luigi was still Italian enough to be a fan of beautiful women, and Celine was right at the top of his list. There were surely other beautiful women among Luigi's customers, but probably none who were such loyal customers.

"Celine, you are a *fattucchiera*, a magician! How ever do you do it: so much good food and always so slim!"

"It's your cooking, Luigi. You're the magician."

I could hardly pick a fight with Celine while Luigi was watching. And then our food arrived and we turned our attention to our meals. At eleven, we asked Luigi for the check. Fifteen minutes later, we were at the hospital.

Unlike the previous time, I had been unable to identify a safe time and date from Frau Krüger. I was a wreck, but everything went off without a hitch. We were done copying the hard drive in no time.

"Is there a john here?" Celine asked just as we were about to leave.

Ha! She was more nervous than she was letting on.

"Yes. Why don't you go the extra mile and use Bredow's private bathroom? If he finds out, of course, there won't be any police or jail. He'll just stone you to death in person."

Celine was enthusiastic about the prospect of breaking more rules so easily.

"Be right back."

She reappeared after a few seconds.

"Hey, I bet you didn't wash your…"

The jest died on my lips. Celine was standing in the open door to Bredow's bathroom. Her face was ashen, but her neck and the top of her chest were flushed.

"There…is…somebody…in…the…bathroom."

Celine was standing stock still. She hadn't raised her hands, and I didn't see anybody behind her with a gun, say, pointed at her. But she didn't look like she was joking either.

"Who?"

"I…think…you'd…better…come."

I walked over to the bathroom. And there was Dr. Bredow hanging, fully dressed, from the transom of his 30,000-euro bathroom. He was still wearing his glasses. His pants had slipped below the waist because the belt that should have been holding them up was instead wrapped around his neck and knotted onto the transom. A stool had been knocked over and was lying at some distance from his feet, which dangled just above the tile flooring. Bredow looked almost nonchalant, hanging there with both hands in his pockets.

"Who is it?" Celine said.

I'd already known at Luigi's that something would go wrong tonight.

"Shit."

"Tell me, who is it?"

"Bredow."

"Can you still do something for him?"

I could not. He was plainly dead—lips swollen and livid, eyes bloodshot and bulging from their sockets. I nevertheless removed his hands from his pockets and felt for a pulse that wasn't there.

"So tell me—can you still do something for him?" Celine said.

"No, not a thing."

I was not a forensic physician and didn't intend to stick a thermometer up Bredow's rear end to try to determine how long he'd been dead. But it was obvious that any efforts at resuscitation would be pointless.

I looked at the corpse. Why did he do it? Who would be the new COO? What did his death mean for the hospital? I forgot why we were here; I forgot Celine. I forgot the time. What would drive a man like Bredow to commit suicide? Was he suffering from depression? From an incurable disease the hospital knew nothing about? What was to become of his family? Who would tell Margret, his lover?

"If you can't do anything for him, let's get out of here."

Celine was right, but I couldn't stop staring at Bredow. I'd read somewhere that people who were hanged had an erection for hours. If that were really true, then nature had treated Dr. Bredow rather shabbily—there was nothing to see. I thought about putting his hands back in his pants pockets, thinking that may have been important to him, but somehow he looked more the way I imagined a hanged man would look with his arms hanging loosely by his sides.

"Felix, let's get the hell out of here."

So we did. Celine had enough presence of mind to turn off the computer and get her hard drive.

Celine slept over with me that night, holding me tight and falling into a deep sleep within seconds despite our shocked state. What kept me awake beside her was that I'd forgotten to put Misha's file back in Bredow's desk. Although Bredow would now never call me about the rediscovered file, I couldn't help but wonder whether his sudden death might somehow be connected to our first break-in. I couldn't shake the feeling that we were partly to blame.

CHAPTER 12

I must have nodded off eventually. How else could I have woken up the next morning with vague recollections of terrible nightmares? But where was Celine? A wave of panic surged through me.

I found her in the living room. She was squatting on the carpet in her shirt and panties surrounded by a hundred thousand printouts and didn't look happy.

"I'm afraid it was all for nothing," she said.

"What do you mean?"

"I mean it all balances. Revenues and expenses, every quarter, every year. No unexpected shortfalls that mysteriously disappear later. Nothing."

That stuck in my craw. We could *not* have been *that* wrong.

"Celine, you're not an accountant or a tax investigator."

She got up from the towers of paper. "I'm going to make us a coffee."

Though she resisted the urge to respond to my last remark, I could read the look on her face as she went into the kitchen. No, it said, I'm not an accountant or a tax investigator but I *am* a mathematician. She'd certainly know if something didn't add up.

Two break-ins into Bredow's office and discovering a dead body to boot—all for naught? I followed Celine into the kitchen.

"Shouldn't you be heading to work?" I asked.

"I'll call in sick and go through everything again. My students are practically on summer vacation anyway. I'll give it one more shot, though I doubt I'll find anything." She handed me my coffee. "Sorry, old buddy."

I'd have loved to have called in sick but feared that might look suspicious.

"Suspicious with respect to what?" Celine asked, in somewhat stilted German.

"How do you know that our good friend Bredow hanged himself from the transom?" I replied. "Won't there be an investigation to see if somebody helped him? Mightn't somebody get the idea that it was us? He surprised us in his office, threatened us with the police or whatever, and we got scared…"

"And so we didn't simply whack him on the head but instead asked him to lend us his belt and place himself on a chair under the transom in his bathroom and then we pulled the chair away. Sometimes you're really bizarre."

I had no comeback. But something else crossed my mind that I didn't want to mention right then. The police would soon discover that Bredow had a lover in the hospital, Margret Steinmayer in the blood bank. And then someone would tell the officers that Margret used to be my girlfriend and that she had left me for him. Though that wasn't quite the way it had played out, the jilted lover wasn't a bad motive.

Celine tried to calm me down. "How can anyone possibly know that Bredow wasn't alone in his office last night?"

"That's easy. They determine the time of death and then see that somebody was fooling around with his computer. And if that person didn't have anything to do with his death, why didn't they call the cops?"

Celine looked concerned for a moment, but then her confidence returned.

"How so, Felix? If I hadn't gone into his bathroom, we wouldn't have found him at all."

I remained unconvinced. I believed our arrest was imminent, or at least that mine was. Since I couldn't think what else to do, I set off for the hospital on a churning empty stomach.

I'd expected to find a lineup of police vehicles blocking the main entrance—after all, the hospital's COO was hanging from the transom in his bathroom—but there weren't any. I didn't even see any Opel Vectra or Ford Orion in inconspicuous gray or blue, the color preferred by criminal investigators.

Then quick as a flash it became clear to me what the missing cop cars meant: a trap! Had I left my wallet on Bredow's desk? Of course not. I could feel it where it always was, in my left pants pocket. Was there a surveillance camera in Bredow's office I didn't know about? It wasn't out of the question, given Lab Dohmke's well-known addiction to electronics. Or had some sleepwalking patient seen us and just signed his deposition? They would be waiting in my office and take me to Bredow's office to confront me with my fingerprints. Or would they arrest me in front of the entire crew during the morning conference? All that for nothing—for a pristine balance sheet for South Berlin Hospital. I wondered whether I should have eaten a proper meal at Luigi's the night before. On the other hand, the slop in the clink couldn't be any worse than the culinary efforts of Hospital Catering Services. I parked my Rabbit and entered the hospital with wobbly knees. My nervous gait alone was enough to convict me.

There were no cops anywhere, not in the parking lot, not in my office, not in the ward bathroom. And Bredow's name was never even mentioned at the morning beds meeting.

I surmised that they may have been waiting for me to make some casual slip, a thoughtless statement like asking about the time of the funeral or a question about who was going to get Bredow's office. But my colleagues showed no interest in me. Maybe they'd been instructed not to look at me. Would Marlies tip me off? I looked at her. She was staring right through me. I couldn't imagine that she'd partake in a plot against me. Or would she?

After the meeting, I ventured a casual remark.

"Marlies, have you seen Dr. Bredow today?"

"Nooo, I haven't. Why should I? Are you pining for him?"

No, I couldn't imagine that Marlies would want to set me up. But in an interrogation afterward she might find my question about Dr. Bredow that morning somewhat odd, at least in retrospect. I'd have to be more careful.

I found it hard to perform the normal hospital routine: brief morning visit to the critical cases, three quick cardiac catheterizations, normal rounds. I delegated the difficult catheterizations to Marlies. Perhaps she would recall that in the future too, but it wasn't as suspicious as my question about Bredow.

It was going on noon when I couldn't stand it anymore. I went to visit Frau Krüger, but only found her busily typing some letters. How would she sign them, I wondered—"Deceased after dictation"?

I asked her whether I could speak with Dr. Bredow. It was important: it had to do with our talk last week about a DOA.

"Sorry, Dr. Hoffmann. You can't see Dr. Bredow; he's in an important meeting."

"Would you please call me as soon as he's free?"

"I'll do that, Dr. Hoffmann."

"Bredow's in a meeting"—Frau Krüger, the very model of a secretary! Maybe Bredow actually was in a meeting right at that moment, negotiating how long he'd have to stay in hell. I wished

Bredow a good defense lawyer at the heavenly tribunal and Frau Krüger a good day.

It slowly dawned on me what was going on. It was entirely probable that our Dr. Bredow—or rather, his corpse—was still hanging from the transom of his bathroom.

Frau Krüger knew only that he wasn't in his office and had understandably not looked for him in his bathroom. Being the discreet secretary that she was, she probably hadn't called him at home—why make trouble for her boss and upset Frau Bredow if her husband had spent the night with his lover? Meanwhile, she'd likely found some excuse to call Margret at the blood bank, hoping to hear some coded message that her boss would be in late today. But even this phone call wouldn't have given her any real indication of when he would arrive.

The Cito Alarm (*cito* meaning quick in Latin) on my pager beeped shrilly about half an hour later and all hell broke loose. Everyone was suddenly rushing all over the building; mobile lifesaving machines were ripped out of their mounts on every floor and rolled through the corridors; loud shouts echoed down the corridors; and several lifesaving units and wheelchairs almost collided with one another. Despite the chaos, the general direction of the action was not difficult to ascertain: Bredow's office, of course.

Frau Krüger had gone in to change the towels in Bredow's bathroom and set off the Cito Alarm.

The Cito Alarm was invented by the same people who installed our new emergency call system last year; it was designed for emergencies that a physician was unable to handle alone. Anyone could simply punch three nines on the nearest phone and all the physicians' beepers would go off, displaying the number that the alarm had been placed from. Drawback number one of this system was that one had to know which room the phone was located in. Drawback number two was that not only was a mass migration triggered but also mass hysteria, which had cost the lives of many patients who were basically curable. It's simple: resuscitating someone alone is difficult but possible, though having two or three trained people is ideal. Any more than three inevitably results in chaos and the patient ends up dead.

By the time I'd pushed my way through to the front of the crowd in Bredow's bathroom, he'd long been intubated and was being ventilated with a bag valve mask. My colleague Dr. Vogel was sweating from the strain of giving him a heart massage. Ulf Vogel, our chief emergency doctor, had perfectly adopted the guiding principle of act first, think later. His job was not to ponder the situation coolly but to intubate, defibrillate, and ventilate as quickly as possible and not to worry whether his actions made sense at that moment or not.

Vogel was a master of his discipline, a magician of resuscitation. He could revive everyone and anyone and had an initial success rate of over 30 percent, which was high. He subscribed to the medical variation on "shoot first, ask questions later."

I left the mob in Bredow's office after a while and disappeared into my ward. I had a few living people I had to worry about. As Prof. Kindel had said recently, let the dead bury the dead.

I still hadn't been led away in handcuffs by the end of the day, so I drove home.

Celine had stayed at my place all day and cleaned the apartment. That was an all-time first and could only be comprehended as a diversion from her shock the night before. I limited my report from the hospital to the facts, sparing her the details of my persecution paranoia and the resuscitation attempts, since I'd been told a number of variations on what had happened. Somebody finally drew Vogel's attention to the fact that Bredow was showing the spotting typical of a cadaver showing livor mortis.

Celine, who is always practical, even when suffering from posttraumatic shock, said that there must be plenty of fingerprints around Bredow's office bathroom by now.

"In any case, we don't have to worry about the cops anymore," I added reassuringly. "Prof. Dohmke has taken charge at last. He saw it as suicide and ordered it to be hushed up. He supposedly said, 'It was an accident, ladies and gentlemen…we don't want policemen all over the hospital. We'll resolve our troubles ourselves.' So there won't be any forensics."

My paranoia didn't resurface until that night. Who had actually told me what Dohmke said, about no policemen and whatnot? Couldn't that have been a trap too? And what did Dohmke mean by "We'll resolve our troubles ourselves"? Did he plan to carry out an investigation himself? One of my brain cells' hobbies was to imagine every possible worst-case scenario. An irritating habit, especially late at night.

Prof. Dohmke took over Bredow's managerial position, in addition to continuing on as head of the privatized hospital lab and as the hospital's medical director. It was said to be provisional, though nobody knew exactly who had given him this authority. He wasn't a bad choice for COO; everyone agreed that Dohmke knew how to handle money. Those who had seen his villa in Dahlem or the "modest" vacation house on Lago Maggiore were of one mind on this.

Two days after Bredow died, Dohmke had Frau Krüger call me in. By then I'd had only one night behind me when I didn't wake up terrified and sweating at least every two hours. I took a deep breath to calm myself down after hanging up, but my own private Eumenides surfaced at once. In my paranoia, I already saw myself behind bars.

Why had I been summoned before Dohmke? The hospital bush telegraph hadn't signaled that all physicians were going to meet with the new COO. Had we left something in Bredow's office after all? Was there an electronic trail? Was I falling into a trap?

I phoned Marlies, but she didn't have an appointment with Dohmke and didn't know of any colleagues who did. The Eumenides within just laughed scornfully.

Dohmke had taken over Bredow's office along with his job. I set out for the administrative wing with a bold step. I had gotten used to the idea of my knees wobbling but was convinced that everyone could see my uncontrollable tremors.

Frau Krüger didn't look happy. She couldn't tell me why Dohmke had called me in.

"You know, Dr. Hoffmann, it was different with Dr. Bredow. I'm now really responsible only for the telephone." She smiled in resignation. "He only calls me in now and then when he can't decipher Dr. Bredow's handwriting." Frau Krüger shrugged ruefully and surveyed her little kingdom. "To be honest, I think my days here are numbered."

That would be bad for her because she was unlikely to find a new position at her age. But it would also be bad for the physicians: Frau Krüger had always been good to us.

"I hope you're wrong, Frau Krüger. Just wait it out until there's a new COO; Prof. Dohmke's only filling in."

"You think so?"

Frau Krüger phoned Dohmke to say that I had arrived, and he called me in right away, which was unusual. He stood up at once and shook my hand. Was that a good sign? The Eumenides weighed in: not a good sign, they chimed in; Dohmke clearly only wanted to gauge whether my hands were sweaty and my handshake was sufficiently firm. I felt they were right.

"Nice of you to come right away, Herr Hoffmann."

What would have become of me if I hadn't come right away? He steered me to the visitor's chair and sat down behind Bredow's desk. The hierarchy was restored.

I took a discreet look around. Dohmke had changed nothing, as far as I could tell. There was no photograph of Frau Dohmke or Dohmke Junior on the desk. He hadn't kept everything the same out of respect; he wouldn't have had any qualms about reorganizing the whole office. But Dohmke was one of those people who neatly separated work from family life—if he even had one.

I was interested to see that both computer screens were on. Dohmke could thank Celine and her battery trick for the fact that the computer Bredow had *not* linked to the intranet computer was still accessible. Had he cracked Bredow's password for accounts and discovered any secrets? Had Bredow defrauded the hospital? Had Dohmke known about it? But that could hardly have been why he'd brought me in.

"Not an easy situation for the hospital to lose the COO so suddenly…there's a great deal of work to be done to keep our ship on course." Dohmke was staring at some spot on the wall behind me. "Prof. Kindel would compare it to soccer. Everybody knows what's supposed to happen, but nobody wants to take responsibility for it or for any unpleasant tasks…" He scratched his ear. "It wasn't easy to break the news to his widow. You know how much of a family man Dr. Bredow was."

I didn't. I only knew he'd had a close relationship with Margret, my former lover, for more than three years and that he hardly ever spent a weekend at home. Dohmke certainly knew that as well but focused on the unpleasantness of his own duties.

"Really—I can tell you it was not a pleasant task, Herr Hoffmann."

He suddenly seemed to realize that I wasn't going to praise him for his achievement, so he carried on.

"But you as an attending physician are not unfamiliar with these situations…"

He was right about that. I'd consoled a great many more fledgling widows, widowers, and orphans than Dohmke had in his career as a lab doctor. Even when his lab apparatus spit out the occasional death sentence for a patient, it was the attending's job to break the news to the patient and his relatives.

But he hadn't called me here to discuss the unpleasantness of expressing condolence. I started to wonder when he'd get down to business. Dohmke looked me directly in the eye for the first time.

"You don't look well, Herr Hoffmann. Are you OK? Are you coming down with something?"

Prof. Dohmke was the last person to worry about the well-being of the hospital staff. The alarm bells in my head—already in overdrive over the last few days—became more shrill and continuous. I was convinced for a moment that Dohmke must have heard them. But he was probably right: Celine had said this morning that I looked like "a dog's breakfast." Still, this was not an ideal topic to discuss with Dohmke, and it wasn't clear what direction the discussion would take. I muttered something about being stretched due to lack of manpower; all that overtime, of course, you know…

Dohmke leaned back, his hands folded behind his head. Not a single shirt button on his stomach strained. It was said that he jogged through the Dahlem greenery for two hours every morning.

"You know, Herr Hoffmann, Dr. Bredow did not implement his cost-cutting policy out of cruelty but because the fat years are over in medicine, too. We all must rethink things, and it's going to get even worse."

It was like a car on the street whose alarm suddenly goes off and nobody puts a stop to it. Was my alarm so loud that I had missed something? Had Dohmke given me a clue? Did he intend to lure me into a trap with his generalities? I still didn't have any idea why I was here. He looked at me absentmindedly, as though he himself was uncertain what I was doing in his new office, and scratched his ear again, this time with the aid of a cotton swab from his lab.

"As for why I've asked you to come…" He was typing something on the computer now, but he'd had me sit in such a way that I couldn't see the screen. "I must get involved, unavoidably, in matters that Dr. Bredow handled until now. You can imagine that as medical director I know by and large what they are but"—he was obviously looking for some piece of information on the screen—"there are always details that only Dr. Bredow knew about. For instance, whether something's important or not. That's why…ah, yes, here it is."

"You see, Herr Hoffmann…" Unfortunately I didn't see, not the screen in any case. "I have here Dr. Bredow's schedule for this week and last week. After all, I have to look after the appointments he made. And I see here that you had a talk with Dr. Bredow. And there's a second meeting scheduled with you for today. Well now, two appointments—so I thought I ought to know what this was all about."

I played for time. Was that only a gambit? Did Dohmke have nothing more pressing to worry about right now?

"I don't know anything about it."

Dohmke looked at me inquisitively, his eyebrows raised.

"What don't you know anything about? You never spoke with Dr. Bredow?"

"Oh yes, I did. I didn't know about a second appointment for today."

"But surely you can remember what last week's meeting was about?"

What had Bredow noted in his electronic schedule? Just my name? Or a key word as well? I thought feverishly; I had to be coherent and precise. Dohmke threw me a bit of a lead.

"Or was it personal matter?"

It was unlikely that I'd have to talk to Bredow about anything personal, but it wasn't entirely out of the question; after all, he had been my former girlfriend Margret's lover. Dammit, what the hell had I told Frau Krüger I wanted to see Bredow about? What could she have written in her appointment book?

"You must understand, Herr Hoffmann. I must know what this is about if it has something to do with the hospital."

Dohmke now had a slightly impatient tone in his voice. Of course he was right. He was now the acting COO. I decided to use the same tactics I had with Bredow.

"It had to do with a former patient of mine who reappeared three weeks ago DOA in the ambulance. I was afraid it might be a case of malpractice and wanted to inform Dr. Bredow to play it safe."

"Malpractice," the magic word. As I said earlier, the hospital is insured against malpractice of course but not against bad publicity. Now I had Dohmke's attention. He frowned.

"Why did you talk to Dr. Bredow and not directly to me as medical director if malpractice was an issue?"

"Nobody said that malpractice was involved. It was mainly about tracking down a patient's file from last October that's disappeared. And Dr. Bredow was responsible for medical records."

Dohmke was eyeing me carefully the whole time. I don't know if my face betrayed something. *His* face betrayed nothing.

"Disappeared? Has the file turned up? Did Dr. Bredow maybe want to see you for that reason?"

"I don't know. Maybe he found the file and wanted to give it to me today."

"You mean, you don't have the file?"

"No, I haven't got it."

"But you think that's the reason for your appointment in his calendar." Long pause. "Can you think of any other reason why Dr. Bredow would want to see you?"

Yes, I could. Maybe he'd want to ask me why I'd burglarized his office and why I'd copied his accounts off his hard drive. And why Misha's file was no longer in his desk. Maybe he'd forgotten his password and wanted to ask me if I'd figured it out.

"Any ideas, Herr Hoffmann?"

On one of my better days, I might have answered that he probably wanted to talk me into a raise or ask me which position Margret liked the best. But since Celine and I had stumbled upon Bredow's dead body, I hadn't had any of those better days and could only muster a feeble shrug.

"Well, OK. I only wish Dr. Bredow had put more details in his planner. This business could have been cleared up by phone. But it might have been something important." Dohmke got to his feet. "Give Frau Krüger the name of the patient who's involved. She will deal with the file. I'm sure you've more important things to do."

The interview had obviously come to an end. By the time I'd got to the door, Dohmke was already tapping away at his computer again.

"Herr Hoffmann, you do look pretty bad. Take a proper dose of vitamin C. And vitamin E. Or you'll get something serious. TB or some such thing."

Dohmke was a devout disciple of Linus Pauling. He thought vitamins worked against everything. They said he took them by the pound.

"I certainly will," I responded. Had Dohmke actually said TB?

"I'm serious. We can't spare anybody on our team right now. And certainly not a good man like you. And, Herr Hoffmann"—I was almost out the door—"go buy yourself a decent suit for the funeral."

Summer is generally a pleasant time, though it has certain disadvantages for old people and pets. While pets are dumped at the nearest autobahn rest area, grandmas and grandpas are delivered to the nearest hospital. A baffling wave of acute illnesses in the elderly sloshes into the hospitals; the frontal wave runs roughly parallel with the start of school vacation in the various German provinces. That doesn't mean there's any less hospital work during the summer holidays, just that the average age of the patients rises sharply. Physicians take their own summer vacations as well, which means more night shifts per week for those left behind, including more unscheduled ones.

An unscheduled night shift hit me for the second time that month the night after my talk with Dohmke. It should have been Schreiber's turn, but he was long gone and I was left holding the bag again.

Celine and I had originally planned to spend that evening analyzing the new data stolen from Bredow's computer. But Bredow's death had rattled us and we kept finding a reason to postpone it. Working on his accounts felt like robbing a corpse. Celine wasn't all that disappointed about delaying our project further.

Misha's blood sample, now with Michael Thiel for testing, appeared to be another victim of the lazy days of summer. I'd called Michael several times, and he'd assured me each time that it was being processed. I imagined that our conversations were automatically being forwarded to his sailboat on the Wannsee; at least that's what I surmised from the background noise. Or was Michael a party to the plot and had destroyed my blood specimen ages ago?

I had to take care of a small matter before my night shift—another visit to my friend Karl in Pathology. I wasn't surprised to find Karl, the chief diener, still in Path so late. He was always there. I'd even heard a rumor that he didn't have his own apartment and slept down there among his silent guests. I found him in his office, which was actually more of a cubbyhole that he'd decorated with photographs of flowers and trees on the walls. Karl wasn't surprised to see me. He probably wasn't surprised by much of anything.

"Dr. Hoffmann! You don't look any better than you did before. Frankly, I'd say you look worse."

He was the third person to tell me that that day. At some point I'd have to take a look in the mirror. Or maybe not.

"Join me for a drink. You look like you need one, believe me."

He opened a metal locker and took out two sparkling clean glasses and a bottle of brandy. The locker was stuffed with books, along with some cutlery, a jar of marmalade, and a pot of mustard. I studied the spines of the books while Karl poured liberal portions. Kierkegaard, Nietzsche, Wittgenstein—Karl, a philosopher? Or had his job turned him into one? People are full of secrets.

"Your health, Dr. Hoffmann!"

We tossed the brandies back without a word like real men, each immersed in his own thoughts. What could Karl be thinking about? About the World Spirit? About man as God's creator? In any case, he knew I hadn't come for the booze.

"The way you're looking, you've probably come to pick out a spot for yourself at Uncle Karl's."

That was his way of letting me know he was ready to talk. He poured me another brandy.

"I'd be interested to know what you did with Bredow. Was there an autopsy?"

Karl looked at me pensively.

"What's wrong with you? First you come down here in a state over some yellow Russian who was refused an autopsy, and now you want to dissect Bredow. Are you nuts? We gave Bredow the full VIP treatment of course, even cosmetics, which is Schmiedike's specialty. I think he used to be a hairdresser."

I was sure that every diener in Path had been something else before. I wondered what Karl had done before as he poured himself another glass.

"What do you think an autopsy or forensics would have turned up in Bredow's case after your colleague Vogel had finished with him? To tell you the truth, we did cut him open a bit. We had to, to spruce his chest up before we could present him to his widow. We poured tons of cellulose into it. And there was hardly a stitch to be seen when we were done with him."

I could picture it. Every beginner learns that he has to break one, maybe two ribs during an effective heart massage. I knew that was all part of a good resuscitation. After Ulf Vogel was done with him, Bredow probably didn't have a single intact rib left in his chest.

I had one more question for Karl.

"Who actually certified Bredow's death?"

Karl smiled.

"Prof. Dohmke in person, so it's all in order. It was an accident. Death by neck fracture."

"An accident?"

"Officially. Signed by our medical director and acting COO."

It was time for me to go.

"Karl, many thanks for your time and the drink. I appreciate it."

"No problem. By the way, I have something that I thought might interest you."

Karl took an envelope out of his locker and handed it to me.

"Maybe it's best if you open this once you're home."

I thanked Karl and pocketed the envelope before going up to Admitting.

It was a surprisingly quiet night; people had apparently dropped off their beloved grandparents for the summer during normal business hours. There was so little to do around midnight that Martin, one of the orderlies, decided to cook up a little something for us. He'd stored an astounding number of supplies in some closet in the staff room. Soon, a magnificent garlic aroma wafted through the ward, mixing with the hospital-specific smells of urine, disinfectant, and fear.

It was a remarkable night: as a rule all hell breaks loose right when the meal's ready, but this time we all enjoyed our sukiyaki undisturbed. I contributed the wine (as a doctor rather well-liked by my patients, I had a respectable selection on hand). Bredow's demise was the main topic of conversation. Everyone who'd been there described Vogel's impressive efforts to revive him. Bredow's liaison with Margret was common knowledge, and given the challenges of juggling marriage, children, and a lover, there was consensus that Bredow hanged himself for personal reasons. Others suggested that he may have been dipping into the hospital's till; after all, Margret was said to have bought an apartment just this past spring. But most agreed that if that had been the case, it would have been more logical for him to grab a chunk of cash and flee to South America. The conversation turned to where each of us would abscond to with a million euros.

Toward one o'clock I retired to the doctors' room. The cot for the physician on night duty is two and a half feet wide at best so it requires a lot of goodwill for one of the night nurses to stay on it with you while waiting for the next patient, but I didn't feel like it that night anyway.

It remained downright quiet on the hospital floor. It was the night shift of every physician's dreams. I could have earned money in my sleep—if I'd been able to sleep, that is. The fewer the patients the better that evening. Not only was I suffering from a sleep deficit but my blood alcohol level was also probably well over 1.0 after two drinks in Pathology and some wine with the sukiyaki. The only trouble was that I didn't have any distractions from my own confused thoughts.

The merry-go-round in my head kept circling back to one thing: Why did Dohmke happen to mention TB, of all the possible diseases? Did he know Misha's X-ray results—"Active tuberculosis cannot be excluded"—from the previous October? I hadn't mentioned that in my talks with either Bredow or Dohmke. Was Dohmke trying to send me a cryptic warning? Was he trying to tell me that he had precise knowledge of Misha's file? Did he know that when I went to visit CareClean, I'd threatened the fat lady with Misha's TB? Was TB a Freudian slip because we were speaking of Misha's file, which he supposedly knew nothing about? Or was TB merely Dohmke's generic synonym for looking lousy?

When I finally nodded off toward morning, I was wracked with nightmares. They were all there: Bredow, dead and alive; Margret, with him and with me; Dohmke, Celine, Misha, Schreiber; the fat lady from CareClean; the Russians in Hostel Elvira; the Eumenides. The police were there too, along with the public prosecutor—it was all about malpractice and computer crime, murder and manslaughter.

Passably refreshed and ready for the new day, I disentangled myself from my two-and-a-half-foot couch. I wouldn't have bought a used car from the guy staring back at me in the mirror as I was shaving, let alone allowed myself to be treated by him medically. On the way to our morning meeting, I remembered the envelope Karl had given me the night before. Since I'd arrived early, I had the conference room all to myself. I opened the envelope. Inside it was the carbon copy of a death certificate made out on June 12 for Misha Chenkov from Kiev, born on April 20, 1971. Cause of death: undetermined. Autopsy: scheduled. Signed "Dr. F. Hoffmann."

I was finally holding evidence in my hand that there were two death certificates for Misha. But what could I prove with it? And who'd be interested? Especially since I still didn't know *why* two certificates existed. I knew nothing, not even how many pieces the puzzle had, but I realized I now held one of them in my hand.

CHAPTER 13

I don't recall how I got through the next few days of work, but a hospital physician adjusts over time to sleep deprivation. My main objectives were not to harm anyone as a result of my limited mental capacity and to slip off home as soon as possible. Marlies hadn't delivered her usual commentary on the day I showed up but had offered to take over my ward that afternoon. I transferred my patients to her around three o'clock.

I discovered on my way to the parking lot that I'd once again forgotten where I'd parked my Rabbit the previous morning. When I finally found it, I realized I'd left my car key back in the ward. After a twenty-four-hour-plus shift, a pilot would not be allowed to fly, and any truck driver would have his license lifted. I frequently felt euphoric after night duty, but today I was simply kaput.

I sped home ahead of the rush hour traffic and even found a parking spot on my block. My luck held: none of the charming kids on my street had a birthday today, and no mothers' collective had organized any cheerfully loud games, which often took place directly beneath my bedroom window. I was looking forward to taking a hot bath with some wine in my toothbrush cup and then to hitting the hay.

But no such luck. The door had been broken in, and I could see pictures had been ripped from the walls, closets emptied, and my clothes dumped all over the carpet. I stepped inside and noted that they'd left the fridge in peace. If nothing else, I could still get myself a glass of wine and sit down on the floor.

I knew that I should call the police, but then I'd have to wait for them for at least an hour, answer their dumb questions and sign all their silly reports. I was so beat I just wanted to go to bed. I hoped I might wake up in the morning to find this was all just my tired, overactive imagination at work, a message from my unconscious that there was too much chaos in my life. If not, then I could still call the police. I was sure they'd never find the responsible party no matter when I called.

In the end, I decided to call Celine. Luckily, she was home. I gave her a brief update on the state of things.

"Nice pile of shit" was her empathetic response. "Probably one of your sweethearts you must have stood up once too often with your night duty excuse. Or one of their husbands. It wasn't me."

"You think I should call the cops?"

"Of course you should call the cops, if only for the insurance."

"Do I have insurance for this?"

"You certainly do: household insurance. Now you can see I've only ever wanted the best for you."

In addition to teaching part-time, Celine sold insurance on the side and brokered a small property now and then. She'd moved into the building across the street about a year before. We met a few days later when she came to my door one evening and sold me four or five kinds of insurance after two bottles of wine. We celebrated her accomplishment with champagne, and she stayed until the following morning. Whenever I called that her standard sales pitch, she emphasized that I had signed up *before* she'd gotten me into bed. And right she was.

"It looks like a tornado hit this place," Celine remarked when she walked into my apartment a few minutes later. "Maybe it was one of your grateful patients?"

She soon realized I was in no mood for wisecracks.

"Have you called the cops?"

I shook my head and didn't move from the floor. Celine called the police. It would take some time, they said; we weren't to touch anything.

"That's stupid," I said. "You could be cleaning up while I throw myself out the window."

"Rope would be better; we've at least got some experience with it. Besides, you're only on the second floor. You would just break something at best and be encased in plaster from head to toe, and I wouldn't have any more use for you."

I went to get the open bottle of wine from the fridge. We sat down on the floor together and waited for the cops. Celine started to think aloud about who wreaked this havoc and why. I had no suggestions to offer her and no desire to think about it. Celine deferred to me and changed the topic.

"You really look like crap, worse than yesterday. You need a massage. Turn around."

I rolled over onto my stomach, and as my back began to relax, a certain tension announced itself elsewhere. Although I was dead tired, my genes apparently didn't give a damn and were always ready to follow their biological program. One of the many things I appreciate about Celine—along with her respect for my privacy, her spontaneity, and her unostentatious intelligence—is that she was one of the few women I know who finds sex fun. And it's fun to have sex with somebody who also finds it fun. It was exactly the right treatment for that moment and went a long way toward relieving my frustration.

"May we trouble you?"

We hadn't heard the two policemen who'd entered the apartment on their own thanks to the broken door, but they'd certainly heard us—or at least Celine, who didn't believe in taking an oath of silence during a good screw. The two cops were straight out of the comic books. The older one, about my age, was short and fat, with pig jowls and a jiggling belly; the younger one, who'd probably just finished his training, was a pimply-faced beanpole in an ill-fitting uniform.

It wasn't clear how long they'd been standing in the middle of my living room. Pimplepuss might have learned a thing or two. Celine had grown up in a commune so she didn't seem particularly embarrassed by their interested stares, but I was disconcerted at being caught with my pants down and felt guilty for some reason.

"You can go ahead and take a look around," Celine said briskly, trying to get Pimplepuss to snap out of his frozen state.

We got dressed and the cops started to poke around. I had the impression that they would disapprove of my living quarters even in their tidiest state.

"Dr. Hoffmann, what kind of a doctor are you?"

Piggyjowls did the talking while Pimplepuss listened attentively.

"I'm a physician. At South Berlin Hospital."

"Right, right. Well then, tell us a bit more about that."

His tone indicated that it would take some effort on my part for him to believe me.

"There's not much to tell." My words sounded like those from TV crime shows, but it was the truth. "I went to the hospital yesterday morning and came back home forty-five minutes ago. The door was broken down and the apartment was in the state it's in now."

"And where did you spend the night?"

"At the hospital. I was on night duty."

He looked at Celine.

"And your wife, where was she?"

"I'm his girlfriend," Celine clarified. "He called me right after he got home."

"So you don't live here?"

"No."

"Then how do you know that he called you right away?"

Piggyjowls checked out of the corner of his eye to see if his young colleague was listening and noting how an interrogation was to be carried out.

"He told me."

"Do you have any idea who might have done this?"

I didn't. Cristina from Italy crossed my mind. She'd once ambushed me in the dentist's waiting room and wound up gluing my apartment door and the lock with Krazy Glue while I was on night duty. She'd probably found a new victim for her love since then. There were certainly other women who'd wanted to exact revenge on me, but not by ravaging my place. Besides, I'd already given the cops enough insight into my private life.

"No, no idea."

"Who knew you were on the night shift?"

"Any number of people. The nurses in the hospital, my colleagues, the patients on the ward. But nobody knew ahead of time that I was going to called up for the night shift last night."

"Why not? Don't you have a schedule?"

"A colleague missed a shift and I had to jump in."

"Right, right. So you had to fill in all of a sudden."

"That's it."

Piggyjowls clearly didn't like me. What wasn't so clear was whether he disliked me personally or just didn't care for doctors in general. Maybe he didn't like the fact that I got to fool around with Celine while he had to drag drunks out of bars or chalk circles around mutilated accident victims. Or maybe Piggyjowls disliked the doctor who, as a student, had taken part in demonstrations that earned him a pile of overtime but also the epithets "Nazi" or "pig police" rather than nice comfy weekends. Why should I tell him I had hardly ever been to a demonstration? I certainly wouldn't do that with Celine around, who counted me among the generation of 1968 protesters from the historical perspective of a twenty-nine-year-old, a generation whose heroic courage she'd heard about as a child at her parents' commune. In reality, I was just thirteen when all that went down and was more occupied with masturbating than world revolution.

"Do you have any drugs here?"

"Why should I have any drugs here?"

I saw what he was getting at. Of course physicians have drugs at home. Right. Since they've got such easy access to all kinds of stuff. Anybody knows that physicians are addicts; they probably deal in all their spare time too.

"Now, listen up, Herr Doctor. You as a physician…"

"I'm a physician in a hospital. That's where I've been for the last thirty hours. Now I'm home. As a private citizen. And very tired. All I really want is to go to bed, but somebody broke into my place and turned it upside down. No, there are no drugs here."

"So, you did an extra night shift, outside of the normal schedule. Do you need the extra money?"

I tried to explain to him that the connection he'd made was wrong and that consequently so was his question, and that I'd already told him I had to fill in for a colleague. But the self-proclaimed detective wasn't so easily discouraged from his search for a motive.

"Are you insured for burglary or theft?"

"Yes, I am."

"For how much?"

"You'll have to ask Frau Bergkamp." I pointed to Celine. "The apartment's insured with her."

"So you first called your insurance agent and then the police?"
Another glance over at his assistant.

"I called Frau Bergkamp because she is my girlfriend, and she'll help me clean up whenever you're finally done here."

Piggyjowls scanned the living room.

"What's actually been stolen?"

"I don't know if anything's been stolen. I haven't noticed anything yet. But I haven't taken a thorough look."

"You're not interested in seeing if something's been stolen?"

"Listen, what I'm interested in this minute is finding out what you plan to do about this other than insinuate that I'm dealing drugs and defrauding the insurance company and God knows what else."

This was a losing battle. I was feeling exhausted, demoralized, and violated. I suddenly knew how a raped woman felt. I growled at the pair of them.

"I'm saying that a crime has been committed here. And I'm saying that that crime was committed by criminals. And I'm saying that it's the police's job to catch criminals, or at least to look for them." I wound up for my knockout punch to make it obvious where the real power lay. "After all, I'm a taxpayer and taxes pay your salary."

The law enforcer looked at me sadly.

"Herr Doctor, do you have any idea how many homes are broken into every day in Berlin?"

Based on my experience with the investigative zeal of these two, I did have some idea. But I was sure I was about to hear more.

"There are two hundred and four breaking-and-enterings a day. That makes eight and a half per hour, or one every eight minutes."

I was impressed. Had he done that calculation in his head?

"You mean there's too many for you to worry about? Maybe there are so many precisely because you don't worry about them enough. You know, in medicine we worry about the common illnesses the most because they affect so many people."

"That's why you doctors have got the flu so tightly under control."

Pimplepuss had weighed in for the first time and he'd landed a direct hit. Even Celine could hardly keep from grinning.

"For starters, we'll take a statement."

Piggyjowls got out his laptop while his adjutant took pictures of the crime scene from carefully selected angles that would ultimately produce a photo album of Celine. She pretended not to notice, but judging from her faux-casual poses, I knew she was faking it. He didn't take a single picture of me.

Meanwhile Piggyjowls leafed through a manual and conjured up an electronic form on the laptop. He listed everything neatly in order, but ran into trouble when the report was to be printed out. Although Piggyjowls had dutifully entered every step that Pimplepuss read aloud from the manual, the report disappeared irretrievably into the RAM and ROM jungle. Piggyjowls's face turned red.

"Calm down, Herr Doctor. We don't know even know yet whether it was a robbery or vandalism. It would be best for you investigate quietly on your own to see whether something's missing and make a list of anything that is. Bring that list to the station tomorrow and sign the report."

They packed up their things. I agreed that it was time for them to go.

"And what'll we do now?" Celine said.

She was bursting with energy after the authority of the state had departed. After all, she was now on summer vacation and had probably been lazing around all day.

"You don't think, for instance, that we should pick up where we left off when we were interrupted?" I suggested hopefully.

"Not a bad idea. But I don't want to overwork you, my dear. One corpse a week's enough for me. Listen, let me take you out for dinner. I'll tidy up a bit in here while you look around to see if anything's missing."

I was ready to drop from fatigue, but I knew I wouldn't be able to fall asleep. And the prospect of having some help with this mess was enticing. I accepted Celine's offer and started to attempt some temporary repairs on my apartment door.

Celine dragged me out to Luigi's. Luigi greeted her with several enthusiastic kisses on the cheek; my welcome was markedly less rapturous. We were given a quiet table in a window niche in the back.

It hadn't taken much time for me to check the apartment to see if anything was gone. There was nothing worth taking except for a few small Romantic period paintings from my art-collecting phase; I'd have paid extra to have my old stereo and the geriatric TV hauled away. But the burglars had shown about as much interest in my Romantics as they had in the cash and checks in my ransacked desk. What had they been after?

"They must have been quite certain that you weren't going to walk in on them," Celine said. "I think they were very well informed about you and your work at the hospital."

"Not necessarily. We don't know for a fact that they were here at night. You're right that that would likely link it to the hospital. But they could just as easily have come in the morning. I've heard that most break-ins occur in the daytime."

"Still, I'm convinced it had something to do with the hospital. Even if they knew diddly-squat about art, they would still have taken your cash. Maybe they didn't want to swipe anything, and it was just supposed to be a warning."

"You think so?"

Luigi dished up steaming spaghetti marinara. Celine dug into hers with zeal.

"Dunno," she said, slurping up her first forkful of spaghetti. "It's not like we've had a lot of experience with this sort of thing. Warnings in detective novels are usually more explicit. Somebody kills your cat and ties a message around its neck, or you take a real whack to the head along with the promise that it'll be bashed in a hundred percent next time if you don't mind your own business."

"So I was really lucky this time."

"Right. As was the cat you haven't got."

"They could substitute you for the cat and tie a message around your neck."

Celine looked up from her plate.

"Watch it, Dr. Hoffmann. That wasn't very funny."

She was right. I apologized and offered to pay for dessert.

"OK, Luigi," she called across the room, "what's your most expensive dessert?"

It turned out we didn't have room for dessert. Luigi always prepared huge portions for us, and even Celine was full. We each ordered an espresso. And I asked for a grappa to boot.

"Don't forget, you still owe me a dessert."

Though she was thoroughly wrapped up in her conspiracy theory at that moment, I knew she wouldn't hesitate to remind me about it.

"No, that was not just a warning," Celine said. "They were looking for something specific at your place. Misha's file, for instance, which you didn't put back in Bredow's desk, or to see if there was a copy of that death certificate of yours. They might even have known about us lifting the data and were looking for a computer."

I hadn't told Celine yet that I had gotten a hold of a copy of the death certificate I filled out. I did some thinking out loud.

"Let's assume you're right that the break-in is somehow connected to the hospital. Does it make any difference?"

"You tell *me*. It's your hospital."

I mulled it over for a minute. There were two dead bodies now. But did Bredow's death have anything to do with Misha's? Misha's cause of death remained unclear, but it was definitely not murder. So there was no real indication that we were in physical danger.

"It doesn't matter whether there's a connection to the hospital or not; I won't shrink down my rabbit hole in fright. Let's go to your place and go through Bredow's hard drive line by line. He didn't kill himself because we were knocked out of the European Championship."

I was about to get up when Celine motioned for me to stay put.

"It's too late, my dear. About Bredow's hard drive data…I wanted to tell you…"

"The data's gone?" My stomach lurched—not a good thing after spaghetti marinara. "Did you delete it all?"

I only saw Celine's efforts to suppress a grin too late. The spaghetti calmed down, but slowly.

"Celine, I'm going to kill you right here. Just tell me what's up with the hard drive."

Celine sipped her espresso with relish.

"You know, I wasn't completely idle last night. Guess what I did."

"You were pining for me, of course. And when I called and told you that I couldn't come over, you cried your eyes out and put on *Sleepless in Seattle* for the hundredth time. And then you cried some more."

"Wrong."

"Did you break into my place?"

"Right. I broke in. But not to your place. I poked around in Bredow's hard drive."

I ordered another espresso.

"You called too late for me to go have a quickie with one of my other lovers, so I had to knock off my two pizzas all alone while sifting through Bredow's accounts some more."

I was finally awake. Was it possible that our second break-in wasn't all for nothing?

"And?"

"What will you promise me if I tell you?"

Now it was advantage Hoffmann. I knew that she was desperate to tell me.

"I don't want to know. Take your secret to the grave."

"You ungrateful wretch."

"Tough luck."

Celine paused graciously, but it was clear she couldn't wait to tell me about her discovery.

"Well, OK. I made a little error when I printed it out, so it still looked like everything was clean. But I was so overwrought last night that I missed something completely when I opened the files: all the quarterly statements were created on just three different weekends."

"So"—I couldn't feign indifference any longer—"they've been manipulated."

"Yes. Apparently all the accounts from the last two years were fully recreated after the fact."

Celine's flushed cheeks led me to believe that that wasn't all she had to tell me. So I did her a favor.

"That really doesn't help us much. It would be different if we could somehow get our hands on the original accounting records."

I patiently put up with her benevolent smile and her brief lecture on restoring the deleted files on the hard drive.

"And presto, there they were! The original data. Like you said yesterday, I'm not a tax investigator. But one thing is clear right off the bat: those aren't just completely *different* figures from the ones on our printouts. Now there are huge gaps that have suddenly been filled in. But I can't get any further on my own. I need more information about the hospital from you, and I desperately need someone who knows a thing or two about bookkeeping."

Celine took a deep breath, a sure sign that she had a surprise up her sleeve. "But one thing is certain: our dead friend was helping himself generously to your firm's treasury."

"Bredow was stealing money from the hospital?"

"Not stealing, just borrowing. Approving the occasional credit to himself."

"And what did he do with the borrowed money?"

"Played the market on a massive scale. He even kept tidy accounts on it."

I was astounded. Bredow had never been an especially good guy, I thought, but he didn't give the impression of being a gambler.

"That's a bit much! How did you find out?"

"More or less by accident. I was surfing around a little on his restored hard drive and suddenly came across a program called RiskMetrics. I didn't know what to make of it."

"And?"

"Then I phoned around a bit. My banker friend Johannes knew all about RiskMetrics. He's an investment adviser."

I was not surprised to hear about banker friend Johannes. Celine probably had a boyfriend in reserve at NASA and in the federal police force as well.

"It's a program banking analysts use to calculate the risk of a particular investment."

"So this program tells me if I'll double my money or lose it? I want to get it too."

"It's not that simple. It only gauges an investment's risk, which means it gives you a profit-to-risk analysis. Investment firms use these programs; they watch the stock market and buy or sell automatically if things trend a certain way. Nothing works today without us mathematicians."

"Are these the programs that cause stock market crashes? While all the analysts are on their coffee break, their computers are cheerfully sending stocks down the toilet. Three cheers for the mathematicians."

Celine played the injured party.

"Do you want to know about Bredow's speculating or to carry on with your speech about mathematicians?"

"Oh, you know that I love, ah, female mathematicians."

"Dimwit! Pay attention. Now, with a little work you can use Bredow's RiskMetrics calculations to reconstruct what he did with the hospital's money."

"How do you know it was the hospital's money?"

"Well, do you think our friend had one million, one hundred thousand euros of private capital for stock transactions?"

"What? One million, one hundred thousand?"

"Euros. One million, one hundred thousand, my good man. That could hardly have been unspent housekeeping money."

I did some rough calculations in my head. Our hospital has about 325 beds. The rate for departments varies between 200 and 300 euros, or over 500 for the ICU. It makes almost 1 million a month from health insurance revenues. Then there are special reimbursements for operations and such, state investment assistance, and of course our private patients—which all added up to at least 1.5 million euros a month in revenue.

"The temptation is great and it happens all the time, according to Johannes."

"The investment banker…"

"Right, investment banker. Lawyers and notaries sometimes speculate with their clients' money; tax advisers often do too."

"Banks do too."

"No, banks gamble legally with other people's money. And if they go into the red, it'll be hidden in some fund or other that they palm off on their esteemed customers."

"Says Johannes."

"Yes, says Johannes, after a few beers. But you know it too. It's a business model that has only two requirements: you must have access to money and have it for some time. A few weeks, at least a month, the longer the better. And you need nerves of steel."

"When did he start doing this?"

Something dawned on me. The previous March, Bredow had announced that there had been an error in the computer program that calculated our salaries. For the remainder of the year, our salary had lagged behind by a month. The problem was elegantly solved in November. In December, the outstanding salary was there, but no Christmas bonus. He'd simply taken four weeks' worth of money out of circulation.

"And how did his speculating turn out?"

Celine shrugged.

"Can't say yet. But it must have been a real test of nerves. Because RiskMetrics evaluated every investment he ran through it as risky."

I was blown away. I'd expected some connection between the hospital and companies like CareClean and Catering Services, some scam for turning profits into losses, but not that Bredow, a man well on his way to becoming an undersecretary, had gambled with my money and possibly blown it all.

"That would explain his suicide," I said. "He finally drove our budget into the ground and bang!"

If that was the case, the hospital was now broke. Or, if it could still be rescued, we'd have to work for half pay. Which would be disastrous. Celine, however, was busy being logical, rather than worrying about my future.

"It would be a motive, that's right. If he really drove the business into the ground, I can still find that out. But there's something that doesn't quite fit."

"And that would be?"

"All these dealings took place last year, from spring until late fall. There are no RiskMetrics numbers from the last seven months."

Now we finally had a clue, but it didn't fit the time frame. And it didn't give us a connection between Bredow's death and Misha's. We still had work to do on Bredow's bookkeeping.

We were Luigi's last customers and asked for the check. I'd forgotten that Celine had invited me, so I paid. Despite my fatigue, I noticed that Luigi had made an error in my favor. I didn't say anything. My little vendetta: he could damn well greet me now and then as heartily as he did Celine.

CHAPTER 14

When I got out of bed, I stumbled over the mountain of old clothes that Celine had stacked up in front of my closet. She had decided the break-in was a fantastic opportunity to finally separate me from my old clothes—at least from those belonging to my student days.

It's a good thing I'm not an avid thrower-outer. Hadn't Dohmke warned me to dress appropriately for Bredow's burial? There it was, the first and last dark suit of my life, bought for the state medical examination back in the day when a suit still could mean the difference between barely passing and sorry, failed. The throw-out pile also yielded a dark tie. I packed them both into a shopping bag and headed out the door.

On the way to the hospital, a little on the early side that day, I speculated whether I shouldn't, in light of the mess in my apartment, call the junk disposal company that always advertised on the same page as the obituaries. The idea of starting over with everything—myself, my apartment, my life—was seductive. It wasn't too late at forty-five to begin a new life. Schreiber's wife, Astrid, was right. I didn't have to worry about anybody but myself. I didn't have to pay off a mortgage or worry about financing my kids' education. But ever since I'd recently discovered my first gray pubic hair in the shower, I knew my days were numbered. Should I stop by the barber's on my way to the hospital? No one would notice if I had the creeping gray veil on my head colored away. Except maybe Celine.

I did not drop by the barber's and did not call the junk disposal company. I didn't feel like stopping by the police station to sign the report either. I decided to give the two cops a little time to retrieve the missing form from the depths of their laptop. If they'd promised me a lineup where I'd be behind a one-way mirror like in the movies, it would have been different. But I hadn't seen a perp. And I was dead certain that Piggyjowls and Pimplepuss wouldn't be able to drum up any suspects for me even if they had the next hundred years to do it. Which was unfortunate, because now that I was a victim, I was changing my bourgeois-liberal attitude toward crime.

It was a short workday. Bredow's burial was set for three p.m. at the Waldfriedhof, and there was an unspoken obligation for everyone who wasn't on emergency duty to be present. Given the choice between the hospital and the fresh cemetery air, the cemetery won easily; the crowd was so big that a microphone and loudspeaker had been set up. The mic was positioned directly beside the grave, which was separated from the mourners by a sea of wreaths and floral arrangements. Bredow would probably have been amazed at his popularity.

Dohmke's eulogy touched upon qualities that the deceased had successfully kept from us. It wasn't a surprise to hear that Dr. Bredow had passed away "due to a tragic accident" but it was news to me what a model of social commitment, paternal leadership, reliability, and sincerity the "man too soon departed from us" had been. As Dohmke explained it, Bredow's door had always been open and he had always been available for his staff. But recently I'd discovered that it was his pockets that were more likely to be open—for the hospital funds entrusted to him. I wondered again whether Dohmke knew of Bredow's double bookkeeping and whether the hospital had been in the hole for a long time.

In the movies, these burials always take place in a November drizzle, but it was July and a magnificently sunny day. I removed my much-too-tight exam suit jacket. The pastor followed Dohmke, intoning "The Lord giveth and the Lord taketh away" and "Ashes to ashes" and speaking comforting words to the family. Margret received no consolation, and I found myself wondering how the pastor would have handled it if he'd been better informed about the deceased's personal relationships.

While the pastor was speaking, I reflected on where and under what circumstances Misha Chenkov had been buried. Who had informed his family? Was there a Frau Chenkov? Were there any children? Was he buried somewhere in Berlin or had his body been shipped back to Ukraine? That was probably too expensive. Maybe he'd been cremated here and somebody had brought his urn home in his hand luggage. Were Russian Orthodox believers ever incinerated? Was he burned anyway to preclude an investigation of the cadaver? I thought I'd better put some pressure on Michael Thiel about that blood sample. I hoped it still existed.

After Bredow's coffin had finally been lowered into his grave, there was the usual moment of discomfiture. Should everyone toss some earth into the grave or was that just the family's prerogative? Did we all have to convey our sincerest condolences to the widow in mourning? And to the children as well? That would take forever—and then some.

Dohmke saved the day by signaling to the gravediggers to fill the grave and escorted the widow to his car. Frau Bredow didn't seem very steady on her feet. Was it from the shock, or had she drowned her sorrow in alcohol? The mourners took the opportunity to leave the cemetery expeditiously but at a measured pace. Many of them had brought bags containing their swimming gear and planned to go for a brief splash in the Wannsee nearby. It reminded me of the times in my childhood when we'd been given an unexpected day off because of the heat and got to skip out of some test that was looming.

I stayed behind and took a closer look at the wreaths and bouquets. I was less interested in the sentiments expressed in these final wishes than in who had sent them. The medical technology departments of both Philips and Siemens had obviously ordered theirs from the same florists—a final gesture of gratitude for our new lithotripter and MIR machine. The wreaths sent by Deutsche Bank and the Bank for Public Economy were a bit smaller. Our hospital's wreath, which Dohmke had dragged along in person, was much more modest. All the others were from companies and facilities that had done well by our hospital in some way or another. What had I expected? A farewell salute from the Association of Speculators with Company Funds perhaps? Interestingly, what I did *not* find was a wreath from CareClean or from Hospital Catering Services.

Margret and I were finally the only ones left in the cemetery. Here was probably the only person with whom Bredow had shared his joys and sorrows over the last three years. She'd waited until now to get up the nerve to walk over to the grave and lay a bouquet of forget-me-nots among the wreaths.

Being a married man's mistress probably involves a long chain of compromises with one's pride and a great tolerance for frustration: planned weekends together suddenly called off; Christmas and birthdays reduced to a few precious hours; and lonely nights when the mistress's partner is away on summer vacation with his wife and children. And if her lover dies, all attention is focused on the woman who was the source of all these frustrations. The mistress, the dead man's real confidant, receives no condolences, no words of sympathy. Her presence is embarrassing at best, and people often simply ignore her.

I walked over to Margret and put my arm around her shoulder. She said in a breathy voice, "Why must there always be so many lies at funerals?"

"No more than in life, I'd think."

"But what's this gossip about a tragic accident?"

"I don't think you use the word 'suicide' in a eulogy."

"If it *was* suicide."

I looked at Margret and decided this wasn't the time to ask questions. Margret and I had, as they say, parted on friendly terms. Everybody knows that in reality there's no such thing, but we nevertheless had managed to part ways without inflicting any gaping wounds on each other. She hadn't told me until some time ago that Bredow had become the great love of her life. I couldn't come up with any words of consolation so I simply offered to take her home.

"That's very kind of you. I've been a bit of a wreck the last few days."

This was my first time in Margret's new place. Her apartment was located in a restored older building right across from Charlottenburg Castle on the other side of the Spree, with a lovely view of the castle and its park. Celine lived in a hybrid space comprised of an office and sleeping quarters, but this was the home of a woman who left work behind when she shut the door to her apartment each night. The walls were a luminous blend of light pastels, and there were decorative bouquets of dried flowers enhanced by the addition of fresh ones. A fat cat was curled up on the sofa and acknowledged Margret's arrival by opening his eyes only briefly.

"Hello, Bella, did you miss me?"

If she had, Bella didn't show it. Margret slipped out of her black pumps, set them neatly in the hall, and disappeared into the kitchen. Alerted by the sound of the fridge door opening, the cat leapt off the couch and took off toward the kitchen.

"Would you like something to drink?"

"Are you talking to me or the cat?"

"I know what my cat wants."

"What have you got?"

"Isn't it time for your Campari Orange?"

Margret hadn't forgotten my favorite rituals—or perhaps Bredow had also liked to unwind with a Campari Orange.

"Good idea. Yes, please."

I took a look around. Her old apartment had been filled with mementos of Margret as a young girl: pictures from school dances, stuffed animals on the bed. I remembered that in the photo of her bed, she'd kept a list on which she'd marked the worst days of her life as a reminder that she'd survived them. Would today have made the cut, I wondered?

Margret appeared with my Campari and a glass of wine. She'd changed from her black outfit into a silk blouse and jeans. I didn't feel particularly comfortable either in my ill-fitting exam suit and took off my jacket and shoes.

"I would never have thought you owned a suit."

"Oh, I manage to take care of myself, even though it may not be the latest style."

"Don't you have anyone who pays a little attention to you?"

"Yes, I do. But Celine doesn't care much about clothes."

"Celine?"

"Yes, Celine."

"Do I know her?"

"I don't think so."

"What does she do?"

"She worships me to high heaven."

"That goes without saying. Does she do anything else?"

"She has a half-time teaching position. She teaches math. And sells insurance."

"Are you living together?"

"No, she lives across the street."

"How convenient for you."

Our relationship had finally collapsed when Margret insisted that we move in together.

"It's convenient for us both. I don't think Celine—or anyone else for that matter—wants to spend every day of her life with me."

"But that's what love is, Felix. People sharing their lives, not just by the hour."

I could have pointed out that Margret's life with Bredow had likely been measured out by the hour. She seemed to read my thoughts.

"Every day that I couldn't be with Knut was painful. And there were far too many of those days. He felt the same way."

"Dr. Bredow's first name is Knut? Did you move on straight from me to him?" Margret nodded.

It wasn't any of my business, of course. And I didn't particularly care. But Margret obviously wanted to talk, preferably about Knut.

"He was my next love after you. As I've said before, he was the great love of my life."

Margret had been quite stoic until now, but a few tears welled up in her eyes. She blew her nose and tried to smile.

"But he wasn't the next man I slept with. That was Boris, the mad Russian."

Her cat reappeared and looked at me unenthusiastically. I was probably sitting in her favorite spot, or maybe she was just afraid of having to share her food with me.

"How did you happen upon a Russian?"

"Actually, Boris isn't Russian at all. He's Ukrainian."

"Aha, and how did you happen to meet this Ukrainian?"

"You won't believe it: I got to know him through Dohmke."

"Dohmke, the number one bastard?"

"Yes, through that bastard, because as you know Dohmke is also in charge of the blood bank. They suddenly showed up after we'd closed one day and the other girls had gone home. Boris is a businessman. I found out later he deals in everything and anything. Dohmke had dragged him in so that I could explain our storage system to him and German regulations on blood supplies. Boris wanted to start up a chain of blood banks in Russia and the other former Soviet states. He claimed there were mobs of potential donors who could be had for a bottle of vodka. Boris took me to a bar that evening and we saw each other off and on for a while after that."

Blood for vodka—nice racket.

"Mind if I have another Campari?"

Margret had hardly gotten up when the cat leapt into her chair. When she came back with my drink, she sat down beside me on the couch. She'd brought the bottle of wine for herself. She'd hardly ever touched a drink during the time we were together. Had she changed or was she making an exception because of her lover's funeral?

"And how was it with Boris?"

"Amusing. And exhausting. There was always something up when you were with him. He was an amazingly active guy. And generous. He was always throwing his money around. One afternoon when I had coffee with him, he gave the waitress a fifty-euro tip. Because she had such a nice smile, he said."

She poured herself some more wine.

"Those were crazy times. I got to know Russian dives you couldn't find even if I gave you the address. When we went out on the town together, it was as though Berlin was a Russian city. Incredible. You have no idea how many Russians live here."

Some died here too, I could have added. But it wasn't the right moment to tell her about Misha.

"Why did it fall apart?"

"It simply got too exhausting. Boris would turn up here at one in the morning and want to go out. It was fun for a while, but it eventually got to be too much for me. Besides, he sometimes got violent when he'd drunk too much."

"Did he beat you?"

"Not quite, though he was occasionally on the point of doing so. He even threatened me with a gun once."

"Doesn't sound too good."

"Oh, well. He was drunk at the time and he was awfully apologetic the next day. He even gave me the pistol. He said I should keep it and shoot him if he ever threatened me again."

"And did you ever use it?"

"Of course not. Russians are always so melodramatic. And anyway it was over between us not long after that."

"And how did you end up hooking up with Bredow?"

"Exactly the way any office affair usually begins. At our Christmas party. But it wasn't a typical office affair. I think we both knew that from the start."

"You certainly knew a different man from the one we did at the hospital."

"I know what you're saying. He hated being the bad guy all the time. In that regard he was very different from Dohmke, who genuinely doesn't give a damn."

"Bredow didn't give the impression of being terribly upset when he cut our Christmas bonuses."

"I'd like to see how popular you'd be if you had so little money to distribute."

"Nobody ever denied that Bredow was good at handling money."

Margret jumped to her feet, her face flushed with rage.

"I think it's time for you to go."

I may not be the most diplomatic guy around, but in this case, I hadn't said anything wrong.

"What's gotten into you?"

The cat lifted her head for a moment to see whether things might take a favorable turn for her.

"Do you think I don't know what they're saying at the hospital? That Knut bought me this place, that I get extra pay, what do I know…"

"There's stupid gossip everywhere. I didn't mean to suggest any of that bullshit."

I really didn't. I didn't plan to confront Margret that day with the fact that her deceased lover had financed his hobbies out of the hospital's cashbox. Of course I had gotten wind of the rumors circulating around the hospital, but I'd always considered them to be typical hospital scuttlebutt. I wasn't so sure anymore after Celine's discoveries on Bredow's hard drive though. Maybe Margret's new home had been one of those hobbies. Which didn't necessarily mean that Margret knew about it.

Margret was still standing there.

"You people haven't got any idea of all the things that Bredow did for the hospital. Last year he really stuck his neck out for you guys. Or you would have been out on the street long ago."

I was able to calm Margret down and convince her that I had no doubts about Bredow's integrity. But my curiosity was piqued.

"What did he stick his neck out for?"

"I can't tell you."

I wanted to know and contemplated suitable ways of getting her to talk, like telling her that she could trust me, her old lover, or that she could say anything now that he was dead. But neither strategy sounded especially persuasive. I chose to give it to her straight.

"No, I think you ought to tell me. Or else you'll create a new rumor about your relationship, even if it's only in my head."

Margret had sat down again in the meantime and poured herself another glass of wine. She absentmindedly petted her cat. She looked afraid that she'd said too much already. But after a while she continued.

"How big do you think the hospital budget is?"

I had a very good idea now that I had seen Celine's data. But Margret didn't need to know that.

"Haven't a clue. Five hundred thousand euros a month? More?"

"Almost a million per month for salaries alone."

"That's a lotta dough."

"Think of it as a total budget of roughly two million a month. That means that amount must be generated each and every month, and that's getting increasingly tough to do. So much so that by last spring our hospital was effectively broke."

"The hospital was broke? How so?"

It had been inconceivable to me until a few days earlier that a hospital could go under just like a screw factory or a fast-food restaurant.

"How is that possible, you ask? Knut explained it to me a couple of times. Even the privatizing of the cafeteria and so on couldn't balance out the losses from the new Hospital Financing Law. It was really looking bad. The hospital was sinking deeper into the hole every month. Knut tried to get help everywhere. The federal government said sorry, you're a private enterprise now, and Berlin said it had an oversupply of hospital beds. Then he went to the insurance companies and explained that almost five hundred jobs were at risk. Here again: sorry, we work for our insured clients and not in labor policy."

"So what did he do?"

"As I said, he put his neck on the line for you and your salaries. Do you remember last March when you all were so nasty to him about your missing paychecks?"

Margret then told me the same story that Celine had told me the night before at Luigi's, with one crucial difference however: Bredow had not sluiced any of the money into his own pocket. In Margret's version, he had morphed into a selfless knight who tried to balance the hospital budget with profits he earned by speculating on the stock market. I didn't know whether to believe her or not, but she seemed firmly convinced of Bredow's noble motives.

"You know, he didn't have to do that. I told him he should simply pack it in. With his qualifications, he could have found another job in no time. But then you all would have ended up on the street."

"And he told you all this?"

"Who else could he talk to? His wife? She had no idea what he did as a hospital COO. No, my dear. He sat right there where you are sitting. And I couldn't do anything but listen."

Now I was doing the same thing. However, I wasn't a completely neutral party. Margret rested her head on my shoulder.

"And now he's dead."

"Did he ever talk to you about it?" I asked tentatively.

"About what?"

"Well, about his…death. About the idea of suicide."

She dissolved into tears. I felt helpless.

"That's just it. Not a word. Of course I could see that something was wrong. He'd been quite depressed lately, but he didn't want to tell me why. But suicide?" She paused, looking at me. "Would you like to know something?" After another pause she said, "We were going to get married."

"What?"

Was Margret already fabricating a legend about her dead lover?

"Yes, really. We were going to run away and get married. Make a new start together somewhere. That's why I don't think it was suicide."

I could understand Margret. If she was the only person Bredow could really talk to, she'd failed and had to feel that she was in some way responsible. It made sense that she would refuse to accept his death as a suicide.

"We always talked about everything. He can't simply have locked himself in his office one night and killed himself."

I couldn't think of a thing to say.

"Maybe something happened that he couldn't tell you about?"

Another torrent of tears.

"You know what's awful? I was at my mother's that night because she was sick. He surely kept trying to reach me. I suppose it's possible that his stock market business had gone belly up and he didn't see any other way out."

I knew, however, that Bredow hadn't played the market since the previous November.

There's often precious little you can do for a person in distress. I spent the night with Margret. There was no longer a list of her worst days in her bedroom. I had one more question.

"Why did you really leave me back then?"

"I didn't leave you, Felix. I simply moved on. You'd never really clicked with me."

That was very strange. Margret had left me because I couldn't give her the sense of togetherness she craved. Then the great love of her life turned out to be a married man. Would Bredow really have married her? Or was he one of those married men who somehow managed to string his mistress along indefinitely with a promise he never planned to keep?

I had forgotten a lot about our time together, but our bodies remembered each other well. Afterward, she cried for a little while, then fell asleep snuggled up next to me. It turns out there are many ways to offer comfort.

CHAPTER 15

I felt I'd done the right thing by Margret but felt guilty with regard to Celine. I called her from the hospital the next morning and we agreed to meet that evening in the Bovril on the Kurfürstendamm.

"So where were you gadding about last night?"

I avoided giving her a straight answer, and Celine was smart enough never to insist on one.

I worked my way through the daily ward routine. Bredow's funeral was not a big subject of discussion at the hospital, though Heinz Valenta remarked that the banks, pharmaceutical companies, and other suppliers would have done better to donate a nice buffet for us rather than wreaths for the dearly departed Bredow. I didn't see Margret all day. Michael Thiel called from his lab just before I went off duty.

"We're finished with your mysterious blood sample. You'll be interested to learn what I found. Best if you drop by."

I was relieved—at least the blood sample hadn't disappeared. I still had some time before meeting Celine and was curious to see what Michael had found out.

He welcomed me, deeply tanned from sailing and in good spirits as usual.

"You want a beer?"

"I want results, gentlemen, as our mutual friend Medical Director Prof. Dohmke likes to say, and yes, I'd like a beer."

Michael got two Budweisers out of the fridge.

"A lab like this saves me a lot in taxes. Every fridge I buy comes under lab inventory. And if I buy a new baking oven, it's considered an incubator."

In addition to his weakness for expensive shirts, extravagant ties, and pretty lab techs, Michael was a professional hobby chef. He might easily have invested 20,000 euros in his kitchen.

"Michael, don't bug me with your tax tricks. What's up with my blood sample?"

"Take it easy, Felix. I can only hope that it's not a sample of your blood. You certainly wouldn't be sitting before me so cheerfully."

"Of course it's not my blood. If I need an AIDS test I'll let you know. So let's have it, Doctor. What's the blood test say?"

"Hepatitis C."

Hepatitis C is a particularly aggressive form of virally caused inflammation of the liver.

"It can't be!"

"There's no mistake. We ran three different kits. Whoever's blood this is, he or she has a massive problem."

"Not anymore, Michael. He's dead. He was already dead when I took his blood. But I can hardly believe it. I would have suspected poisoning, methyl alcohol, something like that."

"Felix, we've never seen C titers as high as what we found in this blood. Why are you so surprised it's hepatitis?"

"It's blood from a former patient of mine, but there were no liver problems. Actually it was a case of multiple bruises and small flesh wounds; somebody had had a nasty conversation with him. He was only my patient because the X-ray guys couldn't exclude TB at the time. He didn't have it. But he got the full-bore lab treatment, including the complete hepatitis panel of course. All negative, from hepatitis A to hepatitis C. I still have his file and I've checked everything."

Michael got us another beer.

"When did he have the honor of being your patient?"

"Last fall."

"What's the problem, then? If he didn't have hepatitis at the time, then he simply picked it up later."

"How's he supposed to have gotten hepatitis? It's not like syphilis; you don't get hepatitis C from a railway station toilet."

"Was he a junkie? If he was hanging around a station, he could have."

"Definitely not. He didn't look like a junkie."

Michael grinned at me.

"Well, think really hard where he might have gotten infected then, Doctor."

It was obvious what Michael was getting at: the best chance of getting hepatitis C was as a hospital patient.

"Shit!"

I told Michael about Harald and the transfusion he'd done for Misha.

"Bingo! Our interns and their invaluable dedication! It used to be that it was the sole prerogative of accredited physicians to kill patients. But we mustn't hold up progress."

"After the transfusion, my man Misha discharged himself. Why, I don't know."

"Maybe one transfusion was enough to get him up on his feet."

"He was completely healthy; I just wanted to have him take a little break with us. I was pretty sure he'd been beaten up and thought that the longer I kept him off the street, the better off he'd be. I have no idea whether he'd just had it with being in the hospital or whether somebody pushed him out. I didn't worry much about his disappearing act at the time. In fact, I wanted to discharge him after the transfusion business before we did him any real harm…it seems we already had."

Michael was enthusiastic.

"Of course I'm very sorry for your patient, but from my perspective it's almost too good to be true. I do hope Dohmke is still responsible for the blood bank. It would be cause for great celebration if I could pin something on that guy. Maybe you can dig up a few more cases."

I had to put a damper on his enthusiasm.

"I don't know. I know that a blood transfusion is a good answer on an exam when you're asked for possible causes of hepatitis C, but the way we test blood donors today, it's highly unlikely that you could get hepatitis from blood."

Michael wasn't so easily deterred.

"But it's not *impossible*. I'm talking about some sloppiness in the blood bank, manpower shortage, something along those lines. It would be nice if we still had the transfusion blood…"

We didn't, unfortunately. But I had something else. I had the original tally sheet for the transfusion in Misha's file. And with that, I could trace the blood back, step by step, through every test, to the donor.

"As I said, Felix, give it a try. If we can somehow beat Dohmke that way, I'll be right by your side all the way. And it's the only lead you've got at the moment for your dead patient."

By the time we'd finished two more beers, we'd agreed on the reasons our highly paid soccer stars had been eliminated from the European Championship. It was almost half past ten when I remembered my date with Celine in the Bovril.

I drove past the restaurant, though I wasn't surprised to see that Celine wasn't there. When I called her, I only got her answering machine. I left a message on it asking it to apologize to Celine for me and telling it that I'd make it up to her. I drove home and checked to see whether her light was still on. Her windows were dark.

The light on the staircase in my building was out again. I felt my way up the stairs and only managed to open the damaged lock on my door after several attempts. I'd barely opened the door when I felt a powerful blow on my right side and a simultaneous kick in the small of my back. I hit the floor and was out cold for a minute.

The fact that the light was out in the hallway should have tipped me off, I thought to myself as I slowly regained consciousness. I should have counted on something like this after the break-in. Especially since I had neglected to change the lock on the door after temporarily repairing it. I kept my eyes closed. It wasn't that I thought my assailants couldn't see me, but I was hoping they wouldn't continue to beat up somebody they'd already knocked out and that I'd buy myself some time.

Could they have been those two characters from the hostel? What stupid questions would Piggyjowls and Pimplepuss inundate me with this time, if I was still in a position to give any answers, that is? Let that be a lesson to the police to investigate future domestic break-ins properly!

"Now don't be shy; open your eyes. I can see you blinking."

So Celine hadn't taken that karate class for nothing. She knelt down beside my demolished body. I didn't move, hoping she'd at least be somewhat concerned about my state.

"I thought karate was the art of self-*defense*."

"You should be happy you're still alive, buddy. You wouldn't be if you'd had some bimbo at your side. I sat around for a whole hour in the Bovril waiting for you while vulgar men tried to hit on me. That's the second time in a week you've stood me up. You should consider yourself lucky."

I sat up slowly and felt my back.

"At the very least, I need a new right kidney."

"Get yourself a new nose while you're at it."

"Does my nose bother you?"

"Take a good look at it in case you're thinking of leaving me high and dry again."

I had a variety of heroic, albeit fictitious, stories ready for anyone who asked about my crooked nose, and it usually came up in the early stages of a new relationship. The trouble was, I couldn't remember which version I'd used to impress Celine. The truth is that my crooked nose came from a run-in with a crib in my early childhood.

Celine defended her attack by saying that she thought from the noises at the door that my burglars had returned. It made sense, but I couldn't shake off the suspicion that she'd recognized me before the last second.

"You've made me a bit of an invalid, but I won't hold it against you. I haven't eaten a thing since this morning. What about McDonald's? My treat."

If I caught Celine at the right moment, I could assuage her more easily with a gallant invitation to join me for junk food than with jewelry or expensive lingerie. The burger joint was the word of the day. I sorted out my guts, Celine her hair, and we headed out.

The burger joint menu offers something for everybody nowadays. Apart from getting modified Creutzfeld-Jakob from a good old hamburger (double your chances with a Double It Up!), you can choose between fish tapeworm (a Fish Burger), salmonella or Hong Kong bird flu (Chicken Bits), or swine fever (Piglets). Celine and I are rather conservative with regard to fast food and settled on double burgers with lots of ketchup. We managed to grab a seat far away from the kids' section—I couldn't help but wonder where all these kids came from at eleven thirty at night.

"I'm sorry if I hit you too hard."

I had learned to listen very carefully to mathematicians. Celine's regret was not directed at the fact that she'd hit me, but at the force of the blows.

"What were you doing in my apartment anyway?"

"Waiting for you. To kill you because you made me sit there like a loser in that bistro. You were lucky I chilled out a bit before you got home."

Not enough, it seemed to me.

"You almost permanently injured me and scared the hell out of me to boot. I thought it was those burglars again."

"What were you thinking? That they'd come back to check on whether you've cleaned up your place?"

I refrained from reminding Celine that she'd justified her attack on me earlier by mentioning the putative burglars.

"I thought about the burglars because I think I know what they were looking for."

I told Celine about my trip to see Michael Thiel, how Misha had hepatitis C, and that the source of the infection might have been our blood bank. Celine tugged at her right earlobe, a sure sign she was thinking hard.

"Can you find out if the blood was contaminated?"

"Not directly. Samples of transfused blood are kept for only a few weeks, but we should have the tally sheets. If everything's been done properly, you can use them to trace the blood back to the donor. The tally sheet is in Misha's file, so the burglars might actually have been looking for Misha's file. I've made quite a fuss about it at the hospital."

"And why would the burglars have come back today it they didn't find the file the first time?"

"Maybe the evil guy pulling the strings behind the scenes said Hoffmann must have the file, so go back and do a better search. What do I know? After all, you've just hit me on the head."

"I did not hit you on the head. That's not part of karate. Tell me, has there been any funny business in your blood bank?"

"If there has, I don't know anything about it. But—here's a rather interesting story about the blood bank. Prof. Dohmke has a Russian friend who wanted to make a big splash in the blood business in Eastern Europe. He took a look at our blood bank and had the storage system explained to him. But there was no talk of his doing business directly with our hospital."

"Aha! And who told you this?"

"The head lab tech of our blood bank. She had a fling with this Russian guy. It seems she had a good time with him, but judging from what she said, he didn't sound like much of a businessman."

"The 'head lab tech of our blood bank,' as in your old girl-friend Margret?" Celine paid attention to detail at least as much as I did. "When did you talk to her?"

I told her a scaled-down version of Bredow's funeral and how I'd gone over to Margret's place afterward. Celine didn't press me on it right then. I knew that I wasn't out of the woods yet, not by a long shot, but rushed to deliver my next piece of news.

"She also explained why Bredow was playing the market with the hospital's money."

Celine looked at me, clearly astounded, and started yanking at her earlobe more intensely.

"She admitted that Bredow was playing poker with all your money? 'Explained' it? I think I need a couple of Chicken Bits."

Celine was visibly on tenterhooks, and I knew I was in the clear for the time being; otherwise, she wouldn't have been over-come by a raging hunger for little pressed chicks after a ham-burger. I went up and ordered, even remembering to ask for sweet and sour sauce, her favorite.

"So what did your old girlfriend tell you about the hospital money Bredow had parked in the stock market? That he spent his profits on Bread for the World?"

"She says he saved the hospital from financial ruin by playing the market, and that Bredow filled the holes in the budget with the profits or else the hospital would have gone bankrupt."

"And do you believe her?"

"She told me all about it of her own free will. Why would she lie to me?"

"I like that about you, Felix. Why would anybody lie to you? Least of all your former lover. Look at it this way: now that her lover Bredow is dead, she must be scared that somebody's going to examine the books and discover this business about playing the market. So she's already constructing a defense strategy for him. For all I know, she may have had a hand in it herself. Or Bredow told her about it, sort of, but still gambled with hospital money on his own account. That's called a partial confession. You reduce your own feelings of guilt by confessing your actions to someone but only do so selectively."

"Could it also be that you simply don't like Margret?"

Celine gave me an innocent look.

"Why should I have anything against that woman? I don't even know her."

All sorts of reasons crossed my mind. Especially because Celine could easily put two and two together and guess where I'd spent the night before. But for the moment, Celine the Mathematician was using her analytical mind to summarize what we knew.

"What we have are two dead men and lots of questions. We have a dead cleaner from Ukraine and a dead COO. Neither death was properly investigated. We've no sign that the deaths are in any way connected. The Ukrainian had hepatitis C; that looks like a proven fact. He may have gotten it from a blood transfusion in your hospital. Bredow played the market with hospital funds; that's also a certainty. He could have done it to save the hospital from bankruptcy, or he could have been lining his pockets.

His bets might have gone down the drain and he might have killed himself because of that, but if so, he didn't do it until months later. We have the still unexplained break-in at your place, a stubborn secretary in a cleaning company that's possibly using illegals, a missing patient's file that you found in the COO's desk, a Russian wheeler-dealer with contacts to your medical director, and a dubious hostel in Uhlandstrasse. Have I forgotten anything?"

"It's an equation with several unknowns, as you mathematicians like to say, right?"

"What this all says to me is that either we stop snooping around"—I looked at Celine in astonishment—"or we still have a lot of heavy lifting to do."

Now the strict schoolteacher was appearing alongside the mathematician. I suddenly felt as though I hadn't done my homework and got a little petulant.

"The glass is half-full or it's half-empty," I said. "I think it's half-full. You say we have a lot of speculations. I think we've a lot of circumstantial evidence and that at least some of it is related to the two deaths. Bredow was the COO of my hospital and Misha was a patient in my hospital. Misha got his blood transfusion in my hospital. His autopsy was blocked in my hospital by a death certificate that replaced the first version, which disappeared in my hospital. And it can't be a coincidence that we found the missing file in Bredow's desk. I think you were right a while back that my motive in this business is this: after all these years, it's my hospital. You can back out if you want to, of course, but damn it to hell, I want to know what's going on!"

A sharp tone had crept into my voice; my night with Margret and my guilty conscience were probably to blame. But Celine didn't seem to notice.

"You'd like that, wouldn't you, for me not to be part of your mystery novel? Well, that's out of the question. We just have to think rationally about how to proceed."

I was sure she'd already cooked up something.

"I'm thinking about another angle: I'll keep working on your COO and print out both versions of Bredow's accounts in their entirety. I'll look at them with somebody who knows her way around an accounting spreadsheet. And you keep working on our deceased Misha. I wouldn't be surprised if our efforts eventually intersect."

I was happy to agree to anything that didn't have to do with the forgotten rendezvous in the Bovril or my night with Margret. Besides, her proposed division of labor made sense. I decided to start by giving CareClean another try.

Nothing had changed at CareClean since my last visit: the stairway with the chintzy living-room wallpaper, the backless benches, the tin cans converted into ashtrays, the disinfectant-linoleum-plastic smell in the rooms. The men patiently waiting in the corridor, at the mercy of the pre-1989 crone behind the reinforced steel door, might even have been the same.

I walked straight into her office without bothering to knock; this time the fat lady deigned to look up. I couldn't tell whether her wide, unblinking eyes betrayed recognition or even a trace of uneasiness behind those strong lenses. I planted myself in front of her desk.

"Dr. Hoffmann, you will recall. Have you been able to find out how long Misha Chenkov worked for your company?"

The fat lady coolly lit a cigarette. I knew that lighter. They were all over the hospital, imprinted with "Hospital Catering Services—Always At Your Service."

"I told you when you were here the last time that I'm not authorized to give you any information about our staff."

As she blew smoke in my direction, I added up her age, weight, probable cigarette consumption, and sedentary lifestyle and arrived at a rather dire prognosis. I wasn't feeling quite so inferior to her anymore.

"So you're saying that Misha Chenkov in fact worked for your company?"

"As I said, I'm not authorized or prepared to give you any information."

A coffee machine standing on a wobbly table nearby contained a full pot of freshly brewed coffee, far more than my friend here could possibly drink in one day. I found it hard to believe that she'd made it for her clients on the wooden benches outside and reasoned that her boss must be in his office. I headed for the door to the next room.

"Maybe it's my lucky day and your boss is in. Shall we see?"

The fat lady jumped up from her chair with astonishing speed, but not quickly enough to block my path to the door. Her boss was there indeed. In fact I knew him. And he knew me. Life was full of coincidences.

"Herr Hoffmann, what a pleasant surprise!"

Prof. Dohmke didn't look surprised exactly. And at this point I wasn't really all that surprised to discover Dohmke in the boss's office of CareClean. The familiar-looking lighter had already given me a further clue of the close tie between the hospital and CareClean. And I'd finally recalled that Dohmke drove a dark blue BMW like the one I'd spotted here the last time. Now I understood: Bredow's plan to outsource some services had been realized by establishing his own companies. So it might not have been just a matter of lower union payments or employee benefits. The way it all was structured, profits and losses could be shuttled among the various companies, or between the hospital and the companies, to avoid taxes. And these connections had further consequences: Misha had been employed by the same people who were running the hospital, perhaps not an insignificant fact in view of the stymied autopsy and the file that had vanished into Bredow's desk.

Prof. Dohmke was leafing through some documents.

"Don't you have anything to do at the hospital?" he said. "Or has your work as a physician started to bore you?"

I could have riposted by asking whether *he* had enough work at the hospital, but he was my superior.

"I'm here because of my hospital work," I replied valiantly, "or at least with the hospital's interests in mind. In the same way exactly that your work here surely serves the hospital's interests."

I asked myself, as I had before, why I couldn't tell that Dohmke had money just by looking at him. He wore an ill-fitting, off-the-rack suit from a low-budget store, and his wristwatch looked like it had been a confirmation present from a stingy aunt.

"You're right there, Hoffmann. God knows I have enough to do at the hospital without having to sift through badly kept records. If Herr Bredow had kept things in better order and not shirked his responsibilities the way he did, I wouldn't be here."

Astounding—Prof. Dohmke had actually allowed himself to be pushed onto the defensive and even felt compelled to justify his presence in the boss's office of CareClean.

"Like our Catering Services, CareClean is an affiliate of our hospital. We fired our cleaning staff when we privatized the hospital and rehired them with CareClean. So now I've got to take care of everything here as well."

I almost felt sorry for our Herr Prof. Dohmke.

"You couldn't have rehired much of the old staff," I said. "It seems that CareClean employs only Eastern Europeans and Africans."

"It's a question of the market, Herr Hoffmann. Supply and demand. Of course a company like CareClean has to buy the cheapest labor it can find. Might be that Dr. Bredow exaggerated.

That's why I'm trying to work through these files. I can't rule out the possibility that mistakes might have been made."

What was Dohmke trying to tell me with the word "mistakes"? That CareClean had been using illegal hiring practices? If that was the case, then why was he telling me that? And why didn't he ask me what I was doing here? Instead he whined about his increased workload since Bredow had died. Not only did he have to run a large hospital laboratory, carry out his job as medical director and continue Bredow's work as head of hospital administration—oh, no—but now he also had to worry about every piddling thing to do with Hospital Catering Services and CareClean.

I was impressed by how much he had to do—he probably hardly had a minute for his investment adviser, and that must have been a bitter pill to swallow. Before I could burst into tears of pity, I asked if he might be able to dig out the contract between CareClean and Misha Chenkov. He looked at me over his glasses, his eyebrows raised.

"Chenkov? Was that the Russian you told me about? He was one of your patients?"

"Dead on. That was the patient who recently came in DOA and should have been autopsied. And whose medical records have disappeared."

I was almost completely convinced that they'd been after the file when they ransacked my apartment; I just didn't know exactly who had been there or at whose behest. Michael Thiel was right: if it had something to do with the blood transfusion Misha had been given at our hospital, then Prof. Dohmke, as head of the blood bank, might be very interested in that file. But he displayed no reaction.

"I remember. It had to do with your appointment with Bredow. And your concern about a possible malpractice suit."

"Right."

"And—have we been sued yet?"

A dumb question. As medical director, Dohmke would have been the first to know about a malpractice suit against the hospital. He was evidently suggesting that I was pursuing a ghost.

"As far as I know, no. Has Frau Krüger still not found the file?"

Prof. Dohmke had asked her to hunt down the records after our conversation at the hospital.

"I couldn't tell you, Hoffmann. At the moment I'm up to my ears in work, as you can see. And I've got bigger problems than tracking down an old file or a contract with someone who's dead."

He was looking for something on his desk. It seemed that he didn't have a supply of his famous cotton swabs here. He bent a paper clip into a surrogate and scratched around in his right ear before he continued.

"I'm still not clear as to why you're so keen on this dead Russian. Are you part of some foreigners' rights association or some such thing? I mean, if you've made a treatment error, you should tell me about it. After all, I'm the medical director. We could smooth over the business internally before you or the hospital would be harmed."

"I am not aware of any error in treatment, Herr Dohmke. All I know is that Misha Chenkov was recently delivered to us dead and lemon yellow. It looked like fulminating hepatitis to me. When this man was my patient on my ward a few months earlier, he was given a blood transfusion."

"You didn't tell me anything about that, about the transfusion. Do you see a connection?"

"I think, Prof. Dohmke, that even first-year medical students can see a connection between hepatitis and a blood transfusion."

"You're right in principle, Dr. Hoffmann. But how did you hit upon hepatitis in our patient? Was it just because he was jaundiced? You know as well as I do that jaundice has hundreds of causes. An infection, for instance, leptospirosis, lues, typhus, try-panosome, rickettsia, spotted fever—there are a thousand pos-sibilities. Your patient's dead and cremated, and we'll never know what he died of. Maybe he tossed a few delicious amanita mush-rooms into a pan and became a victim of Russian cuisine."

I couldn't at that moment quite identify why it struck me that he'd just said Misha had been cremated. I was too busy trying to parry in a convincing manner.

"I don't think it's mushroom season. And from what I could tell, he'd been sick for several months."

"Then think about what's staring you in the face. Methanol, my friend, methanol. I'm a bit older than you and I know the Russians. I tell you, they'll drink anything."

It would have been pointless to point out to Dohmke that Misha was Ukrainian. He would probably only have told me that he knew Ukrainians even better than Russians and that they lived exclusively on amanita mushrooms and methanol.

"It's possible, Herr Dohmke, that Chenkov killed himself with methanol or even with amanitas, but he wasn't autopsied and now we might have a problem. His highly visible yellow skin color is verifiable, as is the fact that he had a blood transfusion in our hospital nine months earlier. If anyone claims he got hepatitis from our blood bank, the hospital could not prove otherwise."

Dohmke reached for another paper clip and was now working on his left ear. At some point he was going to pierce his eardrum.

"Oh yes we could. Our blood is tested very carefully, for hep-atitis among many other things. And the test results are kept for several years. Your patient may have come from Russia, but our blood doesn't."

How interesting. Maybe that was it! Was my hospital import-ing blood supplies from Russia via Dohmke's friend Boris? I definitely had to arrange to see Margret. I objected to Dohmke that there were nevertheless repeated incidents of contaminated blood, even here in Germany.

"But not in our hospital, Dr. Hoffmann. You can relax on that score."

I tried again. It was astonishing that Dohmke had still not told me to leave.

"As I've said, for some reason there was no autopsy. But let's assume that there was nevertheless a blood sample from Chenkov somewhere in a freezer. What if it was positive for serum hepatitis?"

I couldn't read the look in Dohmke's eyes. Was it the sympathetic gaze of a medical director who was being forced to worry about the mental state of one of his attending physicians? Or was he trying to assess whether there really was a blood sample from Misha and whether I posed a real threat?

"This is all getting awfully hypothetical. But OK, let's think about that. Supposing there is a blood sample from your patient. And let's suppose moreover that it tested positive for serum hepatitis. Why would that be? Because of a transfusion of certifiably carefully tested blood from our blood bank? Think about it. Wouldn't a work accident be more likely? You've told me that this Chenkov washed our floors, took out the garbage, and so on. How often do you think workers in our clinic get injured by improperly discarded needles? I'm telling you now: a few every month. Sure, that shouldn't be the case; needles should be thrown into the containers that are provided for them. But it happens all the time. If I dug around here long enough at CareClean, I'd probably even find an accident report on your Russian."

I believed every word. If necessary, he'd surely pull a report like that out of his hat. Bredow's death was an accident. Misha's death was the result of a needle wound. It was his duty as medical director to fend off damages and lawsuits.

Dohmke got to his feet; as far as he was concerned, he'd already given me too much of his valuable time. He put his hand on my shoulder.

"Really, Herr Hoffmann, I appreciate your concern for the hospital. I recognize it very much indeed. I do hope you're just seeing things. Stick with it as long as it doesn't interfere with your work. And let me know at once if you find out anything concrete. I'll take you out of the line of fire immediately. It *is* my job to protect the hospital and the staff. And I mean what I told you recently. I believe you are one of our most valuable colleagues."

As he was talking, Dohmke had efficiently ushered me out of his office and through the fat lady's office out to the stairwell with chintzy wallpaper and that GDR smell. There was no doubt about it: something was rotten here. The fact that the outsourced companies belonged to the hospital hardly justified Dohmke's presence here or the attention he had paid me—hadn't he complained about how much work he had to do? Whatever was going on might very well have something to do with Misha's death, and Dohmke might easily be involved in it.

Nonetheless, his praise was flattering. Our egos are crazy for recognition and, it turns out, not very fussy about where that praise might come from.

CHAPTER 16

It wasn't unusual for me to have trouble getting to sleep, even when I didn't happen to think I was Sherlock Holmes uncovering a large-scale conspiracy at my hospital.

I replayed the bizarre encounter with Prof. Dohmke in my mind. Was my conspiracy theory only a figment of my imagination and our medical director, acting COO, and part-time head of CareClean Cleaning Services just an innocent lamb? Why had he bothered to listen to a physician's muddled concerns about a Ukrainian who had died of jaundice when he was so busy trying to reestablish order in our organization? Or was I on to something really big? Something that could be derailed by a dead Ukrainian with hepatitis C? Dohmke had insinuated that he could pull a written report of Misha's needle wound out of a hat. Had my suggestion that there might be some of the Ukrainian's serum around put me in danger? Was the Hospital Company Ltd. a self-dealing business for the people on the top floors that everybody knew about but me? But once again I would probably be the last to know.

I finally took a sleeping pill. As I began to nod off to sleep, I came up with a game plan for the next day. I decided to go to the police station to sign the complaint about the break-in. And to pay Margret a visit at the blood bank. One last thought flashed across my brain before I fell asleep: Had Dohmke really said that Misha had been cremated? Had that been a guess or an indication that he was very well informed about Misha? At some point the drug overcame my stimulated brain cells, and I fell into a restless, unsatisfying sleep.

I waited until lunchtime the next day so that I could see Margret alone. When I arrived, her colleagues were all out to lunch as expected and Margret was busy dropping serums on test strips with a pipette. Even her carefully applied makeup couldn't hide the traces of what had clearly been a tearful night.

"Doing better, Margret?"

She shrugged.

"What can I do for you, Felix?"

Although her soul was surely longing for consolation, she appeared to have decided that there was no consolation for her current situation. And she was right. I couldn't have done much other than babble some platitude about time healing all wounds, which was the last thing she needed.

"Here's a copy of the tally sheet from a transfusion from last October. I'd like to know where the blood came from, who the donor was, and whatnot."

Margret didn't show any reaction and continued calmly pipetting away.

"Why do you want to know?"

"Can't you simply do me a favor and take a look?"

"Felix, you can see I've got things to do."

"I don't see it, Margret. I just see you making work for yourself. You've got enough people here for this routine stuff."

Margret kept squeezing her droplets into the proper test areas as though I weren't there. She stood up when she'd finished and motioned for me to follow her. I went with her to the blood bank computer. She entered my tally sheet's number, and the information I wanted popped up on the screen.

"Everything's OK with your transfusion, Felix. The blood came from donor HF one-one-seven. He's been one of our regular donors for years. We call him Fat Henry. He gave blood just last week, two bags, and we tested it as usual. No AIDS, no hepatitis, no nothing. Clean as a whistle. Satisfied?"

Of course I was relieved that we did not appear to have transfused an aggressive hepatitis C virus. Even if the transfusion had been Harald's idea, I would have felt partly responsible; after all, Misha had been on my ward. However, I knew that it was out of the question that Michael Thiel had made a testing error with Misha's blood. Could Dohmke's theory about a needle wound be right? But then why the missing ward record in Bredow's desk? Why the blocked autopsy?

"Just a minute, Margret." I studied the screen. No doubt about it: the tally sheet was correct and Donor HF 117 was checked off as a regular donor. The menu bar showed various options for getting further information. Everything appeared to be correct. Fat Henry was regularly tested for every possible thing—that was true—the blood was signed out last year on October 13; that was true as well. But suddenly it was all wrong.

"That simply cannot be, Margret!"

Margret didn't say a word, though she didn't try to interfere with my using her computer. The computer had saved the name of the person who had received the transfusion bag with my tally sheet.

"This tally sheet belongs to one of my patients, not to a woman in Gynecology."

Margret checked my tally sheet against what she'd entered, then shrugged.

"Maybe someone transposed a couple of digits when entering the tally sheet. What do I know, Felix. The tally sheet's almost a year old."

"Transposed numbers when entering the control number? I don't find that very convincing."

I pointed to the scanner that was used for entering control numbers into the computer: they each had a barcode printed on the tally sheet.

Margret shrugged again.

"The reader? It doesn't always work, just like at the supermarket. Sometimes you've got to input the numbers by hand."

I still wasn't convinced. But Margret didn't appear concerned, and her voice remained neutral and calm.

"I think we can find out. Can you look up the original tally sheets? You guys save them for a while, don't you?"

The tally sheets for banked blood have several carbon copies. One stays in the patient's file, the other goes back to the blood bank after the transfusion. That's where we write down whether the patient for whom the blood was required really did get the bag, whether any incidents occurred during the transfusion, and so forth.

"I've really got better things to do, Felix, than hunt up old tally sheets. What's this all about anyway?"

"Are you sure you don't know, Margret?"

Margret was sitting on the office chair in front of her computer and I was leaning against the acid-proof tiled lab counter. We said nothing and avoided making eye contact for several minutes. Margret gnawed absentmindedly at her nails. I remembered that habit of hers from our time together. She always did it when she was faced with a decision. Then she got up, took a full bag of blood from the glassed-in refrigerator, and shoved it into my hand without a word.

"What am I supposed to do with this?" I said.

"It's expired, and we have to dispose of it. Maybe you can find something to do with it. Drop by tomorrow for the original for the tally sheet; maybe I'll have had time to look it up by then."

I took the expired blood bag to Michael Thiel in his lab straight after work. I arrived early enough this time to watch his lab and his female staff in action. Ten of the twelve lab techs looked as though they were eligible for the next Miss Germany contest. I resolved to come and see Michael only during official working hours in the future.

"What have you got for us there, Felix? More hepatitis?"

"Dunno."

I told him about my conversation with Margret. Unwavering in his obsession to stick it to Prof. Dohmke, he assured me that he would thoroughly examine the bag. And promised to work faster this time.

When I got home, I saw that Celine had left a message on my answering machine. She sounded pretty wound up and asked me to come over because she had some exciting news. I went straight over to her place.

Nobody answered the door when I rang, and I figured she had maybe stepped out to grab some wine. I have my own key to her place, so I unlocked the door and let myself in. I'd barely stepped into her hallway when something struck me hard on the head. I should have been armed, I thought, but it was too late. I wondered where the next blow would land. Did my attacker have a knife? But there was no second blow, and the scenario suddenly seemed familiar. It was Belizaar, who had hit me with his big boots once again. Belizaar is a beautiful but quite large item in Celine's puppet collection. Made of hardwood, he was perched right next to the front door. Celine's marionettes were everywhere—hanging from the ceiling, sitting on bookshelves, reclining all over her apartment. I'd banged my head on that stupid Belizaar any number of times in the hallway, but I sensed that a threat or a real attack could come from anywhere at any moment.

Apart from the countless puppets, nobody was in the apartment. Celine's answering machine was blinking, but I didn't pry as a matter of principle, so I let it go on blinking. I retrieved an open bottle of wine from the kitchen fridge and sat down in her living room. Celine was not particularly tidy. The coffee machine had never been turned off that day, and the residue from her morning coffee had boiled down to a black crust. Her navy-blue dress with white polka dots—my favorite—had been casually tossed onto the couch. An open package of black panties and pantyhose lay on the floor. A faded bouquet adorned the coffee table, with several open books facedown beside it. Celine was always reading several books simultaneously. I decided on Hermann Hesse's *The Art of Idleness* and started to read, figuring that Celine would surely be back soon.

Suddenly I woke up, slightly disoriented, shortly after midnight and realized that I'd nodded off. Still no trace of Celine. Her puppets looked at me with dead eyes. Celine and I didn't usually keep each other apprised of our activities, but hadn't she said in her message that she was expecting me? I began to worry. In every second detective novel, the hero's beautiful girlfriend is abducted by evil gangs, and the hero has to make up his mind whether he's going to save his girlfriend's life or keep persecuting evil.

Although I couldn't envision Prof. Dohmke as a kidnapper, he was, given what I now knew and because he was simply so disagreeable, the main villain. On the other hand, if Margret was right and Bredow's death was not a suicide, an abduction wasn't out of the question. An image of the henchmen in the Hostel Elvira flashed across my mind.

I had made a specialty of imagining the worst-case scenario in any given situation. While other people sat in the subway, patiently waiting to get from point A to B, I entertained myself with thoughts of what would happen if the train derailed. So it was easy for me to persuade myself that Celine had been kidnapped. The only question that remained was whether I'd be sent a bloody ear or a freshly cut finger with a note hanging from it saying "Dr. Hoffmann, stop snooping around if you ever want to see your friend alive again!"

My cerebrum and my unconscious together provided a second scenario. Perhaps Celine hadn't been abducted at all but was out cavorting with a new lover while I was paralyzed with fear over her. My brain, ever helpful, drew my attention to a few appropriate details: the torn package with the black panties, which I didn't like; the faded flowers that she certainly had not received from me; even the coffee machine could be potentially incriminating—she was so excited about her new lover that she had forgotten to turn it off. While I was mulling over my various theories—I hate to admit it but I almost preferred the abduction theory; it's easy enough to sew back an ear or a finger—the front door opened and a good-humored Celine made her entrance, alone.

"What are you doing here?" she said.

"Waiting for you. You asked me to come over. Don't you remember?"

Celine tossed her shoes in the corner and got herself a glass of wine.

"Why didn't you listen to my answering machine, smarty-pants?"

Right. It could have been the kidnappers or the new lover. It turned out that Celine had left another message for me, at her place, saying she'd made good headway on the files but needed to ask her friend Beate, a tax adviser, a few questions and she'd likely be back quite late. Celine was wide awake and I was quite well rested, so, despite the late hour, we made ourselves comfortable and got down to business talking about Bredow's double set of books.

"We'll know more when Beate's scrutinized everything, about a mile of printouts. I talked to Johannes, my investment adviser friend, as well. He's going to help us figure out how Bredow played the market. One thing's already certain though: your girlfriend Margret was right."

"That Bredow was murdered?"

"So you admit she's still your girlfriend?"

"Celine! What was she right about?"

"About her claim that Bredow wasn't lining his own pockets. And if I ever find out that you're still involved with her, you're a dead man. And that won't be any suicide."

Celine's way of intermingling different subjects sometimes made conversing with her difficult. But she got back on track all on her own.

"So here's roughly the picture according to Beate: your hospital was broke last spring. It started to go downhill the year before last, a big fat deficit every month in your hospital's accounts. Bredow desperately tried to reduce costs. He eased the situation for a short time by outsourcing the cleaning and kitchen staff, but the hospital budget was still almost two million short last March. It looked rather grim, and Bredow should probably have folded up shop. But lo and behold—suddenly special resources came to the rescue."

"What kind of special resources?"

"Starting in April, Bredow entered between one and two hundred thousand euros of 'special resources' each month under Revenues."

"And you're saying Bredow got these special resources by playing the market?"

"You can't get that straight from the entries, but that's what it looks like. We'll know more after Beate and Johannes have examined the data together. At any rate, the budgetary shortfall gradually decreased."

"If that's so successful, shouldn't we gather up all our cash and invest in the stock market?"

"Listen, it gets even more exciting. As I said, a good two hundred thousand suddenly started flowing into the hospital's accounts with beautiful regularity every month, source unknown, probably profits from speculating. The deficit dropped to just under five hundred thousand. And suddenly, last November—no more special resources and a budget deficit of one point seven million, bigger than ever before."

There was nothing to be done about it: this time *I* had to pee urgently. But I called through the bathroom door.

"That's when he cut our Christmas bonuses. But that can hardly have made up for a deficit of one point seven million. Would be nice if it had."

"Wait for it. The big surprise came on December sixth."

"Saint Nicholas Day."

"Yes."

"New special resources?"

"Even better. Bredow was able to enter revenue of two million on December sixth."

"Then a private patient must have paid Dohmke's lab bill."

Celine gave me a puzzled look.

"Just kidding. Dohmke's bills are well known to be scandalously high, but they're certainly not that high. Did Bredow make another killing in the stock market?"

"No, these weren't gambling profits. Bredow always labeled those under 'special resources.' He entered the two million as a 'Deposit.'"

"A deposit? What's that supposed to mean?"

"Beate says it looks as though somebody bought into your hospital for two million."

I was confused.

"That doesn't make sense. Why would anybody put two million into a business that only generates losses and is up to its eyeballs in debt?"

Celine smiled.

"That's precisely the point Beate finds fascinating too. She's sticking with it though. We need some details from you about the hospital. Total number of beds, percentage of private beds, staffing numbers, hospital and nursing charges, that sort of information."

I promised to get a hold of those numbers, which I didn't imagine would be a problem. Celine had done fantastic work. But we were still faced with the same contradictions we couldn't resolve at Luigi's the other day. Bredow had good reason to kill himself. That would have only made sense last year, in the spring, before the "special resources" kicked in, or in November before he had gotten an infusion of almost two million euros in cash. Why now?

I steered past Belizaar in the hallway and headed home. Celine would sleep like a log, and I had no desire to see her looking so peaceful.

CHAPTER 17

My head began rattling again even as I sipped my coffee the next morning. Though new questions popped up with every discovery, we seemed to be on the right track. I was hopeful that we might discover the reason for Bredow's death from Celine's advisers, Beate and Johannes. We owed him that much; after all, we'd left him hanging from a transom. We hadn't made any headway on Misha, but in this case too, I hoped the loose ends might soon be tied up.

After completing my patient rounds, I got to work on my homework for Beate the tax adviser. I thought it would be pretty straightforward, but it turned out I didn't have any exact data on hand. I went to find Marlies in the next ward, squeezing past several beds in the corridor on the way. Marlies was stuck on the phone, busy with a ward physician's second-favorite job: palming off chronically ill patients who've survived our high-tech medicine to a nursing home in order to get rid of those beds in the corridors.

"Marlies, do you know how many people work in administration?"

She looked up briefly and motioned for me to wait.

"It all depends on how you define incontinence," she said, then covered the mouthpiece for a second. "Yes, I can tell you exactly: nobody," and again into the phone, "Of course he needs a little help; otherwise, I'd send him home."

"Marlies, I've got to know. How many people do we employ there?"

"If I understand you correctly, you appear to only accept perfectly healthy patients…Well, OK. Yes, I'll try again tomorrow." She hung up, visibly frustrated. "At least twice as many as we need, probably two per patient. Or three. Have you got a free bed somewhere? I'm afraid I'm at the end of my rope; I've phoned through my whole list."

"Did you try Saint Margaret's?"

"Felix, what planet have you been on for the past year? They closed Saint Margaret's months ago."

She was right; I had forgotten. Cutting back on the alleged overabundance of beds had become a favorite high-profile game among the city's politicians.

"And what do you need the numbers of the administrative staff for? Are you writing an obituary for Bredow?"

"Something like that."

But Marlies wasn't paying attention to me anymore. She was starting to call the nursing homes outside Berlin—a long trek for elderly relatives who wanted to visit the chronically ill patients. But what was she to do? Her nurses would stone her to death if she didn't magically make those beds vanish from the corridors by noon.

Then the pamphlet crossed my mind. When our hospital had been privatized a couple of years before, they'd put out a very expensive brochure for the occasion. The administration had busied themselves with nothing else for months, and the staff had been asked to gather for a group photograph. Almost a whole afternoon of operations had been canceled, and vacations had been postponed. My copy of the brochure had drifted into the wastepaper basket after a decent interval, but the administration surely had a stack of brochures somewhere. I went to find Frau Krüger.

"Dr. Hoffmann, what a nice surprise. What can I do for you?"

Women over fifty have always been my most faithful fans. I wondered what was going to happen after I turned fifty myself. I started by asking Frau Krüger about Misha's file, and she surprised me with the news that Prof. Dohmke had in fact assigned her to look for it. But an intensive search in Medical Records hadn't turned up anything and the file hadn't been microfilmed yet.

"They're still working on the files from two years ago."

Then I asked about the hospital's promotional brochure. Of course she'd be happy to look for a copy. She asked me why I needed it. I was relieved of the need to come up with a halfway convincing reason by Prof. Dohmke's entrance into the reception area.

"Ah, Hoffmann, most convenient. I was just going to ask you to come see me."

He opened the door to his office and waved me in.

"We've been poking around in the CareClean records. Take a look here; this might well interest you."

He handed me a printed form that had been filled out by hand. It was the report of an injury caused by a used syringe needle from late September of the year before. The injured party was Misha Chenkov, born on April 20, 1971, in his capacity as a cleaner in our hospital while working for CareClean Cleaning Services.

"And are there results from the blood tests?"

When needle injury accidents occurred in the hospital, blood tests for antibodies were done right after the injury and again some weeks later.

"Herr Hoffmann, what more do you want? The only thing that matters is that we can't be blamed for anything, isn't it?"

Who did Dohmke mean by "we"? The hospital? Or did he mean another group of people who couldn't be prosecuted for anything now? I don't remember exactly what I said or what excuse I used to get myself out of his office, but I clearly remember the question he asked as I was closing the door behind me.

"Say, Hoffmann, has the file on that Ukrainian of yours turned up yet?"

I said no.

"You'll want to be quite certain about that. Do another thorough search of the Doctors' Room. Maybe check at home too."

Meanwhile Frau Krüger had dug up the promotional brochure for me and handed it to me in the waiting room. I thanked her and returned to my ward, where I found a note on my desk in rather clumsy handwriting from Nurse Elke. Michael Thiel had called and wanted me to drop by that evening.

Michael had indeed worked on Margret's blood sample more quickly than the last one. Had he hit pay dirt? My talk with Prof. Dohmke whirled around in my head on my way there. Of course it wasn't out of the question that Misha could have been injured by a hypodermic needle at some point while working in the hospital. And the timing of Misha's accident report fit—or had been well chosen for a fake report. He had been verifiably working for CareClean at the time, and it was only shortly before he became my patient. Thanks to Harald's zeal, we'd done liver tests and hepatitis serology, but the results had been negative, since it took a few weeks for the antibodies to show up.

But would Misha actually have filled out the report form for such cases? After all, he hadn't grown up in Germany where one learns early on that there's a guilty party in every accident and usually an insurance company that will have to pay up. He'd probably just looked for a Band-Aid and kept on working. An official report was highly unlikely. Perhaps he'd asked a nurse for a Band-Aid. She might have asked him what caused the wound and then filled out the report form for him. A true criminal investigator would now compare duty rosters, interrogate nurses, compare signatures. I, however, was eager to know what Michael Thiel had discovered.

Michael was busy with some special analyses and was far from getting over the tragic news that the German team had been knocked out of the European Championship. He could talk soccer with me in considerably more detail than with his lab girls.

"You can't be the European champion with a bunch of pensioners on the team."

"Michael, the last time we talked soccer, you made me miss a date with Celine. What's with my blood bag?"

"Easy, Felix, easy!"

Michael was a born lab doctor: one step at a time. At that moment he was still working on an analysis that he couldn't trust to automation in the lab and was manually loading the measuring chamber of his spectrometer.

"Take a look…"

"Is that from my blood bag?"

"No. We still have to make some money here, you know."

A few more specimens landed in the spectrometer; Michael meticulously wrote down the values. I was lucky. The values apparently matched and Michael was satisfied. My patience would probably not have held for another series of tests.

"Who do you think's going to win?" Michael said.

"No idea. The Eskimos? Did you have me come here to ask me that?"

"You're impatient, Felix. That comes from tearing around the hospital. You wouldn't believe how much more relaxing it is here."

"Out with it, Michael. If you keep torturing me like this, I can only think that you must have found something good."

Michael took two beers out of the fridge.

"I've got to disappoint you there, Felix. Your blood bag is clean. No AIDS, no hepatitis, even the blood group's correct."

Michael was right: I was disappointed. On the other hand, what had I expected? I didn't actually believe that all the blood in my hospital was infected.

"I didn't simply take it; Margret gave it to me. She must have had a reason."

"Maybe she did. Or she made a really grave error. Either way, it's not about the blood."

I must have looked as confused as I felt. Michael was grinning from ear to ear.

"Can you think of anything else?"

"Nothing. Let's have it."

He went and got my blood bag from the same fridge he'd taken the beer from. He ran some warm water into the washbasin next to the fridge and put the bag in the water.

"Now be patient, my friend. Just for you, I returned the bag to the state it was in when you brought it in. When we warmed up the bag in the bath to thaw the blood, lo and behold!"

He pulled the bag out of the water and placed it in front of me on the table. I looked at it blankly.

"OK, I'll cut to the chase. We had the bag in the water for a longer time, and then it happened all by itself."

"What happened all by itself?"

"Watch."

The blood bag had the usual label with serial number, blood type, subtypes, and expiration date. With a triumphant smile, Michael pulled off the label.

"Presto! A second one!"

Now it was plain to see. There was a second label under the first one. In Cyrillic.

"A rather unusual way of recycling, don't you think? Has your hospital become so parsimonious that it imports used transfusion bags from the Eastern Bloc?"

I reported what Margret had told me the other day about this guy Boris and his chain of blood banks in Eastern Europe. Michael listened with mounting excitement.

"Incredible. Your cost-cutting commissars in the hospital are smuggling blood bags from Russia."

We were euphoric—Michael because he finally seemed to have something to use against his archenemy, Dohmke, and I because I finally saw some light in the darkness surrounding Misha's peculiar death. Michael decided that this called for champagne. As he began to inspect his stock, I was suddenly attacked by doubt.

"Say, is it illegal to import blood supplies?"

Michael had struck gold and plunked a bottle of champagne on a lab table.

"You're a lousy killjoy! But you're probably right. We're in an age of globalization after all. Nothing's consumed where it's produced anymore. It must first go around the globe once at least. I suppose we send the rice we buy from Asia back to them with an Uncle Ben's label on it. Why should it be any different with the blood supply?"

Our—or Michael's—exciting discovery seemed to evaporate into thin air. The question remained whether we should nonetheless open the champers. Michael was against it. I tried to cheer him up.

"They did stick a new label over the Russian one. At the very least that's gross fraud."

Michael was still skeptical.

"So what? It's what I said. Would you let them give you a transfusion from a bag labeled in Cyrillic?"

"Probably not. But it could still be a matter of upgrading. Surely a German label doubles or quadruples the value of every blood bag. It's like labeling Turkish olive oil to make it look like it came from Lucca."

Michael's face brightened; he understood that analogy. He got his olive oil in Lucca every fall and stuffed the rest of his station wagon with barrel-aged balsamic vinegar and wine.

"Right. That might well be the small but crucial illegal detail that we'll be able to bring him down with."

We were ecstatic that a roaring trade could definitely be carried on in blood supplies. As long as Germany's drivers insist on "Free Speed for Free Citizens," the demand for blood is enormous and that supports the high price. Maybe this explained why Misha and the patient in Gynecology got blood with the same serial number.

Michael now opened the champagne. It was fantastic, and not just because of the label.

I wanted to tell Celine about the label scam immediately, of course. I knew she'd be delighted that there was finally evidence of a plot. But I couldn't reach her. My cerebrum quickly reminded me of the possibility of a new lover.

I had no luck finding Margret either. When I asked for her at the blood bank, her colleagues told me that she'd called in sick. I didn't care to know what they thought of Dr. Hoffmann's sudden intense concern for their boss now that Dr. Bredow was dead and Margret was unattached again. I couldn't get Margret on her home phone either so had to be satisfied with leaving several messages.

I was off on Tuesday afternoon and met up with Celine and her tax adviser at Luigi's. The last few days had not been especially warm, but we could sit outside. Luigi immediately took Beate into his macho Italian heart. Though they'd only asked for a cappuccino, he bowed and scraped before the two of them as though they'd ordered a six-course meal. Celine introduced me to Beate, who was a pretty, short-haired blonde in a skimpy cotton dress, which she kept pulling down toward her knees.

I ordered myself a cappuccino and we got down to business. Beate balanced the pile of printouts on her lap; the table had just enough room for Luigi's obligatory vase and the cups. She'd worked her way through the official books for the last three years and started talking right away.

"So, as you know, the hospital went private two years ago and several of the services it had handled in-house until then were outsourced to outside companies. The feeding of patients and staff was taken over by Hospital Catering Services, cleaning of the building by CareClean, laundry by Spotless. The X-ray department and the laboratory became independent enterprises. The goal was to reduce costs, since outside companies were cheaper than in-house staff. And there were clearly some economies realized in these areas, around twenty to twenty-five percent. But the savings weren't enough to absorb falling revenues. The hospital was still deep in the red."

"And," Celine added, "quite broke by March of last year."

"Correct," Beate agreed. "Celine already figured out how your COO tried to fill the budget hole via short-term speculating. The specifics still aren't clear, but in the end it all seems to have gone bad and the hospital only survived because someone injected two million last December. Then something odd happened: hospital expenses began to increase every month."

"It wasn't because of our salaries," I interjected. "I'd have seen that."

"Correct," Beate responded, "it's not salaries. It's more interesting than that. All of a sudden the whole idea of cutting costs by outsourcing turned into its opposite, because starting last December, the invoices from CareClean, the caterers, the laundry, and so on started growing higher every month. This past June, the hospital paid all those outside companies more than double what they had the previous year."

Beate showed us the relevant places on the printout balanced on her knees. She struggled valiantly with her upward-creeping dress until the printouts were ultimately lying on the ground. I dragged over a second table.

"So the hospital must have slid into a deficit position again," I said.

"But it didn't," Beate replied. "Actually, the hospital is constantly spending more money. The individual amounts are not very high but if you use the available data to project what this year will look like, it turns out to be over ten million more in costs than last year. In spite of this, your hospital suddenly has no problem generating all that money. Unlike last year, revenues and expenses are fairly well balanced. The obvious question is: Where did all that money come from?"

Now Beate turned to look at me.

"Did your hospital expand last year? Add a new private ward?"

"No."

"Are you sure?"

"Sure I'm sure. What are you driving at?"

"Revenues from private patients are suddenly absorbing the hospital's additional expenditures for the outside companies. Here, take a look—two years ago, the hospital took in just under five million from private patients. And this year it's already received four and a half million by June alone. And there's something else that's odd about these private patients: more than half of them pay cash."

"If I understand you correctly," I said, "you're saying that the hospital is making significant profits all of a sudden that are not being passed on to underpaid attending physicians like myself but to companies like CareClean or Hospital Catering Services, though there's nothing extra to clean and God knows the food hasn't gotten twice as good."

Celine had apparently already thought this all through and smiled at me, encouraging me to take my thoughts further.

"So the trick is that these firms suddenly get more money without performing more work."

"And that your hospital isn't performing more work either but is taking in a hell of a lot more money. Or has the number of private patients really doubled?"

Beate pointed out that theoretically the private patients could suddenly be paying twice as much as before. Although I couldn't dismiss that possibility out of hand, the private ward had not expanded, and I hadn't seen—at least not yet—two patients sharing the same bed. And why should they all of a sudden be paying twice the price? In fact, our ward chiefs bitched endlessly that they weren't seeing their usual growth rates for private patients. We hadn't built a landing strip for South American drug lords yet, nor had we rolled out any prayer rugs for oil sheikhs.

I slurped up the puddle in the bottom of my cappuccino cup. The coffee was cold and tasted awful. The two women looked at me eagerly. A zero-sum game of 10 million euros a year. I tried to put on a shrewd face, but it took a little while for the penny to drop. And then it took another little while before I could get it out.

"I think I know what you're getting at," I finally said softly, as though that made it less appalling. "This stinks to high heaven of money laundering."

Celine and Beate gave friendly nods, looking like two school-teachers satisfied by an exceptional performance from an otherwise weak student.

"And whoever turned my hospital into a money-laundering operation would have started by offsetting Bredow's gambling losses last December—that would explain the Saint Nicholas present, right?"

Again they both nodded approvingly. I didn't know what to think of this disclosure. I started out just feeling confused. My hospital, a bastion of service to patients and a battleground against pestilence and disease—a money-laundering operation? I wanted another explanation for the wondrously balanced budget. But I knew that was the only answer that made any sense. And the scam with the private patients was ingenious. Diagnoses were included on patient bills in addition to medical services rendered, which meant that bills were confidential, and the hospital therefore wouldn't have to show those bills to any tax man or any other investigating authority. The money-laundering machine was therefore fed with illegal millions in the form of unverifiable billings to private patients that were then taken over by the owners of CareClean, Hospital Catering, and the like as legal income for services never performed.

"Can this be proved?" I asked Beate.

"On the basis of the documents that you two have given me, it looks highly suspicious. But it's only going to raise suspicion if something's not right. Surely no one will notice when the accounts are routinely made available to the tax office. They're only interested in seeing that sufficient taxes have been paid. The tax office only pricks up its ears if income suddenly declines precipitously or expenses rise considerably. Your hospital's expenses do increase sharply but so does revenue. That's growth—perfectly normal. That's the whole idea of a free market economy."

"Isn't there a danger that there will be inquiries into why, for instance, cleaning expenses have gone up so dramatically?" I asked Beate.

"It could attract attention. In which case the tax man might ask whether taxes might have been evaded by fabricating expenses. If that happens, the hospital will be asked for an explanation and will groan about a change in hygiene regulations or something like that. The tax office is mainly interested in seeing that money gets taxed somewhere along the line. And if CareClean is paying taxes on its doubled income according to the rules, then everything's OK."

I called to Luigi and ordered a double grappa. After all, it wasn't every day that I found out that I'd been working in a big money laundry instead of a hospital. But Beate wasn't finished yet.

"The problem with illegal income is always the same. All of a sudden I've made a pile of money off child pornography or women from Belorussia or drugs. But what do I do now with all that lovely money? I can invest it somewhere where there are few questions asked—in Switzerland or the Cayman Islands or wherever—but at some point I'll want to spend it. That's not a problem if I decide to buy a stolen Van Gogh on the black market. I can lock the painting up in my safe and look at it at night now and then. But if I can afford a Van Gogh, I'd like to show it to other people as well. And eventually somebody's going to ask where I got the money for a Van Gogh or for a large villa or my own plane. Money laundering was invented to solve this unpleasant problem."

Luigi arrived with my grappa. Did his business work for the Italian mafia? Let's say he sold a hundred meals a night and only entered the money for only fifty of them in his cash register; the other fifty would be cash in hand, half of which would go to his friends in Sicily. It's the reverse with money laundering—the restaurant sells fifty meals and records one hundred. I didn't realize that I'd spoken my thoughts aloud until Celine came to the defense of her beloved Luigi. Fortunately, Beate got us back on topic.

"Your restaurant example isn't bad, Felix. But upon closer consideration, a hospital has several advantages as a money-laundering operation. The layman can better understand what goes on in a restaurant than he can what happens in a modern hospital. For one thing, hospital services are in a secret language. With you, an operation is not an operation but—"

"A cholecystectomy or a Billroth," I said, giving her a helping hand.

"Exactly. No man alive can figure out what that means. Let alone what it might cost. The next point is even more important—data protection. I could ask Herr Müller or Frau Maier what they ate at Luigi's, a pepperoni pizza or saltimbocca alla Romana, but I could never ask them why they were in the hospital and what procedures had been performed on them there. With regard to your hospital's private patients, something striking emerges from the documents: almost all the ones who paid in cash stand out because of their foreign names. You certainly can't forbid your hospital to treat out-of-country patients. And you can hardly hold it against the hospital if it accepts cash from foreigners.

"A hospital like this one," she continued, "has yet another distinct advantage over a restaurant as a money-laundering operation: it turns over far more money. Luigi's yearly sales might hit three hundred thousand to four hundred thousand euros. Your hospital's annual budget is over twenty million. It's easy to shelter a few million in illegal funds there."

Was I, in the end, not a hospital physician at all but just a supernumerary in a money-laundering scheme that had chosen my hospital as its headquarters? Was everything bad I'd heard about Germany actually true? Was my upstanding country—a boring stronghold of law and order—in fact no different from any corrupt Central or South American country?

We went through the numbers and Beate reiterated her conclusions one more time, but the facts spoke for themselves; there was no other possible interpretation. And yet I didn't want to believe it. After all, I'd worked with these people every day for years. A wave of exhaustion surged through me, but I had one more question for Beate.

"Did you find anything in Bredow's secret accounts that pointed to blood supplies?"

She said she didn't. I reported on Michael's discovery about the switched labels on the blood bags. As predicted, Celine was thrilled.

"What did I tell you? It's a conspiracy. And it's all about money, naturally."

"What do you think the next step should be?' I asked Beate.

"Celine and I will check the statements from the blood bank. But even if our suspicions turn out to be correct, we don't know who's behind this whole affair. That's what you've got to worry about."

"But how?"

"Go to the Business Registry and find out who actually owns your hospital. And who the owners of Hospital Catering Services, CareClean, and so on are. Then let's meet again."

It had turned cool and we suddenly noticed that the patio had emptied out. Luigi came by and cleared the tables. He said he'd reserved a table for us inside and there was still fresh monkfish. We thanked him politely and paid the tab. I, for one, had lost my appetite.

CHAPTER 18

When Margret showed up at the hospital again, she was wearing sunglasses and it was evident from some distance away that she'd applied a thick coating of makeup to her face. I waited until her colleagues were on their lunch break, then went to speak to her.

"Look at you, Margret—did you fall into a paint bucket?"

"You certainly know how to turn on the charm."

"I've been worried. Didn't you get my messages?"

"Felix, I'm very busy. Is it important?" She tried to keep her face averted but I saw the reason for the makeup anyway: a huge hematoma graced the lower portion of her right eye socket—she had a proper shiner.

"My God, what happened?"

"Why do you think I've stayed home for the last few days? I had a fall. The hall light was out and I tumbled down the whole stupid stairwell."

I pushed a few reagents aside and sat down on her lab counter.

"Did I tell you that Misha Chenkov also claimed he'd fallen down the stairs?"

"And who, may I ask, is Misha Chenkov?"

"The patient whose blood transfusion I was asking you about. I was sure, though, that he'd been beaten up. And if he *did* fall down some stairs, it was not without a little assistance from somebody. For your information, he's dead."

"I don't know what's got into you, Felix. Maybe you're working too hard or you've been watching too much TV. I'll say it again: I fell down the stairs because it was dark. And I'm still alive, as you can see. So be nice and let me do my job."

Maybe her story was true and I was making things up. But after talking to Beate, I had good reason to be suspicious. I deliberately stayed where I was.

"So everything's OK, Margret. That's what you're trying to tell me?"

"For once you're right, my good man. That's exactly what I'm trying to tell you."

She resumed her routine with the test plates and reagents in a determined frenzy. It was pretty much foolproof; the test fields and testing reagents were color coded, and Margret had been doing this type of work for years. All the same, she put the serum both on the blue and the yellow areas with her pipette. She noticed her mistake and repeated the test. It was not clear whether she'd seen that I'd observed her error.

"Well, OK Margret. I've really only come because of the blood bag with the double serial number. You were going to look for the originals."

"Oh, that business. I've checked. The numbers were transposed, wrong entry. Sixty-nine instead of ninety-six or something like that. No reason to get excited. The scanner was probably kaput again and someone was asleep at the switch while entering it."

"Are the two tally sheets still there?"

She looked at me dead on with her big black eye.

"Yes, I have them. I could show them to you, but I wouldn't dream of doing so. Who do you think you are? If you've got any qualms about our work in the blood bank, then please go see my boss. I will not show you anything else without express instructions from Prof. Dohmke."

I slid off the counter and looked her just as directly in the eye. I was already feeling angry when I replied to her.

"Fine, Margret, I get it. I'll go to Dohmke. One last question though: Should I ask him about the expired blood bag you gave me too?"

"You son of a bitch!"

I headed back to my ward, not feeling very pleased with myself.

A pressing directive from Dohmke awaited me back at the ward: "Urgent—Admitting filled to overflowing. Beds must be freed up." That wasn't all that unusual, despite the alleged oversupply of beds. We thought fast about which discharges could be moved up a couple of days and phoned down the list of nursing homes. We'd scheduled Frau Schön's departure for Friday. If I raised her potassium level a little more quickly, she'd be ready to go by the following morning. So I discontinued her potassium tablets and ordered a potassium infusion, signed the order, and dropped it at the nurses' station. Other than that, there was nothing that couldn't wait an hour. I then drove over to the Business Registry in the Charlottenburg district courthouse.

Though I was lucky to come across a very helpful young woman named Karin there, I failed in my mission. Since I could not prove any "legitimate interest" in the ownership of South Berlin Hospital Company Ltd., Karin could only show me the excerpt from the registry that was required to appear in the relevant newspapers.

"I'm terribly sorry, I'd be very glad to help you, but those are the regulations."

The company's place of business was Berlin, its purpose the operation and administration of a hospital. I already knew that. The common capital stock was entered as "€75,000"; the COO was still listed as Dr. Knut Bredow. I copied down the final entry, which stated that "Paragraph 1 (Members)" in the articles of organization had been changed on July 13 the year before. That was the interesting part—the members. I wanted to know who they were. However, my lack of "legitimate interest" proved insurmountable, despite my efforts to charm Karin.

"May I ask for an example of a legitimate interest?"

"Well, for instance, if you want to become a member as well or are thinking about extending credit to the organization."

Karin in the Business Registry reciprocated my charming smile and assured me that if I returned somewhat better prepared, I'd have no trouble finding out the ownership details of South Berlin Hospital Company Ltd. So my legendary charm was not quite yet past its expiration date.

Back at the hospital, I immediately called Beate at her office. She apologized for not thinking of the "legitimate interest" business, but said that it should not be a problem. I actually had a different question for her though.

"Tell me, Beate, have you found any evidence of blood bags deals in the meantime?"

"Just a second, Felix. Stay on the line."

Either she'd left her notes in another room or she was looking for a place to speak in private. A few clicks and she was back on the line.

"I did note something abnormal. There was a line item under Revenues called 'Pharmaceutical Industry.' But the hospital *buys* from drug companies. I figured it must be an expense. What are the drug companies doing under Revenues? That strikes me as odd."

"Not necessarily. Every hospital does some kind of business with the drug companies. It's usually application studies for new medications to establish whether a medication is actually effective or has undesirable side effects. It's not unusual for the industry to pay the hospital for that sort of thing."

"And then the patients get that money in exchange for being guinea pigs?"

I had to grin. Beate's idea had a certain logic but was a far cry from reality.

"No."

"No?"

"Doesn't work that way, Beate. That would be unethical. Patients can't turn their illness into a business. No, only hospitals can. They use the money to add a physician or buy a new piece of equipment."

"And *that* is ethical?"

"Well, it's general practice."

"I understand, more or less. In any case, a large entry under these revenues falls under the rubric 'Blood Bank.' Do they run any studies there?"

I didn't know of any studies that had to do with the blood bank and couldn't imagine what they could be either. I'd have to ask Margret—if and when she ever deigned to speak to me again.

"What amounts are we talking, Beate?"

"I can't tell you exactly until next time because the documents are at home, but I think it was about two hundred thousand a month."

The door behind me opened. Marlies stuck her head in, motioning urgently. I thanked Beate and hung up.

"There's a problem, Felix. I think you'd better go to the ICU immediately."

They'd restored Frau Schön's heartbeat with electric shocks three times; now she was on an artificial kidney. Her relatives were standing in the background, visibly agitated. Valenta took me aside.

"I think it would be best if we made your written order disappear."

I didn't get it. He showed it to me: "Infusion with potassium chloride, 100 ml. per hour."

I had to brace myself against his desk. Had I really written "100 ml." instead of "10 ml."? It was my handwriting, but there was hardly any space between "100" and "ml." A quickly added zero would be difficult to decipher in a handwriting analysis. Valenta put his meaty hand on my shoulder.

"Shit happens, Felix. She'll survive. We've already got her potassium down to six. Right this minute, I'm almost more worried about you. You've looked really crappy lately, totally overworked. That leads to mistakes. Give yourself a break."

Frau Schön was in good hands with Valenta—no question—but going home to bed was out of the question.

I decided to stop by Margret's place that evening. She hadn't fallen down any stairs, of that I was certain. Would my visit put her in danger again? Or would she be in more danger if she did *not* confide in me? Self-serving or not, I climbed into my Rabbit and hoped it was the second option. Question was, would she let me in at all?

The door to her building wasn't locked so I headed up to her apartment. The theme music for a popular TV series wafted over from the neighboring apartment. Somebody was firing up their barbecue one floor up; I overheard fragments of upbeat summer evening conversation and bursts of laughter above me. But there was only silence behind Margret's door. I immediately noticed an obviously new security lock and two large bars across the door. I rang, but there was no response. I rang again, more forcefully this time.

Margret opened the door warily, just a crack, and kept the door chain in place.

"What do you want, Felix?"

She'd taken her makeup off and put on her terrycloth dressing gown, which had worn rather thin during my time with her and was much too short for the present situation. She certainly hadn't been expecting visitors.

"Interesting new lock on your door. Have you had any problems with unwanted visitors lately?"

"Felix, I'm tired and practically in bed. Just tell me what you want."

"I want to know who gave you that black eye."

"I told you what happened."

"And I want to know why somebody gave it to you."

"Go home, Felix, You're not Prince Valiant or Saint George the Dragon Slayer. You're not responsible for me. Do me a favor and go worry about your own life. And stay out of mine."

I leaned on the door jamb.

"Wrong, Margret. It's not a question of your life. Or mine. At least not only that. I don't know exactly what it's all about, but I plan to stay right here until you let me in. And then we'll figure out together what this is all about."

"You can stand there until the end of time. I'm going to bed."

"One second, Margret. I could ring your neighbor's bell and ask them if there was a fight at your place or if you've been falling down the stairs a lot lately. How'd you like that?"

I hated myself for this threat, but Margret heaved a sigh of resignation, unhooked the chain, opened the door, and let me in. I followed her into the kitchen, and she got a piece of cheese out of the fridge. She sat down at the kitchen table and shared the cheese with her cat, who seemed to be as unenthusiastic about my visit as her mistress. I was not offered a thing.

We sat across from each other in silence. The bruise around her right eye had grown considerably larger and was now a mottled blend of blue, green, and yellow edged by red—a sign of lysis of the red blood cells released by the injury. From a medical perspective there was very likely a connection between Margret's black eye and Misha's jaundice. If red corpuscles are not only released locally by a bruise, say, but also die off as a result of a poisoning throughout the body, then you get jaundice, or icterus. I was here to discover whether this connection went beyond the purely medical.

Margret was silent and seemed to be staring at a hidden pattern on the table. I removed the blood bag she'd given me from my pocket and placed it between us on the table. I'd left the German label off.

"You gave me this bag the other day for a reason, didn't you?"

Margret didn't look up. She knew what I was talking about.

"The other day was the other day; today is today."

"Do you mean that the other day was before you had the bad luck to fall down the stairs?"

"Among other things."

"And today you'd no longer give me this blood bag?"

Margret didn't answer. I stood up and got two glasses off the kitchen shelf and a bottle of white wine from the fridge and poured us a drink. Margret took a hearty swallow without looking at me.

"You know, Margret, nobody's beaten *me* up yet. Mind you, two Eastern European characters were on the verge of doing just that when I took a look around the hostel where that dead Russian lived. But still, my apartment's been vandalized, which was almost like bodily harm and could certainly be considered a threat."

"Who vandalized you?"

"I don't know. I'm wondering whether it was maybe the same people who beat you up."

Margret neither agreed nor disagreed with me. She kept studying the kitchen table as though the grain of the wood could point the way out of the labyrinth of her problems.

"I think you're always going to have the same problem, Margret. Should you let yourself be intimidated? Will that ever truly solve the problem so that you're in the clear? Or will it only get worse? Will the first intimidation be followed by a second and a third because the problems of the people who are trying to intimidate you are also increasing? It's like extortion—how can I be sure that a one-time payment to the extortionist will really be the last and not the start of a lifelong installment plan?"

There was a long pause. Tables and chairs on the balcony above were being shoved back to their usual places. I wasn't sure whether Margret had even heard me, and I was startled when she suddenly replied.

"It isn't such a big deal, this blood bag thing."

There was another pause. I gave Margret a chance to keep talking but she said nothing.

"Margret, it looks pretty clear what this blood bag with the label in Cyrillic means—we're pumping blood from Ukraine into our patients. Isn't that it? Wasn't that the real reason your friend Boris, he of those Eastern European blood banks, came to visit you?"

Margret shrugged and finally spoke up.

"So what if it was? It might come from Russia or Belorussia or Kazakhstan. Blood is blood; the patient doesn't give a hoot where it comes from. The blood supply in Germany simply isn't large enough. We used to import blood from East Germany."

"From East Germany?"

"Yes, we did it for years. Didn't you know that? It was an important source of foreign exchange for the Comrades. But now they've got the euro without having to donate blood and they need the blood themselves thanks to all the new cars we sold them in exchange for their new euros. Eastern Europe has replaced them. Blood is much cheaper there than in Germany, and besides, it's not against the law to import blood."

"But—then why stick new labels over the old ones?"

Margret gave the same reason Michael Thiel had.

"Would you want a blood transfusion from a bag labeled in Cyrillic?"

"Not one with hepatitis, in any case."

"Why did you think of hepatitis?"

I explained to her why I'd asked about the tally sheet control number the other day. I told her about Misha and the unnecessary blood transfusion and that he had been DOA. And then I told her that his blood had been full of hepatitis C.

Margret polished off her wine and poured herself another glass.

"But that can't be, Felix. The blood bags aren't from Germany; the labels are false. That's true. But they're clean. They're tested in Russia, in Ukraine, or whatever the country of origin. And they're tested all over again by us. This business may not be clean but the blood bags are. You have to believe me. I run this blood bank, and I wouldn't want to infect even a single person. You do believe that, don't you, Felix?"

"Of course I believe you. But the fact remains that Misha was filled to the gills with hepatitis C. Michael Thiel tested his blood."

"The reason for your crusade is gradually becoming clear, but you're barking up the wrong tree. I haven't a clue where your patient got his hepatitis from. Certainly not from the blood bag. We tested it."

I was confused but relieved. As I've said, even though I wasn't directly at fault for Misha's unnecessary blood transfusion, he had still been my patient. I told Margret what puzzled me: Why had somebody prevented an autopsy? Why wasn't the tally sheet for his blood bag correct? Could somebody have changed the numbers in the computer?

Margret thought that over.

"I don't know anything about the autopsy business. As for the tally sheet, the computer has its own password but of course a whole lot of people know it. Everyone who works in the blood bank, anyway."

"Including your friend Boris?"

"Hmm, I don't think so. If he does, he didn't get it from me."

"Isn't it possible that he could have seen the password when you were explaining the system to him back then?"

"I suppose so, in theory. I still think it was a matter of a simple transposition of numbers. Whatever. That blood bag was definitely tested by us. And it was definitely clean. I can guarantee you that."

It sounded logical. Anybody can make a few tons of dioxin disappear into a garbage dump or make radioactive waste disappear into the North Sea, but nobody would think of dumping infected blood into transfusions in his own hospital—and least of all, selling it to somebody else, if they were interested in keeping a long-term business deal going.

"Margret, I've got a question for you. Why are you going along with this? Whether this business with the Russian blood bags is illegal or not, it's not your style, if I know you at all."

"God knows I'm not proud of being tied up in this business. It sort of began by accident two years ago last summer. We were really short of blood for the holiday traffic as usual. I'd been phoning up and down Germany all day—it was the same everywhere. Then Boris came by—we were just about to go out that night—and he offered to solve my problem: the next day we could pick up a cold pack containing all of the blood groups from the airport. Our reserves were pretty much down to zero at that point, so that probably saved somebody's life."

"And so it became a permanent arrangement?"

"That was my fault. I told Knut about it and mentioned that it was much cheaper than German blood. Knut had to seize any opportunity he could to reduce the budget deficit at that point." She smiled. "Later we called it 'the Russian donation.'"

"The Russian donation?"

"A small contribution from our new friends in the East to help shore up our hospital budget, Knut said. I already told you how Knut risked his neck to save the hospital from going broke. And thereby saving your jobs."

It wasn't the right time to discuss Bredow's motives for doing deals with Russian blood bags and playing the stock market with our salaries. Of course the hospital budget had to be balanced, but in the end it was about Bredow himself and his own future and not about our jobs. He'd wanted to make his mark as a competent manager in an underfinanced health system; the successful restoration of our ailing hospital finances was just another step toward higher positions in the system. At that moment, though, I didn't care to destroy Margret's version of history.

"But Knut Bredow is dead, Margret."

Margret got up and her dressing gown slipped opened a bit.

"You're certainly right about that."

I got up too.

"One more thing, Margret. How many blood bags do we actually use each month in the hospital? I mean, does all this extra trouble pay off?"

Margret pulled her belt tight.

"Felix, I'll gladly ask Prof. Dohmke whether you have a right to know our monthly blood requirements. And if you do, I'll print you out a list for every month of the year. But I'm tired. I'm going to bed and you're going home. And I have to ask you never to come here again. What happened after Knut's burial was OK.

I needed consolation and you gave it to me. But as I've told you before, go agonize about your own life and stay out of mine."

She escorted me to the door.

"There's something else, Felix. If you're on some sort of crusade, don't forget that innocent bystanders are most often the victims of wars."

She bolted the door behind me and latched the chain. A few minutes later, I was back on the street and heading toward my car.

As I've said before, my fourteen-year-old Rabbit was no jewel—God knows—but now the driver's side window and the rear window had been smashed in; the interior was scattered with splintered glass. A fat rat was draped artistically over the driver's seat. I broke a small twig off the chestnut tree in front of the building and carefully poked at it. At least the rat was dead.

It was a little before midnight, hardly the time for a thorough cleanup, so I picked up the rat by the tail and dropped it in the gutter and brushed the glass splinters off the driver's seat as best I could. When I got behind the wheel, I debated whether I was just another victim of rising street crime. But I didn't see any other beat-up cars, and my antique Rabbit could hardly have provoked any hatred of the propertied class.

Was this yet another warning not to stick my nose into other people's business? Was the dead rat a discreet hint of the possible consequences of my curiosity? For my patients, I wondered, or for me? If I was being threatened by someone, didn't that mean that someone felt threatened by me? Margret had described it as a crusade. Was I a noble knight battling against evil or just a Don Quixote tilting at windmills? Why didn't I just let the police handle it all? But what would they be able to do? They wouldn't see any reason to get involved in our COO's accidental death, which had been confirmed by Dohmke, a case of hepatitis with a documented needle wound, or manipulated computer data that I'd stolen.

As I sat in my Rabbit contemplating my next move—or whether I should even make a move at all—the door to Margret's apartment building opened. She'd changed into a pair of jeans and a baggy sweatshirt. I watched as she got into a brand-new Rabbit convertible and took off. Her financial situation certainly appeared to be better than that of someone on your average lab tech's salary. I decided to follow her. She was heading in the direction I'd have to go to get home anyway.

It was a warm summer night, and the sidewalk cafes were still full of people drinking German beer and Italian wine. Traffic was light, and I had no difficulty keeping up with her. We drove at a normal speed—this was no wild chase through red lights with screeching tires. Margret probably had a lot on her mind and had no reason to think she'd be followed.

At first I thought that maybe she was headed to my place and had made up her mind to tell me something, but then she turned left at Roseneck. It gradually dawned on me where she was going, but I wasn't certain until Margret's convertible stopped on Miquelstrasse. We'd wound up in front of Prof. Dohmke's villa.

Margret braked rather sharply, so I was forced to brake hard too. To my surprise, another car slowed suddenly behind me and a dark Mercedes came right up to my bumper. I'd felt like an experienced shadower for the last twenty minutes, but was I actually the one being shadowed? I'd been concentrating so intently on not letting Margret's car out of my sight that I'd neglected to glance in my own rearview mirror.

Margret parked right in front of Dohmke's villa. One of the many advantages of owning property in a swank residential area was that there was always room to park in front of your residence. I drove slowly past the house; the Mercedes passed me. I made a futile effort to recognize the passengers. I realized too late that I should have focused on the plate number. Felix, the all-star detective, drove home disgruntled.

I found Margret in the staff cafeteria the next morning. She was heavily made up as before but had no new wounds as far as I could tell.

"How was Prof. Dohmke last night? Did you thank him again for the neat car?"

Margret paused and looked straight at me. I was afraid for a second that she was about to throw her coffee in my face. She didn't, though.

"Dumbass."

And she walked away.

No one likes to be called a "dumbass." Especially not someone like myself, who's rather proud of his intellectual abilities. But I noticed that Margret's tone of voice hadn't been aggressive or vindictive but sympathetic. She could have said "bastard" or "asshole." I sat down and sipped my weak coffee.

I'd confirmed the night before that I was no ace detective. And I didn't have a whole organization behind me like the police. Even if I had noted the Mercedes's license plate number, it would have taken some effort for me to track down its owner. I couldn't give orders to a surveillance team, couldn't do wiretaps or sift through bank withdrawals, but I had other virtues, and one of them was that I was stubborn as hell.

I tried my luck again at the blood bank toward noon. I figured that Margret must have been lying, at least when she claimed that the Russian blood bags were being imported just for our patients. Otherwise she'd have to clarify for me what else the roughly 150,000 euros a month in income under the "Blood Bank" rubric could possibly mean. By then, I was certain that "dumbass" meant exactly that: I knew nothing and Margret knew a whole lot.

Margret's girls were not at lunch but hard at work. Margret wasn't feeling well, they said, and had gone home after trying to make herself feel better with a cup of coffee from the cafeteria. Their reproachful tone suggested that they thought I was probably to blame for the shape she was in and therefore also to blame for their having to work through their lunch hour. I knew that my patients would have to wait a little longer today for their results from the blood lab.

"Herr Hoffmann, what an honor! Glad you've still got time to see us. Everything under control on your ward?"

It was no great surprise to run into Prof. Dohmke in the blood lab. It was all too clear what he was referring to, and I could hardly object, given that Frau Schön was still on the kidney machine.

The results from the blood lab were indeed remarkably slow in coming that afternoon. I called Celine and asked her to pick up a few things from the supermarket and put them in my fridge. By seven p.m., I decided that my patients' lives weren't in danger regardless of the blood lab results. Maybe I'd get my revenge the next day with a request for a whole battery of time-consuming tests, but for the time being I just drove home. The evening traffic had dissipated, and I stopped at a fruit stand at the Hüttenweg exit that had fresh strawberries.

I kept an eye on the traffic behind me on the way home but couldn't detect anyone tailing me. I hoped it wasn't because my view was partially blocked by the plastic I'd replaced the rear window glass with. If Margret and I were really being monitored, then I suspected there must be a potent enemy behind all this with interests he was willing to protect at considerable expense. I decided to be more careful and wouldn't tell Celine this part of the story. I doubted I would be in any real danger that evening; I just wanted to kick back in front of the TV and then trundle off to bed feeling guilty about the time I'd wasted.

It didn't work out that way. No, my place hadn't been vandalized again, but I came upon a heap of misery on my doorstep. Margret.

She was in even worse shape than she'd been the night before, and I was barely able to understand her whispering.

"It's worse than you think, Felix."

"So it seems. But, you know, it's never as bad as you think. Come inside."

Wise sayings are a well-known specialty of mine. Still, I was relieved to see that Margret didn't have a suitcase with her. She really did just want to talk.

"Can I get you something?"

Margret went out onto my balcony and got busy deadheading the fuchsias and daisies that I'd been neglecting lately.

"Do you have any tea?"

"I do. Would you like anything with it?"

Margret was standing in the doorway.

"Maybe a new life."

"Tea will take less time. I'll put the water on."

Margret went back to puttering around with my balcony plants while I prepared the tea. Her remark about a new life was unsettling. I hoped she didn't mean that she wanted me to take responsibility for her life. I could hardly take care of my own.

It was relatively cool, and what we had to talk about was hardly appropriate for the balcony. I brought the tea into my living-work-lounging room, and I grabbed a beer for myself. Margret took off her shoes, sat down on my couch, put her feet up, and spread a patchwork quilt—a Christmas present from Celine—over her knees. She was obviously finding it difficult to start talking. So I began for her.

"I went to the blood bank at lunchtime today. I wanted to apologize for having waylaid you last night."

"That wasn't so bad, Felix. You know what really upset me? Your lack of trust. We were lovers once after all, and I thought we were still friends."

She was right on the whole. We'd more or less meant it when we'd parted ways with "We'll still be friends."

"I do think we're still friends. But what are friends for if you don't come to them with your problems?"

"That's why I'm here now. I need you."

She took my hand and started stroking it, looking lost in thought. My sympathy was generally rather easily aroused, as was my sexuality. Maybe I was wrong in this case, but if there was one thing that made me angry, it was the feeling that I was being manipulated. I moved my hand away.

"Why do you need me tonight, Margret? Are you having trouble with your new car?"

Margret stiffened.

"That's not fair."

"Not fair? A convertible for your extra work at the blood bank—do you think that's fair?" I was slowly gaining momentum. "Don't you think a convertible is a bit generous for slapping new labels on a couple of blood bags? Isn't there a little more at stake here? Could it be that you all are running a flourishing business?"

Margret flashed me the same "dumbass" look that she had this morning, but again she looked sad, not angry.

"You probably think you're pretty hot stuff right now, don't you? Ace Detective Tails Lab Tech through Nighttime Berlin. Like that's something to be proud of."

"I didn't lie in wait for you last night. I had to get rid of a dead rat that I found lying across my seat before going home. That's why I was still there when you roared off. And then we were on the same road, at least as far as Roseneck. Then I got curious. And I wondered about your brand-new car. Has it got leather seats and a genuine wooden dashboard?"

"OK, Felix, you're right. A bag gets sold now and then. Are you satisfied now? If the expiration date is coming up and we can't use the blood in the hospital anymore, then it gets sold. But it's still clean, thoroughly tested blood."

"A bag now and then? How many bags a month is that? I don't like to be played for a sucker. Maybe a little more of the truth wouldn't be a bad way to start a new life."

For the pharmaceutical industry, blood is a raw material, like petroleum for the oil industry. Modern medicine has an almost unslakable thirst for concentrates from certain blood components, which can be sold for a pretty penny.

Margret finally admitted that it was more than a few bags. She made the same case as before: the first delivery to make up for that summer shortage, she said, had been more blood than the hospital could use. Then Boris the wheeler-dealer had come up with the idea of selling it, and COO Bredow had agreed because of the hospital budget.

"Did the companies know they weren't buying German blood?"

"I don't know. I only do the testing. Knut took care of the rest. And I did it for him."

"I know, the Russian donation. And now you do it for a convertible."

Margret pulled her knees up more tightly and wrapped herself up in my quilt. Even with the protective quilt, she still looked vulnerable.

"I've never had a car straight from the factory."

She patted down my quilt as though she were fondling her new car's leather seats and genuine wooden dash.

"My sincerest congratulations, Margret. What else did you get out of this business? A fully loaded Rabbit convertible can't be the only thing you got out of the deal. Maybe a little jewelry or a few Siberian diamonds? A sable for our cold winters? Or did you fancy an antique gold icon? It's not only a nice wall decoration, but also a fine investment for the future."

I escalated into remarkable self-righteousness. I'd once trusted her, and there was nothing more disappointing to me than seeing that my friends weren't as I wished them to be. Perhaps it still hurt my vanity that she had been the one to call things off. I went on without wavering.

"Have you ever considered who foots the bill for all of this? For your new car and God knows what else? I'll tell you: It's not Herr Dohmke or your friend Boris. It's not the drug industry that's paying German prices for Russian blood. It's me and you and all the little people who finance your deals with their insurance premiums. And now they also have to co-pay for every day they spend in our glorious hospitals."

Tears were welling up in Margret's green-and-blue-rimmed eye.

"Felix, have you ever considered having yourself sculpted in marble? Maybe with an illuminated halo over your head? I told you the truth yesterday. I went along with this blood business because Knut Bredow asked me to. For him and for the hospital."

"And now that your good friend and our COO, Knut Bredow, is dead, Dohmke thinks that maybe a couple of generous gifts to you are in order to keep you in line and the business running?"

"If it makes you feel any better, Felix, the Rabbit was all that Dohmke used to keep me in line, apart from my decorative black eye."

Margret dug a crumpled handkerchief out of her purse; the tear in her black eye had lots of company now.

"They came over a few nights ago, four of them. Dohmke, Boris, and two of their men. I was already in bed. I hadn't even remembered that Boris still had a key to my place. Suddenly the four of them were standing at my bedroom door. Dohmke told me we had to have a little conversation. I could see that there was no use arguing with those two gorillas there. So I threw something on and joined them in the living room. Just to see what would I happen, I said I first had to make a phone call. 'Oh, our dear little Margret wants to call her new old boyfriend,' Boris said.

'Or her lawyer. Of course, Margret, by all means go ahead and make your call.' Then he said something in Russian to one of the gorillas, who ripped the phone cord out of the wall and brought the phone to me with a grin. 'This is Ivor, always at your service. Unfortunately Ivor is a bit awkward and often has trouble knowing his own strength. But if he can carry out any of your wishes, just say the word, Babushka.'"

Margret's voice had become almost a whisper.

"I asked them what they wanted. Dohmke said I should consider this a kind of staff meeting I could report as overtime, though he hoped it wouldn't take up too much of my valuable time. It was about you, 'Your friend Felix.' He'd heard you'd been quizzing me about blood bags in general and about a certain tally sheet in particular. I answered that he should ask you about all that himself. Out of the blue, Boris's gorilla hit me; wham-bang he got me, right-left, and I flew onto the couch. I screamed at the whole gang of them, saying what cowards they were, four men against one woman, and didn't they think they needed a third gorilla? Just the sort of weak-minded stuff my rage inspired. Of course it didn't have the slightest effect. I told them I wasn't going to tell them anything and that I was going to the police tomorrow. They'd certainly be interested in hearing about their profiteering with Russian blood supplies."

Margret paused, touched her eye gently, and continued.

"That's what earned me this beautiful shiner. At that point, Dohmke started talking. He said he was quite certain that I wouldn't go to the police, and asked how I would explain to the police my position as head of the blood bank, and the relabeling of the Russian blood over the last few years. He would only tell the police that Bredow and I had a deal that he'd only discovered after Bredow died. After a few more punches, they finally got the information they were looking for. Most of it at any rate. They were mainly interested in you and your investigations. Dohmke didn't know where you were really going with them. He kept trying to find out who was behind you, who you were making the inquiries for."

"And you told him?"

"What could I have told him? What do I know? I don't even know myself whom or what you're so worried about."

I could see Margret was thinking about hiding her tissue under my couch cushion, a dreadful habit of hers, but she caught herself in time and dropped it into her purse. She looked at me with her freshly wiped eyes.

"What are you going to do next, Felix? Have you got a plan?"

I probably would have confided my plan to her then and there, but I didn't have one. I knew, however, that I had a real adversary now in Prof. Dohmke, even though there wasn't any concrete evidence.

"No, I don't have a plan. And there's nobody backing me."

"You're all on your own?"

I nodded and Margret shrugged.

"Do you see that Dohmke and his friends are actually frightened? When I realized that, I hardly felt those punches anymore. All of a sudden Dohmke threw the keys to the convertible on the table. He said I could use a new car, that it was registered in my name, with taxes and insurance paid for a year. Then they disappeared, and I called in sick for a few days. I spent a lot of that time driving around in the car—to the Havel, the Müggelsee, as far as Rheinsberg. It was really fun. I didn't go to the police. Last night I gave back the car. That's why I went over to his house. I parked it in front of the house and dropped the keys in the mailbox."

Margret heaved a deep sigh. She had told me what she wanted to tell me. I couldn't be sure it was the entire truth, but her story seemed credible. A good cop or lawyer would have stuck with it and gone through her story again looking for contradictions. He would at least have clarified certain details and found out more about Herr Prof. Dohmke's business dealings and those of his Russian friends.

But I was feeling guilty about my earlier accusations and self-righteousness. Why did I of all people get my feathers ruffled over an extra honorarium? Physicians have become so accustomed to the generosity of the drug companies that they don't even recognize them as bribes anymore. Of course it's always for the patients' well-being, from the short lecture followed by a lavish dinner in the most expensive restaurant right up to five days in Paris or Sydney for our so-called advanced training conferences. I knew I owed my familiarity with the finest cuisine and the most beautiful places on earth largely to the pharmaceutical industry. The industry adds this magnanimity on to the sales price, and our patients pay for it in the end via their medical insurance. So who was I to talk about corruption?

I took Margret in my arms; she seemed to need comfort. I slowly slipped back into our old routine. It goes without saying that it was out of strictly humanitarian and unselfish motives.

"Am I disturbing you?"

I was reminded of Piggyjowls and Pimplepuss's entrance after the break-in, when Celine and I were enjoying ourselves on the rug. This time, though, Celine was in the doorway. I knew she had a key to my apartment, but she normally rang and didn't burst in like this. But tonight she hadn't expected me to be here. She'd only stopped by to put my groceries in my fridge. There she stood, grocery bags in hand. I also had something in hand: Margret's right breast. How was Celine to know that I was only practicing humanitarian consolation?

Celine stormed into the kitchen; Margret disappeared into the bathroom. Maybe she really had to go, but I think it was a conditioned reflex. I followed Celine into the kitchen, where she was busily crushing my fresh strawberries with new potatoes from Cyprus.

"Please don't come at me with 'It's not what it looks like'!"

"What did it look like?"

"What do you think it looks like when your paws are wandering all over your supposedly former lover?"

Both of us had mastered the technique of answering a question with another question. We did know our Socrates after all, and who hasn't read an introduction to psychoanalytical techniques?

"Do you think it's a good idea to put the potatoes on top of my strawberries?"

"Do you think it's a good idea to put your paws all over somebody else's tits?" Celine imitated me while placing the bottles of wine on top of the strawberries not already mashed by the potatoes.

I'd had enough of the feeble questions-without-answers game and explained why Margret was here and what she'd told me. Celine was ready to put my precious physician's hands and Margret's bosom on the back burner for a minute, but she remained skeptical.

"And you believe her story?"

"By and large. At any rate it seems more likely than if she'd told me she hit herself in the eye with a wooden spoon or really did fall down the stairs."

"Then why did Dohmke give her a car after having her roughed up?"

"Old tactic: carrot and stick. Until then she'd kept quiet and gone along with it out of love for Bredow. Now Dohmke probably thinks a little intimidation is in order and a little share of the profits to boot. At the same time, having the car was another form of pressure. Dohmke won't be happy she's given the car back."

"Did she really?"

"I saw it myself."

"You only saw that she parked it in front of Dohmke's villa. You didn't see how she left or whether she slept with him, for instance."

I liberated the strawberries from the potatoes. Too late. Maybe I'd make them into jam sometime.

"Celine, could it be that you're a little biased about Margret?"

"I think rather that you're not completely *un*biased. I'm trying to think with only my brain."

I thought it beneath my dignity to react to this allusion.

"I think Margret needs help. It was probably a mistake for her to return the car to Dohmke. That may have put her in danger. It would be better for her to carry on with Dohmke's business. And that's why I think you should leave."

"I should *what*?"

I ducked just in time. The strawberries landed on the fridge door, and strawberry juice slowly slid down to the floor. I didn't have to worry about turning them into jam anymore.

"I'm supposed to beat it so that you can unleash a little more consolation and tender loving care on your former lover? And you'll give me a call when you've finished comforting her? I can*not* believe it. I know we sort of have a so-called open relationship, but this kind of thing, dear heart, is not for me."

"Calm down, Celine. Sit down for a second and listen."

To my amazement, she actually did so. Margret was still in the bathroom.

"Just try to be objective for a minute. I don't want to sound melodramatic, but yes, I do think she's in danger. Would she really want to get into bed with Dohmke? If that were the case, then why did she give me that blood bag with the two labels? She would only have done that if she wanted me to discover the label underneath."

Celine opted for her loving/sympathetic gaze.

"To manipulate you, my dear. Exactly the way she tried to today. Maybe I shouldn't say this but you're awfully easy to manipulate."

I didn't confess that I'd suspected the same thing.

"What did she want to manipulate me into doing?"

"Simple. Dohmke knew—when you showed up at Margret's with Misha's tally sheet or even well before that—that you must have his file and were doggedly pursuing the matter. So they decided on a fall guy. They would allow you to discover the business with the blood bags and let you worry some more about your dead Ukrainian. That would be enough to keep you busy. Margret would see to it that you stayed on the trail and keep Dohmke and Co. au courant. In the meantime, they would have protected their really important dealings for the time being."

I'd never looked at it that way before—nor did I want to.

"I think Margret gave me the bag on her own initiative. Sure she's tied up in this business, but not out of greed; she went along with it because she loved Bredow. And now she wants out. How can she do that though? Go to the cops and lose her job? It's better for her to help me stop this racket from the inside."

Celine reflected for a moment.

"I grant you that that sounds plausible at first blush, but there's one thing that bothers me: Has Margret ever admitted something you didn't already know? Or something she didn't know you knew? If I've heard right, she's only ever responded to your questions or accusations."

Maybe, I pointed out, Margret planned to tell me everything, or would have done if Celine hadn't popped in. Celine replied with a glare that she probably used at school for responding to flimsy excuses for skipped homework. She obviously had her own ideas about how things would have unfolded between Margret and me if she hadn't dropped in just then.

"I don't trust her, which has nothing to do with my natural aversion toward a hopefully former lover of yours."

I wasn't so sure about that, but I was trying to make a different point.

"We both know that this blood deal is just the tip of the ice-berg," I said. "Whether Margret is in cahoots with Dohmke or not, she doesn't have to know your part in this. And that's why I'd like you to leave. Dohmke and his friends know about me—that can't be changed. But they don't know about you, and I'd like it to stay that way. I don't want to put you in any danger."

Celine got up and gave me a kiss.

"You're sweet. But, my noble knight, you're still not going to get rid of me. You want me to step aside now just when it's really getting exciting? I'm to sit quietly at my loom and wait to see whether you return home from war alive? Forget it. Besides, I want to be there when Dohmke's Russian friends beat the shit out of you—I'd hold you down for them."

"Get serious, Celine. You don't fool around with these guys."

"Well, it's much too dangerous for you to go it alone," Celine said, putting her arm around me. "Come on, I'd like to hear your girlfriend's story for myself. And you pay attention to see if she tells us the same version she told you before. Otherwise, we'll just shove knitting needles under her fingernails until she spits out the truth."

We returned to my living room. There was no trace of Margret. And she wasn't in the bathroom or on the balcony either. She'd vanished.

Celine took it in stride.

"She must have picked up that bit about the knitting needles."

I was worried about Margret and cleaned up in the kitchen to get my mind off her. I put five of the six bottles of white wine into the fridge, the potatoes into the food bin, and the strawber-ries into the garbage. I returned to Celine with two glasses and a bottle of wine.

CHAPTER 19

"Do you know what warrants are?" Celine asked.

Celine was lying on my couch. By means of a full glass of white wine, carefully chosen words, and a back massage, I'd convinced her that my feelings for Margret were utterly humanitarian. At least she appeared convinced. But she still harbored doubts about Margret's motives with regard to me, and about her relationship with Dohmke and her old boyfriend Boris. I disagreed with her. For one thing, her argument implied that Margret was looking for more than consolation from me, and for another, that she might have come over today at Dohmke and Boris's behest to sound me out.

At any rate, it was clear that Celine didn't want to back out of this mess. She'd spent the last few days with Beate deciphering more of Bredow's data and talking to her friend Johannes. She repeated her question.

"Do you know what warrants are? I mean subscription warrants."

"Something you can make a lot of money on the market with, right?"

"Or lose a lot of money. To wit, everything."

"Is that what Bredow did?"

"Precisely!"

"Win or lose?"

"Both."

"Can you please explain?"

"Only if you give me another massage."

Celine stretched out languorously on the couch. She was of course champing at the bit to tell me about her discoveries, and I probably could have gotten them out of her without a massage. But I didn't want to spoil things or bring up the subject of Margret again, so I kept working on her back.

"It's not difficult to understand. Shares are traded on the stock market. Let's say you've heard that Mercedes plans to streamline production to cut costs. You'd buy shares in Mercedes because the profits should go up. And when the shares do go up in value, you've done quite well. But if, for whatever reason, Mercedes tanks, you can either sell off your shares at the lower share price and lose money or if you've got steady nerves, you can wait until share prices rise again. Warrants, on the other hand, are all or nothing. Pure roulette. You can, for example, bet on the American dollar. The seller of your dollar warrant places a so-called call. That's the highest amount the dollar will be worth on a certain date, let's say seventy-seven euro cents. If on that date the rate for the dollar is actually seventy-nine euro cents, that makes you two euro cents, which is then multiplied by a hundred to make two euros. The two euros are then multiplied by themselves, which makes four euros."

"Then would I have made four euros on each warrant?"

"Not quite. You still have to deduct the initial cost of the warrant, which leaves you with one euro and twelve cents per warrant."

I did the math along with her.

"So let's say I had half a million euros on hand. If I bought a hundred seventy-five thousand warrants with that, then I'd make almost two hundred thousand euros. Is it that simple?"

"If it rises to eighty cents, you'd make over a million!"

I started feeling greedy. I could certainly borrow fifty thousand. At eighty cents that would come to more than a hundred thousand euros.

"What's the catch?"

"That's easy. The dollar falls and your money's gone. Totally and forever. It's not like with stocks, where you can wait and hope they recover."

"And let me guess. Our good friend Bredow bet on warrants."

"Indeed he did. Quite successfully at first. He'd initially been relatively cautious and put a hundred thousand euros into the German Stock Index. As everyone knows, it performed beautifully last year, so he then raised his stake. He looked around for bigger gains and came across those warrants. He ultimately screwed up to the tune of almost four million in warrants."

"Where did he suddenly get four million in play money?"

"That's not a problem," Celine replied. "If you're a successful speculator, you can always find a bank that will lend you your next bet."

"Four million?"

"Since it went so well at the start, Bredow gradually increased his bets until he'd put in the hospital's entire monthly budget. The bank gave him the rest on credit."

"But that's insane! And if his luck had held, he'd have earned himself a tidy little sum with money borrowed from the hospital."

"It's the old casino problem. Either things go well and normal human greed takes over, until you fall flat on your face, or you lose and then really get going because you've got to make up your losses somehow. Either way, you play until it's all gone."

"So it didn't work for Dr. Bredow. There's no way there's going to be extra income."

"You can say that again. I've already conceded that your girlfriend Margret was telling the truth about that little game. Bredow's gambling really was all part of an effort to balance the hospital's budget. With a little more patience, he might have pulled it off, but he ran out of time. He bet the store—and lost big-time."

I thought back to those delayed salary payments last year and the unpaid overtime—Bredow must have been sweating bullets.

"And how big was the budget shortfall in the end?"

"The figures I gave you a while back were pretty close. He had to get rid of a deficit of about two million."

A lot of people would have disappeared without a trace, but Bredow had bravely kept his eye on the ball. I couldn't even really fault him much for trying to fix things with warrants. After all, a part of the industrial sector earns more on the financial markets than with its products. It made sense to me that you'd take the ultimate way out after such a disaster, even if it was with your own belt on the transom.

However, one crucial piece of the puzzle remained unresolved: our COO had put us 2 million in the red last November but killed himself only two weeks ago. And not because the hospital budget was in the hole, as that hole had been mysteriously filled several months before.

"Have you had any luck finding out which good fairy helped Bredow off the hook? Was it a bank that lent him the money for the warrants?"

"No, not the bank. Banks are no different from the mafia. They'll only lend you money if you pay it back on time. If you don't, the mafia shoots you in the kneecap and the banks in the back. No, our friend got the two million from a transport company," Celine said, looking at the papers she had hauled out of her handbag. "From the Eurotrans Trucking Company—or whoever's behind it. So we just have to find out why a trucking company would give him a handout of two measly million."

I was quite sure I knew the address of Eurotrans, and a quick look in the telephone book confirmed it. I planned to pay another visit to my new friend Karin at the Business Registry and figure out who had bought a piece of our hospital.

Celine looked exhausted but struggled to her feet and went home.

That night, my sleep was riddled with dreams of wild car chases through the streets of Berlin—Dohmke and his thugs were hot on my heels. And I was witness to several versions of Bredow's death, none of which I could stop, because in my dream state I experienced an acute failure to speak as well as some kind of physical paralysis. My default anxiety dream—about my final math exam in high school—also played itself out; my unconscious still knew after all these years that an oral exam would have unmasked me as a math fraud.

The next morning it occurred to me between shaving and brushing my teeth that I had never been seriously threatened in real life. Margret had been beaten up and blackmailed and Bredow had been hounded to death or, as Margret indicated, maybe even murdered. I'd only been vandalized and found a dead rat in my car, and there was not a shred of evidence that these two events had anything to do with my investigations.

Wasn't I entitled to a little more peril than that? I arrived at two possible conclusions: either I was completely on the wrong track with my suspicions and whoever was in charge was allowing me to stumble along blindly, or I was indeed on the right track but nobody was taking me seriously—which was an even more depressing notion than the first. I suddenly stopped brushing, jumped into my clothes, and hurried out to the car.

The question of whether the interested party simply didn't think it necessary to show more than a friendly interest in my efforts agitated me to such a degree that I couldn't concentrate on the usual morning battle for the best lane on Berlin's ring road. I promptly got stuck in a traffic jam just before the Funkturm Triangle. Drivers all around me were well prepared. Cell phones were pulled out and memos delivered into recorders. Right beside me, a real time-saving expert held his cell phone to his ear with his left hand while he shaved with his right. I made a mental note to have at least a toothbrush in the glove compartment from now on.

The traffic jam gave me some time to reflect. Even if Margret had confessed more to Dohmke than she had let on, all she knew was that I was looking for Misha's blood bag. Dohmke had no idea that we were investigating Bredow's secret bookkeeping and the Business Registry. That realization lifted my spirits, and I moved up a few places in traffic with a bold maneuver. I threaded my way through to the city autobahn well before the telephoning shaver.

The next traffic jam caught me just as unprepared, as did my sudden suspicion that my opponents had long ago decided to take drastic steps against me and were only waiting for the right moment to do so. Celine was convinced that the blame for the second zero for the potassium transfusion could be laid at Dohmke's door. If these guys were prepared to risk killing Frau Schön to put pressure on me, why not just kill me outright?

Would my brakes fail at the next stop? Was that the toxic smell of exhaust fumes nearby? Any fatal accident in my jalopy wouldn't inspire any further investigation. I was suddenly thankful for the congestion; moving at a crawl gave me a better chance of survival. I exited the autobahn as soon as the traffic got moving again. I found a parking place on Sophie-Charlotte-Platz, where my expired inspection sticker wouldn't be so noticeable, and hopped on the subway.

I didn't let myself get distracted from my problems during the ride by reflecting, as I so often did, on local public transportation as a backup job for failed city politicians. Either Dohmke and his buddies hadn't cottoned on to the danger they were in yet, or else they were ready to bump me off at any moment. At one stop, I'd be convinced of the former possibility, by the next I'd have changed my mind. While transferring at Wittenbergplatz, I decided to back out of the whole business. And between Nollendorfplatz and Gleisdreieck, I persuaded myself that there were many good reasons for doing so.

It had become quite clear that Misha had not been a victim of the hospital's dubious blood dealings. What did I care about the rest of the story? What did I care about the real owners of the hospital and its various business transactions? It didn't even matter whether I'd personally prescribed the potassium overdose or Dohmke had added that second zero. As long as I limited myself to working as a physician, my patients would continue to receive the care they needed and return home feeling better. If Celine and Beate were right, there was a huge pile of money at stake and the people who were involved weren't going to put up with my messing around in their affairs. Why should I play the hero?

By the time I reached Kottbusser Tor, I'd figured out how to let Dohmke and his boys know that I wasn't after them anymore. I'd simply hand Misha's records over to Dohmke and assure him that I was convinced that he'd picked up his hepatitis while working for us, or even somewhere else, but certainly not from our blood bank. That was probably even true. Dohmke would understand that I considered the matter closed. Celine wouldn't be pleased, but even she might come around to the idea of not skipping through life with shattered kneecaps or a broken thigh.

I made it to the hospital intact. Whether it was thanks to fate or my brilliant switchover to the subway I would never know. I was too late for the morning beds meeting so I marched over to the ICU and took Misha's file out of hiding. There were a thousand urgent problems on my ward but they'd have to wait. I set off immediately for Frau Krüger's desk knowing I'd catch Dohmke in his office after the morning meeting.

Frau Krüger was an absolutely diligent secretary whose workplace was normally immaculate, but that day her office looked like a receiving dock for recycled paper. Frau Krüger sat amid chaotic heaps of file folders, sorting through them and making notes on different colored file cards.

"Hello, Dr. Hoffmann. How are you?"

She was always friendly, or at least polite, even under heavy stress.

"Hello, Frau Krüger. I'm fine, thank you. But you seem to have a problem here."

"You can say that again. We've got a huge mess on our hands. Somehow a virus got into the boss's computer and wiped out all his files overnight. Prof. Dohmke is distraught. So I'm sitting here trying to reconstruct our revenues and bills from the past year."

"Doesn't Accounts have all that?"

"They have most of it, thank heavens. Anything to do with the insurance companies and expenses for purchases—medications and that sort of things—and salaries. But the billing of private patients has gone through this office ever since last year—Dr. Bredow's instructions. Luckily his computer isn't on the hospital intranet. I can't imagine what would happen if the hospital intranet had a virus."

Had Bredow left a time bomb in the form of a virus in his computer? It was possible. But Bredow had been dead for a good two weeks. I didn't know whether Dohmke had cracked the access code to the files since then, but I personally wouldn't give a real hacker that much time for it.

Frau Krüger interrupted my reflections.

"What can I do for you, Dr. Hoffmann?"

"I have to see Herr Dohmke; it's urgent," I said, pointing to Misha's file under my arm. "I've got something here I'm sure he'll want to see right away."

"Prof. Dohmke just left. It seems to be a catastrophic day. There was a fire last night at CareClean and he had to head over there right away."

A computer virus here in the hospital and a fire in Allee der Kosmonauten 116. This remarkable coincidence made an electronic time bomb in Bredow's computer seem most unlikely. It appeared instead that someone urgently wanted to make evidence disappear and that this someone had gotten very nervous, which made me very nervous in turn. It was high time I convinced Dohmke I was harmless.

I couldn't think of any words of consolation for Frau Krüger. At least she'd have a chance to prove that she was irreplaceable and maybe manage to hold on to her job a little longer. As for me, I knew I had to find Dohmke at once. That meant paying a third visit to Allee der Kosmonauten and once again asking Marlies to take over my round. Marlies didn't ask any questions and promised to cover for me until noon.

"By the way, could you lend me your car? Mine wouldn't start this morning."

And she did that too. Marlies was solid gold and I told her so. I really had to take her out to dinner soon.

When I pulled up at Allee der Kosmonauten 116, I counted one rescue squad vehicle and two fire engines in the parking lot in front of the prefab building. Singed and charred office furniture and burnt computers lay scattered outside the building. They'd evidently been heaved out the window so as not to feed the fire.

By the time I arrived, the firefighters were already rolling up their hoses and standing around, smoking. The show was pretty much over. Housewives and pensioners from the neighborhood who'd come to check out the action milled around. A small man wearing a black-and-white plaid hat was even taking pictures. He looked familiar so I approached him.

"Prof. Kindel! You go around looking at disasters now?"

My former boss seemed as surprised to see me as I had been to see him.

"Herr Hoffmann! Do you listen to police radio too? It's exciting, isn't it? More exciting than the life of a retiree in any case. It's these little things that get me through the day now."

I refrained from asking whether the golf clubs we'd given him had gotten much use and instead inquired whether he'd seen Prof. Dohmke. Kindel gave me a look that was hard to interpret.

"Should I have?"

"Well, that's his BMW over there."

The dark blue BMW was parked off to the side, but the license plate was plainly Dohmke's. After the letter *B* signifying Berlin, any dedicated BMW driver would give his right hand for a plate reading *B-M-W*. But Dohmke's plate projected an even greater sense of self-importance. I'd found out that his "B–D 2403" stood for "Bernhard Dohmke" and would hardly have been surprised to learn that he'd been born on March 24.

"Is it?" Kindel replied, then paused. "No, I haven't seen him."

I left Kindel to his hobby and set out in search of Dohmke. The wallpaper in the stairway didn't exhibit any great damage except for a few dark spots. The fire had evidently not spread from office to office through the stairwell. It must have started in different offices. It seemed that whoever had set this fire—and arson was assumed—had only intended to smoke out the offices, not torch the whole building. Which wasn't my idea of pyromania, unless a pyromaniac with an incurable love of chintz wallpaper was involved in the case.

I found Dohmke in the boss's office at CareClean. Either it was the FDGB auntie's day off or she'd been sent home; either way, no one was there to stop me from pushing my way in. Dohmke was standing at a window with no panes, because the entire contents of the office had been hurled through them, and he was talking to a well-dressed man of about fifty. They'd both managed to avoid dirtying their suits, whereas I already had a pattern of black streaks on my light-colored summer jeans.

"Herr Hoffmann! You're developing an astounding affinity for this office."

I suddenly felt rather silly standing in front of Dohmke in soot-streaked jeans with Misha's file in my hand. Had I really gone across Berlin this morning to give him this file?

"Frau Krüger said I'd find you here."

"Well, well. Frau Krüger told you. Our Frau Krüger always knows the score."

That sounded odd. Like he really meant: "Frau Krüger knows about your tiresome snooping and keeps me constantly informed." Or "Frau Krüger knows more than what's good for her and is gradually becoming a problem." I looked at Dohmke and could see that he was waiting for me to explain what I was doing here. Had I become completely paranoid? If not, I'd better start covering my ass. Frau Krüger was old enough to take care of her own ass herself.

"It concerns the Misha Chenkov case. My Ukrainian patient who died recently."

"I remember, Herr Hoffmann. You were deeply affected by his death. It was hepatitis, wasn't it?"

"That's right. You may also perhaps recall that his ward file disappeared."

Dohmke looked at me intently; I held up the file.

"So I found the file this morning by chance, in the ICU. Under a pile of other files. I went through the file right away. Now we can be certain: he did indeed have a blood transfusion, but his hepatitis didn't come from the blood bag."

Dohmke kept eyeing me unswervingly.

"And we can be sure about that?"

"Yes, we can be very sure."

"That's fine, Dr. Hoffmann, very gratifying to hear. I find it very remarkable how rigorously you have pursued this matter. May I have the file?"

He could; I'd photocopied it twice and numbered the pages. It was time for me to leave. As I did so, I emphasized that as far as I was concerned the case was finally and conclusively solved and that there was plenty of work waiting for me at the hospital. Dohmke showed his appreciation and said good-bye. He didn't introduce me to the man who'd been standing beside him all through this peculiar meeting.

When I got outside, I looked for my Rabbit, until I remembered that I'd come in Marlies's car. I got into her Honda and took a deep breath. It was possible that I'd just made a big fool of myself, but also that I'd just saved my own life.

The sun was shining and Berlin's corner pubs had morphed into sidewalk cafes. I saw Prof. Kindel having his second breakfast nearby. I knew that some people, mainly retirees, listened to the police or fire department radio all day and showed up at the most interesting incidents. But why hadn't Kindel asked me what Dohmke would be doing there—or asked me why I'd shown up?

Still preoccupied with my potential murder, I let my curiosity get the better of me and it ended up overpowering my self-preservation instincts. I didn't feel like going back to the hospital right away. Marlies would only have finished about half of my round, and it would knock the nurses off stride if I were to do the second half. I decided to pay another visit to my friend Karin in the Business Registry. Either nobody had ever been following me or somebody had called my tail off by now, if not before. And even

I wasn't paranoid enough to think that Karin might be working part-time for Dohmke and Co.

I found Karin without any trouble. Maybe I reminded her of her older brother or maybe I was just her type; in any case, she accepted Beate's document with her tax business's impressive letterhead without any fuss. It stated that I was there regarding a loan for CareClean Cleaning Services and that I therefore had a justifiable interest in the company's partnership. The box of pralines I'd picked up on the way probably helped a little. I'd guessed right—Karin was a devoted praline fan.

She even helped me navigate the registry's electronic information network. Together we came upon twelve companies all owned by the same partners, all based in Berlin, and all founded within the last two years. Under the umbrella of "General Services," these partners had come to own, since the previous December, my hospital, CareClean Cleaning Services, Hospital Catering Services, and the hospital lab—all the departments that Bredow had outsourced at that time. Some had been established earlier: a German-Ukrainian trade association, the Eurotrans Trucking Company, and a few other businesses whose names I recalled from the cheap aluminum nameplates in the entrance to Allee der Kosmonauten 116.

Though they were a rather mixed conglomerate of companies, they had a common denominator: Boris Zhukov and Prof. Bernhard Dohmke were partners in all of them. I only recognized two of the other partners' names. One of them had only been added as a partner quite recently, and this name was an especially great disappointment to me. It showed me what an incredibly naïve and amateurish detective I was. I drove back to the hospital, frustrated and depressed.

Marlies had done solid work on my ward. The round was completed and the next twenty-four hours in my patients' lives were settled. The request forms for the next round of lab tests, X-rays, and tissue samples were filled out, and medication plans were up to date. The quality of a round can be measured by whether the nurses still have questions for the attending afterward—they had not a single one. By early afternoon I'd checked in my new arrivals and come up with a plan for them through the next morning.

There was nothing more to do. Nothing more to do? I was uneasy, a relic of my upbringing. There must have been a few medical reports that needed to be dictated. But surely, a voice said inside me, a doctor's duties go above and beyond the day-to-day routine. I crossed "dictate medical reports" off my to-do list and went out to chat informally with my patients. We talked about their families, their plans, and their hobbies, but also their hopes and fears. I felt better afterward but ashamed as well. I'd seen strength and courage in people who knew that neither I nor the entire world of medicine could do anything for them—and couldn't help but wonder whether my own problems outweighed theirs.

Marlies dropped by toward five to find out where I'd parked her car. Adding to her long list of good deeds for the day, she offered to drive me to my car on Sophie-Charlotte-Platz. It took her a little out of her way, but that was Marlies's style. On our way there, we got stuck in evening rush hour traffic.

"Where did you go in my car this morning?"

Marlies wasn't the curious type; she just wanted to make conversation to kill time while stuck in traffic. I muttered something unintelligible.

"You don't want to tell me, Casanova?"

"Trust me, Marlies, you don't want to know."

Marlies gave me a quick sideways glance, and then the congestion loosened up. She let me out at Sophie-Charlotte-Platz.

"Not to worry, old pal. If the cops ask me if you were at the hospital the whole time, no problemo."

She laughed, gave a quick wave, and disappeared into traffic. Celine would have riddled me with questions about where I'd been this morning. Not Marlies, though. She knew I'd tell her eventually.

In my excited state that morning, I hadn't noticed that I'd left the Rabbit in a two-hour parking zone. At least it hadn't been towed away; the police had confined themselves to sticking a fifteen-euro ticket behind the wiper. But they hadn't said a word about my missing inspection sticker. I was almost surprised to see that there were no new broken windows and no freshly dead rat on the seat. I got in and drove off.

Not. I intended to drive off. But when I started the car, I felt a powerful bang, and vibrations shook the entire car and me with it. Car bomb! I thought and jumped out of my car. Left to its own devices and the laws of physics, it rattled farther down the lane. Cars braked frantically and drivers honked their horns furiously all around me—but there was no explosion. My driverless Rabbit was stalled, undamaged, and blocking traffic in the middle of Windscheidstrasse. I waited another minute, more out of hope that the angry drivers would somehow disappear than out of fear that something might still explode. The gridlock had spread around me, and a few drivers had gotten out of their vehicles. I ventured out from hiding, muttering something about a defective emergency brake, a lousy repair job, and my abundant apologies. The crowd abstained from stoning me to death on the spot, and two men even helped me push the car back into my parking space.

"You're not going to get very far in that thing anyhow."

This wasn't the first time someone had said this when they saw my Rabbit. But this time they were referring to the reason for the rattling and shaking that had caused my panic. All four tires had been slashed, and I'd been driving over the old cobblestone pavement on the rims. I thanked my helpers, got into my useless car, and refused to accept my fate. A vandalized apartment, a dead rat, slashed tires—what was with all these antics? It wasn't that I was yearning for an actual attack, but these irritations were more like schoolboy pranks than any kind of real menace. And now, pray tell, how was I supposed to get home?

I was disinclined to embark on negotiations with the gas station across the street. Especially since gas stations these days mainly exist to provide fresh rolls, French wine, and the kinds of magazines you'd prefer not to buy at the corner newsstand. I changed my spots, un-leopard-like, and hailed a cab, which was almost more painful to me than the slashed tires. As far as I was concerned, taxis, with their mercilessly running meters, were the height of extravagance. But I was less keen on an hour-long slog on foot.

In the cab I considered whether this recent spate of pranks maybe wasn't so silly if you were savvy about Russian mafia practices. I mulled over the slashed tires. Hadn't Dohmke handed down my capitulation to his foot soldiers yet? Were they just trying to remind me to stick to my resolution? Or had they really followed me this morning but lost me in the subway and slit my tires out of anger at my cleverness? I watched the meter go on ticking at the red light, unfazed by my irritation, and wondered how I could pass the cost of this cab ride on to Dohmke. I decided to put it down as overtime. I felt better at once—until I remembered that overtime wasn't remunerated anymore.

The taxi unloaded me, unharmed, at my front door. I'd begun taking a quick glance to the right and left over the last few weeks but didn't see anything that looked suspicious. There were no passersby standing around unobtrusively, and no gang of innocent-looking young men. I felt relatively safe as I entered the lobby. But only for a moment. I distinctly heard soft breathing near my apartment door. For the umpteenth time, I cursed my laziness. Why hadn't I gotten my hands on some brass knuckles or a can of mace or, better yet, one of those 20,000-volt zappers?

I carefully peeked around the corner. It was a woman, and she didn't display the least sign of aggression. She turned a bloated face toward me, looking at me as though she'd been waiting for several hours and I was supposed to recognize her.

"Felix. At last! I've been sitting here since lunchtime."

Although her face looked vaguely familiar, I finally recognized her from her voice. It was Astrid Schreiber, the wife of the colleague who'd dragged Misha in dead and supplied him with a second death certificate. And who had then immediately disappeared to the States. I could hardly believe that this was the Astrid I'd visited recently. I had to wonder whether she was expecting triplets. Or perhaps she was suffering from preeclampsia, an abnormal retention of water that can occur during pregnancy.

"I hope you won't get into trouble with your neighbors on my account. Or are they used to having young women sitting in front of your door for hours on end?"

"They're getting used to it. Come on in."

Astrid got up with the effort of a superannuated plow horse. Her misshapen figure was draped in a colorful potato sack that might have looked quite stylish when it was featured in the fashion catalog for expecting mothers. She was wearing some kind of flip-flops, and her feet bulged noticeably over the sides. She followed me into the kitchen and plopped herself down on the stool. For a moment, I was more afraid she'd suddenly go into labor at my place than I was of Dohmke, Boris, and the entire Russian mafia. I knew nothing about obstetrics, not even back when I took my exams.

"I thought you'd left to join your husband in New York ages ago."

"Klaus still hasn't found a place for us to live."

She stood up with much more zest than before and inspected my food supply.

"Are you looking for sour pickles?"

"Hogwash. That's something women crave the first month, if ever. Now we just need calories. Have you got something sweet?"

Though I generally didn't, Celine had recently purchased some cookies with a disgustingly sweet chocolate filling. Astrid had already sniffed out the package.

"He's still living in the nurses' dorm. Everything's been held up so long though that I'm worried about getting my baby over the Atlantic."

"If that's the case, you should pay attention to the nationality of the airline. If you fly Emirates, your baby will have free medical insurance for life. And a good pension."

"And we'd suddenly have an Arab in the family. No, that would be too complicated for my liking."

"You'd all have to give up pork."

At that moment, Astrid didn't seem ready to give up any kind of calories—and I didn't want to give up entirely on the prospect of a quiet evening at home.

"Astrid, don't misunderstand me, but why are you here?"

By this time, she'd polished off the chocolate cookies.

"Margret came to see me a few days ago."

Astrid was a hematologist, and Dohmke had offered her a half-time job in the blood bank after her first child was born. So Margret and Astrid had worked together for a while until her next maternity leave.

"And?"

"We talked about you; how you've got tangled up in this dead Russian business and are bugging everybody with questions."

"Why should you care? He was a patient of mine. I'd like to know whether I was responsible for his death."

"That's obviously not the case. You know that. I'm worried about my husband's career. I've heard there's some sort of problem with that patient's death certificate."

"It's a problem because your husband made out two certificates. More specifically, we filled out the first one together and then he wrote up a new one later. 'Cause of death undetermined' was changed to 'death by cardiopulmonary arrest.' I wanted to know why he changed it."

"Maybe somebody asked him to."

"And who would ask him to?"

"There you go with your questions again. I'm worried you'll broadcast this business far and wide and that it will make things difficult for us."

I suddenly got the sense that Astrid's visit really wasn't about her husband.

"Say, Astrid, when you were working at the blood bank, you signed off on the test protocols for the blood bags, didn't you?"

Astrid's look betrayed not the slightest trace of indecision. She still had the look of a pregnant woman whose only concern was the unborn life in her belly. And maybe whether there was a sufficient supply of chocolate cookies within reach.

"I know what you're getting at, Felix. Margret told me about the two tally sheets. So OK, the hospital has a little sideline in imported blood. Wake up, Felix. It's a new era. Treating patients has become a cost-intensive business. Hospitals have always been business enterprises, and with the new laws they're actually required to function that way."

"With illegal dealings?"

"There's nothing illegal about importing blood supplies."

"What about labeling Russian blood bags as German ones?"

"It's only the labels, not rusty old pacemakers or expired drugs. Good God! Do you want to put the whole hospital and all the people who work there in danger with your crusade?"

Now I was absolutely certain that Astrid hadn't come to protect her husband's career. She was in with Dohmke and his friends and would stay in his good graces as long as Schreiber toed the line. I finally realized she'd been sent by Dohmke. Fine, then. I could gladly tell her what I wanted Dohmke to hear.

"I'm not on any crusade, Astrid. And I won't put the hospital in any danger—not my colleagues, not its patients. I've learned that the cause of death on the second certificate was indeed cardiopulmonary arrest. It was fulminant hepatitis C. And it had nothing to do with the blood transfusion he got with us. No more questions, no loose ends. Case closed as far as I'm concerned. I'm a physician—that's a full-time job as you know. I have enough to do as it is. Is that quite clear?"

We moved on to small talk about her pregnancy and home birthing versus a hospital delivery. As we chatted, I came up with a small test for good little Astrid.

"Tell me, when Klaus comes back from the States—I've been thinking it's about time he had his own ward."

Astrid was already on her way to the door.

"He liked working with Marlies, but yes, I think he'd like to have his own ward."

"As you know, I do the scheduling. Maybe he could take over the private ward when he gets back."

"First let Klaus do his year in New York. And let me get through this pregnancy and get over there. I can't think beyond that that right now."

Astrid squeezed by me, waddled to the open door, and vanished into the summer evening. She hadn't swallowed my crafty bait. So what. The main thing was for her to deliver the right message to Dohmke. Otherwise I had one more channel to Dohmke left, as I'd just learned from the Business Registry. But that could wait until tomorrow.

I pulled a California chardonnay from the fridge and spread myself out on the couch with the remote. Two women had messed up my TV plans the night before, and I felt entitled to my one lazy night in front of the tube each week—to be interpreted loosely during special events like the European Championship.

It was Friday evening, and what must have been the fiftieth rerun of *Dirty Dancing* was on one of the cheaper channels. Just what the doctor ordered. It promised to be a cozy evening—until the phone rang.

CHAPTER 20

There are people who can let the phone ring and ring, but I'm not one of them. I also can't throw out old bread or the flyers that show up in my mailbox. I don't ever read them but pile them up neatly and then toss them all in the recycling bin after a decent interval. Celine was on the phone, saying it was a beautiful summer evening and she was feeling a bit animalistic. She wanted to come right over. Celine wasn't dissuaded by my lack of enthusiasm and arrived at my door a few minutes later.

"I thought I'd better call first. Not that I'd be disturbing you…"

"You're in luck: I can work you in on short notice."

Celine's animalism wasn't unpleasant, though I did occasionally wonder what was so animallike about it. I'd only rarely heard of sex orgies among elephants or a sophisticated rhinoceros *Kama Sutra*. I spared Celine my philosophizing and happily succumbed to her hearty appetite.

The next day was Saturday. I woke up refreshed and relaxed for the first time in a long while. Sex seemed to have worked as a buffer against stress—just like with pygmy chimps. The hospital had no claim on me today and it was raining. We opted for breakfast in bed. I scraped together what I could from my kitchen reserves. Not quite fresh toast had to stand in for fresh rolls—which was really a shame because my favorite clerk worked in the bakery on Saturdays. My bed soon devolved into a sea of crumbs. Celine suffered another animal fit, and the crumbs provided an additional erogenous stimulus.

"Have you got anything sweet?"

I wondered why she hadn't asked me that the night before. Sex often seemed to result in an acute drop in Celine's blood sugar—which wasn't particularly surprising given her high degree of physical engagement.

"I don't think so. There may be some honey left."

"What about those disgusting chocolate cookies?"

"All gone."

"What!" Celine propped her head up on her hand and put on her most inquisitorial face. "Don't tell me *you* finished them off. I'll never believe that."

"It was an emergency, Celine. The woman was pregnant."

"Pregnant? Have you gotten perverse as well?"

I told Celine about Astrid's visit and how I thought Dohmke had sent her. Celine, well-known fan of conspiracy theories that she was, suddenly was all fired up.

"I've always wondered how two young doctors with a kid could afford such a chic apartment," she said. "Do you remember the flophouse where their wedding was?"

"They say Schreiber's parents are wealthy. And I don't think Astrid grew up in the poorhouse."

Celine had a point, though. Anything seemed possible after my recent trip to the Business Registry. Was I the last person in the whole hospital who didn't know about the real financial structure of the place—and the only one not profiting from it? Dr. Hoffmann, the naïve schmuck from Ward IIIb.

"So—where do we go from here, Felix?"

"I need to make sure that Dohmke really believes I've stopped investigating. Let's see how things go after that."

"Don't you think you ought to make up your mind?"

"About what?"

"We know that your hospital is in the hands of a criminal gang and that you're working in a laundry operation for the Russian mafia. We know that at least one of your bosses is involved in this business, and possibly more of your colleagues, too. You've got to decide whether you're going to go on working there and let these guys keep doing what they're doing, or whether you're going to try to do something about these crooks. Don't you think?"

"Don't you think we need more evidence?"

"How much more evidence do you need, Felix? We can document that huge sums of money are being laundered through nonexistent patients. Margret and Astrid have confirmed for you how the Russian blood business works. And we know from the Business Registry who's involved in this gang. What more do you want? A confession from Herr Dohmke in writing?"

"I foresee a couple of problems."

Celine's voice took on a slightly strained timbre.

"*You're* the problem, Felix. You'd rather have your ears cut off than make a decision about anything. You can't even choose between Pepsi and Coke. And, while we're at it, that goes for our relationship as well."

The day had started so beautifully—and suddenly I was saddled with a relationship discussion. As far as I was concerned, the sage advice of your garden variety psychologist—that you must talk about everything in a relationship—is only true if you want to end the relationship. I opted for the Kennedy-Khrushchev tactic during the Cuban missile crisis: if there are several issues on the table, pick the least dangerous one—and thereby prevent World War Three. So I ignored the remark about our relationship and focused instead on the first question.

"You're right. We have to do something about these guys. But give me a chance to talk to Margret one more time."

It was a win-win. I'd told Celine she was right but still managed to avoid making a decision and succeeded in sidestepping a discussion about our relationship to boot. That's the way to prevent wars. Celine had realized, naturally, that I was trying to get out of making a decision right now but didn't press me further. She'd made up her mind a long time ago that we wouldn't call off this hospital business.

"Beate's coming over this afternoon. She's been hard at work on the data and we're about to put the last pieces of the puzzle together."

"Sounds good. But it's almost afternoon."

Celine hurriedly packed up and left. I knew a headache would be coming on soon. Always got them when I didn't get up right away in the morning. One of our weekend rituals was cooking together on Sunday night, and it was my turn to get the ingredients. I knew I'd better get going if I didn't want to assemble our Sunday menu from the tantalizing selection at the nearest gas station.

After doing the shopping, I caught up on my postponed TV night that afternoon and surfed American soaps until evening. After the evening news, it was time for me to go pay Margret another visit.

Celine had loaned me her car; our morning in bed had meant that I hadn't solved my tire problem. The rain had stopped by then, but the asphalt still shone on the damp streets and the first autumnal leaves lay under the trees. It looked as though the summer was getting ready to wrap up. How could Margret have ditched a terrific guy like me? Celine was right: I was probably still in love with Margret in my own narcissistic way. Or at least desired her. What did I know? Either way, the prospect of our imminent conversation didn't fill me with joy.

When I'd taken this route in the opposite direction the other night, the streets had been filled with the nightlife of summer and it felt as though a whiff of Paris or Rome had washed over the city. Now, though, the tables and chairs in the sidewalk cafés stood empty, glistening with rain, and Berlin mimicked my mood—it was once again a gray city, more Eastern European than Western.

I'd phoned Margret to tell her I was coming and hung up at once. I hadn't given her the chance to protest, but had left her enough time to leave or get some backup. However, she opened the door when I rang and let me in, and I made it into her living room without a bonk on the old bean. She offered me an armchair but nothing to drink.

"To what do I owe the pleasure, Felix?"

She didn't pretend to be pleased.

"I'm here because I've had it with being the last idiot in town. I'm blindfolded and you guys are playing blind man's buff with me."

"Would you rather play red rover? Or musical chairs? Excuse me for a minute."

Margret's absence gave me an opportunity to quickly inspect the kitchen and bedroom for other visitors. No trace of Russian or Ukrainian auxiliaries. Margret returned.

"So now you don't want to play blind man's buff anymore?"

"Right. Not that, not red rover, not musical chairs. I want to do my work as a physician in peace. I want to come home to an apartment and not find it broken into and turned upside down. I don't want to find rats in my car or slashed tires. I don't want to peek under my bed to see if somebody's there with a blackjack. I'd like you to tell that to your friends. That they don't have anything to fear from me. That my private investigating is over."

The way Margret looked at me it was almost as though she were disappointed.

"Why do you think they're my friends?"

"Because I was at the Business Registry, Margret. And because it says there that you've been a registered partner in their companies since the day of Bredow's funeral."

Tears welled up in Margret's eyes. She dug a tissue out from under a couch cushion.

"What are you after, Felix? Do you want me to always end up with the short end of the stick? Stuck with men like you who are already plotting their exit on our first night together? You maybe think you're something special, but most men either suffer from attachment anxiety or are looking for a new mother to look after them. Knut was different. He loved me and I loved him—it was that simple. We were going to get married but suddenly he's dead, a woman he hasn't slept with for years and wanted to divorce is his one and only heir, and I'm standing at the funeral in the last row. Do you think that's fair?"

Had I really been thinking that first night with Margret about how to get out of it? We'd managed to stay together for almost a year.

"So you went to Dohmke and demanded your fair share of the inheritance?"

"No, I didn't, my dear. Believe it or not he came to me. Just two days after Knut died. And he offered me, as an heir, Knut's shares in the company."

"And a Rabbit convertible as a bonus."

Margret wiped the tears from her eyes.

"What's so terrible about that? He thought I deserved those shares. And I think he's right. Who else cared a fig for me after Knut died?"

I did not remind my old girlfriend that I'd driven her home after the funeral and done what I could to comfort her. It was true, however, that I hadn't presented her with company shares or a car. I was still unclear about a technical detail: How had they been able to cut Bredow's widow out of inheriting the shares?

"Simple," Margret replied. "According to the partners' contract, company shares are not to be passed on but revert to the partnership."

So if a partner died, the company's structure didn't have to be made public—a sly move. That meant that with *these* partners, every one of them had better have somebody taste their food first.

"How convenient for you."

"Get off your high horse, Felix. Do you really think this pretty little apartment I own is paid for? Knut made the down payment and helped out with the monthly installments too. But now? Where was I supposed to get the money to keep those up? From my fabulous lab tech's salary? Or would I be better off being a prostitute? What do *you* think? Would I stand a chance?"

"Certainly, my dear. Of course you'd stand a chance, but the way I see it, you don't have to start walking the streets. Or is Herr Prof. Dohmke not satisfied with you?"

Margret made a move as though she wanted to hit me. I didn't duck, but she stopped midswing and hid her face in her hands.

"Margret, I don't give a damn if you're having it on with Dohmke or your old buddy Boris. Or both. Or whether you really gave the car back to Dohmke or not. I'm not here to argue with you or threaten you. I just want you to assure Dohmke that I pose no threat to him or his enterprises. I think he'll believe you. Tell him I'm giving up. And if he asks why he's supposed to believe that, tell him it's because I've got no desire to wind up like your boyfriend Bredow one day, swinging from my belt with my hands in my pockets."

It took a while for me to notice that Margret was staring at me.

"You were there? You saw him!"

I realized too late that my speech had been a little too precise. Especially the part about his hands in his pockets. I could have protested that I'd gotten my information from Frau Krüger, since she had officially been the one to discover Bredow's body, but that didn't occur to me in the moment. So I admitted that I'd seen Bredow and told Margret about that night in his office. I left Celine out of it.

"I couldn't do anything for him, Margret. He'd been dead for hours."

Margret began to cry uncontrollably. It was some time before she could talk, and even then I had a hard time understanding her.

"Of course you could have done something for him. You could, for instance, have not just left him hanging there. That would at least have spared him those unspeakable resuscitation attempts by Dr. Vogel."

It was no use explaining to Margret why I didn't do anything of the kind. She'd understand that herself when she could think about it calmly. How was I to explain my nocturnal presence in Bredow's office? How could I prove I had nothing to do with Bredow's death? It's not laziness on the part of the police when they arrest the very first person at the scene of the crime as the perp: he usually is.

I left Margret with the same uncomfortable feeling I'd arrived with. I hoped she'd keep Dohmke and his gang of thugs off me.

"Will I see you on Monday at the hospital?"

"I don't think so," Margret answered offhandedly, her thoughts clearly elsewhere. As I returned home, it started to rain again.

Sunday morning greeted me with the headache I'd been expecting the day before. I felt empty and let down. It promised to be the kind of Sunday I'd worked toward all week, but which would turn out to be a big black hole. When I was a kid, I'd been able to pull the blankets over my head on days like this, expecting to find a friendlier world after I'd woken up.

I wasn't in the mood for anything. Not even for Sunday breakfast with Celine, who was keen to regale me with the latest results of her research with Beate. I knew that would only depress me further. I knew that I should drop off some fresh rolls at least.

A polished, gleaming sky outside predicted a beautiful summer day ahead, and my favorite salesgirl was in the bakery. But even that couldn't cheer me up. I brought Celine two rolls and her car keys.

"You've got another date for breakfast?"

"Don't."

I showed her the last two rolls in my bag.

"Maybe she's a muesli fan?"

"Actually, she always wants a rare steak with pommes frites in the morning, because I wear her out so much at night."

It was the sort of day when my only success was derived from infecting other people with my lousy mood, but that didn't make me feel any better. So I chose a more strenuous approach by taking my bicycle out of the basement and heading out for a ride.

I had the whole city to myself; I biked down Berlin's biggest arteries with no hands and no danger to life and limb. All of Berlin had defected to the Baltic, the Havel River, or the Müggelsee, fulfilling a collective desire to eat out at wildly overpriced restaurants and get bashed on the head by Frisbees on overcrowded beaches.

In the Tiergarten, Berlin's Central Park, I could smell the barbecues of the East European immigrants, and then I passed under the Brandenburg Gate, still no hands. By the time I'd reached Unter den Linden, at the Kronprinzenpalais, I'd pedaled my bad mood and headache out of my system. Scaffoldings were everywhere: reunified Berlin was well on its way to becoming a metropolis once again, and perhaps mafia dealings were an inevitable part of its upgrade.

It had become evident to me that the cause of my depression that day was my disillusionment with Margret. It was possible, though, that she'd been forced against her will to become a partner in Dohmke and Co. so that they could put the squeeze on her more tightly. Did she really have any choice? It wasn't obvious who she should fear more: the courts and the prosecuting attorneys or the Russian mafia's revenge. Hardly an enviable choice.

By the time I reached Museum Island, body and mind were in agreement that I'd sweated enough for a hot summer's day; both pleaded for a return home via the Stadtbahn. I still made it to Celine's that evening for our traditional Sunday evening cook-in. I'd settled on duck breast in orange sauce with sugar snap peas; the purchase of the peas and the organic orange had taken quite a bit of time on Saturday. Cooking finally and completely relaxed me. We finished off our meal with a strong espresso from Celine's Italian machine, at which point I was finally ready for her report on Bredow's accounts.

Celine and Beate had done a bang-up job. The printouts displaying Bredow's attempts to grow the hospital coffers were clearly marked in yellow. The private patients' bills from two Novembers ago were in blue, while those from last November were in green. The payments to outside companies like CareClean and Hospital Catering Services were in orange. Blood supply transactions were in red. A visibly pleased Celine sat enthroned above this organized confusion.

"I don't think there are any more loose ends. Whatever else he may have been, your Dr. Bredow was a tidy bookkeeper."

Right on. And the hospital's new owners hadn't wasted any time. By December, the hospital's expenses had risen by almost 200,000 euros—which was completely covered by income from alleged private patients. By now, almost 500,000 per month were being laundered through the hospital—the entry-level price had rapidly amortized.

The blood supply business was less significant but still brought in 100,000 a month. Few of these blood bags were used in the hospital itself; the majority went to the processing industry at a marked-down price, about a third off. These revenues were listed under "Services: Hematological Laboratory for Outside Companies," and here was an interesting detail: the documents included a list of the managers in those companies and their bank account numbers, which were primarily linked to banks in Switzerland and the Caribbean. These managers might not have known that they were working with the mafia, but they must have known that they were dealing in imported blood. No mafia in the world could subsist on underworld contacts and drug addicts alone. The whole racket also depended upon the greed of purportedly serious businessmen.

Celine packed up the neatly sorted printouts.

"I think it's all here. We've summarized the most important data chronologically on the top sheet for an overview."

As I trotted on home, the pounding in my head started up again. I knew what Celine wanted now—a decision. She'd helped me more than enough by getting the data and interpreting it, but now her part in all this was done. It was my hospital, my dead COO, my responsibility.

It goes without saying that I couldn't sleep that night. I went around and around in circles, at times wondering what any of this had to do with me so long as the hospital continued to run, and at others wrestling my conscience over whether connivance also meant co-responsibility. I grew furious when I recalled that recent meeting. What was all that cost-cutting supposed to mean in a hospital whose main function was to be a well-oiled money-laundering machine? Were Bredow and Dohmke really so greedy that they wanted a share of our eliminated overtime?

At three a.m. I made some herbal tea and went through the numbers in the documents once again. I just wanted a distraction; after all, a mathematician and a tax adviser had labored over this. I could hardly believe what I discovered: they'd calculated correctly but—probably in their enthusiasm over how nicely it all fit together—they hadn't compared the numbers for this past June in both files. I worked it out back and forth, at first thinking that I was mistaken, but I wasn't: the hospital budget was neatly balanced from last December on; larger and larger payments to the service companies stood alongside greater and greater revenues from private patients. But suddenly, right before Bredow's death there was a giant, yawning gap in the balance sheet—3 million euros missing again. I almost called Celine in the middle of the night—I'd finally found a motive for Bredow's suicide. Had the money laundry collapsed? Or had our theory?

The discovery had one good side, however: I was able to put off making a final decision about what I'd do with everything I knew.

I felt safe enough on Monday to drive my car. I'd handed Misha's file over to Dohmke, and Astrid and Margret should have informed him by now that I was harmless. I got up early to take the subway to Sophie-Charlotte-Platz. Nobody had bothered to steal my Rabbit; not even the bumpers or headlights had been dismantled. The week seemed to have begun under a lucky star. I went across to the gas station filled with optimism. My luck held: an attendant agreed to take a look at the problem.

"Do you really want to have work done on this car?"

I was getting sick and tired of that question.

"How long will it take to get new tires?"

"You're in luck; I've got tires right here that will fit. I can get them on by noon today. They're ninety euros each. Plus balancing and installation. And sales tax."

A moment before, he'd wanted to scrap my car; now he wanted to sell me new tires for 500 euros.

"Can't you just put in new inner tubes?"

"If that's what you want…" He scratched his ears with oil-smeared fingers. "I'd have to order the tubes first, though; it might take a few days."

I remained unfazed by his extortion attempt and refrained from muttering anything about his "mafia-like methods"—possibly because I was a bit overly sensitive about that at that moment. A few more days on public transportation wouldn't kill me.

"OK, boss, do it," I said. "Order the inner tubes."

"What about the windows?"

The plastic would do for now. I'd wait and see whether the car lasted until fall.

Everything went smoothly at the hospital. I even had a chance to pay down my debt to Marlies a little. She had to leave punctually for a part-time job in private practice once a week, so I promised to wait for her patients' lab results that afternoon and do whatever needed to be done. I wandered over to the blood bank twice on flimsy pretexts, but Margret had stayed home.

By the time I made it to the cafeteria for a late lunch, it was empty except for a few people from Central Sterilization, and the prepared meals had shrunk to dried bits under the warming lamps. I wasn't the only one late for lunch. I had just finished working the dried sauce off my schnitzel when Prof. Dohmke appeared. Since I was the only physician in the room, it wound have looked odd if he hadn't sat down with me. He'd selected a once-fresh salad.

"Herr Hoffmann, *guten Appetit*. You've got no vitamins at all there. Be sure to get your vitamins. You're eating late. Busy morning?"

"Busy enough, Herr Dohmke. I'd be worried if we didn't have enough to do."

"You're right about that, Hoffmann. I think we'll all sleep better when the Berlin government finally decides which hospitals must cut beds and which will be shut down completely."

Overburdened by my detective efforts, I had scarcely been able to keep up with the latest rumors, despite the fact that the papers were full of them. Some claimed that religiously affiliated hospitals were going to be closed, then they disappeared entirely from the chop list. Nurses and orderlies were on strike somewhere. Strangely, we hadn't been on any chopping-block list.

Dohmke made small talk for a while, but it eventually ran dry and I had to contribute something to the conversation. I could think of nothing benign to say.

"Has anybody come up with the cause of the CareClean fire yet?"

Dohmke was busy fishing out a few tomatoes from his salad.

"Nothing concrete as far as I know. The fire department suspects it's electrical, a defect in the wiring or something like that. It doesn't take much of an overload for a computer to catch fire."

I remarked that it was certainly an unfortunate coincidence that a virus wiped out all the data on his office computer on the same day that the fire at CareClean killed all the computers.

"Yes, Hoffmann, you can say that again. 'When it rains, it pours,'" he quoted. "No fun for Frau Krüger, that's for sure. Fortunately Dr. Bredow only kept a few minor accounts on his computer."

I'd have loved to have told him that I could help him out with a complete copy of those so-called minor accounts. But he had already moved on, as optimistic as ever.

"You know, you've always got to look on the bright side. A loss of data like that is also an opportunity to do things a different way. Dr. Bredow was right of course: we have to economize, and the insurance guys will soon be asking us to account for every single hour we're idle. The only question is where exactly I should cut costs. Maybe it wasn't such a good idea to keep squeezing colleagues' salaries and cutting benefits and overtime pay. That surely must de-incentivize staff, don't you think?"

Of course I agreed, but Dohmke didn't give me any time to answer.

"Why should a doctor whose salary I'm constantly cutting care about the medication budget for his ward? And I'm telling you, Hoffmann, that's where there's still huge cost-cutting potential, even more than in salaries."

Now he was picking the hard-boiled eggs out of his salad and pushing them to the edge of his plate next to the mashed tomatoes. He'd probably exceeded his cholesterol quota for the day.

"Not at the expense of patient care of course, but you know how your colleagues think. Just a touch of fever and out comes the antibiotic. And it must be the latest one, which costs ten or even a hundred times more than a time-tested brand that would work just as well. All that when a throat compress would probably have been just fine. I think it's all about motivation. These cost cuts could be passed on to you physicians. Bredow was too much of an administrator. He never understood that you've got to pay good people a good salary. Especially people who are committed one hundred percent. Rest assured, Hoffmann, there are some changes ahead. Those who deserve it will do well. Very well."

His beeper went off. Dohmke went to the nearest phone, put on an important-looking face, and disappeared. I cleared away his half-full salad plate.

What he'd just said was basically reasonable. The hospital probably could save a pile of money without any disadvantages to the patients. But I'd also figured out that it was smarter for me to stop playing detective and knew that my discretion would be rewarded.

My day at the hospital ended with a pleasant surprise. The garage called to say I could pick up my car, since the business with the tubes had gone more quickly than expected. When I got home, I looked around my apartment. I had to admit that Dohmke was right—a little salary enhancement would do my place some good.

CHAPTER 21

I was just trying to figure out which home improvements I might do first when the phone rang. Margret was on the line.

"Something awful has happened. Can…you please come… right away?"

I recognized Margret's voice, but it sounded strange. It had an almost physical urgency to it mixed with an unsettling undertone of resignation. I drove over at once.

Margret opened the door. She was wearing the sort of thing one has on when one's home alone in the evening and not expecting company. Though her hair wasn't a disaster, it clearly hadn't been done lately. Her eyes, however, were bigger than usual; it was almost as though she were wearing strong glasses.

"Thank you, Felix. Come in."

I followed her into the living room, where I saw that she had a visitor. Sitting on her couch was our mutual friend, Prof. Dohmke, who at noon only that day had dangled before me the prospect of a salary raise. He didn't stand up to greet me; in fact, he didn't take any notice of me at all. His upper body was leaning forward slightly, and he seemed to be studying his shoes. It took a moment for me to spot the two small holes, encircled by an almost unobtrusive rim of blood, that pierced the pattern of his shirt.

"Don't bother, Felix. He's dead."

I felt for his carotid artery and looked at his eyes. She was right. Even our efficient Dr. Vogel wouldn't have tried resuscitating him.

"An accident?"

"No, not an accident. I shot the bastard."

Margret didn't look much better than Dohmke, and her voice lacked any modulation. Since nothing could be done for Dohmke, I went to the kitchen in search of some peppermint tea. Works for any problem, my mother used to say.

What was I supposed to say? Margret was right, of course: Dohmke was a bastard. And we clearly wouldn't have an over-population problem if shooting all the bastards were permitted, but who would guarantee me that I wouldn't be a target myself?

I was perplexed. I wondered whether I should call the police or a lawyer first—my friend Burghard for instance? Or had Margret gotten me over here so that I'd help her get rid of the body? Meanwhile the water started to boil. I'd found some peppermint tea bags and poured enough for the two of us.

Margret was sitting in an armchair across from Dohmke and staring at the ceiling.

"Really, Felix, he deserved it. He killed my lover."

"Watch out, it's hot." I handed her the cup and sat down next to her. "I don't think Dohmke drove Bredow to commit suicide. Bredow had painted himself neatly into a corner, quite apart from your Ukrainian blood bags. You must have known he was gambling illegally with hospital funds and had piled up a lot of debt and that he ultimately sold the hospital to the Russian mafia as a money-laundering operation. That was maybe a few more balls than he could keep in the air at once."

Margret sipped absentmindedly at her peppermint tea; I might just as well have put used motor oil in her cup.

"You found out everything, didn't you?"

"I don't know. But I know it wasn't only about blood bags."

Margret studied the ceiling some more.

"Dohmke underestimated you."

"Did he? He offered me a hefty raise in a sort of roundabout way."

"Those are their tactics. First money, then threats. Then more and more new things they want you to cooperate with. It was the same thing with Knut."

We sat there for a moment in silence. *Still Life with Dead Man.* I winced when Margret spoke again.

"I didn't say that he drove Knut to his death. He killed him. Either he did or Boris did or their guys did. Any which way, it was murder."

I understood that she somehow had to justify what she'd done, even if it was just to herself.

"How do you know?"

"You told me yourself."

I didn't know what she meant.

"Don't you remember? You told me how you discovered him that night. I'll never forget your words. You told me what I was supposed to pass on to Dohmke: 'And if he asks why he's supposed to believe that, tell him it's because I've got no desire to wind up like your boyfriend Bredow one day, swinging from my belt with my hands in my pockets.' That's exactly what you said."

I guess it was.

"Don't you think it's strange that somebody would have his hands in his pockets when he hangs himself?"

It had seemed odd to me, it was true. I remembered thinking about whether to take his hands out of his pockets.

"That's the way the Russian mafia kill people who've embez-zled their money."

"By putting their hands in their pockets?"

"Yes. Boris explained it to me back when we were together. It's like the Boy Scouts or the Ku Klux Klan. Men always need a secret language. If the mafia wants to threaten somebody, they put a dead rat in front of his door or in his car. If they kill an informer, they cut off his member and stuff it in his mouth. If one of their people helps himself to their cash box, they cut off his hands; unless it's supposed to look like suicide, in which case they put their victim's hands in his pockets."

I must have been looking at her in disbelief.

"Don't worry, Felix. There's no mistake about it. Dohmke confirmed it for me himself a little while ago."

She kept on talking. Dohmke had shown up this evening to bring her to her senses, as he put it. She wasn't to get any stupid ideas, he said. Or else they'd do to her exactly what they did to Bredow.

"Why would they have wanted to kill Bredow?"

"Because he wanted out. He'd had enough. He was happy at the beginning, naturally, when they got him out of a bind with those warrants. After that, he didn't really have a choice but to go along with them. But suddenly he was only the accountant for their ingenious money-laundering scheme. He got scared when he noticed two weeks ago that somebody had gotten into his computer." Margret took another sip of her tea and stared into her cup. "We wanted to go away, far away. He transferred a small annuity to Switzerland for us, and it cost him his life."

Although I was beginning to feel sorry for Bredow, I was relieved. The last hole in Bredow's accounts was explained. The 3 million euros had gone off to Switzerland! Not a bad retirement annuity.

"How did they find out?"

I thought I saw a flicker of a smile cross Margret's frozen face. "They didn't find out anything. Knut did it very cleverly. And they probably wouldn't have found out about it until long after we'd disappeared. It was simply bad luck. As I said, Knut had invested most of the money in Zurich. But he'd also transferred a few hundred thousand euros to the Cayman Islands as start-up capital so to speak. That's where we wanted to go initially. But the Cayman Islands bank belongs to the Russian mafia—some of Boris's distant friends. Isn't that crazy? They were curious to know where the transfer had come from. Nobody expects them to do such a thing, but it's something mafia banks always do. They know that transfers often involve illegal funds and check to see whether there might be a little extortion in it for them. They were able to trace the transfer back to the hospital despite Knut's precautions, and they let Boris know. That was it."

Poor Margret. Instead of enjoying the Caribbean sunset with her lover and chatting about the best way to invest 3 million in Zurich over tropical cocktails, she was sitting with me and a bullet-riddled Dohmke in the living room of a home that wasn't paid off, not by a long shot.

"The last time Dohmke, Boris, and his gorillas showed up here, they didn't only pump me about you but also wanted to beat the Zurich account number out of me. It was pointless though—I know the bank but not the access code."

We were silent again until Margret asked, "You know the worst thing about it? It's all my fault."

"What are you talking about?"

"It's true. I was the one who first let Boris and his blood into the hospital."

"Your summertime shortage of blood bags. You told me yourself."

"But that happens almost every summer. Knut first learned how much cheaper those foreign supplies are through me. It's like I personally handed the hospital keys over to those people."

I didn't see it that way. It wasn't until Bredow went broke that the hospital suddenly opened as wide as a barn door. Margret had hardly been listening; she wanted to get the rest of the story off her chest. Dohmke had told her everything, evidently to brag about the extent of his power and expertise. It turns out that my flippant report on Misha at that beds meeting had actually scared him into thinking that the blood business might be discovered. He'd taken care of the new death certificate by applying some gentle pressure on Schreiber plus a ticket to the US and was thereby able to block the autopsy.

It really got serious when Bredow noticed that his computer had been hacked and pointed the finger at Dohmke, who immediately sized up the danger. When I started asking about Misha's file and he found out about my visits to the Hostel Elvira and CareClean, he knew who he was dealing with. But even with the break-in at my place and his spies Margret and Astrid, he couldn't be absolutely certain how much I knew or what evidence I had. So he tried to keep me busy following the blood trail to prevent me from discovering the infinitely more important money-laundering scheme. He assumed that I wouldn't make a big fuss about the blood business because of Margret. Of course Dohmke had also been responsible for the 100 ml. of potassium, which he'd intended as a warning and to put me under pressure and discredit me as a doctor. To be on the safe side, they'd eliminated all records by means of the virus in Bredow's computer and the arson on Allee der Kosmonauten. Dohmke's preemptive measures would probably have worked—if he hadn't been up against Celine.

And now Dohmke was dead, a victim of his own network of deception and extortion. And ultimately murder. Celine had once again been proven right: there were only two motives—money and love.

"Where'd you get the pistol from?"

"From Boris—I told you. After Knut's funeral."

Right. She *had* told me. She was supposed to shoot Boris dead if he ever hit her again. What would he say now that the gun had plugged his partner instead?

"Where do we go from here, Margret? How can I help you?"

Margret was staring at Dohmke's corpse. She spoke so softly I could hardly understand her.

"Don't worry about me, Felix. I'm at peace with myself. I know what I've done and it was the right thing to do. I just wanted to tell you the whole story." She got up. "Excuse me, I feel sick."

She disappeared into the bathroom. I was thinking about making her another peppermint tea when I realized what a goddamn idiot I was. I rushed to the bathroom—too late. Right then a shot rang out.

I thought it wouldn't take the police very long to get there. But I still had enough time to realize that I was a more of a knucklehead than I even secretly admitted to myself. You don't have to be a doctor to imagine how mentally unstable a person must be just after killing someone. There ought to be a law against being that stupid. The first thing I should have done was take the pistol from her. Even my rookie pal Harald wouldn't have let Margret simply walk off to the bathroom alone in that state of mind. I was still in shock when the police arrived.

Two ordinary patrolmen had come, fortunately not my friends from the break-in. They were calm and collected and very professional. After looking at Dohmke, they went in to see Margret. She'd evidently heard that the surest way to kill yourself was to hold the gun in your mouth pointed at your brain.

They asked if I'd moved anything. I had. I'd puked into the bathtub. They nodded in understanding as they put handcuffs on me, claiming that it was purely routine. We all fell silent and waited for the detectives to show up. A female detective and her trainee soon walked in. The party slowly got under way as a police doctor, forensics, and a Head Detective Müller arrived on the scene. Photographs and fingerprints were taken, they ran a vacuum cleaner to identify any fluff; they took my fingerprints and checked my hands for traces of gunpowder.

I had to tell my story a couple of times. I couldn't tell whether they believed me, but they took off the handcuffs after they'd run me through the federal database of criminals. Detective Müller soon got to the crucial point, the motive. But I'd had some time to come up with an answer and didn't mention the mafia, money laundering, or the faked suicide. I figured I could always plead posttraumatic shock later.

"It probably began with the suicide of our COO, Dr. Bredow, three weeks ago. He and the dead woman had been an item for some time; it was a rather close relationship. We at the hospital think that Bredow wasn't up to the stress of his job anymore. As COO, he worked closely with the medical director, Prof. Dohmke. And Dohmke put considerable pressure on Bredow—you're surely aware of the precarious financial state of the health care industry. Margret was convinced that Dohmke ultimately drove her lover to his death because of all this pressure."

"Did she tell you this?"

"Well, it was clear to me that she held Dohmke responsible for Bredow's death."

"Did Frau Steinmayer have any other possible motives?"

"She'd hinted that Dohmke went after her after Bredow died."

Which wasn't a total lie, though in a somewhat different sense.

Müller didn't take any notes. That's why he had a detective and her trainee.

"What was your relationship to Frau Steinmayer?"

I'd been waiting for that question, and I knew they'd ask around at the hospital.

"We were friends."

"Very close friends, Dr. Hoffmann?"

"We once had a close relationship, about two years ago. Not for very long though. We've been friends ever since."

"Who ended the relationship?"

What was going through Müller's head? Did he think that I, the enraged jealous lover, had knocked off Bredow, Margret's new lover, then Dohmke, and then, when Margret showed no gratitude for this proof of my devotion, that I'd bumped her off too?

"Actually nobody ended the relationship. It had just run its course and then petered out."

Here we were, sitting between two dead bodies, and my pride was still doing the answering. I wasn't sure whether Müller believed my reply, but he moved on. His next question caught me off guard.

"Do you know where Frau Steinmayer got the weapon?"

To be on the safe side, I decided on a definite no. I thought the timing of my reply was right on the mark, not too quick and not too slow.

"Did you know Frau Steinmayer owned a gun?"

"No."

Several men arrived with lockable metal tubs and removed Dohmke and Margret from the premises, a sight that made me viscerally aware of the finality of the evening's events. I began to shiver uncontrollably. Müller didn't tell me that I was not to leave town, and I wondered whether that was something that was only said in the movies. He did say, however, that I should make myself available to give my statement tomorrow and sign it. The detective and her trainee were to take me home, which I thought was a humane gesture.

But it wasn't. When they dropped me off at my place, they politely asked me for my clothes so that they could be checked out. Yes, underwear too. Frau Detective waited in the next room, but the trainee made sure that I dropped the right clothes into his plastic bag. I briefly wondered whether I'd put on clean underwear this morning.

I was sure that the female detective had taken a look around my place while she was waiting, but Bredow's printouts were at Celine's place and the copy of Misha's file was in the ICU.

I had the pleasure of seeing Head Detective Müller three times during the next few days. He had to eliminate me as a possible suspect early on, regretfully or not. There were substantial traces of powder on Margret's hands, and none on mine. Same with the fingerprints on the gun. The only thing they found on my clothing was my puke.

The detective and her trainee poked around the hospital a few times and confirmed that Margret had gone into a deep depression after Bredow died. My remarks about Dohmke's efforts to win Margret over were corroborated when they found the papers for the Rabbit convertible he'd bought and registered in Margret's name.

Müller, however, didn't appear altogether pleased with the results, especially regarding the motive. But he couldn't find anything concrete to hang his hat on. He had a quite tidy closed case: a classic lovers' triangle with a fatal ending for all parties. Whether he was convinced or not, the important thing was that the case could be closed with halfway credible circumstantial evidence.

They surely had countless unsolved cases and were thankful that they could stamp this one "Solved," a crucial designation for their statistical records. It's just like at the hospital, where we sometimes discharge patients as healthy without having obtained a satisfactory diagnosis. I imagined Müller's final report on Dohmke's and Steinmayer's deaths would look a lot like some of my medical reports: though it probably didn't reflect the real truth, it was sufficiently logical and convincing to close the case.

I wasn't especially concerned that they'd pin the deaths on me. I primarily needed to come to terms with my guilt and figure out what I was going to do about the hospital. Right after the detective and her trainee had left with my clothing, I'd fled to Celine's place. Celine wasn't given to high drama but looked frightened when she saw me.

"Good God! What's happened?"

I told her about the entire evening in extensive detail, including my unimpressive role in it.

"Felix, you didn't hand Margret the gun and you most certainly didn't fire it. If you'd taken the pistol from her, she'd have jumped out the window or thrown herself in front of a train."

She meant well, and it was what I wanted to hear, but she was wrong. My sequence of cause and effect was different: by investigating Misha's death and the blood supply—and definitely with our first break-in to Bredow's office—I had triggered a 3 million euro panic in Bredow that ultimately led to his murder. My Victim Number One. Informing Margret that Bredow's corpse had his hands in his pockets had caused her to shoot Dohmke. Victim Number Two. And that in turn had caused her to commit suicide. Victim Number Three.

Müller had a few questions for me over the course of the following week. I wondered repeatedly whether I should tell him more and put a stop to the crooks' little game by giving him Bredow's printouts. But I feared the consequences. For one thing, my survival would probably depend on my joining a witness protection program—not a reassuring prospect judging from what I'd read in American mystery novels. For another, it would guarantee the closure of the "mafia hospital." The Berlin government would be delighted with such a simple solution. And I'd be to blame for the loss of over five hundred jobs. Who'd given me the right to make a decision about the lives of five hundred people? I was not especially happy during those days.

I'd been expecting a certain call shortly after receiving Müller's message that the case was closed. When the caller identified himself, I was hardly surprised; on my second visit to the Business Registry, I'd seen his name listed as a founding member of that honorable company: Prof. Kindel, my revered chief of Cardiology, and now, according to his own words, an amateur photographer and keen listener of police radio. I hadn't told anyone about this.

He said it was urgent that we meet; he had something important he wanted to discuss with me. Our meeting took place in the grocery section of Berlin's renowned deluxe department store the KaDeWe, where I was looking for ingredients to try out with my wok the following weekend. I'm not a fan of the famously over-the-top food selection at the KaDeWe, but then I was no longer a fan of Kindel's.

Our conversation was brief and predictable. Kindel said that he and Dohmke had been watching me very closely the past few weeks. And he could understand that some goings-on in the hospital probably made me a bit uneasy. But he also told me he could guarantee that it was all happening to ensure our hospital's survival and our jobs.

"I'm delighted that you took my recent admonition to heart, to always keep the hospital's well-being in mind. You might easily have steered the police investigation in the wrong direction with an ill-considered statement."

That's actually what he said: "steered in the wrong direction"—what chutzpah! I'd just found a can of coconut milk when he came out with his offer: sharing in the "General Services" Company, with the level to be negotiated.

I remained astoundingly calm. "I'll have to think about it."

"Fine, Hoffmann, but don't think about it too long. I for one would like to have you onboard. But there are other shareholders who aren't so keen on you."

I promised to let him know soon and could only imagine how the other shareholders would feel vis-à-vis my future role in their company.

"A question, Herr Kindel. What were you actually doing at CareClean that day?"

"Taking pictures for the insurance company. Somebody has to pay for our damages," he replied. Tipping his shepherd's checked hat in an old-fashioned way, he disappeared.

The effrontery and greed of these people was mind-boggling—they were turning the fire they'd set themselves into an insurance claim. My anger surged into a veritable rage. Who did these people think they were, just buying out everything and everyone? I forgot my coconut milk at the counter as a result.

While searching for my car in the parking garage, I began wondering how much these people thought I was worth. And what price could I be had for? I would never snatch up a twenty-euro bill an old lady had dropped, but what about a million, say, tax-free in the Caymans? That million would presumably just be languishing in some other account anyway. So why not in mine?

As I started the car, I imagined what it would be like to be a member of this honored association. I had very little desire to join it in the first place and absolutely none when I recalled Bredow swinging from his transom. I was, once again, faced with a decision, and had to do so pretty much alone. I certainly didn't want to drag Celine into it. Ultimately, my choice wasn't so difficult, since it was now mainly about me. By the time I got home, I'd already made up my mind to see Müller in the morning. I was perfectly satisfied with my life without a million euros tucked away in the Caymans.

However, I decided not to call Head Detective Müller. Instead I called Prof. Kindel, who congratulated me on my decision. Then I made an appointment with Beate, as I needed a first-rate tax adviser. After all, I was about to become the newest partner in the General Services Company.

CHAPTER 22

The meeting of the partners of the General Services Company was held in the renovated offices of CareClean, where new furniture, new windows, and new computers had all been installed. A faint singed smell still permeated the building. I was the last to arrive.

The company had five partners at that point in time. They were sitting around a new boardroom table in the office where I'd found Prof. Dohmke. Prof. Kindel was the only one that I knew personally, and he introduced me to the other gentlemen with a satisfied smile. Boris Zhukov was, as I'd suspected, the man I'd seen with Dohmke after the fire. I couldn't fault Margret—Boris was a good-looking man of about fifty with a powerful build and a pleasant voice. He said he'd heard a lot about me and was pleased to meet me at last.

I was somewhat familiar with the third man at the table, if only from seeing occasional pictures of him in the paper. It was Arthur Roth, the undersecretary in the Berlin health administration. He greeted me with a campaign smile and was clearly the reason why our hospital hadn't graced any bed-cutting list, not to mention any of the lists of closures. The two other men muttered their Slavic names to me and displayed no enthusiasm for their prospective new partner.

Although the table was round, Boris Zhukov was plainly the alpha dog in this association. However, he left it to Kindel to welcome me.

"Yes, my dear Herr Hoffmann, we thank you for coming. And may I congratulate you once again on behalf of all those present on your decision to work with us. Herr Zhukov has already mentioned that we have kept close tabs on your actions over the past few weeks and, I must say, at times with some misgivings. Although you have gained some insight into our firm during that time, you still do not have the big picture. And that could have led you to the wrong conclusions, with embarrassing consequences not only for this company but also for the survival of our hospital. And that, Herr Hoffmann, is the key point and primary concern of our company: to ensure our hospital's survival."

Every word he'd spoken thus far was true—there was no question about it: they would do anything to keep their wonderful money-laundering machine running.

"What you cannot have known, Dr. Hoffmann, is that the hospital would quite likely no longer exist without the help of General Services. Dr. Bredow drove the hospital into bankruptcy last year through some unfortunate financial maneuvering. You would be out on the street today, along with the hospital's five hundred other employees. Of course, Herr Hoffmann, we are not a charity or Good Samaritans. We are businessmen who have demonstrated that a hospital can be run economically and perhaps profitably, even in times such as these, when money is scarce."

I couldn't find any rhyme or reason to Kindel's calling me "Dr. Hoffmann" versus "Herr Hoffmann." It didn't help to distinguish between truth and lies, because until now, as far as I could judge, he still hadn't lied.

"It will take some time for you to fully understand how our company operates. In fact, you won't even need to grasp every aspect of it. We do not require your advice on finances or other business-related matters; rather, we would like to be able to rely on your medical expertise. We need you to serve as an intermediary between us and the hospital, especially since Herr Dohmke and Herr Bredow have been ruled out."

Ruled out. What a nice euphemism. He pressed on, undeterred.

"This position requires not only expertise but also tact and discretion. And you have, happily, demonstrated both over the last few weeks."

Prof. Kindel was finished with his little speech. I waited to see whether Boris or our undersecretary had something to add. But it seemed that I was now expected to say a few words.

"What kind of involvement did you have in mind for me?"

Kindel continued to do the talking.

"You will be a chief physician with a salary to match. But more importantly, you will be a partner here."

"So you would assign shares in your company to me?"

"As I explained to you recently."

"And what would this share amount to?"

"It would be Dr. Bredow's share, or Frau Steinmayer's. Seven percent."

"Would I be expected to put any money into the company?"

"Your contribution is your competence, your expertise. And your goodwill."

I took a look at my future partners. They appeared to be perfectly ordinary businessmen—try as I might, I couldn't detect so much as a whiff of the underworld on them.

"Seven percent, you say. May I ask what that would mean on an annual basis, approximately?"

Kindel replied again.

"It's difficult to say exactly in the world of business. But rest assured that it would more than compensate you for your commitment to the company."

"But there are surely numbers from last year?"

Boris joined in at this point.

"Well, Dr. Hoffmann, we have a problem with the exact figures for last year. We had a fire here recently, as you know. In all the offices. Just about all of the documents were burned up in the fire, as were the computers storing the data."

It was time for me to play my trump card.

"You know, gentlemen, I can help you out there. Nothing would be more unpleasant than to build our future relationship on missing data. I'm in the fortunate position of being able to give you a complete list of your business activities relating to the hospital, CareClean, and Hospital Catering Services. One moment, if you please."

I went to the door and asked Celine and Beate to come in; they'd been sitting in the waiting room. The partners all jumped to their feet, but none of them offered the ladies their seat. Boris was the first to regain his ability to speak.

"This isn't a kiddies' birthday party, Dr. Hoffmann, where you're welcome to bring along a few neighborhood friends. This is a confidential meeting. If you must consult with these ladies about something, then please do so outside."

One chair at the table was unoccupied. Had it been Bredow's? Dohmke's? I remained standing and seated Celine and Beate in two other chairs. Beate put a thin folder in front of each person.

"Please be seated, gentlemen. These ladies represent my business expertise; that's why they're here. May I suggest that you listen to what they have to say?"

My partners *in spe* sat down again in silent protest.

"You have before you a compilation of the relevant numbers for the last two years regarding the dealings between your company and the hospital and your company's subsidiaries, such as CareClean," Beate said. "You owe this precise accounting to your Dr. Bredow. It came into our hands before this data was unfortunately wiped out by a virus. You can see, therefore, that we should have no trouble talking about exact figures."

Beate displayed no signs that she was nervous as she became the focus of attention of a company of criminals. Maybe tax advisers were accustomed to it.

"What are they offering you, Felix?" she asked.

"Seven percent of the partnership's shares."

"Which, projected onto the current year, would be around three hundred and fifty thousand euros."

The amount was neither confirmed nor contradicted by the gentlemen at the table.

"Do you consider that acceptable?" I asked Beate.

I was standing between Celine and Beate, one hand on the back of each chair.

"Absolutely not."

I felt a wave of tension surge through the room. Kindel was filled with righteous indignation.

"Dr. Hoffmann, may I point out that you have until now only made trouble for this company. We pay based on performance. That means your share in the firm could go up depending on what you do for the company. And don't forget your promotion to chief physician."

"I'm glad that the performance principle is in effect here, Herr Kindel. But you're wrong if you think that I haven't been actively working on the firm's behalf. If you would please turn to page eight in the folder before you."

I gave them time to find the right page.

"Here you have written statements from your partners in the pharmaceutical industry. They affirm here that they had no doubt that the blood bags and blood products from your company were

German blood bags and that, if that should *not* be the case, the business relationship with our hospital would be terminated immediately."

Our undersecretary woke up, stirring to life for the first time since I'd arrived.

"They can't do that!"

Human greed really knows no bounds, and I watched, astounded, as Undersecretary Roth gradually turned beet red with rage and indignation. The blood business only came to 100,000 euros a year, a paltry sum compared to these gentlemen's other wheelings and dealings.

"Why not, sir? You are perhaps thinking of the payments deposited into certain special accounts as so-called compensation. These companies have no knowledge of them. Do you have receipts for these payments, or must I remind you of that unfortunate night when your records were burned up?"

"Don't be so sure that we don't have any of those documents," Kindel interrupted.

Boris gave Kindel an angry look. So Boris still had the names hidden away somewhere and maybe the sums as well. But that didn't affect my plan; all that was important was that *we* now had complete documentation.

"Well, OK, let's say you've still got the records of your dealings with your friends in the pharmaceutical industry. Do you want to ask for your so-called compensation back? Sue them for breaking contracts? Press charges?"

Kindel said that I could easily figure out for myself what my shares would look like if there were lawsuits because of the fact I'd cast doubt on the very foundations of the company's business.

"Herr Kindel, I am to become an associate in your company, your partner. For that reason, we should agree to be a little more open with each other. You'd have me believe that it was only a matter of having Frau Steinmayer stick a different label on your Russian blood donations and sending them out with new documentation. Let me tell you, Herr Kindel, what I think about this blood business. I think your partner Boris Zhukov isn't all that interested in the blood bag money. He only needs the blood deals to keep the hospital participants under tighter control. He could probably even terminate this sideline—and you as well—without endangering his real business with our hospital."

Boris stepped in a second time.

"OK, Dr. Hoffmann. I've looked over your little dossier here, and I'll admit your documentation is more extensive than we thought. Let's get back to the main purpose of this meeting. Why don't you tell us what share of the company you'd find appropriate? After all, we're reasonable businessmen. But, Dr. Hoffmann, please don't put us in the position of having to look for an alternate solution to bringing you on as a partner. I would deeply regret that."

I was astounded at his German and his correct grammar. Had he worked for President Putin back in his KGB days when he'd been stationed in the beautiful German city of Dresden? Celine had sat quietly up to this point, but she became flushed after Boris's threat. Maybe she was just angry, but I was scared shitless. I knew that threats were to be expected of course, and propped myself up more firmly on the backs of the chairs.

"You know, Herr Zhukov," I began, hoping that no one else detected the quiver in my voice, "you've been lucky until now. Bredow took great pains to record all the company activities but made one big mistake: he didn't copy his data to any external source; even his lover, Margret, didn't have any copies. Rest assured, gentlemen, that I'm not going to make the same mistake. You can be sure that everything will immediately be sent to the state prosecutor's office if something should happen to me. And the same goes for the two ladies here."

Kindel made a futile attempt at protest.

"I think it would be a mistake to put such sensitive material into the hands of some random lawyer we know nothing about."

"Nice try, Herr Kindel. I am sure you would be able to recommend a lawyer you trust. But who said the documents are with a lawyer? Wouldn't a bank safe deposit box be a possibility? Or, for instance, an e-mail that will automatically get sent to a certain address if I don't cancel the order daily with a specific password?"

Prof. Kindel looked quite helpless. He could picture the lawyer and the safe deposit box, but electronic blackmail must have sounded like the devil's handiwork to him. Boris, on the other hand, appeared unruffled. He remained at all times the composed businessman seeking a sensible solution to a business problem through a sensible conversation.

"I don't want there to be any misunderstanding, Dr. Hoffmann," he said, "but I'd like to repeat my earlier question. I asked what share of the company you would find acceptable."

"The question is easily answered, gentlemen."

All heads swung around toward Beate.

"Dr. Hoffmann requests the complete, one-hundred-percent transfer of all shares in South Berlin Hospital Ltd. and the companies CareClean and Hospital Catering Services to his name. He will take over these companies with all of their assets and liabilities as of today's balance; we will have to come to an agreement on the figure. Dr. Hoffmann has no interest in the building at Uhlandstrasse 141 or Eurotrans Trucking Company. As a quid pro quo, all the documents pertaining to these companies now in our possession will be destroyed."

That was what we'd arranged. What was I supposed to do with a building on Uhlandstrasse anyway? I also didn't need a trucking company, since I had no plans to move in the near future. If our little plan here didn't pan out, I'd have to move to the ends of the earth anyway.

The group erupted in protest, complete with tongue-lashings and abusive threats. Beate waited patiently until the excitement had died down somewhat.

"Our offer is valid for three days. If you find a way to accept it, the documents will not be sent to the relevant authorities. I'll leave you with the contracts to be signed. There is no provision for changes."

We had assured our own safety at Allee der Kosmonauten 116 by means of the documentation we'd safely deposited, but we were nevertheless relieved to get out of the meeting alive. Celine had to go to the john right away, and we were all suddenly ravenous. I didn't resent Luigi's enthusiastic doting on Celine and Beate today; they had put on a magnificent performance.

Boris, Kindel, and Co. really had no choice. Either they handed General Services over to me or they'd have to kill us. And that would of course be an unreasonable choice because they'd go bust along with their company. But who was to say that these guys were reasonable? It did occur to us when we considered the situation more closely that they could pressure us to reveal where we'd stashed our reinsurance. They could also kidnap one of us and use the documents as ransom. Or they could simply kill one of us—which would surely motivate the two survivors to rethink their stance. Maybe it hadn't been such a brilliant idea after all to bring Celine and Beate along with me to the meeting.

By the time we'd polished off a few glasses of soave, we'd made up our minds. We had to disappear together until the honorable society had come to a decision. Beate suggested taking the next plane. Voted down. Boris would only have to station his gorillas at the Berlin airports to nab us; besides, taking a plane left a paperwork trail.

"Let's leave by car," I suggested.

Also vetoed. Our cars could easily be watched and a rental car left clues behind. Celine, ever-practical, suggested we head out to the On the Green Banks of the Spree Hotel.

"Last time I forgot my hairdryer. We'll take the train and pay once we get on. They can't watch every station in Berlin."

We arrived in the Spreewald that afternoon. I called in sick— even physicians aren't always healthy—and Celine was on summer vacation anyway. How Beate was so simply able to skip town was never clear to me. Torsten Römer picked us up at the station. Though it was midweek, he only had one room available, which had a large double bed and a not very large couch. I suggested that the girls draw straws each night to decide who got to go to bed with me. However, majority rule vetoed that and *I* ended up on the couch. Only once, after I'd fixed their bikes for them en route, was I permitted to lie between them for a back massage. When I described their massage as wonderful foreplay, they tossed me out of bed.

By day, we explored on foot, on our bikes, and by canoe, heading deeper into the enchanted world of the Spreewald each time we ventured out. By night, I took sleeping pills. The swirl of Russian mafia, hospital, murder, and kidnapping gradually receded a bit into the background. I had blisters on my hands and feet by the third day and left Celine and Beate to take the eight-hour hike they had planned by themselves. I had something else to do that they didn't need to know about. I borrowed Torsten's car and was back in time for dinner.

The two girls came back in a state of excitement.

"Look at the cool things we found!"

They showed off the various examples of *Pecten opercularis*, *Avicula semisagitta*, *Cytherea meretrix*, and *Lima squamosa* that they'd picked up, all of which gleamed iridescently in a gorgeous array of colors. My little surprise had worked, in spite of the delay. They had found the South Sea shells I'd buried on the bank weeks ago. I congratulated them on their sensational find and saved the disclosure of my triumph for a later occasion.

We telephoned daily from different phone booths to speak with Herr König, a lawyer and notary. We'd picked his name out of the phone book and deposited the Boris and Co. contracts with him. Incidentally, we really had left the accounting records for General Services and Bredow's accounts with my Internet provider, along with the proper electronic instructions to send an automatic e-mail to Head Detective Müller. Every morning Celine reset the e-mail from my laptop. König must have wondered about his new clients, but it was just a standard contract changing the number of a partner's shares in a company. All he had to do was take the partners' phone calls because his new clients had to be out of town for a few days.

Our partners reported to him on Friday, one day after my secret excursion. I wasn't surprised. They were in agreement and proposed to sign the contracts the following Monday. We celebrated with champagne and stayed in the Spreewald over the weekend, changing hotels just to be on the safe side. We drove back to Berlin Monday morning. Celine had forgotten her hairdryer again but was already talking about going back soon to look for more seashells.

By Monday evening, I was the owner, sole partner, and CEO of our hospital, CareClean, and Hospital Catering Services. And all three of us were in the best of health.

What did it feel like to own a hospital? It didn't feel so hot. I was suddenly burdened with taking responsibility for my colleagues, the nurses, the lab techs. For maintaining decent bed-occupancy figures. For negotiating with the insurance companies and the state government. For planning the number of beds needed. Even for making sure there was an adequate supply of toilet paper. All in a hospital that wasn't even making a profit.

I'd had a strategy session with Celine and Beate before the big meeting in Allee der Kosmonauten. Part one of our plan had worked astonishingly well. Now it was time to implement part two. I had absolutely no desire to be the owner, sole partner, and CEO of our hospital.

Nonetheless, with Beate's help, I quietly pushed through two decisions during the short time I was dictator. I ordered that the staffs of CareClean and Hospital Catering Services be paid the going rate for their services. The second matter was a bit of petty, self-indulgent revenge. I had the fat cadre secretary yanked off her comfy five-legged office chair at CareClean and transferred to our step-and-fetch-it service. She now had to spend all day bringing blood samples to the lab, taking files from Records to the wards, and transferring X-rays all over the hospital. After a few days of this, she called in sick and then brought in a doctor's certificate.

My last attempt to intervene also went awry: Michael Thiel turned down my suggestion that he take over the management of the hospital lab and the blood bank. It was too bad, because he'd have succeeded his archenemy, Prof. Dohmke. But he preferred to keep working in his own lab with the pretty lab techs of his choice.

Nobody in the hospital had any idea that I was their boss. I did my job as attending physician during the day and discussed the problems of managing the hospital with Beate in the evenings. She was on leave from the office where she worked and was now acting as our administrative director. She called a general staff meeting to get part two of our plan under way.

Beate had hammered out my vague ideas for reorganizing the hospital into a communicable plan, which she presented persuasively at the meeting. The staff was speechless; there was not so much as a murmur through the ranks. They were to become partners in the hospital; ownership of the hospital was to pass to them. They themselves would be responsible for the cost-effectiveness of their work and for their salaries.

I had run my plan by my closest confidants at the hospital, including Marlies, Heinz Valenta, Nurse Elke, and Frau Krüger. Once they'd bought into the plan, they convinced the rest of the staff of its merit. Clueless group that they were, none of them even asked how this had had all come about. A week later, Berlin had its first self-administered hospital and I, I hoped, finally had some peace and quiet.

Though I was pleased that our plan had become a reality, our solution was still marred by a sizable blemish—and their names were Boris Zhukov and Prof. Kindel and Co. Though we'd inflicted a serious financial blow, they still weren't in jail where they belonged and would probably soon find some new money-laundering setup. I wondered whether I'd failed in the long run. But what would have happened if I'd had that conversation with Head Detective Müller, as I'd originally planned to do? With some luck, I might have survived until I got myself into a witness protection program. And then what? It wasn't just a matter coming up with a new name and a new driver's license. What would have become of my physician's diploma? My medical license? My specialist credentials? How was my retirement pension going to be transferred to me and my new identity? All kinds of people would have had to be let in on the secret, knocking more and more holes in my protective screen. I knew that the Russian mafia's reach extended far beyond Boris and Co. As for the hospital, you can bet that it would have been closed in a heartbeat.

I hadn't eradicated evil, but I didn't think that was possible anyway. Even if I'd managed to put Boris and his comrades behind bars, they'd have been replaced in short order by a new Boris and

new comrades. I could justify our actions to myself. It was like
weeds in the garden: they'd never go away completely, but you
could keep them in check by repeatedly digging them out and
replacing them with something else. Though the self-administered hospital model had its flaws, it was harder to corrupt than a
hierarchical model. Furthermore, I consoled myself with the idea
that people like Bredow and Dohmke did a better job of doing
each other in than our justice system ever could.

I was skeptical, of course, about the success of our self-
administered hospital, but I was still able to persuade Beate to
give up her job in the tax office to become the hospital's permanent administrative director. And I knew she would make every
effort to make our model a success.

The following Sunday was once again a properly hot and cloud-
less summer's day. Celine and I treated ourselves to another lazy
day on the Wannsee beach. I dozed off. I mused over the chaotic
nature of our world and how it just got more chaotic every day.
The Second Law of Thermodynamics at work. How could I orga-
nize this chaos somewhat, at least for my own life? I asked Celine
if we ought to get married.

At that very moment, a football landed on me, and I realized
I'd only been dreaming—long enough, however, to feel the prog-
nostic symptoms of a new sunburn. Celine was jumping out of
the water like a colt, hardly aware of the grace of her movements.
In the end, I knew I ought to be grateful to Dohmke, Bredow,
Boris, and the whole crew: they'd brought us much closer. And
now I properly belonged, in Celine's eyes, to the generation of
1968. I was (almost) a hero. The game was worth the candle.

Would marriage and starting a family really bring order to the
chaos of my personal microcosm? I had serious doubts. I wondered what Celine would say if I really asked her. She'd probably

laugh and change the subject. But maybe not? I'd never find out. Probably not, anyway.

PS I reread my report on the weeks when Misha was our DOA and must admit I came off rather well. Like Jesus and the money changers in the temple, I freed my hospital from the clutches of an avaricious clique and put it in the care of those who kept it thriving through their work. The ideal result of a truly selfless act.

But I was nevertheless struck by a few inconsistencies. For instance, was the mere threat of my going public with their dealings enough to bring Boris and Co. to their knees? I would have thought we'd have to share Bredow's fate, if nothing else as a warning to others. And why did I up and leave the Spreewald that day when Celine and Beate went on their hike?

There was indeed a connection: it had to do with the 3 million euros that Bredow had hidden away in Zurich. I have just written an account of human greed. There must be some kind of primal instinct behind greed (so lovingly described in the Declaration of Independence as "the pursuit of Happiness"); why wouldn't I be at the mercy of it as well? Didn't I deserve a little reward for my efforts?

Margret had revealed the name of the Zurich bank to Dohmke and Co.—and to me—but not the code that would give us access to the money. My premise was simple: nobody wanted to keep track of a hundred different passwords, and we knew Bredow's computer password. It seemed worth a try. So I borrowed Torsten's car, drove to Leipzig airport, took the morning plane to Zurich, and called on the Züricher Kredit- und Handelsbank.

I'd imagined it would be far more difficult than it turned out to be. Not only had Bredow used his password "minister" here as well, but the gentlemen at the bank found nothing unusual in the fact that I wanted to withdraw all the money immediately in cash. I was back at Leipzig by early afternoon.

I'd already made plans for a good 2 million on the return flight. But then I began to have doubts. How long would it take Boris Zhukov and Co. to trace the 3 million, only to find the account closed? By then, my threat of exposing the evidence would surely have passed its expiration date. In their own criminal way, Boris and Co. were businessmen, so I decided to invest my carry-on luggage with all those pretty little bills in a life insurance policy with these same businessmen rather than in a very short future.

I went straight from Leipzig to Berlin and put my 3 million into a rather special "life insurance" with Boris Zhukov. Which is why I wasn't surprised when König called to tell us that the other party was prepared to sign over the company: the mafia had gotten their 3 million euros and now were willing to play by our rules.

It was too bad about the money. However, I didn't feel any obligation to hand over the interest that had accrued on the money as well. Which means there's a nice trip with Celine next year in there—to a place where there are fabulous seashells.

Honestly, Herr Kindel, Herr Zhukov, Undersecretary Roth— now I've really said it all. I've destroyed Bredow's books and my records along with them. And only readers of thrillers will get their hands on this version. But you needn't worry: nobody will believe this story anyway.

PPS Undersecretary Roth is still a big cheese in the health administration, and people say that odds are good he'll become department head after the next election. One of the reasons for this is the initiative attributed to him that created Berlin's first employee-administered hospital. His speech on that occasion was printed in all the local newspapers, and excerpts of it were picked up all over Germany.

ABOUT THE AUTHOR

 Cardiologist and Agatha Christie prize-winning author Christoph Spielberg lives in Berlin, Germany, where his mystery novels have gained national notoriety. Spielberg was awarded the prestigious Friedrich Glauser prize from the German Crime Writers Association for *The Russian Donation*, the first in his ongoing Dr. Hoffmann crime series, and his books have been translated into both English and Japanese.

Critical acclaim for the Dr. Hoffmann series has prompted the German ZDF television network to produce a run of TV movies based on the novels. Today, Spielberg continues to draw from his medical experience, writing novels, short stories, and providing medical care to his patients.

TRANSLATOR'S ACKNOWLEDGMENTS

I wish to thank Christoph Spielberg first of all, particularly for his helpful and energetic contributions to the many English versions of his first novel. Dr. John Truman at Columbia University generously provided expert help in linking German medical terminology to American. My colleague George Thomas at McMaster University kindly handled the Russian transliterations. AmazonCrossing again deserves gratitude for finding a home for the volume in its enterprising program, especially Gabriella Page-Fort and her negotiating skills, among other things. Christina Henry de Tessan and Marcus Trower deserve recognition for their editing know-how. My wife, Nina, was once again my first critical reader of another of my translations, and I owe her, as always, my heartfelt thanks.

ABOUT THE TRANSLATOR

Gerald Chapple is an award-winning translator of German literature. He received his doctorate at Harvard and went on to teach German and comparative literature at McMaster University in Hamilton, Ontario, choosing to take early retirement in 2000. He has been translating contemporary German-language authors for more than thirty-five years. His recent prose work includes *The Zurich Conspiracy* by Bernadette Calonego; two books by the Austrian writer Barbara Frischmuth, *The Convent School* and *Chasing after the Wind*, completed with co-translator James B. Lawson; Michael Mitterauer's probing history of Europe from 600 to 1600, *Why Europe? Medieval Origins of Its Special Path*; and Anita Albus's wonderfully idiosyncratic book *On Rare Birds*. He lives in Dundas, Ontario, with his wife, Nina, an architectural historian, and two Labradors. When not translating, he can usually be found studying birds, butterflies, and dragonflies, reading, or listening to classical music.